Fire's Field

Book 2
The Elementals Trilogy

Jillian Jacobs

Published by Green Moose Productions
Copyright 2015 by Jillian Jacobs

ISBN: 978-1-942313-04-5

Cover art and logo design: www.shelbybertsch.

DEDICATION

For my sisters.
For all the times I made you sing and dance to Pointer Sisters' songs.

ACKNOWLEDGMENTS

To the sensational six! My beta-girls. You fired this story up!
Also thanks to Linda Carroll-Bradd. Best editor ever.
Any mistakes are my own.

PROLOGUE

1324 Kilkenny, Ireland

They were coming for her.

On the eve of her mother's 25th birthday, Sorcha fought back chills as the braying of bloodhounds echoed through the forest. A single red stroke, mixed with the faintest purple, lit the darkening sky as the night, along with death, crept closer.

At the banks of River Nore, the young witch rocked back and forth, tears of innocence-lost escaping down her cheeks. Heart splintering, the seven-year-old searched her memory for a spell to ease her mother's torment. With her hands locked in the fabric of her mother's woolen dress, she chanted pleas to the Goddess Isis to hear her cries and heal her mother.

To no avail.

The only answer came in the form of the demon's sickness dripping from her mother's mouth in a sludge of grimy gray mud.

Fear unlike anything she'd ever felt iced her heart as once more she begged, swore her very life in exchange for the continued beat of her mother's heart.

A piercing pain shot through her overburdened mind as the beast fought to break through her mental shields. Weakened by her angst and untested youth, Sorcha left a crack exposed, and the beast slipped in. Squinting her eyes closed, entire body shaking with the will to deny the sick beast's entrance, she couldn't prevent his foul words from seeping through.

"Your mother paid for her defiance, for her inability to accept this gift only I could give her. Look at you, simpering and shaking. If you weren't so weak I'd use you, but no matter, I'll be back."

Drained from holding back the tempest, Sorcha let loose true sobs for the loss of the deepest love of her life, her solid fortress during every storm, the lyrical voice singing away her nightmares. Ignoring her drenched skirts, Sorcha released all her agony against her mother's breast, barely catching the beat of her mother's weakening heart drowned out by each moan torn from the depths of her anguished soul.

No one came to her aid. No one soothed her broken spirit.

The hounds drew closer, their howls a mad cacophony in her surreal world. The yellow glow from fire-tipped sticks created a mystical glimmer in the woods before her. Snaps and cracks of branches reverberated across the forest as the frenzied townspeople advanced to accuse and convict one of their own—a powerful witch.

Then, upon the breeze, Sorcha heard the faintest whisper of her name.

She gazed into her mother's eyes and glimpsed a momentary ray of lucidity in their violet-blue depths.

Her mother licked dry lips, narrowed her eyes and, with a strength the girl could only dare to imagine, lifted a hand to caress her daughter's face. Her mother's jaw clenched and, though on the very cusp of death, her words rang strong and true. "Avenge me."

Keeping her mother's gaze, Sorcha simply nodded, red hair bouncing around her shivering shoulders.

She'd apprenticed at her mother's side, learning the ways of the witch, but she still had much to learn. And learn she would.

Avenge me.

Releasing a feral scream against the folds of her mother's dress, she accepted the challenge. Moments later, hidden from detection by a cloaking spell, Sorcha could only watch in helpless horror as the townspeople arrived and carried her mother away.

Avenge me.

The words scored a bitter ballad across her heart, burning their unceasing tune through her soul.

Avenge me.

That vow carried the young beauty throughout her life. The two words rang in her mind as she dredged through all forms of magic, seeking, gaining power, and embracing the mystical world—light and dark.

Enchanting each man she came across, Sorcha used them for money and power, financing her desire for revenge and retribution, until, at last, she was heavy with her own child. In that moment, all her planning, all her forays into the black beat of dark magic, came to fruition.

On the first day of her twenty-fifth year, Sorcha, now a powerful witch in her own right, lay beside the river where her mother had spoken her final words. As with all things mystical, numbers held meanings. Numbers served to cement a witch's will upon the realm of enchantments with a solidity created through similar figures. Her mother had died the day before her twenty-fifth year, so this spell, in this place, on the cusp of her own twenty-fifth year, was permeated with significance.

The river ebbed and churned around her, as if wishing to wipe clean the dark magic she began painting upon the canvas of time. Yet, she held back every drop of water, using the magic gifts she'd honed over the years. Intent on her purpose, she painted her pregnant belly with a mix of earth, water, fire, and air, though nature's pure beauty was tainted with the blood of a goat and the ashes of twenty-five stillborn babes. Surrounded by vibrant tufts of wild violets, she massaged the thick coating over her skin and whispered a spell that would carry through her line, ending at the twenty-fifth girl.

Until that day, Sorcha would wait in the shadows, guiding each child along the proper path. Then, on the glorious day of retribution, on the day that dark monster was erased from this earth, she would stand at her future descendant's side and witness the fulfillment of her vow.

With a thin, razor-sharp blade, she sliced twenty-five cuts along the top and down to the underside of her rotund belly. Mixing her blood as an offering to those dark spirits watching, sealing her resolve with each slice.

"Mother, on this ground you struggled. On this ground that beast from another sphere took everything from you, from me. But on this day, with each drop of blood, I seal an end. With this spell, I honor my vow. I avenge you."

"Black death marked before her time

Maternal mother down the line
From my core, a child I'll spawn
Twenty-five to make her strong
Rise once more from withered beam
Violet bloom along light's beam
Four petals span against the foe
A single petal arching low
From the elements one shall rise
Burning light into her eyes
Shadows scorch
Remain unseen
Reaper hold thy scythe 'til then
White field from my future line
Clasp your golden hand in mine
Together, vengeance we shall see
I shall hold thy place for thee
As I will, so mote it be."

At the end of her spell, she watched the river bubble and churn before parting, and from the fold came a woman—tall, ethereal, flowing with a spark only the purest nature could provide.

Mother Nature.

"What have you done, my child?" Mother's musical voice drifted through her mind.

"I have fulfilled my vow." While rising, Sorcha fought back a wave of dizziness then adjusted her skirts and walked up the path to the dirt road.

"You've done nothing but damn your line."

As Mother's words trickled through her mind, Sorcha stopped, but didn't turn to face this being who thought to judge, who had arrived eighteen years too late. "So be it." Jaw clenched, she studied the remnants of the spell's mixture on her hands. "Sacrifices must be made, since you seem incapable of destroying the beast on your own."

"But will this enchantment end the dark-matter creature? He shall evolve. Your spell will remain the same. Turn your heart from this path. Save your future child the pain."

"Pain is all I have to offer." Sorcha continued along the dirt path to her lover's carriage waiting at the top of the hill. *"My will is done. My vow complete. You may be the Mother of Earth, but you turned a blind*

eye to my mother's suffering. I alone remained at her side." At the top of the knoll, she turned and studied the woman remaining by the river's edge. "Do not think to hold my hand now, fairy creature. Vengeance is mine."

CHAPTER 1

Vibrant autumn leaves skittered along the pavement. Mixing with a light mist, they lined the roadsides in clumps of brown and black, yet in the fading evening light, a few glints of red and gold remained. The spicy fragrance of her favorite season filled her senses, and though slightly chilled, she soaked up every nuance.

Shaking wet beads from her hair, Violet Levina scanned the neighborhood, lit only by a single lamppost at the end of the block. An eerie fog blanketed the street, matching the sense of foreboding in her heart. For months, throughout her hiding spots in Switzerland, the Elemental, Flint, had been hot on her tail. However, embroiling him in her destined task seemed unfair, not to mention deadly.

Since last seeing the fire elemental, she'd considered his existence more than she cared to admit. *What happened to peri-mortal beings when they died? How hot was his internal body temperature? How did his internal organs function under such conditions? Could he create fire without using the three necessary elements?* Over and over these thoughts waved through her mind, driving her mad.

Enough! Keys in hand, Violet clicked open the lock to her co-worker's flat and headed for the kitchen.

Then stilled.

Heat filled the room from a roaring fire, crackling and popping in the fireplace, flickering with welcoming warmth, and yet, her friend was still out of town.

"Good evening, Violet."

A deep male voice, tinted with a faint Russian accent, drifted into the kitchen and sparked goose bumps across her skin.

He'd found her.

Violet fumbled the grocery bag in her arms before placing the burden on the counter. "How…how did you locate me?" She peeked around the corner into the living room, and there he sat.

Resting on his lap, a large bouquet of yellow roses popped with color against the darkness. The tissue paper crinkled as he shifted in the chair. "Pillar told me." Flint's raven-wing hair and amber eyes were only discernible by the flickering light dancing across his angular features.

Violet heaved a heavy sigh. "She's developed a big sister complex where I'm concerned. This continual belief that I don't know what's best for my own life is insulting, not to mention ridiculous. My IQ is 185. So, this condescending attitude is quite unfair." Glaring at the man sitting in shadow, she let the silence stretch for a moment. "I realize you may have reservations about Pillar, due to her past with Quint…and the whole relationship with…ah…Nodin." Violet leaned against the doorway. "But she's trying to change. You should give her a chance."

"Don't." His tone turned harsh. "Don't give that salty square your allegiance. She sought me out. That should speak for itself." Flint waved a hand.

His gesture suggesting everything should be perfectly clear.

It wasn't.

"You've known Pillar for many years." Leaving her friend's blatant disloyalty for another time, Violet focused all her wits on this fiery Elemental.

"Unfortunately, yes." Flint sniffed, and then picked at a yellow petal. "She may have led me here for reasons of her own, but I would have found you. Pillar's sudden need to redeem herself now that Quint's been hurled back to where he came from doesn't concern me, or allow for any pity. She's been against us for a long time."

"And you've never chosen the wrong path? In all your years?" Violet folded both arms across her chest, remaining in the doorway between the kitchen and living room, caught between her wish to flee and her foolish attraction to this man. "She's making amends. Why not forgive her?"

"I've survived too many years to worry about insignificant things like forgiveness." Flint waved a rose bud through the air by its stem. "We live, we move on. No need to dwell, or force alliances with people who don't know their own minds, or are so warped by love lost they choose to disregard humanity. Pillar is a fool." He paused for a moment, flicking a loose leaf off his dress pants. Those amber eyes lifted once more, and he raised a brow. "A better question would be, do I have any regrets?"

"Regrets?" Violet crossed the room, drawn by the fire's warmth. When she shifted a candle on the fireplace mantle, she started as the wick suddenly lit. Glancing over her shoulder, she met his gaze. "As you say, in one lifetime, who has time for those?"

"Ah, but I've lived many lifetimes." He smiled and tapped the yellow rosebud against his knee.

"So, you've found me." Arms braced across her chest, she waved a hand in his direction. "What now?"

"Now, I make sure you don't have any regrets."

Violet stuttered out a laugh. "You won't control me. I can easily destroy you."

"Ah, now, my Violet, *that* I would regret."

The evening's chill dissipated in his presence. Should she flee? Use her powers to shock him? Powers she'd been cursed with, or so it seemed at times. *No regrets.* That viewpoint was easy for a man who knew he would live more lifetimes. She blew out the candle and turned to study the human personification of fire lounging in her leather recliner.

A hazy gray aura surrounded him, blocking, creating distance. To keep others at bay? A subtle warning? Yet, he wasn't the only one with power.

Flint steepled his fingers against his chin. "You've been elusive prey. But once I set my sights on a prize, I generally win."

"And I imagine you do that by using your Elemental gifts." She leaned against the fireplace, tapping the iron poker against her foot.

"For what I want from you, I won't need any gift." Flint flashed a smile that was all teeth as he stood and placed the roses on the coffee table.

Just what was he suggesting? Stepping back, she knocked over a copper tin filled with fireplaces matches. "Blast it." With shaky hands, she quickly gathered them together and stuffed the wooden sticks back into the pot then glanced at Flint. "Listen…I-I don't…you won't…you must understand. I have a responsibility, and though Pillar believes I should join your Elemental team, I do not believe that is the wisest course." She wouldn't let his bright smile and floral offering sway her objection to his presence. "My duty is to my family, and to...well...to the world, to fulfill a prophecy laid down by my ancestor in 1342."

"A prophecy, you say." Flint raised a brow. "I haven't heard of anyone believing such nonsense since the Moscow plague and riot in 1771." He stalked across the room, a single rose in hand. "What about me frightens you?"

"First of all, the prophecy is not nonsense." She tightened her grip on the fireplace poker. "Secondly, I am not frightened of *you*." Violet refused to retreat, even though he reminded her of a heat-seeking predator—a coiled pit viper using infrared-detection to locate its prey. And she was certainly Flint's prey, for reasons she hadn't quite grasped.

"Not frightened?" He removed the poker from her hand, setting it back in the stand before tilting her chin with his finger. "Then why lead me on this merry chase across Switzerland?"

Turning from his touch, she ignored the heat sizzling along her skin. "I've led you nowhere. I have not asked for your pursuit."

"And that makes the chase all the more...stimulating." Once more, Flint clasped her chin between his forefinger and thumb, forcing her to meet his gaze. "Months ago, you left your mark upon my skin." He opened his hand and ran a finger across the pink welt marring his palm. "I can't let that go unanswered." He combed his fingers through her hair while brushing rose petals across her cheek. "Your bravery in the face of so much danger was a beautiful sight. There you stood, framed in broken glass. Red hair flowing around your face. Energy pulsing from your body. More powerful than any force I've experienced in over five hundred years. Glorious. And when I watched you shoot that beam through Quint's chest, I fell in love a little."

Violet rolled her eyes. "No doubt for the fifth time that week."

Flint hummed out a chuckle. "The violet has a little sass, does she?" He rocked back on his high-dollar shoes. "You'll need it." He clasped her hand in his. "You belong with us, Violet."

The fireplace flames danced and sizzled, reveling in his presence, leaping at the chance to underscore his purpose. Burning in a blaze that seared an unwelcome heat across her skin. Yet for a girl who'd walked alone her entire life, this concept of sharing her burden, of opening herself to another, was too much. Too intense.

Flint squeezed her hand. "Months ago in Quint's office, you proved the five of us can be so much more together. Asking for help, needing another, isn't in my nature." He tapped her nose with the rose bud. "But Terran insisted...and I...I will admit, we need you." He wrapped an arm around her waist and drew her against his warm body. "I need you."

"No." Violet braced a hand between them and eased away. He would not seduce her with his overused bag of tricks. Was her body steaming from his presence, or her proximity to the fire? And weren't they one and the same?

Focus. Study him analytically, as if he is the subject of scientific observation. Lost in thoughts of the fire triangle, she realized he was speaking about Quint.

"...if you think to face Quint on your own, think again. Terran and I—" His brow furrowed as he glanced at the window.

"Flint, please. I must fulfill the spell. I am the 25th daughter." She took the rose and ran her thumb across a thorn. "Therefore, the responsibility lies with me, and you are an unwelcome distraction." And there were too many thorns to bear before she could ever welcome the rose.

He barked out a laugh. "I am the distraction?" With a searing smile, he trailed a finger along her bottom lip. "I'll tell you what I am. I am the heat that smolders through your body, burning, blazing as desire. I sense each red stroke, flaring toward mine." Flint placed a hand upon her chest, just above her wildly beating heart. "Red and blue swirling into a heated pulse of violet. I resent this connection as much as you, but after living for almost six centuries, I...I can't believe I'm going to say this...I want to feel."

He ran a hand through his hair and then rested his forehead against hers. As if the weight of the world had dropped on his shoulders and he could no longer bear the burden. "Stop running. We both must stop running."

"I can't...I will never be that girl for you." Why did her heart suddenly ache? Why must she stay in this cold existence, never allowing the touch of another to melt her defenses? She had accepted her solitary existence, and this desire she felt for Flint was an unfair temptation. "I have no future," she whispered against his lips.

"Then I'll share some of mine." He nudged her mouth open with his own, teasing with light kisses, and then slanted his mouth over hers, again and again.

Though she could stop him, this…this heat, this instant spark, electrified her soul. Why now, when she was so close to fulfilling her ancestor's spell, was this opportunity for an emotional connection offered? These feelings racing through her body were too intense to quantify with simple words. With each stroke of his tongue, he made her believe she could lean on him. Grasp the support of his muscular body, hide behind his fiery protection, and build a wall of flame that no one could extinguish.

The scared, abandoned girl who craved the love of another, a soft touch, a warm embrace, allowed the kiss to go on and on, until he stilled and murmured a soft curse.

Stalking to the window, Flint yanked open the blinds, then once more raked a hand through his hair. "Damn it. There's a fire in town." He turned for the door but glanced back over his shoulder. "Wait for me here."

"No, Flint, please." She stepped across the room and tugged his sleeve. "Please, listen. I appreciate Terran buying me more time to prepare, but I must face Quint alone. The probability of your demise is too great. And if I discovered that dark-matter parasite controlled one of you, I'd still have to—"

"That won't happen." Flint gripped her shoulders. "Terran's knowledge of how to destroy Quint will only aid you. We need your power to finish this task, and we *will* face the final battle together. No more solitary forays. Terran almost…he could've…" Flint shook his head and heaved an exasperated sigh. "We can discuss Terran and Quint later, among other things." He wrapped a hand around her waist and bumped their hips together.

"Stop." She braced a hand against his solid chest, ignoring the flare of heat coursing through her body. "Your efforts at seduction won't sway my course."

Flint narrowed his eyes. "Think what you will about my reasons." He shrugged. "Disappear if you must, but know this, I will find you." He met her gaze, a bright glow of amber that flickered golden beside the firelight. "I will not abandon you."

How unfair. He must have used his Elemental gleaning gift to read her thoughts while her defenses were down. "Of all the things you could say to me, please, never that." Violet shook her head. "I have nothing to give."

"Your scientific mind may analyze and dissect all your softer emotions, but—desire, passion, love—those feelings do exist." Again, he glanced at the window.

"Those emotions have no place in my life." Violet dropped her gaze to the floor.

"Then, together, we'll find a place." He lifted her chin until she met his gaze. "I'll be back, Ms. Levina. We have unfinished business." He winked before walking to the door.

His demeanor was so sure, so confident, in a way she had never been—except in her studies. Science had never let her down. As she watched his solid frame disappear, she trailed a finger across her damp lips.

This feeling he brought about in her body was natural enough. Flint's tall, powerful frame, coal-black hair, and amber eyes were so masculine he could melt the sheets. *Actually, quite literally.* His features had obviously pushed her hormones and pheromones into overdrive. Her body being in its most fertile portion of the feminine cycle explained her white-hot attraction. This ache remaining at the core of her body would, in theory, fade once a potential mate was no longer available.

Simple enough. Yet, not simple at all. There were times in her life when she did crave the attentions of a man, a soft kiss. But, her life was not her own, hadn't been since she'd been born cursed with an ancestor's spell. Yet, there was a catch to this enchantment, one only she and her grandfather knew. This reason, among many others, was why she resisted joining the Elementals. She really had no way to help them, and they wouldn't understand her limitations; they'd want more, and she couldn't deliver.

Violet shook her head and felt something jostle in her hair. After brushing a hand through her wavy strands, she found a yellow rosebud with a broken stem. As a single tear escaped, she crushed the silky bud in her hand, allowing herself a moment of regret for all she could never have.

After all, she was a violet, not a rose.

CHAPTER 2

A heavy blanket of smoke eddied and churned. Black ash, flickering with orange and yellow, fluttered through the air before landing on his skin. Flint breathed deeply of the aromatic blend of his life force—fire.

He had no time to wallow in the blaze. With his elemental gifts, he'd detected a young female's faint heat signature on the second level of the building.

Pounding up flame-engulfed stairs, Flint braced an arm against a collapsing wooden beam. After regaining his balance, he shoved away the beam, but not before flames licked a hole through his white shirt. "Damn it, this is Valentino." He flicked the black char remnants off his designer dress shirt and sighed.

The intensity of the fire built— a cracking, hissing, popping symphony that would end in a crescendo of falling ash. Yet, Flint remained in his element. Only fire kept his peri-mortal body alive. Together with Nodin, who was air, Maya, who was water, and Terran, the newest little piggy in the pen, they represented the Elementals. Mother Nature had bestowed upon them "the gleaning", the ability to read and compel minds. They used their elemental abilities to protect the Earth and its people.

An elemental connection linked their minds, and although they allowed each other as much privacy as possible, no distance was too great for them to communicate. Right now he could use a little help from Nodin, but the man was likely blowing smoke up someone's ass with his ridiculous philosophy quotes.

Flint bit back a chuckle and refocused his energies. Though he'd rather be relaxing by the fire with a certain gamma-girl, his elemental duties obligated him to save the human trapped on the second floor. He'd reflect on Violet's world-weary indigo eyes, flaming red hair, and petite body when he didn't have a human to save.

As he traveled farther up the staircase, he reveled in the flames licking and caressing his skin in waves of orange, yellow, and red. Each sizzling and crackling flicker, fed his life force.

Under the weight of his hand, the burning banister crumbled. In the distance, he heard the faint whirl of sirens. Toasted wooden chunks disintegrated under his feet. Sniffing, he detected a simple accelerant—gasoline.

At the top of the stairs, he gathered his bearings. Flames waved along the walls like colorful orange curtains fringed with black-gray frills that danced and billowed.

Heading down the hall, he spread his arms wide as he walked through a flame wall, savoring the blaze.

Blinking through the smoke, he used his elemental senses to locate the human girl. Overhead, beams shuddered and groaned, snapping and cracking before falling, and striking his body with chunks of burning embers. As they landed on his exposed skin, the embers sizzled, and then disappeared.

Little time remained to rescue the human. If he didn't move fast, he'd be discovered and end up wasting time altering the minds of witnesses who questioned his ability to walk out of a roaring fire unscathed. Time Violet could use to slip away. Focusing, he closed his eyes and searched for his mark.

There.

He dashed up the hall and entered a sparsely furnished room. Flames and smoke curled around a solitary mattress. An emaciated girl lay on the floor in a corner with a wet rag covering the lower half of her face. Flint absorbed the flames dancing across the floor, and then lifted her in his arms.

Racing back down the hallway, he jumped across wooden floor joists barely capable of holding his weight and dashed for the stairs. Weakened by the fire, the bottom step crumbled, and his foot broke through. He tumbled with the girl in his arms, but quickly twisted and landed on his back.

A shout erupted behind him.

A firefighter, dressed in gray highlighted by yellow stripes, crept along the floor on all fours. He grabbed what remained of Flint's charred shirt and tugged him toward the front door.

Arms still full of the unconscious girl, Flint stood and stepped away from the scorching heat. His elemental duties screamed for him to return to the flames and absorb what he could before the fire spread. He shook his head, gathering his bearings. If he recalled correctly, this building's origins traced back to a premier woodsmith who'd created skis for the wealthy aristocrats traveling to Switzerland in hopes of taming the mighty Matterhorn.

"*Êtes-vous d'accord?*" His rescuer shook his shoulder.

Though his French was a tad rusty, Flint knew the man asked if he was all right. He answered in English. "Don't worry about me, help this girl." After passing his light burden to an awaiting EMT, Flint returned his gaze to the beckoning flames, the tempting blaze of red, yellow, and black, wishing they could rage around his body, that he could gather strength from each flicker, but his elemental identity must remain a secret. Too many witnesses now clogged the area. Fire trucks and emergency vehicle lights flashed red and blue across the dark night. A light mist brushed across his skin as the firefighters doused the flames with their hoses.

The persistent fireman shuffled Flint toward an EMT, guiding him in the same direction as the girl.

"Stop for a moment." Flint grabbed the fireman's arm and gazed into his eyes. He used his "gleaning" gift to re-align the man's memories and thoughts. "*You will not remember me. An unknown man rescued a girl. I was—*"

A microphone suddenly blocked his line of vision, breaking his trance-like lock on the man's mind.

A bright light blasted into Flint's eyes from the camera hoisted on the shoulder of a local station's cameraman. Blinking against the glare, he covered the lens with his hand.

A perfectly-coiffed blonde reporter in a blue suit cleared her throat, dabbed at her watering eyes with a tissue, and then shuffled along at his side. "*Excusez-moi. Qui êtes-vous?*"

"Who am I? I'm whoever you want me to be, baby." Flint flashed a smile and a wink, and then walked away.

He didn't have time for questions. Violet was likely escaping, meaning he'd have to go through the trouble of finding her again. Not that he didn't enjoy the chase, especially if he received more heated kisses as reward for his troubles.

Shouts erupted by the ambulances. He glanced over his shoulder and saw the girl he'd saved stumbling across the parking lot, racing in his direction. Lights from the fire trucks illuminated her wide, blue eyes.

"Wait, please wait." The girl halted before him, dropped to her knees, and hugged his legs. Voice scratchy from the smoke, she cleared her throat. "I knew you would come."

Flint gleaned the impulse control disorder—pyromania—burning through her disturbed mind. "How did you know?"

"The dark shadow said there were four, but one was just for me. I brought you here. I created you from the fire."

Flint pulled her to her feet. "Look at me." He met her gaze and seared new beliefs across her warped mind. *"You conjured no one. You barely escaped with your life. You will no longer play with fire. This madness ends now."*

Laughing, the girl shook her head. "No. No. No."

The dark miasma of her mind made changing her will almost impossible. She seemed half-lost on another plane of existence.

"The shadow said you would come, and you did...my fire man. Mine."

Her raspy words stunned him. Flint studied her. Unkempt blonde hair fluffed around her head, her eyes red-rimmed, and the tears leaking from each corner left pale pink streaks on her soot-covered cheeks. Her clothes—blue hospital pants and matching shirt. Had she escaped from a nearby facility? How had this girl learned of his link to fire? And what had she said about there being four?

No matter, he'd tattoo a new truth across her mind. After tonight, she would not remember a "fire" man. Once more, he locked his gaze with hers. Glimmering into her mind, he redirected her thoughts, yet, her madness fought against his Elemental will. *"Fire burns. Destroys. Do not seek me again."*

With a shake of her head, the girl simply rubbed her wet cheek against his half-charred shirt.

Scuffling shoes sounded on the pavement. An EMT approached and hooked his hand around the blonde's elbow.

"Miss, please come with me." The medic shot him a glare before leading away the pyro-girl.

Flint shrugged off the man's attitude and surveyed the scene.

Firefighters had most of the fire snuffed. A cacophony of sizzles and hisses came from smoldering remains. Ash drifted and circled through the air. He clasped a piece of the floating debris and studied the white and black scrap in his hand.

An odd sensation shot a heated warning over his skin. He shifted his gaze and saw pyro-girl watching him.

She smiled, but her eyes—was it a trick of the light, or had they turned fully black? She blinked, and once more they were blue.

He stiffened and watched her retreat into an ambulance. Had he imagined the darkness? Or had Quint found a way to return?

Once more, his Elemental team was in danger, and his plucky little Violet would need his help now more than ever.

CHAPTER 3

"What shall I do, Heisenberg? Should I continue on my own? Complete my studies with the funds left from Quint's now-defunct drug company?" Lounging in his makeshift office, Veimhet Schwarz handed a bit of leftover bacon to his German Spitz, Heisenberg. "Yes, I know curiosity killed the cat. I'm very aware you'd much rather do that, my little Spitzy." He tucked the fluffy black dog into his leather bag before heading to the library across town.

The dusty smell of used books usually comforted Schwarz, but he was anything but comfortable with his current situation. He hadn't heard from his employer, Quint, in months, although the bank accounts remained open. Their last meeting had revealed a new world where the mythology of the elements and science combined.

"Stay still and be quiet. We'll only be here for an hour, and then I'll take you to the dog park as a reward." As he studied the library patrons, Schwarz shifted in the creaky, wooden library chair and sipped the last drop from his to-go coffee cup.

Each discreet meeting brought Schwarz one step closer to completing his last assignment—capturing Violet Levina—a girl with immeasurable power.

Prior to his disappearance, Quint had directed him to Kilkenny, Ireland. His orders included investigating the history behind Petronella de Meath, a supposed matriarch of witches in fourteenth century Ireland, and the first recorded witch to die by burning at the stake.

Schwarz had heard rumors of Violet's lineage during his studies of Germany's forays into the occult throughout WWII. He alerted Quint to what he believed were grim witches' tales, but a grain of truth resided in all fiction. Schwarz believed Violet could harness the power of the entire Electromagnetic spectrum. Microwaves, gamma rays, radio waves—each allegedly under her control. Limitless energy. With a flick of her hand, she could disrupt all electrical signals by generating an EMP, electromagnetic pulse. She could trigger radiation burns, or radiation sickness with X-rays or gamma rays. What brought about an intense wave of giddiness in Schwarz was her ability to boil a human body using microwaves. Since the body is composed of sixty percent water, vibrating water molecules would, in essence, heat a subject from the inside out.

Schwarz shivered with excitement. "We'll have to wear sunscreen around Ms. Levina so she doesn't burn us with her ultraviolet light." He chuckled. "We won't let her hurt you though, Heisy. No, we won't." Schwarz scruffed his pup's head. When he noted a woman sitting a few tables down glaring in his direction, he merely cleared his throat and raised a brow.

Dressed in an all-black suit, a shady character sporting mirrored shades pushed open the library door, scanned the area, and then weaved his way through the tables.

Schwarz placed a bookmark in his Celtic lore tome. "This candidate looks promising, Heisenberg."

After an extensive search through back channels for individuals willing to take on a very specific challenge, he'd indicated where he would be every afternoon at 3:00 p.m.

The man sat across from him, but he did not speak.

Several moments passed in silence.

Schwarz almost rolled his eyes at this ridiculous man's game of who-will-speak-first. *These bounty hunters and their eccentric ways.* "Good afternoon, sir. Are you looking for a specific book?"

"No. I understand you have task." The burly man tapped a finger against the table.

He wasn't Irish. Based on his accent he was something else, perhaps Ukrainian. Light brown hair, prominent nose, flared "cauliflower" ears, pale skin, and clothes that Schwarz believed were tailored. He shrugged. "Yes, a simple task, really. I need a woman."

"Easy enough." The man adjusted the sunglasses on his nose.

Schwarz studied his reflection in the frames and refrained from rolling his eyes. Again. "No. Not easy. You must hire others to retrieve this woman, and then deliver her to me. Alive. Unharmed. No one who has seen my face, or yours, can be involved in her capture."

"The price just went up." The Ukrainian sank back in the flimsy wood chair, folding both hands across his stomach.

"Did it?" Schwarz tapped his empty Styrofoam coffee cup on the table and adjusted the knot in his green tie.

The man smirked.

"This conversation is over." Schwarz stood and straightened his cuffs. He'd had enough of bulky bullies believing they held all the power. Brains beat brawn every time.

The man pulled his mobile phone from the inside front pocket of his suit jacket. He flipped around his phone and scrolled through photos of Schwarz in many different locales. "We know who you are. We know where you're staying. We know you eat Muesli for breakfast, and you typically eat barley stew with farmer's bread for lunch, followed by a light fruit plate, and then you take a walk. You come to the library every day at three p.m. and stay exactly thirty minutes. We know you worked for Aether Pharmaceuticals. We know of your 'secret' experiments. Do not believe you are working with amateurs, Mr. Schwarz."

Schwarz studied him for a moment as preconceived notions about this bounty hunter's abilities realigned in his mind. Decision made, he passed over a single card with two words written in black ink.

Violet Levina.

CHAPTER 4

"What are you doing?"

Violet jumped as Pillar shifted into the bedroom, flipping her white-blonde hair over a shoulder. Though not an Elemental, Pillar existed in order to maintain the balance of salt on the Earth—in essence, the human personification of sodium chloride.

Watching her friend cross the room, Violet mentally recited *Matthew 5:13*, "You are the salt of the earth; but if the salt has become tasteless, how can it be made salty again? It is no longer good for anything, except to be thrown out and trampled under foot by men." Had Pillar's nature brought about the initial characterization of the phrase, "salt of the earth"? Had ancient cultures recognized and celebrated her as a person of great worth and reliability?

Her friend tilted her head. "What are you thinking about?"

"Nothing, just packing." Violet bundled her own unruly red mass into a large clip, then continued folding her pants before settling them in her suitcase. Even though she didn't have time to properly fold each item, she'd attempt some sense of order. Her life was chaotic enough. Not to mention the threat of a fired-up Elemental soon to return, offering kisses and roses, and who knew what else.

"Packing? You're leaving?" Pillar ran long, pale fingers over the blue-flowered bedspread. "Why?"

"Have you seen my coral top?" Standing outside the closet, Violet ripped the dry-cleaner's wrap off her shirts before tossing them on the bed.

Avoiding situations that caused inner turmoil was something she'd developed when, at the age of seven, her mother had abandoned her. Violet had never understood the why's of her mother's disappearance. She only knew one morning her mother was there, and the next she was not.

Perhaps her mother had been frightened of her daughter's curse, or perhaps she no longer wished to be a mother. The enchantment devised by her ancestor, Sorcha, daughter to Petronella de Meath, had carried down through the centuries. As Violet was the 25th daughter born in Sorcha's line, she was the supposed final solution to Quint's dark stain on the earth. Final—a word Violet had struggled with her entire life. Her stomach churned at the thought.

Pillar grabbed the beige sweater from her hand. "Violet, if you would stop running for five minutes and just speak to the man, everything would be over. You know what he wants. Tell him no, and he'll move on."

"I did. Flint was here, earlier tonight." Violet brushed two fingers across her lips, remembering the heat he'd generated, and then recalled how he'd found her in the first place. She glared at Pillar. "But you should already know that. You do realize my co-worker was just letting me stay here during her business trip. What if she'd come home early and found Flint lounging in her living room?"

Pillar simply shrugged.

"How could you?" Violet clenched her fists to hold back the gift that seemed to manifest in Pillar's presence. The tips of her fingers heated against her palms. She took a deep breath and released it slowly, searching for calm. "You know the danger involved. The full magnitude of my powers needs further study. If I were angered or distressed by one of the Elementals, I'm not sure what would happen. I'm not fully prepared. How many times have we discussed this?"

"So you think to escape fate?" Pillar raised a pale blonde brow. "What kind of life is this, always on the run? You've known the inevitability of your existence since you were sixteen."

Violet sank onto the bed and lined up several pairs of socks before folding them neatly. "Flint's like a fire-breathing dragon hovering overhead, just waiting to blaze down when I least expect it. I don't like surprises. I need order." She bit her bottom lip and glanced at Pillar. "He…he frightens me."

Not the whole truth, but partial. Feelings, in general, created a sense of anxiety. Emotional attachments were not something she had ever studied or researched, therefore, not something she could comprehend.

"No. I don't believe he invokes fear." Graceful in her pale blue dress, Pillar dropped beside her and settled against the headboard. "Flint excites you. And who can blame you, with all those muscles, those feral amber eyes, that thick black hair? I've always had a weakness for men with dark hair."

"I agree. He is quite...virile, but he's utterly maddening." Violet studied the dull white socks in her hand. "His relentless pursuit on behalf of the Elementals is all for naught. This duty is my own. I'll not have him...I-I mean them, harmed in the process."

"You use that ridiculous spell as an excuse to hide from life." Pillar nudged Violet's hip with her foot. "No one says you have to marry the guy. Just use him for a little fun."

"His power—"

"Is no match for your own, Gamma-girl." Pillar laughed then took the socks from Violet and slipped them on her feet. "Consider joining them. You'll need their combined strength."

"And you, Pillar? What will you do?" Violet wiggled her friend's big toe.

Pillar heaved a world-weary sigh. "I may...my time here...the choices I've made during my long existence are irrelevant." She swung her long legs over the side of the bed and rose to stare out the window. "The Elementals can help you prepare for Quint's return. He'll come back stronger, wilder, bent on revenge."

"The inevitability of Quint's return isn't something I like to be reminded of, Pillar. Why do you insist upon it?"

"Because he *will* return. If that is your destiny, if that is what this prophecy portends, then he will come back." Pillar turned and gripped her shoulders. "Quint is likely only slightly incapacitated after Terran struck him down in battle. You have no idea the unending power that personification of dark matter wields." Frowning, she shook Violet's shoulders, her pale-yellow eyes blazing almost fully white. "Five against one just might be enough. Add in the full potential of the electromagnetic spectrum raging inside your body, and then maybe, just maybe, you can destroy Quint forever. You have to try. Please. He'll come for me, bent on revenge, and I...I..."

With a trembling hand, Pillar covered her mouth and turned away.

"Please, sit." Violet took Pillar's hand and pulled her back to the bed. "Let's not talk about Quint if the topic upsets you."

Pillar wrapped both arms around her middle. Her honey-colored gaze seemingly focused on the white socks covering her feet. "I'm scared. I'll admit that only to you, dear friend. I've made so many mistakes." As she shook her head, her long blonde hair skated back and forth across her lower back.

Violet wrapped an arm around Pillar's shoulder. Her friend rarely spoke of her past, and refused to answer any questions related to her "salty" existence.

Though if Violet considered sodium chloride from a historical perspective, and the immeasurable impact salt had in shaping the world, she couldn't help but wonder what fascinating moments in time her friend had experienced.

Had Pillar educated each culture in salt's uses? Was she the reason so many different civilizations recognized the chemical for its various purposes? Had she perpetuated one of the greatest discoveries in history?

From the earliest days, humans used salt for its medicinal and therapeutic benefits. Salt was a food-preserver, exfoliate, cleanser, religious offering, currency, trade product, and a spice. Human blood was composed of 0.9% of sodium chloride, so the importance of maintaining the substance's health was crucial if you considered the ramifications should it not exist.

Upon reflection, her friend deserved so much more. Praise, adulation, respect, and yet, here she sat frightened and seeking comfort.

But, what could Violet say that would offer solace? How much had this woman endured during her long existence? She brushed her hand up and down Pillar's upper arm. "I will destroy Quint, but first, I must discover a way to contain him. The solutions are within my family's spell and ritual books in Castle Nemon's library. It's critical I study them again to find some way to immobilize Quint, so I can perform my final duty. The day I helped Maya by the lake, I was unprepared. I've neglected my studies, because I…because I don't want the spell to be real. I've tried to bury these unrealistic notions in science, but after facing off with Quint in his office, I've begun to understand the depth of my power and duty." Violet brushed a hand through her hair. "In that moment, I became someone else, my entire being filled with hate and a desire for revenge. That sensation frightened me, and until I understand why I lost control, I believe staying away from triggers is the best course."

"Books won't have the answers, Vi. You need a full-fledged command center, because only suffering and death will follow Quint's return. Darkness, pain, complete annihilation. You must prepare. I cannot protect you."

"I would not place that burden on you." Violet patted her friend's shoulder. "I only ask that you travel with me to Ireland. You were with Quint for many years. Perhaps you might recall something that could give me an edge."

"Years wasted." Pillar tightened her fists in her lap. "The Elementals, you see…Nodin and I…we…our past…they don't trust me, for very good reasons."

"I'll convince them you've changed." Violet bumped her shoulder.

"That's the problem, my friend." Pillar flashed a tight-lipped grin. "I don't know that I have."

Violet studied Pillar. Her ivory skin seemed to pale with each passing day. "I think the Elementals do have reasons to trust you. Especially after we helped them fight off Quint months ago."

"That only proved I'm capable of changing allegiances." Pillar threw up her hands. "I found someone who could destroy that dark matter parasite. You. The Elementals actually hindered our plan by confronting Quint before we were ready."

While Violet understood the difficulties that lay ahead, she felt bound to make Pillar believe her efforts were appreciated, no matter how late in the game. This creature beside her came from a different century, one where women had to fend for themselves because they had no rights. Was it any wonder Pillar was jaded?

"Try to look at what happened from a more positive perspective, Pillar." Violet nudged her friend's knee. "I had a chance to use my gifts. By utilizing the particle nature of the electromagnetic spectrum, I hit him with a high-energy beam of photons and converted his dark matter into regular matter. A test-run, if you will, before the final battle." Destroying Quint was her destiny. Her burden. Having a friend who knew her purpose was welcome, but at the same time she understood, at the end, she'd face Quint alone.

Throughout her life, Violet had avoided intimate relationships, focusing instead on her job as Director of Research and Development of Quantum Mechanics at CERN. Her life revolved around reading, studying, and gathering facts, because science didn't deceive or abandon you.

"Pillar, I've spent my life researching dark matter and dark energy. So, do not fear." Violet brushed Pillar's hair off her shoulder. "I will do everything in my power to keep everyone, and every being, safe."

"Your power won't be enough. You can't defeat Quint alone." Pillar stood, and then cupped Violet's cheeks in her cool, slim fingers. "You must change. You must find something worth fighting for. Destiny. Prophecy. Duty. None are enough. You must feel. Only then can you win. I know, because I...I no longer feel. I've lost all purpose. Let Flint be the light in your world of shadows."

Violet remained still as her friend left the room, yet she felt Pillar's words resonate across her soul—her heart. A heart that ached for everything Pillar had endured throughout her unceasing lifespan.

Studying the chipped, pale pink polish on her toes, she contemplated Pillar's words—her quiet plea.

Did she live her life in the shadows? Hidden. Gray. Bundled away from life.

What would happen if she lit her life's short wick? If she illuminated her world with a passionate blaze like Flint, would she find release from this pounding, aching loneliness? This void she'd felt since he'd left her by the fire. What had he altered within her? And how much would remain when he burned through her life, leaving nothing but the smoldering embers of her heart?

CHAPTER 5

"What are you doing here, Earthman?" Back home in Kostroma, Russia, Flint shivered from the autumn breeze drifting across his bare skin as he leaned against the faded wooden doorframe of his glassblowing workshop.

"What? You don't like people invading your space? Imagine that." Terran, his fellow Elemental, stood with both hands stuffed in the front pockets of worn work jeans.

His jeans—a personal favorite actually, though they were long overdue for the scrap pile.

"I could smell you a mile away, Pigpen. What'd you do to my jeans?" Flint flicked a hand in Terran's direction.

"I found this rope on the workbench and looped it through. Makeshift belt." Terran tugged at the frayed string wound tight around his narrow waist.

Flint shook his head and grinned. "You should know better than to think you can fill my pants."

Terran chuckled and ran his fingers through his brown locks. "First of all, the nickname is getting old, but then again, an ancient relic like you shouldn't strain your over-fried gray matter. Secondly, don't worry about what's in my pants. Third,"—he waved a hand toward the shelves—"you have nothing to eat, not even a Green Moose beer. Real hospitable."

Flint shook his head then grasped Terran by the shoulder and brought him close for a gruff, one-armed embrace. "Isn't there some eco-disaster somewhere? Maya send you?" Though he'd never admit the truth, he enjoyed these visits with Terran. He stifled the thought before the brainiac Earthman gleaned his pleasure at this unexpected visit.

"Many disasters, many places, but you come first." Terran pounded a sturdy love tap against his back, and then stepped away. Picking through the glass items on the table, he lifted a vase streaked with reds and blues. "We haven't heard from you in a while."

Flint sensed the energy thrumming between the glass and Terran's hand. As Earth, Terran bore the greatest connection to the elements.

"Aren't you still in the honeymoon phase with that water-girl of yours? Maya bored of that little twig already?" Flint picked up a red glass rod and tapped it against his Kevlar work gloves.

"Is that your not-so-subtle way of asking how Maya's doing?" Terran chuckled. "A minor chemical spill occurred. She's cleaning water in the Appalachian Kanawha River region. It's known as Chemical Valley. Plus, Mother said we'd been on vacation long enough and needed to get back to work." He shrugged and placed the vase on the table. "What's the status on Violet?"

Withholding his concerns over Maya working alone, Flint focused on his report. Terran had taken the lead in their band of elemental misfits. Someone needed to hold the reins, sure as hell wouldn't be him. "Pillar led me to Vernier, Switzerland, where Violet's been hiding. I had her in my grasp, but then a girl started a fire. Kind of odd." Flint met his friend's gaze and mentally projected his memories.

"Pyromania." Terran rubbed his chin. "Huh...that *is* worrisome."

"The girl was a tad off her rocker. She said, 'I knew you would come.'"

"What else did you glean from her thoughts?" As Terran paced the narrow dirt path between the workbench and the supplies littering the floor, he tapped his bottom lip with an index finger.

The head-hog was obviously in problem-solving mode. Flint refrained from chuckling at his overly-analytical friend. Violet was likely the same. Lord help him if the two ever put their mighty brains together. "Pyro-girl was a psychiatric patient. Her mind couldn't be turned, too broken by her mental illness." He scratched the back of his neck. "Violet's been...elusive. I don't understand why she's afraid. She mentioned some prophecy, or enchantment. After the fire, I went back to her friend's apartment, but she'd fled. I can't even find her through gleaning. After five hundred years of easily detecting and changing human thought patterns, I'm a tad irritated by this roadblock."

Terran halted pacing and met his gaze. "The very waves, radio waves, that carry our gleaning gift are part of a wave-length she can control. We are like CB radios. We can send and receive signals from each other through our elemental link. Her own link to those same waves allows her to elude your attempts." He leaned against the worktable and tapped the stainless-steel punty rod against a charred wooden sawhorse. Silence reigned a moment, broken only by the continual clink, clink, clink of the hollow shaping tool against the wood. "Maybe you should search for the absence of thought. The void."

"What? Why?" Flint scrounged a pair of jeans and a flannel shirt from an old trunk set back in the corner. Flying as smoke from Switzerland hadn't allowed for clothing, and he was well aware of Terran's continued unease with their frequently necessary nudity. *Piggy was a prude.*

"Just because I don't want to see your hairy ass doesn't make me a prude." Terran huffed.

"For someone so sensitive about others reading his mind, you sure find it easy—"

"Back on point, please." Terran jabbed the steel rod in his direction. "You say you can't detect Violet. Well, instead of searching for her life force specifically, let's search out areas of emptiness."

Well, hell. Flint stepped across the room and grabbed his friend's shoulders. "Of course, Terran. You're a genius." Heat coursed down his spine, illuminating the answer. "Take my hand." Excitement flared over this possible channel to locate his wayward redhead.

"You want to hold hands?" Obviously unnerved, Terran tried adjusting glasses that no longer perched on his nose, a human habit he hadn't broken since his transformation into the Earth elemental less than a year earlier.

"Last fall, Maya, Nodin, and I joined hands to hunt down diseased wolves in order to capture them before they infected their pack. We combined our gleaning gift and tracked their location. Since you know what to look for, you can direct our combined power."

"Sure." Terran shrugged. "It's worth a try." He stilled for a moment, and then jabbed Flint's chest with the punty rod. "Another thought…this just came to me…we could use the earth's magnetic field to look for distortions due to her massive amount of stored energy."

"Hey, careful with that rod, Pigpen." Flint rubbed his left pec. "You get laid much, speaking all that nerd lingo?"

"Stick and stones, Flint. Sticks and stones." Terran snapped his fingers, creating a flame, and then he formed a pool of water in his other palm and drenched the fire.

"Yes, I know, little piggy hogged all four gifts." Flint remained irritated over Mother Nature granting Terran the ability to control each element. Still, he was Earth—the center. Without earth, no other element—fire, water, or air—would exist.

Flint sank to the floor, yanking down Terran beside him. "If I discover you've told that philosophical air-bag Nodin I used his method, I will burn a pig snout tattoo across your forehead."

Terran shoved away his hand. "If you think he won't glean this moment from my thoughts, you're a fool."

A fool, was it? He may have allowed Terran the lead, but that didn't mean he blindly followed direction. "Let's get started. Or do you need to phone the little lady first, and let her know you made it here okay?"

"Maya knows." Narrowing his gaze, Terran sniffed.

Flint quirked a brow, and then delved into Terran's memories. A red-hot vision seared across his mind—Maya smiling down at Terran, blonde hair flowing around her shoulders, lips slightly parted while she rocked back and forth. "Damn, she's—"

Terran raised his fist and streamed gallons of water over Flint's head. The workshop's dirt floor rumbled and cracked. The fire in the hearth flickered and leapt in their direction as the Earthman growled out through gritted teeth, "My mind is off-limits."

"I see my water-girl's been getting lots of exercise." Water droplets sizzling on his skin, Flint waggled his brows.

Terran punched him in the jaw while mumbling a few choice words about Elementals and mental privacy.

With a chuckle, Flint worked his jaw back and forth before grabbing Terran's clenched fist. "Let's do this."

"Maya's right. You are a flaming ass." Frowning, Terran settled across from him.

"Tell me something I don't know." Flint shrugged, though secretly glad Maya was content with her lot. *Or pigpen.* At the thought, Flint fought back a grin.

Terran wet the dirt floor at his sides then rubbed the mud on his hands before clasping Flint's fingers. "Concentrate on a blank room. An area where no thoughts, memories, or dreams exist, and then follow that colorless wave back to its starting point."

Flint closed his eyes and concentrated on connecting with Terran's mind. Riding earth's frequencies to locate a vibrant violet who would soon realize she wasn't always the brightest bloom in the room.

Pigpen just might have her beat.

Mentally drifting across the ether in a blur of greens, blues, and browns, they found and followed an empty white trail.

Flint swore he could smell Violet's faint floral bouquet.

They were close. Gaining ground.

A vision appeared of a white car with rental tags on the bumper, traveling down the highway. Locking in on the location, they approached the driver's side window and—a familiar chuckle broke their concentration.

Mind back in his workshop, Flint heaved a long, heavy sigh and opened his eyes.

Nodin stood behind Terran in all his Native American glory—jet-black hair, loose and flowing past his shoulders, red-brown skin, sky-blue eyes, and his lean build evident due to his nudity.

"Great." Flint released Terran's clutch on his hands. "What are you doing here?"

"What am *I* doing?" Nodin placed a flattened hand upon his breastbone. "I believe the more pertinent question is, what are *you* doing?" He waved his fingers in their direction while raising a single brow.

Nodin's grin was far too wide for Flint's taste. He closed his eyes and muttered a silent plea for forbearance.

Nodin chuckled. "Well, I *was* here to inform you of Mother's directive to investigate Veimhet Schwarz. He's in Kilkenny, Ireland, which I hardly believe is a coincidence, considering Violet's ancestry. But now, I find I'm quite interested in what kind of endeavor was being employed here."

31

Refraining from answering Nodin's primary question, Flint headed for his trunk and dug out clothes for the air Elemental. He whipped a pair of sweatpants at Nodin and then leaned against his worktable.

Nodin slipped on the pants and tightened the drawstring. He glanced at Terran. "Spill, brother."

"We were tracking Violet." Terran kept his gaze on the ground as Nodin dressed. "We started by following a void in thought patterns. Another option would be to search for a large energy field." He shrugged, and then adjusted the tie on his jeans. "Flint said you'd done something similar before."

Nodin chuckled. "I'm sure he said plenty more besides. The poet Robert Service says, 'It isn't the mountain ahead that wears you out—it's the grain of sand in your shoe.' Let's tackle each grain of sand, one at a time. I'll join your circle."

Flint poked at the fire in the furnace. The yellow-orange flames flickered impatiently, waiting for him to work his glassblowing magic. "Before we start, let me get this straight: Mother Nature wants you to investigate Schwarz's purpose in Ireland? What could that menace to science find there?" He mentally weighed the time involved traveling to those green shores versus focusing his efforts on locating Violet. He refused to withdraw from the hunt, regardless of Mother's wishes.

"He could discover certain aspects of her history." Nodin shrugged. "The answers to the present always lie in the past. Schwarz poses a threat to more than just Violet. His inhumane scientific practices must be stopped." He banged a fist against the table, jostling shards of broken glass. "This man justifies his foul experiments in the name of science."

Terran scraped his hand across the dirt floor. "Many scientists throughout history have done the same. Look at General Shiro Ishii or Josef Mengele." He shook his head. "However, that is a discussion for another day. Our primary focus here is to find Violet, and if Schwarz hinders our plans, then we'll deal with him, as well."

Sometimes, Flint could just kiss his rational friend, but he'd leave that to Maya. "Good call. Nodin, let's wrap this up. Pigpen is itching to spend a little more time at the water trough."

Nodin slapped Terran on the shoulder. "Can't say I blame him. Although Maya is—"

"Water trough? Really?" Terran dusted his hands against his

pants. "It's a good thing Maya isn't here, or neither of you would be standing."

Flint glanced at Nodin before they sank next to Terran. After a quick glimpse into Nodin's mind, he detected a swirling jumble of thoughts. *Maya. Pain. Schwarz. Experiments. Ireland. Pillar. Guilt.*

Nodin hissed out a breath, caught his eye, and slightly shook his head. "Let's concentrate on finding Violet."

Flint hesitated a moment, and then joined hands with his elemental brothers.

With Terran leading the way, they rode along the white wave until they came to a road surrounded by vineyards. Flint recognized the area as the Burgundy region, or Côte-d'Or, in the eastern part of France.

Locks of red hair fluttered out the open driver's side window. Static was replaced by some classic rock tune that sounded a lot like…"Ramble On" by Led Zeppelin. On the passenger side, a husky, scratchy voice sang loud and clear. A flash of white-blonde hair—Pillar.

Flint caught Nodin's quick inhalation before his friend's concentration broke. "Damn it, Nodin. We had her." Flint shoved Nodin's shoulder.

"Do you really think ole' Pigpen didn't root out the route?" Terran reached across and tapped Flint's knee with a fist. "They are on the A-39, heading toward Dijon. Besides, I'm sure you can find her easily, now that you know how to focus your gleaning." Terran stood, helping Nodin to his feet. "I don't believe Pillar means Violet any harm."

"Why would she harm her?" Flint scoffed. "Violet's her only safeguard against Quint." When around Nodin, he attempted to mask his opinions about Pillar. Though he believed Violet could hold her own against that devious blonde saltshaker, he worried over the false beliefs the woman could implant in his innocent flower's mind. What kind of deceptive information was Pillar feeding her about their elemental team?

Nodin drifted across the room to the doorway.

A slight breeze rustled Flint's hair. He didn't delve into Nodin's thoughts again, because he detested seeing the guilt the man still carried, even after more than three hundred years. His long-time friend believed he alone bore the blame for Pillar's downfall. Not entirely accurate from an outsider's viewpoint. However, Nodin was correct in noting history held the answers. Not that those answers ever eased any lingering pain or heartbreak. "Nodin, you have a job to do. A responsibility. Whatever Pillar's reasons, she can't be of concern. Violet is our focus, and concerning that, I agree with Mother that perhaps you should delve into Schwarz's purpose in Ireland."

Nodin remained at the door. "I don't need you to remind me of my duties."

Flint nodded, and then glanced at Terran. "I'll head out after I spend some time in the furnace."

Terran kept his gaze on Nodin for a moment before fiddling with the tools littering the workbench. "I imagine it's easier to work glass when you can actually stand in the fire." His brown-eyed gaze shot to Flint. "Maybe you could teach me glassblowing. Maya would love one of these trinkets."

Flint arched a brow. "Trinkets?" Vanity came hand-in-hand with his otherworldly abilities. Hell, he was just vain, period, but these *trinkets* were a point of pride—a stopgap to the continually fading memories of his human life. Creating glass sculptures had kept him grounded over the centuries. Terran would understand the importance of such human attachments after a few hundred years. *Maybe.* He grabbed a sketchpad, ready for these invaders to leave him at peace.

"Speaking of Maya, I just left her and Mother." Nodin waved a hand at Terran. "They were making some progress, but Mother delivered her back to her sea cave due to the toxicity of the chemicals."

And just like that, all thoughts of peace dissipated.

Terran gasped, transformed into a flurry of dust, and disappeared. In his wake, the table contents unsettled enough to knock off a glass vase.

Nodin caught the red-streaked vessel before it crashed to the ground and set it back on the table.

Flint glared at Nodin. "Couldn't you have eased into Maya being back at her cave? Last time she wavered on the edge of true-death, due to Quint's attack. Real smooth, Airbag."

"Once again, don't tell me how to handle my duties." Nodin jabbed a finger on the table. "My goal was to get Terran to the cave.

Mother didn't say how, just to get him there so Maya would heal faster."

"That bad?" Flint hated to think of the blonde beauty suffering.

"No, not like before, but Maya will be calmer with Terran beside her."

"So, I'm stuck with you, then?" Flint shoved more wood into the furnace before sinking into a worn rocking chair he'd made many, many years ago. Getting the curve just right was the hardest thing he'd ever done.

"As you say, I need to pay a visit to Schwarz. We could go to Ireland together."

"I need to find Violet."

Nodin leaned against the worktable and crossed his ankles. "Terran's been researching ways to help Violet contain Quint."

"He mentioned something before about combining their powers." Flint tended to zone out when Terran spoke in science-tongue.

Nodin rolled his eyes. "His 'science-tongue' may be the only thing getting us out of this mess."

"Stay out of my mind, air-boy." Flint winged a piece of glass at Nodin's head.

After catching the flying shard, Nodin tossed it on a table. "Listen, Terran read me this physics article which theorized on containing matter in a magnetic field and then converting it to dark matter by using a high-energy magnetic field." He kicked Flint's knee. "You paying attention?"

"Kick me again, and you'll see attention." Just because science talk wasn't his strong suit didn't mean he wouldn't step up when required.

Nodin nodded. "So, that being said, maybe we can reverse the effects. Terran could contain Quint's dark matter using Earth's magnetic field, then once he's trapped, Violet could convert him into regular matter. After which, in theory, he would be as fragile as any human, and we could disperse his energy into another form."

Tapping his index finger against his bottom lip, Flint rocked back in his chair. "Terran did a damn fine job facing Quint on his own. I'm still pissed I wasn't part of that showdown."

Earth served as the Elementals stabilizing force—their grounding plane. Destiny had led Terran into Maya's arms. Their connection was like wet leaves scattered across a forest floor. A necessary combination that meshed together blues, greens, and browns in a never-ending chain that fed nature.

Flint craved a similar connection. To feel again. To love. Too many years had passed as a solitary flicker on earth's surface. He wanted to burn brighter, illuminate his heart in a vibrant mix of red and violet.

Nodin stopped in the middle of his monologue on Terran's theories and Mother Nature's warnings to clasp Flint's shoulder. "I didn't realize you were so—"

"Don't." Flint brushed him off. He didn't appreciate Nodin gleaning his thoughts. "You should probably go."

"I understand, Flint. At one time, my heart was more than an empty hollow." Nodin sighed and was silent a moment as he gazed through the soot-covered window. "Guilt still batters me during quiet times. How much of who Pillar has become is my fault? I'll never know. But I cannot live my life with the expectation she will change. I made the choice...I made it...I have to wonder if perhaps...if perhaps our love wasn't built on anything but mutual loneliness. Antoine De Saint-Exupéry said, 'Life has taught us that love does not exist in gazing at each other, but in looking outward together in the same direction.' I don't know if Pillar and I ever had the same goals, the same understanding of the future. Our desire was so heady, we couldn't see anything else."

Flint stood beside Nodin and bumped his shoulder. "You want a fucking tissue?"

"Nice flower tattoo, you do that yourself?" Nodin pointed at a purple violet Flint had recently inked above his heart. "Next thing we know, you'll be wearing pink."

Flint shrugged. "Hey, you know what they say, 'real men wear pink.'"

"So you're saying the next tattoo will be pink?" Nodin chuckled. "How old is this autoclave anyway?" He opened and then slammed shut the door to Flint's tattoo tool sterilizer.

"Stop messing with my stuff." Flint slapped his hand. "I don't like visitors, so get out of here. I've got places to be." He slipped out of his pants and headed for the furnace.

A brisk breeze and airy laugh whipped through the room as Nodin exited.

Flint considered his easy friendship with Nodin and Terran. He'd watched new personifications of water, earth, and air come and go, while he remained constant. Mother Nature always transformed another for their team. The reasons others left this life behind were their own. Could he do the same?

Rubbing his eyes, he stepped into the blazing furnace. When was the last time he'd truly loved? His Elemental duties led him from one corner of the earth to another. He'd been driven mad many times by his lack of a real connection and frequently escaped into a fiery pit until the emptiness passed. Which was why, when Violet placed her hand in his and he'd felt something new—a slight flicker in his heart, he'd had no choice but to pursue her.

She also felt their connection but ran from the truth. Their destiny.

Not him, he always forged straight ahead. Ms. Levina would learn that very soon. But would he, could he, love her? Could he remain in her life and watch her grow old, then die? How many years would they truly have together? Twenty? Thirty? Was asking her to stay by his side fair?

For the first time in many years, a question ignited—Would he forego this elemental life?

Rejuvenated by the flames, he stepped out of the furnace but tumbled to his knees, thrown by the direction of his thoughts, by the actual consideration of leaving this world behind. But for now…he'd work through his churning emotions as he always had—by creating art.

Bracing a hand on the table, Flint stood then gathered his tools.

Preheating the tip of the blowpipe, he dipped it in the molten glass bubbling in the furnace. After gathering the molten glass onto the end of the blowpipe, he headed for the marver, a flat slab of marble. Very clear of the vision he wished to create—a vivid purple violet with a red heart at its core.

CHAPTER 6

Schwarz's re-purposed delivery van idled on a shrubbery-lined road down the hill from Castle Nemon, Violet's ancestral home.

Heisenberg shivered and whined in the passenger seat, distressed over his wet state.

Earlier, they'd hiked along a worn path at the rear of the castle where the trail crossed through ancient stone ruins. Over-time, bright green grass had crept up the sides of the relics. At the edge of the grounds, Schwarz stepped onto the castle's freshly mown lawn. He jumped back as a strong electrical current buzzed up his leg, and then froze in fear when Heisenberg yelped and tumbled down a small hill into a muddy drainage area.

After recalling the nightmare, Schwarz brushed a hand over his still damp dog. "My poor, Spitzy. Are you all right?"

Heisenberg growled and bit at the hot air blasting from the vents.

Since a backdoor approach no longer seemed an option, Schwarz contemplated his next step while pretending to study an unfolded map.

Had witchcraft served as the castle's electrical security shield? And who wielded the power? The owner of the castle, Violet's grandfather, Eamon, was a reputed wizard. Had he set a magical boundary spell to keep out intruders? Or was a security system buried underground and set off by motion?

Schwarz still fought to explain events in a rational, scientific manner. His entire lifetime had been spent never believing in witchcraft or mystical beings, but one evening, his entire belief system altered.

Months ago, in a fine fury, he'd plunged a knife into Quint's chest, only to observe black ooze pouring from the wound. That night, he'd learned Quint was a being composed and created from dark matter—a parasite whose greatest wish was to inhabit an Elemental due to their perpetuating or peri-mortal life force. Quint's darkness destroyed a human host too quickly, so he strove to merge with a body he could inhabit forever. He'd pursued a plan to inhabit Terran Forrester, as Earth was the strongest Elemental, however, those efforts must have failed, or Quint would be here, wouldn't he? Was this all some sort of test?

Schwarz sighed and sank against the driver's seat before glancing at the witchcraft and Celtic lore books mixed with theory pamphlets on dark matter scattered along his van's dash. Maybe he'd find a spell that would help him fulfill his life's work—creating a super-soldier impervious to pain, disease, and injury. He, too, had lofty goals. The Ukrainian bounty hunter came to mind. He'd make an excellent test specimen.

Ready to leave, Schwarz ruffled the fluffy, black fur across his dog's back. "Why are my studies looked upon with such horror? Aren't dying soldiers a condition humanity should remedy? Just one of my super-soldiers could do the work of ten, twenty, maybe even fifty, men. Aren't my experiments worth saving the lives of sons, husbands, and fathers?" He patted Heisenberg's head. "Not all experiments over the years have been ethical, but would healthcare be what it is today without those scientists who worked outside the lines? Let others hide behind platitudes. I shall not."

Stomach grumbling, Schwarz refolded the map of Kilkenny, and then adjusted his seat before shifting the car into Drive. One minute he was tapping his fingers to Beethoven's "Für Elise," the next, he swerved to avoid a naked man who appeared out of thin air.

Whipping his van to the left, Schwarz crashed into the hedgerow. After throwing the van into Park and getting his bearings, he picked up Heisenberg. "Are you all right?"

His dog whimpered and licked his face.

Schwarz gazed out the windshield at the cause of the disturbance.

In the middle of the road stood a man with jet-black, shoulder-length hair, red-brown skin, and a sharpness to his body and face, as if he'd been honed to an edge by the very winds of time.

Quint had warned him, but Schwarz hadn't really believed until observing this man appear out of nowhere, his form seemingly created from the very breeze that battered the bushes and rippled through the naked man's hair.

This was an Elemental.

For a moment, Schwarz continued his study of the man before crawling across the seat. His mind spun with the possibilities. Oh, the experiments he could perform on this creature.

Heisenberg barked and growled from his perch on the front seat armrest.

"No need to worry, my pet." Schwarz tamped down the bristled fur on Heisenberg's back. "He won't harm you. Quiet now." He exited from the passenger side, stepping out onto the road.

"I see no introduction is necessary." The man spoke.

Odd. The man had blue eyes, which didn't seem indigenous to Native Americans.

"I know you're in Ireland on behalf of Quint, Schwarz. In case you hadn't heard, he's been sent back where he belongs. Destroyed." A violent wind broke against the hedgerows, waving the branches, pummeling the leaves. "As Einstein said, 'The world will not be destroyed by those who do evil, but by those who watch them without doing anything.' I'm done watching you. This little reconnaissance trip you've taken to Violet's home was a grave miscalculation."

"Who are you?" A stiff breeze whipped against Schwarz, thrusting him against the van.

Heisenberg jumped, snarling against the window, frantic to protect his master.

"The more important question is, who are you? Why use your intelligence for such barbaric endeavors? You could do good, if only you turned your heart." The man shifted closer, yet he hadn't taken a step. "But I can see changing who you are is lost in the wind. So, I've come to serve notice. You will cease all barbaric experiments, as well as this investigation of Violet Levina."

Who did this man think he was? This Elemental was merely a naked being standing in the middle of an isolated back road. With Quint on his side, Schwarz feared no one. "I will cease nothing."

"I'd hoped you'd say that." The man quirked a half-smile that didn't reach his eyes.

As a strong wind punched him from behind, Schwarz grabbed the side mirror. "How's Pillar, Air-man?" Based on these atypical wind gusts, Schwarz clarified which Elemental he faced—Air, or Nodin. Quint had related the man's sorrow over losing Pillar. The Air Elemental was correct in that he did use his intelligence to fight, and why fight, if not to win?

Nodin narrowed his stormy-blue eyes.

"I think we understand each other." Schwarz leaned against the van's side.

"You understand nothing." The Air-man widened his stance.

"I know a few quotes of my own, *Nodin.*" He smiled as the man's gaze tightened. "Karl Brandt said, 'Ethical obligation has to subordinate itself to the totalitarian nature of war.' And there is always war, and those who profit from the spoils. Why shouldn't I be among them? War is power, and I'm on the right side. Do you realize how insignificant you are compared to Quint? Dark matter is infinite, everywhere. I'll be ready when he returns. Will you?"

"Quint's return is nothing you'll ever celebrate. I'm here to make you forget. So enjoy those memories while you can."

Schwarz chuckled and did as the man commanded, allowing free reign to every lascivious thought he'd ever had of Pillar. Every demented dream.

The Elemental roared.

Schwarz laughed as a gale force wind toppled him to the ground. *Bad play, Air-man.*

Never show your weakness.

CHAPTER 7

After arriving in Reims, a city in the Champagne-Ardenne area of France, Violet settled in her seat at a small outdoor café. While sipping the region's bubbly amber liquid, she watched tourists mingle around the Fontaine Subé. The four statues surrounding its pedestal represented the area's rivers. A golden angel, or "Victory", rested one foot on the summit as if landing on the tip, her wings spread wide and her skirt flared out behind her.

Oh, to be that free, to soar above it all. Yet, that wasn't her destiny. Violet blinked away a tear, and then stilled as a trickle of heat trailed down her spine. She could blame the warm shudder on the half-empty bottle of Champagne, or admit she possessed a connection to Flint, after all.

He'd found her again. How, he'd likely never say. Pillar had poofed from the passenger seat yesterday afternoon and hadn't returned. Perhaps, her friend had run off to tattle again, or perhaps Flint had simply found a way to track her.

Her heart pounded a rapid beat, and though she wished the emotional turmoil was fueled by distress, she admitted the fluttery feeling stemmed from pleasure at his reappearance. She searched through the crowds, trying to locate the approaching Elemental, all while attempting to locate her reason, her will, a small bastion of resistance, anything to hold strong against these foreign flares of pure need. Was she truly attracted to this man, or merely entranced by his existence? She'd kept her softer emotions hidden for so long. Why not do as Pillar had suggested and bask in the heat? If she was to be

Flint's conquest, couldn't she lay claim to the same?

Her prize weaved his way through the tourists crowding the Place Drouet d'Erlon, Reims' Main Square. Flint's urbane masculinity drew the gazes of all around him—male and female. Perhaps an aspect of his aura shouted man-out-of-time, or maybe their stares were based on pure attraction. He certainly had her squirming in her seat and re-thinking her wardrobe. In his superbly-cut, black suit, Flint took wear-it-well to a whole new level.

Arriving at her table, he moved the metal patio chair beside her and sank onto the seat.

So many sensations churned in her mind and her body—all uncharted and unwelcome. Yet, desire didn't follow reason. It simmered along without logic or predetermined path. Violet shook her head.

"What?" He quirked a brow.

"You look very…nice." She waved a hand over his fashionable ensemble.

"Why shouldn't I enjoy nice things?" He shrugged, causing the white dress shirt to tighten around his chest. "I've earned them."

"Earning and stealing…I just don't think…they aren't…" She wobbled her hands up and down, imitating a scale. "They aren't… quite the same."

He reached across and clasped her hand. "I enjoy the feel of fine fabrics on my skin. The caress, the brush of quality, is like nothing else, except one thing."

Breathless from his touch, Violet shifted forward in her seat. "What one thing?"

"Your skin." He trailed his thumb across her palm.

Holding back a shiver, Violet breathed deeply, and then hardened her resolve. She may be drawn to his light, but that didn't mean she was a bright-eyed fool. "First of all, I'm not pleased that you've found me. Second, please don't say things like that." With her free hand, she tapped her Champagne flute on the table. Avoiding his gaze, she watched the water spill from the fountain's various spouts. Over and over, the clear liquid flowed, trickling into the pool, unceasing, just like the undeniable certainty of her destiny. "My entire life, I've followed a clear path. A simple direction. These sexual impulses you evoke are not welcome. I don't like being a game, a toy. Besides, I doubt you'd even be interested if not for my ability to destroy Quint."

Flint squeezed her hand. "Violet, look at me." He tipped her chin with his index finger. "Regardless of what you think of me, or why I'm here, the fact remains, our futures are linked."

"My future ends in death." She turned away and yanked her fingers from his grasp. Releasing his warm grip created a slight twinge in her belly, as if her body had already accepted him as the missing puzzle piece. "Is that the link you want? Because I refuse to take anyone with me." With a white-knuckled grip on her wine glass, she continued, angry and frustrated at all she could never have. "I refuse to take *you* with me."

Flint wrapped his hand around the back of her neck. "Ah, Violet, it's a mistake to think you can refuse me. I am forced to prove you wrong." He leaned in and kissed her, hard, yet with a mastery honed over hundreds of years.

A skill that said, 'I will take and you will follow', and follow she did. Her lips met his in the ancient dance, aligning, caressing, seeking steamy pleasure with dueling tongues. All thought lost as, for once, she allowed herself to just feel the pleasure two lovers could create.

Pulling back, he met her gaze, his amber eyes sparking with red-gold glints. "My inner flame rages, Violet. My life force perpetuates, but, for the first time in five hundred years, I no longer find it necessary to wallow in the bubbling depths of a volcano. The flame exists within you." He placed a hand over her pounding heart, and then brushed his fingers down her chest, cupping her breast.

She gasped as he kissed his way along her jaw to her chin before lightly brushing her lips.

"Deny our connection if you must, but this fire between us does exist. It smolders, and someday I'll show you just how hot." He bit and tugged on her bottom lip.

"You'll not show me anything in this public place." Yet, turning from his touch, his blazing words, she remained overwhelmed by the lust electrifying her body. "Even if we have a connection, that won't matter, because neither of us will be standing at the end." She squeezed his hand. "I'm frightened for you, Flint. I won't be responsible for your death."

Flint brushed her hair behind her ear. "If we fall, we'll fall together." Gaze intense, he bent and kissed her cheek. "No regrets. Come out of the darkness. Let me be your light."

Violet had to turn the tide, pull away from these foreign feelings. "I've never had a choice in what I want." She shoved against his chest, needing space before she surrendered to something, anything. "I wouldn't even know where to start."

"I know exactly where you can start." He waggled his brows.

Violet laughed and rolled her eyes. "You just can't help yourself, can you?"

"I do it to shake you up." He ruffled her hair.

She peered from beneath lowered lids. "Why don't I believe you?"

"Because you're a fine..." With those twinkling amber eyes, he gave her a blatant once-over. "Finely...educated woman." He winked then sat back and filled her Champagne glass.

Damn him. She didn't understand why she enjoyed his ridiculous banter. Her world had always been gray, but what would happen if she ripped back the shades and allowed a sliver of Flint's light?

What color would her world be then?

CHAPTER 8

Feet propped on the queen-sized hotel bed, Flint shifted in the lounger and watched two guys blow up a soda bottle with mints on the television's science channel.

The things these humans enjoyed.

"I'm ready." Violet's voice sounded over the whoops and screams of the wacked-out scientists.

When the door opened, he chuckled at the steam pouring from the bathroom. Her petite frame was adorned in a simple black dress with capped sleeves and a hemline that landed just above her knees. Fabulous toned legs led to not-so-fab shoes.

Flint stood, and then circled her still form until pausing in front of her. "You look beautiful. However, the lack of color in your wardrobe will need to be addressed. I'd very much enjoy seeing those lovely legs in cherry red, sky-high heels."

She poked his chest. "I wouldn't be in those heels for long, because I'd fall and break my neck. Or suffer a Lisfranc fracture. It's named after the arch joints involved."

"Arch joints...hmmm..." he purred against her lips. "Then perhaps, you could wear them in the bedroom...with nothing else, while...*arching.*" He reveled in her swift intake of breath before wrapping his hand around her back and pulling her close.

She shoved away and studied her scuffed shoes before murmuring, "I tried really hard to look nice tonight, especially since you look like a walking magazine ad for some Savile Row tailor."

"Why am I not surprised you're familiar with central London's premier area for tailors?"

She shrugged.

Watching Violet's self-conscious movement, Flint experienced a jolt of awareness. Someone had done a number on this girl's confidence. Never one to delve to deeply into other's feelings, Flint realized Schwarz wasn't the only one who wanted to exhume her history.

Ready to offer reassurance, he reached for her, but just then, a tingling blaze of awareness shot down his spine.

A fire. Close.

He inhaled deeply, and then headed for the patio doors to whip them open. Flint noted a slight tinge of gray to the air, billowing around his elemental senses, beckoning. A red-hot flicker rose in his mind's eye from a location very near. "We need to evacuate. Now." He grabbed her hand and led her from the room.

"What is it?" She fell in step beside him.

"There's a fire."

"Where?"

"Below, somewhere. I need to get you someplace safe before I can locate the source." A familiar dark aura filled the air, a danger he'd detected before. A tinge of recognition sparked and sharpened all his fiery senses. Stepping into the hallway, he glanced around for signs of danger.

Violet clutched his arm, stumbling a bit while he pulled her down the hall toward the stairwell.

After scrutinizing the lobby for threats, he led her outside and stepped alongside two twenty-something parking attendants. "*Parlez-vous anglais?*"

"*Oui.*" The two nodded in unison.

"Good. Do not let this woman out of your sight."

Violet blocked his path. "Flint, let me—"

"No." He refused to allow her close to the flames. As the smell of smoke intensified, he quickly scanned the area. This fire seemed a little coincidental. Was someone attempting to draw him out? If so, who? And why? He clutched Violet's shoulders. "Stay."

The two young attendants withered against the vehemence lacing his tone, so he softened his next words. "Something seems off." He directed his attention to the older of the two attendants. "I believe a fire is nearby. Call the fire department."

At their furrowed brows, Flint recalled the French word for fire service, "*Sapeurs-pompiers. Hurry. Vite. Vite.*" He clapped, and then flicked his fingers toward their phone.

With no time to spare, he followed the elemental call to the parking garage.

Violet's whispered, "be careful," carried across the wind and offered a small comfort.

Gray smoke, rolling in thunderous clouds, greeted him at the stone entrance to the underground parking structure. He followed the billowing vapor to its source. Three overflowing metal garbage cans were clustered together, flames pouring out their tops. He absorbed what he could of the flames before detecting another's presence.

A raspy laugh sounded behind him.

He turned, hands gathered into fists.

There she was, the blonde pyro-girl from Switzerland. *What the hell?* Was she following him? And if so, how?

He stomped over, noting her mad smile and glazed eyes. "What have you done?"

She giggled, covering her mouth with a black-smudged hand. A hand loaded with a cardboard box of matches. "He said you would come. He brought me here. You came, you came." She spun in a circle, and then hopped up and down.

"What's in those cans? Are there explosives?"

"Fire." Eyes wide, she pawed at his chest. "He said to tell you… to tell you… um…he said, he'll 'keep her burning after you're gone.'" The blonde threw back her head and laughed. Her sunglasses fell from their perch on her crazed head and splintered against the pavement. "Ooopsie." She picked up a broken piece, settled it on her nose, and sang, "I wear my sunglasses at night. I wear my sunglasses at night." She laughed again. "You better run. Run, run, run." Shoving against his chest, she bolted out of the garage.

Following her out, Flint roared, "Stop. Now."

A sudden explosion ripped from the cans, propelling him against the cement wall. Ears ringing, he stumbled and braced his hand against a car's bumper to stand. Waving away the smoke blocking his vision, he studied the partially collapsed garage and burning cars while biting back the pain from the shrapnel embedded in his skin and the searing laceration on the back of his head.

Violet.

Was she injured? He searched for her signature but, overcome with contusions leaking out his life force, he fell to his knees. Fire beckoned, flaring in his direction, responding to his need to heal.

Shuffling over to a burning car, he wrenched open the door and collapsed onto the fire-filled seat. Flames rolled over his skin, and he breathed in the red-gold air. The cuts and bruises on his body simmered away, and the pain in his head subsided.

Had Quint somehow sent that crazy blonde? Was she, even now, carrying away his woman? This new move by Quint was not anything he had expected. Perhaps Terran hadn't injured him as much as they'd believed.

Sirens sounded outside the building. Smoke poured in white-gray waves across his eyes, and car alarms blared in wild echoes across the shattered concrete lot.

Flint ran a hand along the charred car seat, smearing his face and arms with soot. That, along with his ripped and burnt clothes, should create enough of a "survivor's" costume. After stepping from the car, he climbed over the concrete boulders blocking his path, a barrier to his redhead.

On his way out, he absorbed what he could of the flames. Yet, the healing peace found in walking through his life force did not come. Now his center revolved around Violet.

Once away from the rubble, he spotted a fireman and, in an effort to play his role, crumpled to his knees.

The firemen directed him to an ambulance while bombarding him with questions. *Was there anyone else in the garage? Did he know what started the fire? Was he injured?*

He shook them off and glanced through the sea of bodies for Violet.

She stood behind the firemen and, upon their parting to let her through, she rushed over and wrapped him in her arms. "Oh my goodness, Flint. What happened?" Wide-eyed, she ran her hands over his body, his face. "Are you all right?"

"Just a wee fire." He shrugged, and then let his ancient warrior nature take over, kissing her with unbanked need, cooling his inner heat with each brush of their lips, relieving his worried mind by delving into her soothing caress, over and over.

With both hands, she patted his head, the sides of his face, his

49

chest. "I'm okay. It's okay. Are you hurt?"

"No. Are you?"

Tears trickled down her cheeks, but from either too much smoke or fear for his safety, he couldn't say.

"The bomb...it went off...and I...and I...what happened?" She grabbed both his shoulders and gave him a shake. "Don't ever leave me like that again."

And just like that, he had to kiss her again.

She seemed to forget her previous aversion, and all the reasons they couldn't be together, as she settled into the kiss.

Breaking away, he fought the distraction of her wet, plump lips. "We need to leave." He refused to remain in the area with a mad pyro-girl on the loose who had a seemingly direct cell signal to Quint. To his mind, there was no other way she could have tracked him. The parasitic bastard must have found a way to return. *Not good.*

Violet studied him with a tilted head and furrowed brow. "But, the police and firemen will have questions." Her voice was a tad raspy, and she coughed, clearing her throat. "You should stay and explain. I'd like an explanation, as well. How did you survive the explosion?" Violet squeezed his hand as he led her away.

"I'll explain what happened later. Right now, we need to move." While weaving through displaced hotel patrons, he mentally stretched and erased the memory of his presence from anyone who tried to approach. He didn't appreciate having to block their thoughts when his mind needed to focus elsewhere.

Dealing with a pyromaniac would only distract him and create more danger in his mission of protecting Violet. He'd task Maya and Terran with delving into the mysteries of this blonde menace. Hopefully, they could track her before she lit more matches in her mad desire to keep him running to her fire-fueled beck-and-call.

Violet rubbed her eyes, seemingly irritated by the smoke now flowing from the collapsed garage. "Did you know that at the Chernobyl disaster, the firefighters weren't aware of how radioactive the smoke and debris were? The fire there was finally extinguished by a combined effort of helicopters dropping sand, lead, clay, and..."

He doubted Violet was aware that, when flustered, a chaos of words tumbled from her mouth. How could such a little head contain all that knowledge? Zoning out, he let her natter on about neutron-absorbing boron and liquid nitrogen, because falling back into fact seemed to settle her nerves.

While he was more knowledgeable than most about history, he knew that resulted from living through actual events rather than by study. Besides, history books rarely got everything right. True history wasn't bold, black print on white pages. True history was stained with red.

Finished with her history lesson on the Ukrainian disaster, she was quiet for a moment, following him away from the scene before beginning a long dissertation on safety precautions they'd added to her lab in case of fire. At times, her nerd-speak was actually calming.

Studying the redhead beside him, he almost faltered in his rushed escape route. If Quint had found a way to return, then Flint's time with Violet was short. *Too short.* For a man who'd lasted centuries, who'd stopped measuring the passage of time—each second with Violet was a wonder. A blessing.

Quint would not snuff her out. Not now. Not ever.

CHAPTER 9

The sound of a crowing rooster lurched through his mind. Schwarz blinked and studied the dirt floor at his feet. From the aromas wafting through his nose and after a heavy-lidded glance at his surroundings, he realized he sat on a metal chair in a barn of some sort. How had he arrived?

And where is Heisenberg?

Muffled voices broke through his dazed mind—an argument between a man and a woman. The woman's voice seemed vaguely familiar.

A horse whinnied behind him and dust stirred.

The scent of hay fanned through his nostrils. Struggling against the urge to sneeze, he kept very still and quiet, attempting to eavesdrop on the conversation.

"Where is Violet?" The man's voice demanded.

"I told you, I don't know."

"You do realize keeping her from us isn't helping anyone."

"I've realized a lot of things lately."

Ah, the woman's voice was Pillar's. His blonde beauty had come to pay a visit. How fortuitous. Which meant the man speaking was the air Elemental, Nodin.

"George Bernard Shaw said, 'A Native American elder once described his own inner struggles in this manner: Inside of me there are two dogs. One of the dogs is mean and evil. The other dog is good. The mean dog fights the good dog all the time. When asked which dog wins, he reflected for a moment and replied, the one I feed the most.' You keep feeding the wrong dog, Pillar, and one of these days it's going to bite."

"I am amazed you even care."

"Why shouldn't I?"

Schwarz heard a heavy sigh and an abrupt bang against something.

"Nodin don't do this, please. I'm happier on my own."

"Are you?"

Schwarz bit his lip and scrunched his nose, fighting an impending sneeze so he could continue snooping on their conversation.

"I take happiness when I can, because when Quint returns, my existence will be forfeit. He'll take great pleasure in exacting revenge."

"Then help us stop him."

Silence reigned for a few moments.

"It's too late," Pillar said. "Look after Violet. She is too innocent to truly understand Quint's evil. He'll try to weave into her life, using every sort of deceit imaginable. I find...I-I like her. She is inherently good. My opposite."

"Pillar, don't say—"

"It's true, Nodin." Pillar scoffed. "That girl is only twenty-five. Twenty-five. And she talks like a walking encyclopedia. Pure nerd, ninety-nine percent of the time. She's clueless as to the darkness in this life, and I hate...I hate that she'll see just how horrifying this world can be, and soon. Too soon."

"Sounds like you—"

Unable to contain his twitching nose, Schwarz sneezed

"Well, well, look who's awake." Nodin sauntered over.

"Keeping me here is pointless." Schwarz glared at his captors and stood, only to be shoved back down. "The wheel is already spinning."

Nodin shrugged. "Wheels break."

Schwarz shifted his attention. "Pillar, nice to see you again. I had a lovely dream about you the other night. Would you like to hear it? In detail?"

Pillar scowled.

Schwarz let his gaze skim up and down her body.

A strong wind tossed him off his chair and knocked him against a horse's stall. The unrelenting blast blew dust and straw against his body, snapping his clothes. His eyes burned, and he couldn't catch his breath.

"Nodin, enough."

Pillar's plea was barely audible over the gusting gale.

Nodin clutched the front of Schwarz's shirt. "Stay away from Pillar and Violet."

"I am." Schwarz wiped his dripping nose with his sleeve.

Nodin's eyes narrowed. "I see that." He tapped his own temple. "You've hired others to find her."

Though he could interpret Nodin's words as a question, Schwarz knew they were a statement. Quint had explained the Elementals could read and alter thought patterns. *No worry.* Schwarz had prepared for every eventuality.

"Do you see how easily I obtained you?" Nodin shook him. "Look at me."

"No." Schwarz closed his eyes, not sure if that would prevent Nodin from entering his mind, but he'd attempt the block anyway. "I know about your "gleaning" gift. I know everything. Most importantly, I know Quint will return. I will rule at his side. You can't stop the plans I've set in motion." Lifting his chin, he smirked. "Violets *are* Quint's favorite flower, you know."

"And how do you think Quint will feel when he comes back and sees you've turned his flower into some science experiment?" Nodin shoved him against the stall.

"I'm not quite following, sir." Schwarz opened his eyes and studied Nodin. "At the roadside, you said Quint was destroyed, yet here you say he'll return. Which is it?"

"You both know better." Pillar interjected with a huff of laughter. "Though, Schwarz, you're not as clever as you believe. Quint will chew you up and spit you out. I've never understood why people serve rulers who use threats to gain allegiance. Yet, I followed your same path before recognizing that serving Quint was my biggest mistake." She shook her head. "I've roamed this earth and seen it all. Nothing is new. In the end, these games men play always boil down to who wants the prize most. The good guy doesn't always win, but then, I haven't always rooted for the home team."

"You will desist all foul practices against humanity." Nodin's voice battered through his mind.

Schwarz erupted into the first verse of "Das Deutschlandlied",

Germany's National anthem, as he fought against the voice breezing through his mind. "I want Violet, but would settle for an Elemental, or even you, my lovely Pillar."

"Return to the states. Desist your research into Violet's past."

He fought against the barrage shaking his will. "I could conduct ex…ex…stens…sive re…researrsh…"

"I've seen your 'research.'" Pillar's disgust broke through the miasma in his mind. *"You're demented."*

Schwarz closed his eyes and sent his own mental message. *"There are places and circumstances where nothing is detectable. Air vanishes. Salt dissolves. Fire is snuffed out."* He shook his head against the overpowering mental modifications battering his brain.

Nodin's voice echoed through his mind, pounding against his reason. *"You will cease all immoral science. Use your mind for good."*

Schwarz fought against the billow of influence. *Why is he here again? Who are these people?*

A coarse, female voice whispered. *"Forget."*

Then nothing.

#

An unceasing buzzing accompanied a riot of sloppy doggy licks upon his face.

Bzzz. Bzzz.
Bzzz. Bzzz.

Allowing a moment for his eyes to adjust to the dark, Schwarz shifted and glanced around the room.

Where am I?

"Enough, Heisenberg. I'm awake." Taking in his surroundings, he realized he rested on a flea-ridden bed in some seedy hotel. Paint cracked and peeled from the walls. Stains from frequent leaks littered the ceiling. The drip of a faucet plopped over and over. A foul stench of leftover tobacco filled the air.

He sat up and opened the single curtain that stretched across the window, not recognizing the adjacent building or the surrounding area. An overwhelming need to book a flight back to the States had him searching for his phone. New plans clicked in his mind. Update his resume. He'd work on curing cancer—no, heart disease.

Bzzz. Bzzz.

"What is that sound?" His little Spitzy only yipped in answer.

Bzzz. Bzzz.

His mobile's reminder chime.

After finding his phone on the side table, he studied the daily reminder text, which had popped up on the screen.

Watch video.

A splitting headache assaulted his temples, feeling like two giants battled for dominance in his mind. Clenching his jaw, he fought to remember something real, his purpose in being in this place. Where was his van? Had he driven here? And if so, to what end? "Heisenberg, what is going on? How did I end up in this disgusting hovel? I feel quite...odd."

Heisenberg pranced by the door, showing his readiness to leave.

"Give me a moment, and we'll find you a patch of grass."

When his phone buzzed in his hand, he opened a second reminder text, which again directed him to a watch a video. After wetting his dry lips, he hovered his thumb over the video's play button. Then jumped half out of his skin when his phone rang.

"He...Hello?"

"Mr. Schwarz. I call to say money will soon be mine. We find girl."

"I'm sorry." He glanced at the caller ID, but didn't recognize the name. "Wh-who is this?"

"Eh?"

"What girl?"

"This not Veimhet Schwarz?"

"Yes, I am Veimhet. What girl?"

"Do not play games with me, science-man. I find her, and I find you too. Get money ready. We'll have exchange soon." After that incomprehensible statement, the caller disconnected.

"Wait...what?" A sickness rose in Schwarz's belly as he tried to recall something, anything, about a girl. Again, he glanced at his phone where the video was queued, and after taking a deep breath, pushed play. Hoping to find answers, he sat braced against the headboard as the video began.

On the small screen, he watched himself fiddle with a camera for a bit before sitting in a chair in an office of some sort. His camera self nodded at another person in the room then he turned and stared directly into the camera. "Veimhet, listen very carefully. On a daily basis you are set to watch this message. If you do not remember your purpose, if your plan is to go home and do horticulture, or something equally ludicrous like curing cancer, then you must listen. An Elemental being has altered your mind. Your purpose has been removed from your mind. You are Veimhet Schwarz. You must fight against their gleaning influence. Now, go to..."

CHAPTER 10

Once the initial disorder created by the explosion had subsided, the hotel patrons were given dinner vouchers to local restaurants so the hotel security, Reims police, and the National Gendarmerie could sweep the area before allowing guests to return to their rooms.

Flint sat next to a simmering Violet in a tiny bistro's booth after their heated argument regarding breaking and entering a men's clothing store in order to acquire proper high-dollar couture. Whether from anger over his late-night shoplifting or the basic events of the evening, he noted her hand shook as she took a healthy sip of wine. His tough I-can handle-Quint-on-my-own girl was finally showing signs of distress.

"So, what really happened? Do you think the explosion was a terrorist plot? Is a secret government official staying at the hotel? Perhaps the fire was meant as a diversion?" She nibbled on the end of her thumb while flipping through her phone.

He should have known her rational mind would search for reasonable explanations. Too bad a twisted pyromaniac was the answer. "Violet, we need to get rid of your cell phone."

She blinked and took another sip of her wine. After three water glasses and quite a few glasses of wine, the rasp due to smoke inhalation had yet to clear from her voice. "Why? My whole life is on this phone."

"Exactly." He squeezed her knee. "Listen, there is something you should know."

She huffed out a laugh. "What else could there possibly be? I find exploding parking garages are quite enough for one day."

Flint hesitated. "A man is investigating you and your family. His name is Veimhet Schwarz. A true mad scientist. We must be careful, all right? I have a feeling he knows what you are. We believe Quint sent him to Ireland to learn more about your history."

Violet bit her bottom lip. "I have a vague recollection of that name. I believe Pillar has mentioned him before. He worked with Quint at Aether Pharmaceuticals, right?"

"Yes. He could be a very real threat. So, whether you like my presence or not, I'm staying." He removed her cell phone from her grip. "Your mobile phone registers its position with cell towers every few minutes, whether the phone is being used or not. Unscrupulous people can learn a tremendous amount of detailed information about you with mobile monitoring software. You're a target, Violet, and if Schwarz has your number, he can track your activity, including call log history, GPS location, calendar updates, text messages, emails, web history, basically everything."

She tilted her head, studying him with wide-violet eyes. "Where did that come from?"

"I *have* learned a thing or two during my vast existence. So, yes, I am more than just a pretty face."

She rolled her eyes. "Moving on. Do you believe the explosion was caused by Schwarz?"

"I'd really rather not upset you with this, but you need to know." Flint tapped her cell against the table. "This fire and the one in Switzerland were started by the same girl. A blonde pyromaniac who somehow knows who, and what, I am. I believe she's been infected by Quint."

Violet's swift intake of breath proved his words startled her, so he took her hand. "I won't let anything happen to you."

"She tried to blow you up?"

He smirked at her indignation. "Worried about me?"

"A little, yes." Violet scoffed. "Who is this blonde girl?"

"I plan to ask Terran and Maya to research her background, but Maya was unwell last I knew, so a few days may pass before they can begin."

"How do you know it was the same girl?" Violet drummed her fingers against the table.

Avoiding her gaze by studying the label on the back of the wine bottle, he explained what happened prior to the explosion. Then, to lighten the mood, he tipped more wine in her glass. "How about more red, Red?"

"One would think, given your longevity, you could come up with something more creative than Red." Violet sidled closer in the booth, peering at the wine list for a moment before she shook her head. A smoky scent emanated from her long locks. "The degree of force needed to generate that amount of destruction had to be created by some sort of device. I imagine she's quite adept at constructing various explosives. By the very nature of her disease, she'll be compelled to continue."

Flint shrugged. "Yes, but she's met her match. I am the king of pyros."

"This isn't something to joke about, Flint." Violet slapped his arm. "She could have killed someone."

Unnerved by her belief he didn't comprehend the ramifications of a loose fire-starter, he volleyed back, "I realize that, Violet. I apologize if you believe I'm not taking my Elemental duties seriously. I have been fighting fires for more years than you can count." He shifted away. "Sometimes levity is the only way through the chaos."

"I'm sorry." She brushed his hair off his forehead. "I didn't mean to offend you."

Luckily, the waiter chose that moment to appear with her meal.

"Are you sure I can't get anything for you, sir." The waiter hovered at his side.

"No." Flint winked at Violet. "My diet is a bit restrictive."

"Of course, sir." The man nodded and walked away.

Smiling, Violet rolled her eyes. "Poor fellow doesn't know what to make of you."

"Most people don't." He waved a hand at her plate. "Go on. You'll need your strength." As he watched her dig in to her meal, he considered that with these increasing threats such moments of quiet companionship would become less frequent.

"So, you don't like Red as a nickname?" He tilted her chin with his finger. "Shall I come up with other names, in other languages?"

She pushed aside her half-empty plate. "What languages?"

"I typically save them for more intimate moments, but if you wish, I'll share a few right now." He leaned over and kissed her flaming pink cheek.

Violet braced a hand against his chest.

"I'm compiling a list, and believe me, Red, I'll use every one." He would, but for now, intimacy shifted her focus from explosions, pyro-girls, and crazed scientists.

"I'm going to Castle Nemon to prepare. If Quint has returned through this girl, then I'm running out of time." Violet grabbed the container of sweeteners and started filing the packets by color. "Containing Quint, and controlling this..." She waved a hand at her chest. "Understanding this energy inside my body must continue as my primary goal. I wish this Quint problem was mathematical, because then I could formulate a clear answer." She dug her fingers into her hair and sighed. "I hate this waiting game." With one big gulp, Violet finished off her wine.

Apparently, she hadn't been taught to sip and enjoy the subtle flavors on her tongue.

"Are you sure you're all right after that blast?" She touched his arm, her indigo eyes red-rimmed from all the smoke.

He held back a smile and nodded. Unless he was mistaken, the wine was starting to drench his little flower.

She flicked a blue packet across the table. "Do you know what's in these? Artificial sweeteners. They're really not good for you. People should just use real sugar or honey." She brushed at the crumbs on the table and then shot him a glance from under wrinkled brows. "What was I saying?"

"Honestly, I have no idea."

"Oh, right." She nodded and tipped the empty wine bottle into her equally empty wine glass. Frowning, she jabbed a finger against his chest. "I remember. Your sweet talk. The sugars. So, you see... I can't pursue this attraction with you, even though I'm tempted at times."

What he wouldn't give for five minutes in that complex head, but her shields were still up. "Violet, look at me." He shoved away the sweetener packets and held her chin in his hand. The candle on the table flickered higher, responding to his fierce resolve. "I have no doubt you are prepared. So take a breath, and trust me. You've already let Quint win by hiding in the pages of science books."

"Hiding?" She waved an index finger back and forth in front of his face. "I'm not hiding. Let me make something very clear, Mr. Pyro-king." She tapped a finger against the table. "In order to destroy dark matter, I've studied every facet of its existence." Violet pounded a fist on the table, jostling the silverware on her plate. "No mystical rainbows highlight my journey. In my world, rainbows are simply reflection, refraction, and dispersion of light in water droplets. I stopped believing in fairytales the day my mother left." She turned away.

But not before he watched a tear escape down her cheek.

"I don't think this...this situation between us...will work. I can't...I'm not..." She shook her head and wiped at her cheeks with her napkin. "Pillar will return. Maybe...maybe it would be for the best if I continued to Ireland with her."

Not happening. That salty-square would never take his place in Violet's life. "Pillar is of no concern to me. She is only your friend because she fears Quint's return. She's using you."

"And you're not?"

Anger flared in equal measure at himself and at her. She was right. He had only found her because of her gift, but he didn't question the whys of life, just reveled in the spoils. "You want the truth, *Red?* I am here because of who you are. Go ahead and damn my purpose as selfish, because in the end, the truth remains and the truth lies much deeper. The truth lies with this—" He nudged the table back then yanked her onto his lap, locked his hand in her hair, and kissed her. Refusing to recognize her fists pressed against his chest, he released enough inner heat to slowly melt her resolve, brushing her lips with light kisses, leading, teaching, and gentling her to his touch.

Their elemental link vibrated and hummed, heating the air.

With each stroke of his tongue in her sweet mouth, he freed his white-hot nature.

She joined in the heated molding of their lips. Needy gasps escaped from her mouth. Her hands unclenched and clenched his striped dress shirt before she broke away. "This will...I can't...this will ruin everything. The prophecy states—"

"I thought you were a scientist." He seared kisses along the curve of her neck.

Violet bit her plumped lower lip. "I am, but you see—"

"Why would you believe in something as scientifically unsupported as a prophecy?"

"Because I come from a line of witches."

"A witch, is it?" He nudged her with his hips. "Would you like to see—"

"Don't you dare say it." Violet glared before bracing two fingers against his lips.

"Say what?"

She leaned back and studied face. "You know exactly what you were going to say."

He hunched his shoulders and raised a single brow. "I was just going to ask if you wanted to see the dessert list."

"I doubt that."

"Why, Violet, you seem disappointed." He stifled a grin. "What exactly did you want me to say?"

She poked him.

A tiny electric pulse shocked, then burned, his neck.

"Ow!" He jerked and pushed away her hand. "Damn it."

"Understand this, I don't find your perverse innuendoes funny."

"Woman, I may be an Elemental, but I can still feel pain." He rubbed his neck and pondered why her jolt had actually sparked a sexual response.

Violet shrugged.

Her indifference sent a blaze of fury down his spine, lighting his elemental nature. She really had no idea who she was dealing with.

He arched a brow and flashed a searing grin. "If offending you ignites your inner spark, then I'll do exactly that, because that is who you really are. That is the woman I want unleashed." He kissed her once more before settling her stunned form back in her seat.

Ms. Gamma-girl needed to understand she wasn't the only one who could deliver a shock.

# # #

Violet strove to calm her raging heart—and libido. Right now, thoughts of prophecies, mad scientists, explosions, and escape were all muddled in her mind, burned to ash by a kiss that had scorched all thought except for him—taking him, and leaving everything behind. A foolish fantasy, and even though she'd declared otherwise, she did wish she could see the mystic behind the rainbow.

Funny how the room began spinning, and her eyelids seemed impossibly heavy. Was that due to his kisses, or too much wine? Her lips felt numb, so she licked them.

Flint's breath hitched.

Under lowered lids, she took in his too-handsome features, and then quickly looked away from the simmering need in his amber gaze. He really should stop kissing her. Although...she shivered at the memory, the raw emotion, the passion. These feelings coursing through her body were oh-so-foreign. Her skin felt heated beneath the surface, and she ached, just ached.

What was she doing? Thinking? Glass after glass of red wine had soured her brain. Wait a minute, why were two empty bottles on the table? When did that happen?

She shifted in the seat and rested her head back against the padded booth, willing the room to stop spinning. "Did you know Egyptians left detailed descriptions of their wine production through tomb paintings? According to these paintings, grapes were harvested with a curved knife, and then gathered in a wicker basket. I imagine they made the baskets out of reeds of some sort, but anyway, the grapes were then placed in vats of acacia wood and stomped on. I can't imagine that practice was very sanitary."

Flint tapped a knife against the table. "I imagine wine's flavor has changed quite a bit since my last drop."

"You miss out on a lot, don't you?" Why did that fact make her feel like crying? She never cried.

Something like sorrow flickered across Flint's face before he masked the emotion with a smile. "I try not to miss much." He resumed his tapping. "Although, if I could have back one human habit, it would be sleep. I miss sleeping."

"Oh." What would life be like with your eyes always open? How much more would you see? Did he never rest? Never take a break from his Elemental duties? "I'm sorry, Flint. I remember when I was studying for my Masters, I always felt like sleep was a distraction. A weakness. I wonder, if the necessities of everyday life were taken away, how I would feel. I know I'd miss tea, and I'd definitely miss wine." Violet twirled her empty glass between her fingers.

"Did you know the color red has often served as a symbol of virility?" Again, she licked her lips, trying to focus through the wine's rouge-colored haze. "Studies have also shown that red signals a readiness for sex. Though that may have to do with strong blood flow." Violet leaned over and trapped Flint's head between both her hands, holding him still so she could focus on his face.

"Female baboons and chimpanzees, for example, make public their ovulation by displaying redness on their genitals and chest. Hence, the underlying theory that red may have become, over time, a substitute signal for reproductive potential. Is that what you are, Flint?" Violet brushed a kiss across his bottom lip. "A flickering red ornament, teasing me, enticing me?" She laughed as she tried to unbutton his shirt. "Can I see your red breast?"

"Violet, honey, I think you've had enough red everything tonight." He refilled her water glass.

"No, no. I'm seeing things more much clearer...more clearlier...clearsome. Why won't these stupid buttons work?" She yanked until the button popped off and danced across the table. "Oops."

Flint took her fingers and kissed them.

"Why do you do things like that?" Wasn't he a callous womanizer? She blinked and studied the dark hairs on his chest. "I've lived my life with a bleak cloud hovering overhead, but with you, everything clears...I see everything... and I hate you for it." She climbed onto his lap and bit his nose. "I hate your stupid mouth, too." She pushed back his lips with her fingers. "I hate your stupid teeth, and I hate your...well I don't hate your tongue." Laughing, she threw back her head. "I don't know why I like your tongue, but I do. Actually, let me do an experiment."

Flint gently extracted her hand from the back of his neck. "Violet, no. Come on. Let's get you to bed."

"I want more wine. *Garçon. Garçon!*" Violet grabbed her napkin and waved it in the air until the waiter glanced her way. "Another bottle of your finest, please." She slapped his shoulder. "I've always wanted to say that."

Flint performed secretive hand movements with the *garçon* who'd come running at her call. "Thank you for the lovely meal."

"What are you doing?" She flicked a hand at Flint, accidentally bumping his nose. "Did you order more wine? Mr. *Garçon*, just ignore him. What's your name?"

Flint's chuckle rumbled through her body. "Don't laugh." She poked his chest. "This situation is all your fault. It's all his fault, Mr.

Garçon. I normally don't drink, but he's making me crazy with his stupid face." Violet pressed Flint's lips together until he looked like a goldfish. "See?"

"*Oui, madam,* his face *est un problème.*" The man winked at Flint, and then walked away.

Oh, my goodness. "He was totally flirting with you."

"Why, Ms. Levina. Are you jealous?"

Violet huffed out a laugh. "No." The rumble came from her stomach this time. "Oh, I'm not feeling so good."

CHAPTER 11

Attempting to move without moving, Violet very slowly tried to wet her lips. No such luck. Maybe after a few gallons of tea, she'd finally restore her lost fluids. *What is that sound?* Each mumble was like a ton of bricks dropping against her skull. She carefully removed the pillow lying on top of her head. Who'd left the TV blaring? And where was Flint?

Nature was calling, yet she had no desire to answer.

She sat up and breathed through the nausea. Gripping the hotel phone in her hand, she gently pressed each number for room service and ordered two pots of tea, dry toast, and a bottle of aspirin. Or a sword, which would probably be the best option—removing her head from her body. She rested until the knock came at the door. When she got up to answer, she realized she was naked. *What?* How had that happened? She searched the floor and found Flint's dress shirt, then noticed all her clothes strewn in a colorful disarray across the room.

Oh my God.

That's right. She'd—No. No! She wouldn't think her ridiculous behavior until after caffeine fortification. Humiliation always went down better with tea. Or maybe it didn't, she'd never really experienced such a thing before.

After she tipped the delivery boy and settled her tray, she ripped open the two packets of aspirin. Hands shaking, she swallowed the first two with scalding hot tea. Violet slowly chewed each bite of toast, and then took the other two aspirin.

After rifling through her bag, she found her most comfortable clothing and hit the shower. As the water trickled over her, she realized her head was only halfway better. She'd need another round of aspirin before they traveled to Calais.

How had she gotten in such a state? She vaguely recalled fawning over Flint, and how she'd been wrapped around his body as he put her to bed. She may have even done a little striptease, based on the way her clothes were flung all over the room. Humiliation was too small a word to describe that hideous dance debacle. She buried her face in her washcloth, scrubbing away her pink-cheeked embarrassment.

And yet, the whole thing was his fault. If he wasn't such a virile man, her hormones wouldn't be screaming for attention. The little devil on her shoulder, that looked a lot like Pillar, shouted, 'Take him now and forget the future. Why not experience what he'd freely give?'

"Shut up, Pillar-cifer," Violet growled as she squirted shampoo onto her hand.

Fate hadn't played nice with Flint, either. Last night, she realized they both hid behind masks. His was layered in innuendoes, and hers was hidden behind useless trivia, because neither knew how to relate to the real world.

Maybe, since she understood both who and what they were, and maybe if she held back her heart, maybe, just maybe, she could learn about pleasure. Was that too much to ask? Hadn't she gone long enough without knowing? Without the feel of a man's hand against her skin? Without the connection of two bodies in the barest, most natural, way possible? Could she let someone that close without melting her heart, especially someone who could burn through her life like Flint? Maybe he'd be amenable to just one night. Surely he'd had many one-night stands over the years. Why shouldn't she be among the hundreds, or thousands, or however many? And why was she bothered there had been so many—a whole lot of many. Maybe she shouldn't be thinking about sexual pleasures, with Veimhet Schwarz and pyro-blondes doing whatever they were doing.

As she wrenched the shower knob to Off, Violet groaned. Too many maybes churned in her head. She hoped Flint wouldn't return anytime soon. She needed to rebuild her mental shield. Yet, that salty

Pillar-cifer still sat on her shoulder and whispered, 'Think about the pleasure. He'll make you scream.'

Horrid little creature.

After drying, dressing, and then swallowing the dregs of her tea, Violet finally made her way out the door. Refusing to wait for Flint, she rolled her bag down the hall and stopped by the lift.

A beautiful Asian woman, also waiting, asked her the time.

Violet pulled out her phone and gave the time in English. She was fluent in both French and German, since she lived in Switzerland, and while the majority of Swiss spoke German, French became more prevalent the closer you traveled to the border. However, with her Irish roots, speaking English was a welcome change.

The woman gave her an obvious once-over. "You have beautiful skin."

Violet cleared her throat. "Thank you." Kind of an odd comment, since she was sure her skin was some hue of green. Perhaps this woman was interested *in her.* Heat rushed across her face, and she was sure her cheeks now blazed pink.

How lovely, a pink and green face.

Inside the lift, her nerves hummed. The woman stood right beside her, even though they were alone.

Violet punched the L button. "Did you know that in 1743, a counter-weighted, man-powered, personal elevator was built for King Luis XV connecting his flat in Versailles with that of his mistress, Madame de Chateauroux?"

"A mistress? Sounds intriguing." The woman's painted red lips curved, and she eased closer.

Violet scoured her wine-drenched mind for something else to say. "Many years later, Elisha Otis, an American industrialist, founded the Otis Elevator Company. The company invented a safety device, which prevented elevators from falling if the hoisting cable failed."

"Smart is so…sexy." The ebony-haired lady licked her lower lip. "Will you be in town long? Maybe we could meet later for a drink…or something?"

Violet shivered as the woman ran a finger down her upper arm. Sure her face had now turned beet-red, Violet stammered, "I-I'm with someone." For once, she was actually glad to use Flint as an excuse.

"I don't mind a threesome." The woman smiled, and then squeezed her arm before stepping out of the lift.

Stomach flipping, Violet followed her out then scanned the lobby for a coffee shop. Obviously, this day required more tea, and a very large roll of antacids.

CHAPTER 12

Just before dawn, Flint had exited the employee door of the men's clothing store, which was nestled in a small corner of the hotel lobby. He'd left Violet to sleep off the effects of alcohol before he did something he'd regret. After her wine-fueled striptease, he needed a moment to regroup, and since he'd gleaned no imminent danger, he snuck downstairs to pilfer some new clothes.

He'd also conducted a scratchy mental conversation with Terran and Nodin about the pyro-girl and Schwarz. Terran stubbornly remained at Maya's side, but agreed to assist once she was well. Nodin indicated Schwarz was temporarily out of service. However, they all agreed Nodin should maintain his observation of the slippery scientist.

As Flint straightened the sleeves on his new suit jacket, he considered how Terran, and now Violet, would chastise him for his thievery, but at the same time he couldn't walk around nude, could he? Riots were frowned upon these days, weren't they? He smirked at the thought. The way he figured, pilfering goods was actually payment for all his noble deeds. Who knew how many beatings, deaths, hell, even wars, he'd prevented during his time? The fact his taste ran to finer fabrics, well, that was something he couldn't and wouldn't change.

He crossed the bustling lobby and mentally searched for Violet's energy trail. Damn woman still hadn't dropped her shields.

Over the years, he'd become very familiar with particles left in the universe. He'd received one other gift upon his transformation—

a gift he'd only used three times in his Elemental existence—the ability to suspend time. His first time had been at the end of the Polish-Muscovite War in 1618, after the signing of the Truce of Deulino. After celebrating with two especially buxom ladies and smoking for days from a very potent pipe, he'd declared a halt to time. Mother Nature quickly arrived and dropped him in the closest volcano to break the spell. The second and third times were used to stop death—only he'd failed, because Death always found a way.

In the beginning, Mother Nature had made one fact very clear: Elementals could not cause, or stop, death. With his brash and imperious nature, Flint had tried anyway, yet suffered the same result each time. The Grim Reaper's scythe only floated, waiting in mid-air until time resumed, and then the blade hit its mark. Elemental gift— zero. Death—infinity.

Many times, he'd been tempted to use his gift on Terran, just to keep the man from asking so many questions, but Elementals were immune to the halting of time. Sometimes, having just the four of them in a stock-still world didn't seem like such a bad idea.

But not being at Violet's side *was* a bad idea. So he concentrated his gleaning gift until he located a bright white void which trailed a path to the parking garage. Damn woman hadn't waited in the room. Did she have no recollection of his warnings?

Once outside, Flint strolled over to the enclosed parking area, melted the security code box outside the gate, and weaved through the cars, following her path. He wiped his image from the shocked security guard's mind and left him with hopes of Reims' football team, Stade Reims, winning another Ligue 1 title.

Out of the corner of his eye, he caught a shock of red hair as Violet bopped through the lot. The flare of relief, and even hotter rush of lust, had him chuckling. He'd thought himself too jaded to feel anything this intense.

Yet, he wasn't the only one with passionate feelings for Violet. Menacing thought patterns flickered and burned across his mind.

Danger. Darkness. Chloroform. A sharp silver blade and an underlying thrum of something sexual.

Assassin.

Damn it, he knew that cell phone was going to cause them trouble.

Flint searched the parking lot and located an Asian woman

hiding behind a hotel van. She moved to follow Violet, her smile in no way matching her malicious mind. Her first plan involved becoming Violet's travel companion. If that didn't work, Plan B called for a straight abduction. But the woman hoped Violet would comply, because she was very attracted to his innocent redhead. And while Flint understood the attraction, he didn't share. Ever. Well, almost never. There was one time back in the 1860's when…and maybe that one time in…when was it?

He shook his head. No time for those kinds of memories right now, Violet faced danger. His untamed wild flower was about to learn why he served as an excellent escort.

Clueless to her danger, Violet sipped her tea, and then placed her paper cup on the hood of her rental car. Probably lost in thought about tea leaves and how they were grown, and all the processes involved in getting the liquid into the cup. Flint bit back another chuckle.

The assassin shifted closer to Violet then approached.

Flint watched as the woman spoke and they both laughed. "Assassinette" murmured something about meeting again. When had the damn fool woman met this insane chick? Hadn't he warned her?

The woman settled closer to Violet, brushing a hand down her arm. "I'd like to see you again. Where are you traveling? Perhaps we could journey together?"

Violet bit her lower lip and wove her fingers together. "N-no…as I said earlier, I-I have a…um…a man…a travel partner, sort of…and he's a man. So, sorry, but no. Thanks, but no."

Flint shook his head at her apology to a woman who meant her harm.

The woman's mind turned, now frustrated by Violet's lack of interest. Plan B kicked in gear as the tiny assassinette slammed Violet against her car and wrapped a hand over her mouth.

Flint strolled over, his smooth motion in severe contrast with the roiling riot of anger searing through his body. Why wasn't Violet gamma-blasting the woman? Using her gifts? Shoving her away with an energy wave? She really needed to have more faith in her powers.

Leaning against a stone pillar, hands shoved in his trouser pockets, Flint cleared his throat. "Well, well, ladies. What's going on here? Lovers' spat?"

#

Violet glared at Flint. Fear remained, yet she knew he would handle the situation.

Until…the woman pulled a gun and aimed the barrel at Flint's chest.

A wave of wine or tea, she didn't know which, catapulted in her stomach. Could he die from a gunshot wound? Would this woman kill him? What was wrong with this lady, anyway? One minute they were chatting, the next the woman had her pinned against her car.

"Wait, please, don't shoot him." Violet breathed deeply to settle her racing heart, and then lifted her hands in the air, palms up, while studying the woman's weapon. "I see, based on the barrel size, you have a 9mm with a silencer. Perhaps…perhaps you were unaware, but Hiram Percy Maxim, an…ah, um…American is noted as the inventor of the "Maxim Silencer." Did you know that the silencer isn't actually silent? You see, depending on which suppressor you have—"

"Shut. Up." The woman grabbed a handful of Violet's hair and once more shoved her against the car. "I don't give a shit about elevators, or silencers." Then the woman turned, and time seemed to slow as she fired two shots into Flint's chest.

His body jerked backward and he toppled to the ground.

Violet remained frozen in place, a horror-filled scream locked at the top of her throat. Using spare air from her diaphragm, she moaned out an unearthly bellow that sounded like a dying moose. Would Flint get up? Should she find a fire source? What did he need? Matches? She'd seen some cigarette butts, maybe one was still lit. That would work. Sure, it would work. It was fire, right? He just needed fire.

Another tug on her hair startled Violet from her irrational thoughts.

"Get in the car." The woman poked the gun against her side.

"Do you smoke?" Violet quickly studied the ground around her, looking for something, anything.

"What?"

Her elevator companion wasn't so friendly now. "Smoke. Cigarettes. Would you have a lighter? Uh…you see…my nerves. I'm a little frazzled."

"Frazzled?" The woman shook her head and bumped the gun's muzzle against her side. "Just shut up and get in the car. I'll get you something when we're on the road. Now, do as I say. I'd rather not mess up that pretty face."

A rustling sounded on the pavement behind them.

Violet steadied her hand against the car before turning. A relieved cry escaped from her mouth, echoing across the lot. "Oh, thank God."

Flint stood and dusted off his pants. "I'm getting real tired of ruining perfectly good suits." He swiped the lady's gun.

Easily. Apparently, none of her other victims had survived two pointblank shots to the chest. At the thought, Violet released a burst of nervous laughter. But, after catching a glimpse of Flint's flickering amber eyes, she quickly stifled her wayward giggles.

Flint gazed into the Asian woman's eyes and held his hands firm on each of her shoulders. "Who sent you?"

"Go to hell."

"Go to hell, really? You couldn't come up with anything more original?" Flint shoved the woman against the car. "Violet, get behind me."

As she moved to stand behind him, she almost tripped when he handed her the gun. While she understood the basic mechanics behind a gun's operation, she'd never actually fired one. Still, she pointed the gun at the woman. For reasons Violet refused to contemplate, the fact the woman had shot Flint really pissed her off.

The woman spat out a string of words in what was likely her native tongue.

Flint just smiled. "I don't really need you to speak the answer. Let's see what's buried beneath all that silky black hair."

Refusing to be left out of his mental gleanings, Violet shook Flint's shoulder. "What are you seeing?" She jostled Flint's shoulder again when he didn't respond. "Tell me."

He turned, arched a single brow, and then glanced down at the barrel pointing at his back.

"Sorry." She quickly lowered the gun.

"I'm seeing a phone call she received a few nights ago. An assignment alert. Pictures of you in various locations. A male voice, with some sort of Eastern European accent, likely Ukrainian, on the other end of the line. Coordinates on hotel stationary. And, pulsing at the very forefront of her mind is a serious lust for a certain redhead."

"What? She wants...well, I don't..." Violet slapped his back. "Stop it."

Flint chuckled and eased away from the woman who had remained immobile the entire time. "Not interested, Red?"

"You do understand I'm holding a gun?" His levity when she had a loaded weapon in her hand and a hired kidnapper leaning against her car was not appreciated.

Flint flashed a smile then turned back to her would-be abductor. "Go back to your home. Your job here is done. You will not remember today's events, or Violet." He glanced over his shoulder. "What shall she be, Red?"

Violet shrugged and moved to his side. "Umm..." She glanced at her paper tea cup. "Barista? Pastry maker?"

"How about a cupcake artist?" Flint chuckled. "We can't push her that far over the edge. My gifts do not erase who she is, in essence." He met the woman's gaze again. "Go outside and get a cab. Go to the airport. Go home."

After rubbing her temples, the woman blinked a few times, and then shook off Flint. "Get your hands off me." She seemed dazed, as she turned in a circle before stopping and staring at Flint. "Who the hell are you?" She walked a few steps away, and then turned back. "Do you...do you know...um...can I get a cab around here?"

"Absolutely." Flint hooked his arm in hers and led her outside.

Violet watched as he carried on what looked like a perfectly normal conversation with the lawless woman. With a shaky hand, she slowly placed the gun on top of her car's trunk, before accidentally shooting someone—most likely herself.

What did that woman want? Violet took deep breaths, one after another. Where was she planning to take her? And what kind of monster killed innocent bystanders? Not that Flint was innocent, but still, he'd taken two bullets. Two bullets likely meant for her. She clutched her stomach and bent over.

Oh God, why did I take this trip?

She should escape back to her lab. Security was tight. Her instruments surrounded her in comforting hums and beeps. Everything there aligned perfectly in place. Disorder was nonexistent in that sphere. She leaned against the bumper and scrubbed both hands over her face. "I'm not ready for this. Why? Why make me do this?" She pounded the trunk with her fist. "I don't even know how to fire a gun. What were they thinking, spelling me?" As always, no answers. No succor. Only an endless march to death.

As she watched Flint make his way back through the lot, she made a mental note—get matches, lighters, anything with an easy flame—because that feeling of loss, of helplessness when he'd fallen, was not something she ever wished to experience again.

Yet once more, fate worked against her.

Seemingly unsteady on his feet, Flint bumped into a car, setting off its alarm.

Violet rushed to his side and brushed a hand over his chest. Two round, burnt circles were visible on his shirt. "Are you all right? Do you need medical attention? Gunshot wounds through the chest can injure your lungs or your heart. Blood in your lungs can cause—"

"Violet, my organs don't work like a human's, remember? Let's go. She may not be alone."

#

Flint settled Violet in the driver's seat, trying to stifle his very real, all-consuming fear that those two bullets could have landed in Violet's chest. What would happen then? How would they defeat Quint? And how would he go on? Because this time...this time...*damn it*, how had Violet burned across his heart so quickly? Fear was an emotion he hadn't experienced since...well, since Eva. The last woman he'd loved, and though he'd stifled those memories, he still ached over that tragedy.

After slamming shut the passenger door, he glared at the redhead sitting in the driver's seat. *Literally.*

"Nodin! Terran! Come now." He mentally shouted for his Elemental teammates across the earth's frequencies.

His need for recuperation by fire had hit critical status minutes ago. The two bullets, though melting, remained lodged in his chest. Still, he refused to leave while Violet faced possible danger. He hadn't detected a partner in the assassin's mind, but someone had hired her—someone who would send another. "What the hell happened out there? Do you realize she was trying to capture you? Why in the world would you talk to her?"

"Flint, enough with the questions." Violet slashed a hand between them, keeping her gaze forward. "I'm still a little shaken."

"A little shaken. I see." He gritted his teeth, grinding down hard, but his next words still came out in a harsh roar. "Why in the hell didn't you use your gift? One zap"—he jabbed the dashboard with a finger—"and she would've been down. You just stood there and—"

"Stop yelling at me."

"I'll yell all I want, woman." Flint grabbed her chin. "Understand this, that venomous wench was taking you to who-knows-where, to have who-knows-what done to you, and you didn't think to burn or shock her? Why the hell not?"

With her tiny nose in the air, Violet used two fingers to push away his hand. "I'd prefer to wait until I've calmed before discussing the matter."

"Well, you'll have to wait until I've calmed, which will be this side of never." He raked a hand through his hair. "Why did you take on this journey if you weren't willing to protect yourself?"

Violet poked him with her finger.

The high-energy pulse bolted through his body. Flint growled out, "Third time, Ms. Levina, and you know what they say about three strikes...so I don't suggest you use that gamma-ray finger on me again." Especially since her little love zap drained even more of his reserves. "Brilliant, by the way, because now you've fried the car and probably every other vehicle in this lot."

Violet tossed the keys against the dash. "Why do you even care?" As she shook her head, her red locks skated back and forth on her shoulders.

"Why? Because, you burned me that day in Quint's office. You threw down the gauntlet, and don't try to convince yourself otherwise. Any woman capable of stepping that close to the fire has my regard and overwhelming interest." He blinked away the gray haze smoking across his vision. "We were made for each other."

"That line work on many women?"

"All the time." He winced and undid his seatbelt.

"Oh my God, what's wrong?" Frowning, Violet tore open his shirt. "Unbelievable. Why are you sitting here chastising me when you need to leave?" She shoved his shoulder. "Go. Now."

"I will, as soon as I make something clear." He brushed her hair over her ear, and then circled the tiny shell with his index finger. Her skin so pale, so delicate. Freckles sprinkled across her nose and cheeks. Or were those black dots, forming as his vision faded? "You're stuck…with me, because…that "cupcake artist,"—he flicked air quotes with his fingers—"will remember…once she…returns. She'll remember, and you…and…you." He focused on each word as he slumped against the car door. Pain, his old friend, fired hot pokers through his chest. *"Nodin. Terran. Now. Shot. Violet."*

"Flint, please." Violet's cool hands brushed across his overheated skin. "I don't know what to do."

A strong billow of air rushed through the car's open window.

Violet huffed out a gasp.

Nodin appeared at the side of the car and opened the passenger door.

Without the car door bracing him, Flint tumbled to the ground. *"I have to go."*

"Nodin, will he be all right? Maybe you should go with him."

Violet's pleas became muffled in Flint's mind. Keeping his body still against the pain boiling under his skin, he registered the tug of Nodin removing his clothes.

"Go. I'll take care of her until you return."

Trusting Nodin's words, Flint released his human form and drifted with the wind. High above the earth, he fired south as a dark thundercloud until diving headfirst into Mt. Stromboli's bubbling magma.

CHAPTER 13

In a churning pool around Flint's body, bursts of magma splashed against his skin as he floated along, absorbing the erupting flares. His body pulsed in various shades of orange and black. Under his skin, the bullet remnants sizzled and popped, and then trickled out in a trail of copper and lead. Running a hand through the bubbling pool, he rubbed the thick, boiling yellow-orange mixture over his wounds.

"Flint." Mother Nature's lyrical voice broke into his worries over Violet's safety.

"Yes, ma'am."

"I await you in the village of San Bartolo."

"I'll be there shortly. One favor, could you procure some clothes? Preferably, no tourist wear."

"I'll see what I can do."

Recuperated after his dip in the fires of Mt. Stromboli, The Lighthouse of the Mediterranean, Flint shot out of the volcano and headed for San Bartolo—a small village on the northeast side of an island north of Sicily. Year after year, Mt. Stromboli lit up the sky, and he'd wallowed in its depths over many an hour, day, and month during his centuries on earth.

In his smoky form, Flint crept under the familiar bistro's bathroom door and found a bag of clothes waiting. Standing in front of the mirror, he adjusted his collar and combed his fingers through his hair.

Stepping outside, he caught sight of Mother Nature basking in the sunlight as she sat at a patio table. She'd muted her beauty, yet no one who looked at her would think her anything less than stunning. After dropping a kiss on Mother's red-gold locks, he sank onto the black resin patio chair. "How's Maya?"

Mother smiled and spoke with a soothing tone. "That your first question would be for your Elemental sister pleases me greatly." She squeezed his hand. "She is still healing. Terran is a tad disturbed, to say the least."

Flint leaned back in his chair. "She should know better."

"This, from you?" Mother raised a perfectly sculpted golden brow.

He sniffed and glanced away. His fellow Elemental, Maya, had poured her sweet waters across his heart long ago. Though, due to her relatively new life as an Elemental, she still required tough love. He hated to hear of her pain. Terran, the over-educated bastard, was a lucky guy.

Speaking of smart people. "What do you know of Violet's prophecy? She's stubbornly locked on this ancestral prediction, regardless of its absurdity. I've never known such a contradictory woman." Flint plucked a flower from the vase on the table and ran a finger over the velvet petals. "Actually, I take that back. All women are walking contradictions. This one, however, is my woman. So, what do you know?"

"A man who lives by fire speaks of contradictions?" Mother pursed her lips and met his gaze.

Flint shifted in his seat and cleared his throat.

After a whimsical laugh, Mother tossed her hair over her shoulder. Light sparkled from each autumn-colored strand. "The spell was cast by Sorcha, daughter to condemned heretic, Petronella de Meath. Petronella served Dame Alice Kyteler, who just happened to lose four husbands before fleeing the country and leaving Petronella to suffer for her sins. During those times, even the faintest whiff of witchcraft meant persecution and death."

"Were you there?"

"I was, but I arrived too late. I am but one creature on this vast earth. There are times that I…some days, I wish I was more." Mother's soft words carried along the tropical wind floating in from the Tyrrhenian Sea.

The floral mixture of jasmine, bougainvillea, and plumbago

burst through the air as if each flower were spreading its scent in hopes of offering comfort. "Don't." Flint lifted her hand and kissed her knuckles. "You are the most selfless and compassionate creature on this planet." He squeezed her fingers and held her gaze. "You have me. You have the Elementals. We do what we can. I understand your frustration, because I know there is much we cannot do. The earth, as with all things, will die. The burden of its care is not yours alone."

Mother remained quiet for a moment before continuing. "Thank you for your words. I find comfort in them." She cupped his cheek with her hand.

In doing so, the gesture brought memories of a mother's touch— a touch he hadn't felt in far too long. He shook his head at her offer of support, when she was the one needing consolation.

Breaking the mood, a waiter arrived, practically dumping the complimentary plate of figs and olives on Flint's lap because he stared at Mother, obviously entranced by her beauty. He blinked and finally settled enough to ask their order.

Flint ordered a bottle of Malvasia. In the Aeolian island region, this dessert wine was known as the "wine of the Devil", due to the slightest aftertaste of sulfur. Not that he could drink it, but he enjoyed the scent.

After the fawning waiter left, Mother related the tale of Sorcha's sorrow and vow of retribution. "At twenty-five, Violet's ancestor divined this enchantment.

"Black death marked before her time
Maternal mother down the line
From my core, a child I'll spawn
Twenty-five to make her strong
Rise once more from withered beam
Violet bloom along light's beam
Four petals span against the foe
A single petal arching low
From the elements one shall rise
Burning light into her eyes
Shadows scorch
Remain unseen
Reaper hold thy scythe 'til then
White field from my future line

Clasp your golden hand in mine
Together, vengeance we shall see
I shall hold thy place for thee
As I will, so mote it be."

Flint absorbed the words and tried to garner their overall meaning.

"Petronella had served as Quint's host for many years." Mother's hair rippled with glints of deep red. "Sorcha watched her mother commit heinous acts while under his control. Then he exited Petronella's body, leaving her to bear the burden of his wicked deeds." Mother clenched her fists on the table, her strong emotions creating a gust through the outdoor café. "Sorcha spoke the spell with no concern for the future, or the fact she damned the 25th girl in her line. Her only focus was fulfilling a promise to her mother. Over the years, the de Meath line has strengthened, powered by Sorcha's solid will, which was forged by her deep forays into the shadowy side of witchcraft."

The waiter arrived with their wine.

Flint took that moment to regroup. "Does Violet know all this? Her history?"

"Yes."

"And you believe this spell is real?"

"I believe in magic, yes. As should you, or else, how do you exist?"

His existence, and the hows of it, were not details he chose to dwell on. He'd turned that thought over and over in his mind far too often during the initial years of his Elemental life. In the end, he embraced who he'd become and never looked back. "I have to believe what I am is more than magic."

"If that is what you wish."

He sighed. Women and their vague statements that meant you were either full of shit or completely stupid.

Mother smirked. "Not *completely* stupid." She ruffled his hair. "I do feel you should know one other thing. Violet's grandmother fought off Quint five years ago and died during the struggle. Violet has no idea Quint is responsible for her death." She met his gaze. "Luckily, at that time, Quint was unaware of Violet's potential. He only wanted another de Meath as his host. Now, however, he's very aware of who Violet is and what she represents—his end."

"What does Violet think happened to her grandmother?" Flint raked his fingers through his hair. "Do you really think lying to her is fair? She's not a child."

"She believes a stroke led to a massive heart attack."

As sympathy for his redhead filled his heart, Flint replayed the prophecy's words in his mind.

Violet bloom along light's beam. Four petals span against the foe. A single petal arching low. From the elements one shall rise. Burning light into her eyes

Though the phrase was oddly stated, he sensed he was the "light" in this prophecy, and the petals were the four Elementals. What was Violet's interpretation of her ancestor's curse?

Lost in musings, he came to attention when he caught a rush of pure adrenaline exuding from a passing tourist. The man was preparing to scale the volcano, yet fear of some cataclysmic explosion had his heart beating fast. These humans and their fear of death were such a foreign concept. One Flint refused to entertain when it came to Violet. "She believes she'll die."

"And yet she may."

Flint whipped around and glared at Mother. "I won't allow it."

"She is human. She will die."

Narrowing his gaze, Flint straightened in his chair. He hadn't avoided death for over five hundred years for nothing. "Again, not going to happen. It's time to step up, Mother. Stop skulking around the sidelines." He fired a finger in her direction. "You know how important Violet is to our cause. Without her, Quint comes back and is free to continue, as he will. What's the point of all our gifts and powers if Violet must sacrifice her life?"

"Flint, she is human and will remain so. You know I can't stop death." Mother patted his hand. "Keep her safe. Show her there is more to life than prophecies, duty, and death." She tipped his chin with her long, twig-like finger. "This will be a good lesson for you, as well."

"Someone tried to kidnap her."

Mother nodded. "Yes, that is what I wished to discuss. The scientist, Veimhet Schwarz, still serves the darkness. He has hired many to capture her, offered a large bounty. He hopes to contain her until Quint returns."

"And will Quint return?"

"The prophecy declares it so."

"It?" Her vagueness at times like this was annoying as fuck.

"Quint's return, his presence, his being." Mother waved a hand in the air. "Dark matter is a vast, expansive creature. One I have no quarter in. Though you may believe otherwise, his presence has always disturbed me greatly. He is an aberration against nature. My nature. I've had to stand by while his blight marred everything I've built. Every blade of grass darkened by his black touch batters against my very being." Mother's moss-green eyes turned a stormy shade of blue.

On the table, the glass salt and pepper shakers tinkled together as the ground rumbled, and the flowers rising from the tiny metal pot folded shut their petals.

"Enough." She pounded a fist against the table. "Each day dawns anew. As time marches on, death finds us, each and every one. And each choice we make ripples across the waves of time, ever flowing, never ceasing. You will have many choices in the following days, Flint." Mother reached across the table and brushed a stray lock of hair off his forehead. She smiled and met his gaze, her eyes sparkling with every shade in the rainbow. "Choose with your heart. Love is not a failing, but a vibrant mesh of life's brightest colors. And though you believe your soul burnt to ash many years ago, I still see that glowing life force swirling at your breast, flickering in a never-ending flame." Mother stood and kissed the top of his head.

A cool calm coursed through his overheated body.

"Believe in something, my son. Believe in love."

"You understand what it means if I believe again? What will happen? If I love her...I won't leave her behind." Flint locked his gaze on Mother Nature's now blue-green eyes.

Mother closed her eyes for a moment, and then once more met his gaze. With shimmering gold fingers, she caressed the side of his face. A single crystal tear dripped down her apricot-colored cheek. "I comprehend with all my heart, but if I lose you to love, I can think of no greater surrender."

CHAPTER 14

Every afternoon, those damned Irish stopped working for teatime at 2 pm, which fell after lunch, so essentially, they were off work nearly two hours each day. *For tea.* Schwarz growled as he passed his lounging workers. Yet, he hadn't hired the best and brightest, just a bunch of pillocks desperate for a few quid. Desperation was something he was becoming all-too-familiar with these days.

Preparing four specially equipped chambers to inhibit each Elemental's gift hit crucial status after his abduction by Nodin. Now that they'd gleaned his plans, who knew when they would arrive and attempt to prevent whatever foul practices they falsely assumed were being conducted behind these walls. At this point, he was so far behind schedule he had no chance of stopping them.

When would his hired minions deliver his ultimate prize?

Schwarz stopped beside the lead member of his construction crew, who was pouring foul-smelling tea from his thermos. "Sir, I thought I made clear yesterday that these breaks would not be tolerated. My schedule does not allow for these frivolous teatimes. As of today, I shall deduct an hour from each man's pay."

"Ah, Mr. Schwarz, right you are. We'll just sip this bit and get back to it." He waved his steaming thermos. "I've been meanin' to say, me cousin's second son works as a doctor over in Hillside. His nurse come to him fresh and bright-eyed from Heidelberg, Germany. Name's Schwarz, too. Like to turn his head, she is, chipper lass."

"I do not find that information useful or relevant." Schwarz clenched his jaw and fought to maintain his professional façade. "Now, I realize every culture has its traditions, but I really need more working and less drinking." With that, he turned on his heel and headed to his office before the fool corralled him into further useless conversation. Yet, with each step the reality of his incomplete mission pressed harder on his shoulders.

Glancing back, he met the foreman's gaze. "The magnitude of this endeavor is on a scale you could never grasp. If I fail in this, believe me, I'll know who to blame, and I won't be responsible for the consequences." Content he'd made his point, he entered his office and slammed shut the door. "Heisenberg, why do these Irishmen always go on about some relative who has done something or other? As if I care about these familial connections. What has family ever meant to me? You're the only one who understands my purpose." Feeling grateful for his fluffy friend, he dipped into his mini-fridge and broke off a sliver of braunschweiger.

Heisenberg licked the meat from his fingers.

"This constant pounding of nails and stalling Irishmen is building nothing but migraines." When Heisenberg yipped and spun in an excited circle, Schwarz groaned. "Don't worry, Spitzy, I'll make sure the work is complete before Quint returns. The water chamber is complete, as is the fire chamber. Air and earth have been trickier. Constructing a chamber with the absence of air is quite difficult." Lost in thoughts of the perfect vacuum, he patted Heisenberg's head.

Over the past few months, interruptions, hammers banging, radios blaring, men talking and slurping tea, had grated on every last one of his nerves. Times like these, he regretted leaving behind his own ambitions. Why continue? Was this a fruitless endeavor? Still, each day one fact broke through the Irish muck—dark energy made up sixty-eight percent of the universe, and dark matter made up twenty-seven percent so, in essence, everything else constituted less than five percent.

Numbers didn't lie.

Quint's return was inevitable. Using that combined ninety-five percent, he'd revive and reform.

Schwarz understood that drive. Nothing should stand in the way of the evolutionary process, and Quint was the next link in the never-ending chain. Proving the existence of dark matter, and that it could live inside a human host, was a scientific discovery that would immortalize Schwarz in every future science book.

But for now, his focus must remain on the present. Preparation for his potential Elemental guests must enter the final stages.

Sinking into his office chair, he pulled up his detailed inventory lists. This morning, he'd ordered the last dry ice batch. His special shipment of Halon, purchased through back channels, was scheduled for delivery later this week.

"I've got extra special plans for that fire Elemental, Heisy." Schwarz kicked the dog's bone across the room. "Sit in your bed for a while before we head to the library."

Months ago, Flint, had destroyed his lab, turning to ash his super-soldier research. "Never mess with a scientist. Would you like to know why?"

His dog yipped and spun in a circle in his bed.

"At high temperatures, Halon will squelch flame even when adequate fuel, oxygen, and heat remain. I'll destroy that fire creature as he destroyed *my* creature. I was so close, and then he burned my soldier to ash."

Heisenberg whined.

"Flint will pay. With each breath of Halon blanketing whatever passes for organs within his body, he'll come one step closer to his final death."

His burner cell's ring hummed through the locked desk drawer.

"Never a quiet moment." Releasing a deep sigh, he fished his key from his pocket, clicked open the lock, and answered the pay-as-you-go phone he'd picked up at a nearby petrol station. "Schwarz."

"I'd like to meet." Odd voice. A bit distorted, as if the pitch was manipulated.

"If you're calling this number, you already know where I'll be at three." Though he'd hired many for the hunt, he would keep meeting bounty hunters until someone brought him Violet. Statistically, the more people working on a problem, the sooner the job would be done. Unconcerned who he provoked by hiring more than one group, his only goal was retrieval. Although, at the pace these bar bums worked, he'd have to keep her locked up in his office, and that would never do, because then he wouldn't be safe from the Elemental rescue crew.

"Come alone," The wobbly voice continued.

"I always do." Schwarz hung up and then dropped the phone

back in his drawer. He had a few hours before his daily library meet-and-greet, so he scooted his chair over to his workbench and picked up the Hans Berger helmet, named after the German neurologist who had created the electroencephalograph—an instrument for measuring and recording electrical activity in the brain

He'd love an opportunity for a test run. In theory, this contraption would weaken the Elementals gleaning power. This hat, lined with electrodes, would create subtle shock waves through his brain, using a steady pulse of light electrical jolts.

The heavy battering outside his office door was soon forgotten as Schwarz focused on soldering wires to each connector. Satisfied with his progress, he propped up his feet and read a research article on the hippocampus, the area of the brain believed responsible for short and long-term memory. Lost in brain cells inside his own mind as well as on paper, he started when his phone chimed. The clock read 2:30 pm so he left for the library, but not before packing a long, thin knife with a poisoned blade.

Because, when at war, it paid to be prepared, and while a blade injured—poison killed.

CHAPTER 15

After another rejuvenating dip in the depths of Mt. Stromboli, Flint fired back to Violet, anxious now that he'd learned Schwarz was behind the bounty hunters.

Following Nodin's mental trail, he landed, pilfered some clothes, and honed in on their location. Spotting her sitting at an outside café with her head thrown back in laughter, he decided next time he'd leave her with Terran. She was enjoying her time with Nodin a bit too much. No doubt, the dusky air-puff was dusting off his flirting skills.

France was known for love, and sitting at a table for two in a Calais café provided the perfect environment. A half-bottle of red wine, cheese plate, fruit, and bread sat half-eaten on the table before her. What kinds of thoughts were spinning through that clever mind? Not being privy to her mind's inner-workings seemed a trifle unfair.

Sitting in the shadow created by the umbrella shading the table made Violet's vibrant red hair dull. Her pale skin seemed muted by gray light, not to mention her hideous brown button-down shirt.

As he approached, he removed a rose from a tiny vase set on a nearby table. Then, he procured a spare chair, dropped beside her, and wove the stem through her hair above her ear.

Violet jumped at his sudden disruption of their little tête-à-tête. "Flint. Oh, my goodness, you startled me." She waved a hand at his chest. "Are you better?"

"Yes, thanks for your concern. I'm fully rejuvenated." He shot his friend a salute. "I'll take over from here." Adding a sharp kick under the table for emphasis, he blazed a mental message to his airy friend. *"Nodin, get lost."*

Violet furrowed her brow as she stared at his chest for a moment, then, after slightly shaking her head, favored Nodin with a bright smile. "I was just asking if he's seen Pillar."

Nodin reached over and clasped Violet's hand. *"She likes me."* He smirked before answering out loud. "I have seen Pillar, yes. But I am unaware of her current whereabouts."

Flint jerked his head. *"So go find her, Windbag."*

"Violet and I were in the middle of a discussion about her research at CERN." Nodin arched back in his chair and settled an ankle on his knee. "Before we were interrupted, we were discussing the validity of Terran's assessment. Violet is on board with using Earth's magnetic field to contain Quint. It would be best if Terran took over from here. They have much to discuss."

"Sounds like riveting lunchtime conversation." Flint wrapped his arm along the back of Violet's chair. While listening to her ramble on about magnetism, he sent Nodin another mental message. *"The great-grandchild of your philosopher, Albert Camus, just found a 'til-now-undiscovered book of quotes. Better get shopping."*

"Maybe if you spent a little time getting to know Ms. Levina, instead of being a crude, overbearing brute, she would enjoy her time with you, too."

"Book supplies are limited. Two copies left, last time I checked." Flint fingered strands of Violet's hair before massaging her neck.

"The only thing in limited supply here is your brain matter. Now, start being a gentleman, or I'll have Mother pull you from this mission."

"Try it." Flint shot out of his chair.

Violet stuttered to a stop in her explanation of Michael Faraday's magnetic field research, glancing back and forth between the two men. "What's going on?"

Nodin rose, clapped Flint on the shoulder, and smiled down at Violet. "Nothing. I just remembered I have somewhere else I need to be." He ruffled her hair. "Remember, I'm just a call away. And if this lava lump gives you any trouble"—he jerked his thumb at Flint—"I'll handle it."

"Oh, you'll handle it, will you? Get on your lily-white Pegasus and fly the fuck out of here."

"You don't really have to go, do you?" Violet stood and enveloped Nodin in a hug.

Behind her back, Flint flipped the interfering ass the bird.

Nodin just held her tighter, grinned, and then kissed her cheek.

The outdoor umbrella burst into flames.

Shaking his head, Nodin chuckled and blew out the fire. "I'd best get back to my duties." He released Violet and slapped Flint's shoulder with a little more force than necessary. *"Later, brother."*

Violet waved Nodin off, turned, and then sniffed. "What's burning?"

#

Settling back into her chair, Violet studied the Elemental beside her, and she felt an overwhelming sense of relief. While she enjoyed Nodin's company, she craved the wild, yet assuredly inappropriate, banter she experienced with Flint. His bold comments and amber eyes were something else she'd missed while he recuperated. She'd even worried he wouldn't return. But here he was, dressed to the nines in a black suit and a white shirt with an open collar, revealing a spattering of dark hair. Didn't the man own a pair of jeans? And if he did? *Goddess, have mercy.* Flint in jeans and nothing else. The vision aroused lustful sensations through her body. She arched a brow. "What happened to the umbrella, Flint?"

"That?" He waved a hand. "Slight accident. Not real keen on seeing you in another man's arms."

"So, in other words, jealousy is not a safe emotion for a fire Elemental." Violet sipped her wine and studied her enigmatic companion.

"Don't know." He shrugged. "Haven't felt this way in a long time."

"Logically, you shouldn't feel anything. You've known me a very short time."

"Who said I was logical?"

Violet dropped her head on the table. "I have no idea what to say to you. Our conversations are exhausting."

"Come on. Let's take a walk. We'll come up with something."

Violet fell into step beside him as they strolled along the Calais cliffs and watched the ferryboats load and unload. With each step along the Strait of Dover shoreline, Violet became more unnerved at Flint's continued silence. She squeezed his hand. "When does a battery go shopping?"

"What?"

"It's a joke."

"Oh, what did you ask, when does a battery shop?"

"Yes."

"I don't know." He shot her a glance. "When?"

"When it's out of juice."

Flint chuckled and shook his head. "So, along with science trivia, you've got science jokes under all that red fluff."

"Would a fluff know this? See the opposite coastline? The white cliffs of Dover."

"Yes. The sky's clear enough to see across today." He stopped and stared across the English Channel.

A light breeze ruffled through his dark locks. She fought an urge to lift her hand and do the same. Gaze locked on the white cliffs, she pondered the sturdy wall, which had existed for hundreds of years, yet slowly crumbled over time into the sea. As she realized her heart had done the same, she gasped. Fallen. Plunged. Lost and floating within a fiery sea.

She loved him. Desperately needed his illuminating presence. He was the light mentioned in Sorcha's spell, but would she be the end to his flame? Her mood now matched his—melancholy. In an effort to cover her rioting emotions, she fell back to the one thing that offered succor—science.

Though her voice seemed shaky at first, Violet spouted what she knew of the area. "Did you know the cliffs are composed mainly of soft, white chalk with a very fine-grained texture, composed primarily of coccoliths, which are plates of calcium carbonate formed by coccolithophores, single-celled planktonic algae whose skeletal remains sank to the bottom of the ocean during the Cretaceous period, and together with the remains of bottom-living creatures they formed sediments? You're there, too."

He simply raised a brow.

Undeterred, she continued. "Flint and quartz are also found in the chalk. Speaking of that, what's your real name?"

"I suppose, after your tantalizing strip show the other night, we should be on a first-name basis." He snuffed out a laugh.

Violet slapped his arm. "I have no idea what you mean." A small smile slipped from her lips as she met his gaze.

"Shall I remind you?"

"Absolutely not." She continued along the path, sure her cheeks had pinked, but not from the sea's brisk breeze.

Flint reached her side and clasped her hand, matching his stride with hers.

With each step, Violet tamped down her disappointment that Flint had not answered her initial question. Was the slight deliberate? Did he refuse to share his human name with others? Was keeping that part of himself hidden a way to maintain an emotional distance?

"What do you know about the Elementals?"

She glanced at him, still unclear of his mood. "Everything. Pillar gave me a very thorough run-down before we traveled to the States. Although, I don't quite grasp your limits. After being shot, if you hadn't returned to a fire source, would you have died? And could Quint really inhabit an Elemental, as he wished to do with Terran? Would you have destroyed your friend if Quint had overtaken his body?"

Flint gazed at the distant shores of Dover. "Terran has become a solid member of our team."

Once more, the wind rippled through his hair as if, just like her, it was attempting to break into his secrets. "You seem a bit out-of-sorts today. I expected a less thoughtful response." Where was her innuendo-laden hot shot? This new dimension of his personality only added to his complexity—and his attraction.

"Destroying Terran is not something I find amusing." Flint stuffed his hands in his pockets. "His entire life changed overnight, without any choice. Before he'd even had a chance to grasp the bare essentials of this Elemental life, he faced off against Quint with no backup. Not a humorous subject."

Violet grabbed his hand. "I understand." Her family tree was littered with the ash of Quint's destructive swath. "In case you are injured again, I'd like to be of more assistance. I bought some matches and a couple of lighters. Will those help?"

"Yeah, those should help." He quirked a smile and then wrapped her in a hug.

Flint and affection, how odd. What happened during his recuperation? If she didn't know any better, she'd say he seemed a little introspective.

"How high a temperature can you tolerate? Where did you go to heal? I know active volcanoes are located near Italy." She ticked them off with her fingers. "Stromboli, Mount Etna, or maybe you healed in

Kīlauea in Hawaii, since it's generally considered the world's most active volcano."

Flint nudged a hand against the small of her back, leading her along the grassy path back toward the hotel. "You're worse than Terran with all your questions. Don't you have an off switch?"

"That's rather the point of my questions. I refuse to stand helpless the next time someone injures you." At the thought, she shivered and leaned into his heat, seeking shelter from a gusty wind blowing in from the harbor and the memories of Flint stumbling to the ground with two holes in his chest. "Doesn't it get tiresome? What year were you born? Do you ever wish this service, your life as an Elemental, could end?" What would happen if his flame snuffed out? Would he immediately fade into nothingness?

Flint was quiet for a moment before taking her hand and kissing her wrist. "Yes, at times this Elemental life gets tiresome. I was born in 1405. Do I seek an end to this life?...I suppose that would depend on the day."

Layers. He was like an onion buried deep in the earth. If she pulled him free and dusted him off, would she ever slice through each layer? And if she did, how many tears would she shed as she peeled back each one? Even now, she blinked back tears at the thought of his fiery presence no longer lighting up the world. She should have known better than to believe she would remain unmoved. How did he view her? Was she a means to an end? Was any part of her touching his heart? Or was she, once again, in this alone?

"Rurik Skuratova."

"What?" Violet halted and met his gaze, her heart pounding as one of his layers fell at her feet.

"My name is Rurik Skuratova."

CHAPTER 16

So long.

Such a very long time since he'd uttered those two words. His human name no longer represented who he was in this world. He was Flint. Fire. He'd been burning a swath across the earth for so long that, for some reason, hearing his name—a symbol of his human life—almost brought tears to his eyes. Her questions about the endlessness of his life edged too close to his current inner turmoil. Too close to his flickering thoughts of abandoning this Elemental life—for her. Yet, in all honesty, an end appealed. An end where he could rest. Just close his eyes and be...average. Be a father. Be a husband.

He glanced at Violet and noticed the goose bumps covering her arms and her pink-tipped nose. "Come on. Let's get you to your room. You're chilled."

She nodded and glanced away.

Oh, now that would never do. After revealing a deep part of himself, he wouldn't let her remain hidden behind that distant shield. Plus, making her blush was a lot more fun than considering his future path. "Or maybe I'll just warm you right here." He wrapped her in his arms and gave her a swift kiss on the lips. "I love seeing your cheeks pink when I touch you. Knowing I'm the one burning under your skin, breaking through that barrier you've erected to keep everyone out. Too late, Red. I'm in." He brushed kisses across her cheek, and then bit the tip of her nose.

"I like it when you touch me." Looking down, she scuffed her shoe against the wet grass. "I shouldn't, but I do."

"No more shouldn'ts. More shoulds." Flint tickled her sides.

She squealed and ran from his embrace.

He smirked then followed the bounce of red hair as she ran back to the hotel. Falling into step beside her once more, he stepped into the elevator and punched the number to her floor.

"Last time I was in an elevator, I was with an assassin."

"What?" He snapped a glance over his shoulder. "When?"

"The Asian woman, she befriended me in the elevator."

"There was no befriending, Violet."

"Well, of course, but anyway, I explained a little about the history of elevators, you see—"

Flint fired down upon her lips. He had no intention of listening to what was surely a mind-numbing lesson. He'd rather be numbing her lips. He locked her hands above her head, then backed her into the corner and teased her mouth with his until the doors pinged open.

Walking down the corridor to her room, he tried to regain control, baffled that a simple kiss could light his wick so quickly. He shoved his hands in his front pockets to keep from slamming her against the wall and kissing her until she was pliant and heated, ready to take all he would so willingly give. He grunted out a groan. *Not happening.* "You should get some rest."

Violet cleared her throat and stepped into her room. "Flint, would you come inside? I don't feel comfortable being alone quite yet."

"I should stay out here and glean the thoughts of the hotel's occupants." He cleared his throat. "In case there's danger…or another bounty hunter."

"Oh, I see."

No, no you don't. Flint sighed. "Being alone with you…it isn't the brightest idea, Red." He scraped a hand across his chin.

"Would you at least stay until I'm done showering?"

"Showering? Are you trying to kill me?"

"Please, Flint. I don't want to be alone."

Flint suppressed an inner groan. "Fine, I'll come inside." Those violet eyes always did a number on him. How the hell would he distract himself from thoughts of her soapy body? And there she went slipping off her shoes, revealing those dainty feet. Mother save him from innocent females. He stepped over to the window so he wouldn't see her pulling underthings from her bag.

Violet rustled and murmured to herself for what seemed a tortuous amount of time. "Why don't you watch some TV? I'll be right out."

Flint flicked on the TV, even though he was sure the view behind the shower curtain would be much more to his liking. Toeing off his shoes and hopping onto the bed, he found an action movie where the bad guy was actually winning, and then situated a mound of pillows against the headboard. Bad move, but then, he'd never been able to walk away from a beautiful woman.

Eventually, the running water stopped, and moments, later the bathroom door slid open.

Though he knew it was a mistake, Flint glanced at the vision appearing out of the steam. Her semi-dry hair lay in strands against her shoulders. Her pajama top made obvious she wasn't wearing a bra beneath, and her shorts revealed trim legs. Her smell evoked thoughts of a field of flowers in some forbidden land where you could look, but not pluck. Hell, forget plucking. What he wanted involved total annihilation of her body, marking her with his fiery tattoo. Burning across every inch of her skin until she melted in the overwhelming blaze. But there wouldn't be any burning or marking. She was innocent. And though he'd sear down that path soon, tonight wouldn't lead him anywhere but out the door.

Violet sank down next to him and brushed a hand over his knee. "Flint, may I speak to you for a moment?"

Speak, torture, at this moment they were the same thing. "Sure." He muted the TV and propped a pillow over his lap. He was harder than a piping rod. Damn his filthy mind. He glanced at the TV again, trying to focus on something besides her squeaky clean virgin body.

Violet fingered a stray string on the bedspread. "You know my destiny." She waited until he nodded before continuing, "I've spent all my time studying science, not really having a lot of time for social interactions, because well, what was the point if I am to die anyway? Plus, psychologically speaking, I have a fear of abandonment. While I understand this about myself, I've never done anything to alter my path." Releasing a shaky breath, she shrugged a shoulder.

Flint refrained from watching the shirt slide up and down her body.

After clearing her throat, Violet ran a hand farther up his thigh, making her way under the pillow. "However, tonight, I…I would like to have sexual intercourse. I-I have…ah…I've never done this before and would like to experience sexual relations before I die." She cleared her throat and glanced at him while attempting to chew a hole through her bottom lip. "You are well-suited for this endeavor, as you have a vast amount of expertise in the subject due to your longevity." She cleared her throat again. "I imagine, anyway."

Her body seemed to pulse with an energy he'd never sensed before. He needed to leave before she shocked him like a bull charging an electric fence. Only, at this point, he wasn't sure which of them was the bull, especially when she continued her journey closer to his now-raging cock. Hell, why should he stop her? Wouldn't hurt to let her feel how much he wanted her.

He shifted against the pillows. "You're not going to die."

"I disagree. So far, everything has come true. My ancestor's spell is very real." She leaned her body against his, so she laid half on top of his legs, her bold hand shaping him, working beneath the pillow. "Show me what I've been missing by burying my nose in science books all these years. Show me the pleasure two people can find together."

He rocked his hips against her. "Why do I feel like some kind of test subject? I'm not some battery-operated dildo that will buzz on command." Though at this moment, his battery *was* fully charged. Still, he refused to make this moment some scientific study and halted her wandering hand. "When I have you beneath me, our connection will be more than an experiment. Expect a white-hot nuclear fusion, burning down everything you've ever known, hotter than the fucking sun until you beg me to burn across your body over and over again, but not tonight. You're not in the right mind-frame. I won't just fuck you."

Violet shoved against him and shot off the bed. "How many women? How many?" She glared from her stance at the side of the bed before pacing. "You've lived for more than 500 years, and let's just say for the sake of argument, you've had sex twice per week." She started mumbling and flicking her fingers one at a time. "Born in 1405, died, or whatever in 1438." Rolling her eyes, she waved a hand in the air. "If you take into account 365.242 days per year, with 52.1175 weeks in a year, at 2 times per week… that is 104.355…" She murmured some more, moving her lips in what seemed to be silent math equations. Her gaze locked on the ceiling as she multiplied ridiculous numbers in her head. "Then if you multiply by 576 you get...60,108.48 times you've had sex." She locked her hands on her hips. "So based on those calculations, I imagine you are quite proficient."

Something about a smart woman turned him on every time. "Twice per *week*. Really? I can remember some days when I went twice per—"

"I do not want to hear it." Violet slapped his shoulder then stepped back and lifted off her shirt.

Every primal instinct locked on her body. His eyes scorched by her trim figure, enhanced by a very enticing set of perfectly rounded, pink tipped...no, no, no. He'd bypassed sanity many times in his life. This was another moment to add to the list. The torture continued as she began that adorable rambling.

"The human sexual response cycle is a four-stage model of physiological responses to sexual stimulation. The stages are the excitement phase, plateau phase, orgasmic phase, and resolution phase." Again, she ticked each point with her fingers. "The cycle was first proposed by William H. Masters and Virginia E. Johnson in their 1966 book, *Human Sexual Response*. I believe I am in the excitement phase, because my heart rate and my breathing have accelerated." She fluttered a hand in front of her chest. "I imagine, based on your experience, you can easily lead me into the orgasmic phase."

"Woman, could you make this anymore clinical? Don't you know the man is supposed to take the lead?" On the verge of stomping out, Flint turned off the TV and slammed the remote on the side table. He wasn't a man for hire, running women though ridiculous stages. He should. And would. Leave.

But...orgasmic stage?

Maybe he could show her that stage without actually taking her. With that thought, his dick dripped sorrow-filled tears against his pants. *Sorry, buddy.*

"Maybe 600 years ago the man led, but I am a modern woman. I do not understand why it should be so hard to give me something you've surely given to hundreds of women before." She flounced back and forth along the side of the bed, wildly waving her hands. "Perhaps even to a woman you'd just met, or even paid for the night."

"Paid?" Flint shifted to sit on the side of the bed then grabbed Violet's hips and pulled her between his legs. "You want to know what I would do to a woman I paid? I'd throw her down on the bed." He suited actions to his words. "And I would plunder her body until she begged to pay *me*. Only not in coins, but in pleasure." On his knees, Flint rose above Violet and locked her arms above her head. "I'd bind her. Take my tongue and scorch every inch of her skin, until she was steamy, aching, sizzling with need."

Violet's indigo eyes flared. "Yes, that's what I want." She wet her lower lip with her sweet pink tongue.

A thrum of blue-flame vibrated along his skin. "Are you going to pay me, Red? What kind of currency can you offer?" Flint kissed his way from her neck down to her chest, and then rubbed his lips against her peaked nipples. "What phase are you in now?" He raked both hands through her hair and kissed her.

Gone. So gone. Why had he ever even considered being a gentleman?

Denial was not in his nature. He'd blast through each phase until she understood there was so much more.

Lips locked against her mouth, he released her hands and exulted in her frantic movements, up and down his back, but then groaned when she rocked her hips against him.

He shifted up so they were both on their knees, her back to his front. Diving his fingers across her lean stomach, he shimmied down her shorts, so they rested at the crook of her knees.

"This phase is that first crackle of lightning across the night sky." He kissed her neck and ran a hand across her breasts, tugging and plumping until she moaned and bowed against his body.

Twisting her neck, he fit her mouth to his in a feverish sideways kiss as his hand explored the silky hair at the apex of her thighs, and he circled her spot of pleasure. "This phase is that warning rumble of thunder."

Her breath stuttered as he hit the right spot over and over until she gasped against his mouth.

He kept up the assault. Kissing her, one hand skating over her breasts while the other hand broke past every silky barrier. "This phase...tell me, what phase is this?"

"I don't know, but show me. Show me." Writhing under his

touch, she nipped his chin and gripped his wrist as he fingered her wet folds.

"That's right. This phase is the pouring rain. You'll shower over my hand, as I take you to that final stage. That thunderstorm roaring though your body." He entered her slick channel with one finger, brushing against her clitoris.

She buried her face in the side of his neck, panting sweet breaths against his ear. "Yes, take me."

"I'll take you to where the lightning strikes, but this time, it's inside you. This time, the bright bolt fires through your body, electrifies your skin, and everything you used to be washes away with the rain."

She shuddered against his hand.

"Rain for me, Red. Hit that final phase." As he nipped her neck, he felt her entire body clench before she screamed out his name. Her svelte form rode out her release in his arms. Words poured past her lips in incoherent murmurs as her body melted against his hand, and she found solace in the storm.

Body lax, she turned and collapsed in his arms, and then promptly burst into tears.

Flint held her close, rocking her against his body, crooning soft assurances and combing his fingers through her hair until she calmed and fell asleep.

If he hadn't known before, he knew beyond a doubt now. He may have taken her through the storm, but in doing so, he became her lighthouse forever—a constant, burning beacon, awaiting her, guiding her, and comforting her from life's tempests.

A sturdy fortress, a home, he, too, would return to time and again, seeking shelter, and finding it with her. Only her.

CHAPTER 17

"I don't care who brings her in, just see that she's delivered, unharmed." Schwarz tapped the spine of his book against the library table, barely refraining from banging the tome in frustration. Days had passed since the failed memory swipe by the air Elemental, yet the threat remained, and Schwarz wasn't any closer to obtaining his prize. He did know Violet was traveling to Ireland, which aligned perfectly with his plans.

He glanced at the fool sitting across from him. These hired hunters were like schoolchildren who'd lost their teacher and now wandered the halls, clueless.

And on top of that, the cauliflower-eared Ukrainian with his ridiculous mirrored shades barged through the library and stopped beside his table, hands braced on his hips.

Schwarz flicked his wrist. "I'm presently occupied with another."

"What is this?" the Ukrainian belted out in a voice sure to bring the librarians running. Not good, as they were already eyeing him.

"Wait your turn, lad." His current appointment sneered.

"Gentlemen, may I remind you that we are in a library?" A silver-haired librarian stomped over and wagged her finger under their noses.

For some reason, they all hung their heads and whispered, "Sorry, ma'am" and "Yes, ma'am".

"I'll be in touch." His burly Irish companion removed his cable knit wool cap and bowed to the librarian. "Forgive me, miss."

The Ukrainian took the vacant seat and tore right in. "What is this game you play? Who is this...this Violet Levina? My operative, she does not remember her assignment or recall her time in France. She even consider getting out of business. What happen out there?"

"Just do the job." Without any sympathy for the man's troubles, Schwarz made a note on his tablet to revisit his voltage calculations on his Hans Berger helmet.

"But, what happened to my lady? I never see her like this. She almost...eh...housewife." The Ukrainian spat the word as if it were filth on his tongue. "Her brain is mush. They must use...eh...mind-altering drug. No?" He whipped off his sunglasses and tossed them on the table.

"She'll have to fight through the mire on her own. I can't help you." Schwarz sank back in his chair and crossed both arms over his chest. "I find this entire conversation tedious and irrelevant. Unless you have news about Violet, I have somewhere else to be."

"I need answers. What happened to her?"

"Every job has a certain degree of danger. Obviously, completing this mission is more difficult than you realized." He flashed a thin-lipped smile. "Abducting Violet will take more than brute strength. Use your mind. I'm sure you have one hiding behind all those muscles."

The Ukrainian leaned forward, clenching his hands into fists on the table. "I need money. We send more men."

"The pay remains the same. The compensation is more than reasonable. You aren't the only player in this game." Schwarz studied the dark tattoos on the man's arm. A Reaper's scythe, dripping with black blood. Did the man possess no original thoughts? "You stomped in here with all your photos and research. I suggest you do the same with this assignment. Getting to the girl will prove almost impossible."

The air in the room seemed to still. A hazy shadow crossed the table and transformed half the man's face from light brown to faded gray. The Ukrainian convulsed in the chair, gagged, and coughed. Without blinking, the man met his gaze. "Almost impossible. Is that so, Schwarzy?"

An icy chill slithered down Schwarz's spine, and beside him, Heisenberg whimpered. "Just, uh...just make sure the job doesn't trace back to me."

A momentary wash of black filled the man's eyes.

"Quint? Is that you?" Schwarz's heart pounded in either hope or fear. With Quint, he never knew which emotion won.

The man shook his head and visibly swallowed before experiencing an intense coughing fit. After gasping for breath, he spat into a hanky he'd pulled from his front jacket pocket. When he met Schwarz's gaze again, the inky soot had disappeared, and black tears drizzled down his cheeks and onto his shirt.

The first glimmer of hope ignited in his heart. Perhaps his master, Quint, was fighting to return.

Fighting...and winning.

After wiping his nose on his sleeve, the Ukrainian tapped his sunglasses against the table. "What was I saying?" He blinked and stared at the black tar on his shirt. "What is this? I need more tissue."

Still in a daze, Schwarz searched through his bag until he found a Kleenex multipack and then tossed it over. Why had Quint only returned for a moment? Where was he now? Why tease him with just a glimpse?

Schwarz glanced around the library, staring a little too long at each patron. Was Quint inhabiting one of these people even now? Was his struggle to return finally coming to fruition? And if so, what did that mean for Schwarz's mission? His need to find Violet now surged with urgency. He would not fail.

"You are man of science?"

Breaking through his thoughts of Quint, Schwarz once more focused his concentration on the man across the table. "Yes, I am. Are you feeling all right?"

The Ukrainian nodded. "Too much dust in this place. If you are man of science, why not use your mind, your knowledge, to trap this woman?"

"Not that simple." Schwarz bent his elbows on the table and tapped his index finger against his lower lip.

"Explain."

Schwarz shook his head. "I don't take orders from you."

Heisenberg sneezed.

Schwarz lowered his hand and patted his dog's head. "Almost done, my pet." He met the man's gaze across the table. "Hunting is your department. You came in here so smug, so sure this mission would be easy." Schwarz tapped a finger against his own temple. "I suggest you work smarter. With the amount I've got on the line, I believe you could retire."

"Or I could just take you." The Ukrainian sneered. "Hold *you* for ransom."

"You're a fool. I alone hold the keys to the kingdom. Don't waste your time making ridiculous threats. Just find the girl." Schwarz shuffled his notes together on the table and speared his pen into his shirt's front pocket. "I will, however, offer one piece of advice. Get her alone. If there are any...ah *people* hovering around her, do not even think her name. Be patient. Observe and strike when she is not guarded. That is the only way you'll win."

The Ukrainian studied him for a moment, like there was actually a brain spinning behind that thick head.

"I accept your challenge. I will win." With that, he shot back in his chair.

"Wait." Out of all the villains he'd met with so far, Schwarz believed the Ukrainian would succeed. He studied the man's form, wondering if he would be willing to submit to some...enhancements. The hulk of a man would make an excellent subject for his Überlegen soldier program.

"Yes?" The man tapped his sunglasses against his leg.

"Perhaps we can work together." Schwarz gathered the bag loaded with his books and dog then stood. "Are you comfortable with modified weapons?"

CHAPTER 18

Violet started as something jolted against her side.

Did I fall asleep at the lab again?

"Violet, wake up." A husky voice with a faint Russian accent flickered against her ear.

"What? Qubit factors are...wait, what? Where am I?" Violet rubbed her eyes and glanced around the room.

Flint smacked her bottom. "Get up, Gamma-girl. The ferry leaves in an hour."

Violet groaned and braced her forearm across her eyes. What was she supposed to say this morning? He'd seared her body with his touch, so now what? Would he touch her again? Now? What was the proper protocol for "the morning after"?

She sat up and brushed her hair from her face. "Um...good morning. Did you eat?"

From his stance by the window, Flint merely arched a brow.

"I'm sorry, that's right. I'm a little disoriented this morning." Make that a lot disoriented. Violet scratched her temple.

Bag. Where is my bag? Get the suitcase and escape.

"Fifteen minutes and I'll be ready. Would you mind ordering tea and toast?"

"On its way, Red." Flint stood by the balcony, staring out the windows. What thoughts passed through his mind? With five hundred years under your belt, how differently did you view the world? These philosophical meanderings would be better suited for a discussion with Nodin. Violet shook her head and headed for the

107

bathroom.

As she showered and felt the water sluicing over her skin, she recalled the trickling glide of Flint's touch. The man had spelled her. With each brush of his fingertips over her body, he'd seared a love potion across her skin. Overnight, the heady brew had sunk down deep and infiltrated her heart—a heart that welcomed this foreign substance with open arms. Wasn't that fate's plan? The prophecy laid out in real life.

Violet bloom along light's beam…Burning light into her eyes. Perhaps she'd been wrong earlier in dismissing rainbows, since she clearly felt each end of light's spectrum as a vibrant wave of color glowing under her skin. She would embrace this feeling, embrace Flint, for as long as she could. Because why not? *Why not?*

Finishing, Violet dried off, and then studied her reflection in the mirror. No more gray. Not in her multi-colored world.

After dressing, she stepped out of the bathroom and glanced around until she found Flint waiting by the door. He held her suitcase in one hand and a to-go cup of tea in the other.

Smiling, she kissed his cheek. "I don't care what the normal protocol is after a night like ours. I refuse to act like nothing happened, because it did. I must say, my calculations were correct. So, thank you." Glancing upward, she caught his amber gaze. "Just, thank you."

The suitcase landed with a thump as Flint wrapped his fingers in her hair and kissed her until she couldn't breathe.

"I like a woman who speaks her mind." He handed over her tea. "Here I thought I knew all about sex, and then I discover I had to go through phases." He smirked.

She slapped his arm with her free hand. "Shut up."

"Quite an educational experience." He tugged a lock of her hair. "Everything about you is brilliant…except for this dull brown shirt you're wearing."

"I agree." Violet refrained from rolling her eyes. "It's time to add a little color to my wardrobe, especially when you put me in the spotlight."

"A spotlight, is it?" He braced both hands on her waist and rocked her side to side before bumping her hips with his. "You planning another striptease?"

She elbowed him, eliciting a startled "oof", and then rolled her suitcase out the door.

"How many phases would that take, Red? First phase, hit the stage. Second phase is, what? You shimmy that tiny ass?"

She refused to answer or look over her shoulder, but a smile tickled the corners of her mouth.

The melancholy shadow dimming Flint's mood yesterday seemed erased by the morning sun shining bright over a new day.

Yet, would the dawn's yellow and gold embers glinting through the hotel window touch her spirit, as well? Relieve her burden?

She'd reveled in the storm of his touch and found that golden treasure at the end. And a treasure it was, because like all things that glittered bright gold, the shine would eventually tarnish. So, for now, she'd bask in the light. For now, glory in that elemental glow.

CHAPTER 19

After idling in the long line to board the Calais-to-Dover ferry, and discussing, of all things, the weather, Flint finally drove their rental car onto the ramp and parked. "You know, travel would be much easier and safer if I just had Nodin fly you to Ireland. Or Maya could get you there, you'd just be soaked once you arrived."

"I'm kind of enjoying the journey." She shrugged. "Basking in each phase, if you will."

"Why, Violet," Flint shook her knee. "Was that a double-entendre?"

She smiled, avoiding his too-sure gaze. Window down, she exulted in the sounds of the squawking birds and the fragrant scents of the sea. Shaking her empty tea container, she got out of the car and stretched, and then peered through the window. "I'll be back in a minute."

Flint stopped fiddling with the radio. "Where are you going?"

"I'm human, and humans have certain…requirements. So, I'll be back in a minute." Did she have to explain everything? Tea plus long wait plus human equaled one thing, and on top of that, she needed more caffeine.

"Hang on. I'm going with you."

Violet cleared her throat. "Uh…I'd rather handle this on my own, please."

"No." Rounding the car, he placed a hand against her lower back and guided her toward the stairwell.

Halfway up the stairs, Flint stopped, grabbing a fistful of her shirt. A blast of heat flared against her lower back.

Violet turned to ask what was wrong, but Flint's gaze was locked on a man coming up behind them. Her back began to burn where he touched her. "Flint, you're—"

He pulled away and growled out, "Stay."

Wearing a congenial smile, the approaching man stopped on the stair below Flint. "Good morning to you. Lovely day for a drive." His gruff British accent came across kindly, but the knife glinting in his hand and pressed to Flint's side wasn't friendly at all. "How about you let the girl come along with me for a while?"

Flint pressed her behind him. "She has her own transportation. Now, move along. The thin edge of that blade is nothing compared to my mood this morning."

"I just want the girl." The tip of the knife disappeared into the folds of Flint's shirt.

"I'm quite aware." Flint nodded. "What's your plan here?" He folded both arms across his chest. "How will you get her off the ferry? She's a bit of a screamer."

Violet smacked his back.

"That tranquilizer gun you're carrying won't work on me, so scurry back on down the stairs." Flint flicked his fingers. "Be gone with you."

The dodgy man sniffed and wiped at the sweat on his brow. "Hand her over, and no one gets hurt."

"Well, you see, that isn't happening. She is mine. A fact I established quite thoroughly last night."

How dare he! Violet pinched his shoulder, this time.

Flint merely chuckled, and then glanced over his shoulder. "Violet, now do you understand why it's important I stay at your side?" He turned more fully to face her and clasped her hand. "Don't feel pity for what I'm about to do, because this man has a penchant for beating innocents. Wife, prostitutes, his child. One thing I cannot abide is a man who abuses children. So close your eyes, Red."

"I trust you to serve justice." Violet shifted back and forth in the cold stairway. "Still, could you kind of hurry things along a bit?"

He glanced down at her dancing feet and smiled. "Right, sorry. Human. Gotcha." He winked.

"What the devil are you going on about? Miss, come with me, or I'll gut him." The ridiculous man waved his knife.

Flint turned his attention back to the red-bearded, black flannel-wearing man. "Are you a pirate?" He scoffed. "Ahoy, matey. I'll gut you like a fish." Flint spoke with a high-pitched voice. "So unoriginal. You're not even wearing an eye patch." He sighed, and waved a hand in the man's direction. "I miss the old days when less incessant banter preceded battle."

"Enough of this." The man lunged for Violet.

With a hand around flannel-man's throat, Flint thrust him against the wall on the opposite side of the stairs. Then, he grabbed the hand wielding the knife and slammed it against the wall above the man's head.

A red glow emanated where Flint's hand touched the man's skin. Burning, searing, scorching a brand of the knife into the man's palm.

The villain opened his mouth to scream.

"No. Quiet now." Flint blew a puff of smoke into his face. "You started this, now I'm going to finish it. You will return to your vehicle, and then go home. You will not remember Violet Levina's name, and if you ever hear it mentioned again, you will feel this same burning sensation in your palm."

The man released a pained sob as tears poured down his cheeks.

Flint maintained his grip. "Do not raise your hand against another in anger or violence. Walk away from this path, or you will burn."

"Flint." Violet touched his arm. "Let him go."

Keeping her gaze, Flint released his hold.

Eyes wide, the man clutched his blistered hand and raced down the stairs.

Red glints flickered in Flint's amber eyes. He took a deep breath and blew out a gust of swirling gray smoke.

Violet stood transfixed as she watched his body relax.

The smoke eddied around her body before dissipating.

In awe of his elemental gift, she braced a hand against his chest. Heat emanated in waves from his skin. She longed to rest her head against his warmth, rest her cares at his ever-kindled fire.

How did his body work? What was going on inside? She unbuttoned his dress shirt and frowned at the crisp, white T-shirt that greeted her.

"What are you searching for?" As he gripped her hand, Flint's voice fired across her nerves.

"How does it work? The fire. Where does it come from? How can you alter their minds? And what…what did that man want from me?"

"The sum of fifteen million danced around in his head. And as for what he wanted…I won't say." He clenched his jaw. "Although I will say, had you not been here, his punishment would have been much more severe."

"Are you all right? Will you need to rejuvenate?" Violet met his gaze, worried he'd leave her again.

"Are you offering your services?"

"My services?" She ran a hand up over his shoulder and through his hair then whispered against his lips. "What do you mean?"

Smoke once more filled the stairwell, wrapping them in a world all their own.

Flint wrapped both arms around her waist.

A puff of white smoke broke across her lips before she felt the warm touch of his kiss, heating her mouth. Thoroughly stoking their simmering embers by sliding his tongue across her lips and then delving into her mouth. With each rough glide, he offered reassurance. Each meshing touch ignited a blaze across her heart. She let him ease her worries and calm her fears with each skilled caress. She wanted to melt into him, clasp his hand, and beg him to blaze through the previous night's stages once more, regardless of their public location.

Yet, more than one primal need was making itself known. *Stupid tea!*

With a quiet murmur, she pulled back, but braced a hand across his chest, over his heart. She'd found the sun in his arms and refused to break away, no matter the cost. How could she keep him safe from the coming danger?

Flint studied her with a tilt of his head, and then brushed her hair behind her ear.

"Perhaps I should call my grandfather. He could get us safely to Ireland."

"If having him at your side makes you feel better, then so be it. Although, I'd rather not have a chaperone." He crowded her against the handrail.

Dizziness threatened. Perhaps from a release of excess

adrenaline now that the threat was over, or perhaps she was overly-stimulated by Flint's all-encompassing heat. "No...no chaperone." She ran a hand under his shirt, caressing his heated skin. An instant addiction formed for the burn, the passion, ignited by holding all that fire in her hand. She hadn't been frightened of the knife-wielding man. Flint would protect her. Yet, this easy reliance on someone remained foreign.

Under his shirt, her hand began to glow white. Afraid she'd burn him, she pulled back. *What was that?* Was their connection so strong he'd brought forth her gift without her conscious thought? "Did I burn you? What just happened?"

Flint clasped her hand and kissed her palm. "I'd say that cements our connection, Gamma-girl. While most women burn in my presence, they typically don't emit light waves." Grinning, he tapped her nose with an index finger.

Violet slapped away his hand. "You are absolutely conceited and completely ridiculous."

Perhaps, she *should* call her grandfather. She needed his guidance. He'd see things with a much clearer head. Hers was fogged over with Flint's smoky presence, not to mention the lust hazing her brain.

"Come on, let's get you back to the car in case someone else decides to steal you."

"No, come up with me. I need another cup of tea, and maybe some chocolate." Turning, she headed up the stairs.

"Chocolate?"

"Yeah, it's the cure-all. And right now, I need the biggest bar they've got."

"Well, if it's a thick bar you're looking for..." Flint tugged her back against him.

"Oh, sweet Goddess, save me." Violet bumped him away and headed for the bathroom with an entirely too-goofy grin lighting her face.

# # #

After tossing her paper towel in the bin, Violet shrieked when Flint grabbed her arm.

"We need to get back to the car. Now."

"What...what is it?" Had another bounty hunter appeared? Where would they run? They were trapped aboard this boat.

Alarms blared across the ferry.

Silent for once, Flint intently scanned the area while leading her back to the car.

"Flint, please, tell me what's happening." She tugged his arm.

Frowning, he glanced over his shoulder. "Fire."

Men with extinguishers raced between the parked cars, heading for the ferry's entrance.

"Get in and lock the doors." Flint whipped open the passenger door and pushed down on her head.

Exasperated by his actions, Violet shoved away his hand. "Quit treating me like some criminal being stuffed into the back of a patrol car."

Smoke billowed through the open ferry, gray and white swirling with the ocean breeze across the tops of vehicles. People huddled beside their cars, gaping toward the front of the boat, trying to catch a glimpse of the fire's source. Ash drifted through the air and landed like autumn leaves in the black strands of Flint's hair.

"Maybe someone tossed a lit cigarette into a bin." Violet leaned out the window.

Glaring, he handed her the keys. "Roll up the windows." Upon giving that order, he moved toward the back of the rental car.

She settled into the seat, coughing from the smoke, but didn't close the window, because at this point, she'd just lock all the air inside the car with her. She wished she'd had time to purchase some tea. These frequent disturbances were really cutting into her caffeine intake. While digging into her handbag for a piece of gum, she heard cheers erupt. They'd likely snuffed the flames. As she considered all the safety precautions the ferrymen would now be required to complete in order to secure the boat, she sighed. How much longer would they sit stagnant?

Flint didn't move from his position. His gaze remained locked on something at the back of the ferry.

Violet twisted in her seat and shouted, "What are you looking at?"

He didn't answer.

Following the direction of his gaze, she went on instant alert as she realized it wasn't something, but someone.

A blonde girl, standing by the stairwell, stared back at Flint.

"Oh, now this is unacceptable." Violet opened the passenger door and started after the blonde pyro who'd dared to challenge Flint. Was the girl, even now, planning to blow-up this boat?

A hand gripped her elbow.

"Where in the hell do you think you're going?" Flint tugged her back toward the car.

"That's her, right?" Violet pointed at the blonde. "She's your pyro-girl. She and I need to have a little girl-to-girl chat." Fury turned her fingertips bright blue, so she tucked her hands into her pockets, worried she'd injure Flint instead. Remaining calm when her gift presented was crucial, or she'd be the one injuring travelers.

"Violet, your gift is showing." He flicked a finger at her hair, which had turned purple at the tips. "Calm down. You cannot 'chat'"—he tossed up air quotes with his fingers—"with an irrational, mentally-damaged person." He blocked her path, but no longer touched her. "She doesn't look at the world as you do. Fire is the only thing she understands."

After taking a deep breath, Violet bit out, "She could have killed you."

"No. Come on, let's get back in the car before you turn into a glow stick."

Remaining by the passenger door, Violet waved her hand toward the blonde. "So, she just gets to burn down this ferry?"

The air thickened around them and crackled with barely leashed energy. The hair on Flint's head started to rise from the static. "I gleaned her mind, Red. She lit that small fire to let me know she's still around."

"I don't understand. How is she tracking us? I tossed my phone."

Flint nodded, and finally he ventured to touch her shoulder.

His warm touch served to soothe the potent power waiting to explode from her body. Never had her gift presented this strong before. Violet bit her lip and tried to concentrate on the pain of her digging teeth, so she wouldn't accidentally erupt.

"I think...I believe, perhaps she's been infected by Quint."

Oh, please no, those words were not helping her tamp down this overwhelming urge to destroy something. She gasped as a wave of hate, a desire to punish, seeped forward from somewhere deep in her soul. No, she didn't hate. Where was this foreign expression of emotion coming from? Her whole body began to shake. "Flint, I need you to back away. It's my duty to—"

"No, Violet. Calm down." He gripped her shoulders, and his eyes flared red. "Listen, she's not fully infected, just a small seed. I see swirling darkness in her mind, and her willingness to heed its call. A small sliver of whatever Quint is exists within her. He's always been able to track us. I believe that's how she's following me. But she has no grander scheme today. This was just her having a little fun."

"Fun? You call this fun? I'm fighting for control, holding back a magic dying to teach everyone here a new definition of that exact word, so don't treat this situation lightly." Violet wrenched open the car door and collapsed onto the seat. Bending over, she braced her elbows on her knees and scrubbed her hands through her hair. *Focus. Don't let it out.* After taking a deep breath, she studied her shoes for a moment before glancing at Flint. "Will you speak to her?"

"I refuse to recognize what she's doing." He leaned with one arm along the top of the open door. "The fact she's following us just makes tracking her easier for Terran and Maya."

"I'll let her go…for now." Eyes narrowed, Violet met his gaze and jabbed a finger against his stomach. "However, next time when I'm not surrounded by traveling families, I'll show that girl what happens when she hurts someone I care about."

"Gonna zap her with your gamma-ray?" Flint nudged her shoulder.

"If I can, yes." Violet sniffed and shifted in the seat.

After rounding the front of the car, Flint joined her then reached across the seat and took her hand. "Violet, at this point, continuing to travel by car isn't wise. Let me call Nodin. He can take you to Castle Nemon in a matter of minutes."

"Not yet. Please, just a little more time." Her life was short enough, why couldn't her final days be filled with a fiery Elemental? Violet glanced at his profile and took in his clenched jaw. Maybe protecting her had become too much? Trying to lighten the mood, Violet attempted her best pirate voice. "Land sakes, matey, let's sail these stormy seas together."

"What in the hell was that?" He shot a glance her way.

"My pirate impersonation."

A wide smile lit Flint's too-handsome face. "So you're a pirate, now?" He raised a brow.

"Maybe."

"I thought pirates plundered. So..." he waved a hand down his body.

"Does everything come back to sex with you?" Violet shoved his shoulder.

"What did you say? You want sex?" He grasped her hand and pulled her across the seat, locked an arm around her neck, and brought her close for a very thorough kiss.

"I don't think pirates kissed each other like this," she whispered against his damp lips, glad she'd distracted him from thoughts of transferring his duties to Nodin.

"I thought you were the pirate, and I was the prisoner."

"You *are* the prisoner, and I'll not let you go. Travel with me." She kissed his nose. "Or I'll make you walk the plank."

Flint heaved a sigh. "That isn't an actual fact."

"What?"

"Walking the plank, that's some over-imaginative author's version of history."

She jabbed a finger against his chest. "I find it hard to fathom that in this exact moment you, of all people, wish to discuss the accuracy of pirate lore."

A chuckle rumbled through his chest. "And I find it equally unbelievable that you would ever believe such utter—"

This time, Violet silenced him with a heady kiss. Today she *was* a pirate, sailing the open seas, and as she deepened the kiss, she reveled in the spoils.

Pyro-girls be damned.

CHAPTER 20

Flipping down the visor after attempting to finger-comb her thoroughly ruffled hair, Violet glanced at Flint. They were driving off the ferry ramp and heading for the main road after spending a short time getting better acquainted in the front seat. He'd held her back when people started returning to their cars. There was a family van parked beside them, after all.

Once away from the traffic, the GPS voice blared out its wish for them to take a legal U-turn at the next crossroad. "Where are you going? The GPS is set for Birmingham."

"I thought we'd visit Stonehenge."

Violet pressed cancel on the navigation system. Flint had probably traveled these roads many times before. Roads unpaved, then paved. By horse, by carriage, as smoke. So many trips across the globe.

"I don't understand. One minute you're suggesting I travel with Nodin, the next, you're stopping at a very public tourist site?" With crazed scientists sending bounty hunters and fires popping up at every location, why would he stop? Though she'd chosen to prolong her journey with this fire Elemental, in the end, she was a goal-oriented person. "It's imperative I stay focused. I've been sidetracked enough as it is. Though I wish it were otherwise, I must travel to Castle Nemon so I can study the spell books in grandfather's library. I've neglected my duties for too long." Not to mention her fear that someone else was attempting to control her power when she did use her gift.

How much of Sorcha's spirit remained in the spell? *Clasp your golden hand in mine. Together, vengeance we shall see.* Apparently, the "together" portion of that spell was more than just words. Only, Sorcha was much stronger, more sure in her magic. How could Violet stand with equal strength?

Once she'd turned sixteen and learned her fate, she'd stepped away from everything magical. Denied her true nature. And now she suffered the consequences of her resistance.

Violet glanced at Flint. "I have a vague recollection of a binding spell. Using that, I can contain Quint long enough to destroy him, then I shouldn't need Terran's assistance." She tugged at a loose string on her shirt. "When my mother left, I blamed magic, and then again, when I learned of Sorcha's spell. I turned away from my ancestry and embraced science."

"That's what this detour is about." Flint waved his hand toward the windshield. "To show you there is deep beauty and wonder in magic. There is love."

"Cite an example, please." Though Stonehenge was believed to be a site for various rituals, she'd never heard of any love stories attached to its history.

"I'll explain when we get there. Trust me, the story is worth the detour." He tugged on a strand of her hair. "Sometimes you just have to stop and smell the violets." He winked and chuckled.

"It's three hours to Wiltshire." Violet rotated her neck in a circle, trying to ease the strain caused by too many hours in this rental car. Flint started singing along with a pop song, and she bit back a smile. "Did you know that in order to receive AM/FM radio stations, a radio antenna must be used? However, since the antenna will pick up thousands of radio signals at a time, a radio tuner is necessary. This is typically done through a resonator."

"You'd know all about radio waves, right?"

"Sure, they *are* part of the electromagnetic spectrum. A part of who I am, I suppose." She shrugged and, as a way to calm her nerves, continued her lecture on radio waves, then switched to microwaves, gamma rays, and light rays until they arrived at the ancient stone structure.

Once on site, they walked through the pedestrian tunnel and past a bundle of darkly dressed Goth kids smoking freshly rolled cigarettes. Suddenly, the tips of their cigarettes flared with yellow flame. Screams followed as they spat out the blazing white sticks, and then stomped out the fire with their ridiculous black boots.

In the cacophony, Violet heard Flint's chuckle. She shook her head.

"What?" Linking their fingers, he pulled her along. "They're too young to smoke." He flicked his free hand toward the startled teens. "Trust me, I'm very clear on the damage smoke can cause the human body."

"It *is* a nasty habit." Violet wrinkled her nose.

"Ever tried it?"

"Absolutely not."

"Hmm, and no, I don't need you to elaborate on the hazards of smoking. Because for you, my little fire engine, there aren't any roadblocks to this smoky trail." Flint ran a finger down his body.

"Is that so?" Violet shot him a sassy smile.

"Why, Ms. Levina, I do believe you're flirting." Flint wrapped his arms around her waist and kissed her, oblivious to others observing their blatantly public display of affection.

Violet turned in his arms and studied the more than 20-foot-tall sarsens, or stones. "What practices occurred here in ancient times? What was the purpose?"

Flint nudged her forward with a bump against her hips. "Sit with me, and I'll weave you a fairy tale. Only, this tale is true."

She sank onto the damp grass with Flint bracing her back. His arms came around her waist, and he toyed with her fingers before kissing her temple. "You want to know the truth behind Stonehenge?"

"Why? Do you know the truth?" Relaxing in the warmth of his arms, she yawned and struggled to keep her lids from drooping.

"Stay awake, Red." His deep baritone vibrated along her back. "You'll want to hear this."

Violet released another jaw-cracking yawn and settled against him. "I'll listen." She closed her eyes as his deep, lightly accented voice drifted across her ear.

"In the beginning, there was nothing but life and death. Mother was life. And death was, as always, just an end. There is no evil to death, just a welcoming embrace at the end of life's journey. Death has always been reviled, yet truly, he brings nothing but peace."

"You feel sorry for death," Violet mumbled, touched by the

sympathy in his tone.

"He's the kid no one likes, but you're stuck with him on your team." Flint was quiet for a moment, and then brushed his chin over her bared neck. "Anyway, that isn't the point of the story, at least not in full. Stop distracting me."

"I didn't—"

"Shhh." Flint nipped her neck and continued. "Mother Nature's maternal hand swept across this newly-formed globe and created the elements—air, fire, water, and earth. Many have served before me. I am not the first, nor the only fire Elemental to walk this earth, and Maya and Terran are not the first Elementals to fall in love. The truth behind Stonehenge is the truth behind everything. Love."

At the word, a sizzle of something broke across Violet's heart. The feeling had her opening her eyes and studying the landscape before them in an entirely new manner. Entranced, she gripped Flint's hand as he continued his tale.

"When all was new, Earth was said to be a beautiful queen, floating across the globe like a halo of gold, touching all with goodness and prosperity. Air and Water served as her sisters. Yet, they felt the absence of Fire.

"Then Mother transformed a skilled warrior from a clan high in the hills of what is now Scotland. A hulk of a man with arms and legs the size of tree trunks and eyes so green, you'd swear they were blades of grass."

"Mmm…a Scot. What color was his plaid?"

Ignoring her question, Flint pinched her side and continued. "Fire blazed into their lives. Charming, smug, and exulting in his new-found gifts. Yet, at heart, he was a good man. And when he saw Earth, it is said his fiery heart burst from his chest and fell at her feet. Earth was appalled at his masculine manner and gruff attempts to court her. Still, he didn't give up. Each time he was sent away, he simply smiled and promised to return.

"And as is the way of things, Water fell in love with Fire. She didn't understand her sister's reservations, because here was a man. An equal. Someone who boiled her waters with lust and hope for more.

"Fire discouraged Water's interest, as he loved another and would not create a divide between the sisters. Knowing his absence for a time would be for the best, Fire spent many years alone, focusing solely on his elemental duties, growing stronger, believing in his purpose as no other before or since. Earth, of course, learned of his devotion, and her heart softened.

"After traveling to his side, Earth saw beneath Fire's brawny frame to the fiery heart that burned bright for his elemental purpose, and with love for her. Hours, days, months spent at his side turned her admiration into a deep, abiding love. Together, they forged a bond that circled around them in a blaze of golden amber."

"Brilliant. I love a happily-ever-after."

"But, I'm not finished."

"Oh, well." Violet waved a hand. "Continue, then."

Flint rolled his eyes at her imperious gesture and refrained from noting *she* had interrupted the tale. "Water became jealous and turned to a great sorceress of the time. Lost in darkness, they worked on a deadly spell for Earth. Fire learned of Water's treachery and, in sacrifice, fell under the curse.

"When Earth learned of her sister's foul deed, she struck out in a thundering rage, destroying Water and the sorceress. But at the same time destroying herself, because, for an Elemental, there is one forbidden act—Death.

"Earth understood her time as an Elemental was at an end, and she collapsed on this very field. Her hands clenched in this very dirt. She called on her element one final time, asking for a stone crown for her Fire King. A crown to stand as an eternal symbol of his strength and service. A crown built in a circle, symbolizing their never-ending love. A love standing strong and resolute against all the elements, for all time."

Violet sniffed and shifted upright. "I don't like this tale. Though, I see the visual of the crown with the stones, I don't particularly like the ending."

"That wasn't the end." Flint kissed the top of her head. "After the rocks formed into what you see today, Earth collapsed in the middle of the stones, surrounded by her final gift to her Fire King.

"Mother Nature came and took her hand.

"Earth cried in agony, begging for escape, and asked to join her Fire King on the other side.

"Mother and Earth's sister, Air, wept as death's blade delivered Earth's final wish.

"Yet, even now, the lovers walk amongst the stones. Hearts

bound together as proof love does endure, remaining as strong as the stones still standing over centuries, bringing wonder and joy to all who see."

Quiet for a moment, Flint drew a deep breath and ran his hands up and down Violet's chilled shoulders. "That's the truth behind these stones, Red. One of many truths passed down from Elemental to Elemental."

Violet wiped at the tears on her cheeks. "Why do the deepest loves always end in such tragedy?"

Flint tightened his arms around her. "Love is at the center, though. At times it divides in various shades of jealousy, anger, lust, sadness, and hope, but at the core, love is very simple and long-lasting. In the end, Earth and Fire won, because for the time they had together, they loved without reservation, and in return, they have eternity together."

"Do you really think so?" Violet whispered. These lovers' fairy tales were lovely to hear, but how true were they? The loss of a loved one, the hurt from the betrayal by a sister, was easier to comprehend. When had this man, with his arms wrapped around her, become such an advocate for happily ever after?

Once Flint let her past his surface, just like the Fire King before, she saw the bright flame beneath, burning, reaching for something. Did he want the happy ending? Would he use his gifts to immortalize her? Wasn't he already tattooed on her heart forever, and if so, what would that cost? Because their tale would also end in tragedy. No, her tale—her story, not his. Never his.

She closed her eyes and considered all Flint had done for humanity over his vast years on earth. All he'd done for her in just a few days. Did he understand that his light changed people's lives? Did he know he'd changed hers?

What could she give back? She could level the playing field. A little. A very little. Breathing deeply, she noticed the air possessed a vibrant scent of clarity, as if somehow Flint's tale had opened her senses to all the shades of blue lighting the sky.

As he said, the beginning started with life and death. He was life and she was...death. But until that final peace came, she'd take some of his life, his verve, and give it back. Explore parts of her personality previously leashed and frightened, like a quivering dog abandoned in the woods. At first, she'd been skittish with Flint, but now she trusted him and looked forward to their moments together. She was satisfied with the results of her seduction last night, and she couldn't wait to try again.

With that in mind, she stood and stretched, a thousand points of lust and hope radiating through her body. "I believe your story." Violet took Flint's hand and drew him to his feet. "I'll never forget this moment." She rose on her toes and kissed him.

Holding his hand, she led him closer to the stones. A warm breeze stirred across her skin, though the day was clear and brisk. "They *are* here." Violet closed her eyes and spun in a circle.

Glorying in the moment of being alive, she twirled and twirled until she became dizzy, so dizzy. She collapsed to the ground, laughing. A sudden wash of heat coursed over her body, and a fragrant scent like a bouquet of roses leapt across her senses. Her gift thrummed within her body, not from fear, but from an immense feeling of joy and love.

Lying still, she opened her eyes. A large man with a cocky smile, long black hair, and only a scrap of clothing covering the lower portion of his muscular body, stood over her, and beside him was a gloriously beautiful woman with bountiful waves of golden hair.

Unclear of the vision, Violet squinted, yet with each thrumming beat of her heart, she knew. The burly man held out his hand, and the woman beside him smiled, the vision radiating her already magnificent face.

Violet blinked, and a foreboding chill shot down her spine when a woman's whispered warning surged through her mind. When she again opened her eyes, she saw only Flint holding out his hand, helping her to her feet.

Feet firmly on the ground, she noted her hands were shaking as she cupped his face. "They were here."

"Of course, they are." Flint brushed her hair over her shoulders. "We'll come back again to visit." He smiled and kissed her cheek before tugging her across the street to the parking lot.

Sparing a glance over her shoulder, Violet shivered as she recalled the words drifting through her mind. A message delivered with lyrical splendor by an ancient Earth queen. *Don't let the flame burn out.*

CHAPTER 21

An early evening mist fell over the stones, cloaking the Stonehenge visitor's car park. A half-hour before closing time, most visitors had left, their arms burdened with souvenirs, and their voices murmuring theories on the sarsen's true purpose.

A flash of bravado over her next move had Violet rushing to the car. The sense of foreboding from the Earth elemental's words, along with the inevitable end of her time with Flint, had her feeling braver than usual.

With Flint's hand in hers, she took a deep breath and stopped beside the passenger door. "I want to explore what we started last night."

Flint smirked. "In the middle of a parking lot?"

"Why not? Open the back door."

Flint surveyed the area, and then dug the keys from his pocket. "Never took you for an exhibitionist."

"Not an exhibitionist, but an…experimentist." She tucked her hair behind her ear, sure that if he kept her waiting one more minute, she'd lose her nerve.

"No such word, Red, but I'm liking the thought."

"Shut up." She shoved him against the car door and kissed him, overcome by raw emotion. Time closed in from all sides, and she wanted to mark each minute with *her* fire Elemental, and if her heart broke, like the fated Earth in Flint's tale, then so be it.

Flint returned her kiss, sliding his tongue across her eager lips. His own eagerness evident as he delved deep and stroked the walls of her mouth, tangling his tongue with hers in a flagrant, teasing dance.

Smoke billowed around them, turning the air an even hazier gray.

Violet felt for the car door handle at his back then turned and beckoned with her finger as she slid into the backseat.

Following her down, Flint pushed up her skirt, his fingers burning a path along her upper thighs. "What phase are you in now, Violet?" He caught her gaze, a simmering grin lighting up his face, yet something glimmered in those amber depths.

"I've been in the resolution phase since the first moment I met you. I fought this." She tapped a fist above her heart, which thumped a wild beat. "But resolve is all I have now. I may not have a choice in my future, but I choose this moment. I want to feel the same connection Earth and Fire from the legend had together. Shouldn't I get the same chance at bliss? For one day, why can't I be a normal woman, fulfilling her desire for a man?"

An orange glow flickered for a moment in Flint's eyes. "Be whatever you need to be, Violet. Don't hide behind prophecies or rules. Break free."

"I want...I need your help. When I consider your story, I understand Earth's initial reticence, but like me, she saw the man burning inside. Tonight, I want Rurik, not Flint."

He closed his eyes for a moment, his jaw clenching. "The things that come out of that mouth." He shifted and shut the car door. "You may think you want Rurik, but that man...that uncivilized brute would drag you out of this car and carry you to the stones, drop you on the grass, and fuck you until you screamed."

"Yes, that's what I want." Her pulsed quickened and her skin flushed pink as the erotic visual of a grimy, sweat-soaked man taking her, owning her, flashed through her mind. Would he really fulfill such a carnal offering? She would go, if only he'd asked. In fact, she'd race him to the center.

"Violet, you deserve more than that. I'll do what I can, but it's tight quarters in here. Lean back against the door."

Violet settled against the door and ran her fingers through his warm, dark hair.

He transformed into half-man, half-smoke, and glided along her body. Turning into his element caused his clothes to drop across her legs.

She kicked them onto the floorboard. Heat billowed along every inch of her skin. A deep moan escaped when his fingers traveled along her thighs once more, and then spread them wide.

Gray smoke filled the backseat, blocking her vision, until the weight of a fully formed man settled against her body.

Flint braced her head between his hands and kissed her, bruising her lips with his vigor. "You may want the man, Violet, but I am no longer that being. I've crossed too many divides to ever return to who I once was, but hearing you say that name does something. Makes me long for my humanity. Makes me wish to become Rurik once again. For you."

She had no time to digest his words, his meaning, because with a single fiery finger, he singed a line down her shirt, burning it open.

Flint brushed away the white cup covering her breast, and then bent his head and caressed her peaked nipple with hot swirls of his tongue.

Arching against him, Violet frantically tugged at her skirt, but then gave up, as her hands were too shaky. "Burn it off."

A chuckle was all she heard before Flint once more rolled into smoke.

Shifting in the seat, she jumped when a heated puff worked up her thighs, caressing, sizzling along her skin.

Flint's human hands transformed, and she watched them delve under her panties, working magical, heated fingers into her wet slit.

So hot. This smoky creature burning up and down her body. Steaming, bringing heat to her core. Violet closed her eyes, letting the mystical moment take her to another place.

One sensation led to another as a hot lick rasped against her core. "I want the man. Rurik, take me to the stones. I want you. Please." Violet begged as each hot slide of his tongue sent shockwaves along her skin. Waves that coursed through every nerve in her body and then centered once more, creating a steady pulse right where she ached most. "Rurik, please."

Weight once more settled on her legs as Flint coalesced back into his human form, though he remained under her skirt, licking, sucking on her bud.

With a tight hold on her hips, he tilted her closer, and then slid two fingers inside, stroking along her G-spot in time with each stroke of his skilled tongue. Settling her higher against the seat, he plunged over and over.

Clutching a thick hunk of Flint's dark hair in her grip, Violet rolled with each surge as it took her further from the shore. Shuddering, arching, lost in the heavy caress of his tongue, she writhed with each flick sending steaming swells across her core. Then with the continual thrust of his fingers, he propelled her out to sea where, afloat on sensations, she broke over and over in time with his torturous caresses. Words tumbled out her mouth. Curses she never used spilled forth, each murmur exalting in the waves of bliss flowing through her body.

Sated and gasping against the seat, lost in the sensation of Flint's touch, Violet trembled as he kissed and nipped his way along her chest, her neck, and finally her mouth.

Rising above her, he kissed her—languidly.

As if he had all the time in the world to explore the intricacies of her mouth. She wanted more. More of the same, yet with him filling her—in every way. Her essence remained on his tongue. An elemental flavor. Yet, wasn't this part of the ritual of lovemaking? The sharing of everything, each taste, each touch. A touch she should return. She reached for his erection, pressed solidly against her stomach, but he drew away her hand.

"You wanted the man, Violet, but as I said, Rurik is primal," he gritted out. "I know you are untouched, but right now, I would strip you of everything. Tear through that barrier without a care. I want too much. So, don't tempt me." He forced out a shuddered breath, and when he opened his eyes, they flickered with red.

Energy surged through her body, and she reveled in the knowledge that she had created such carnal need in this elemental creature. Though she ached to connect their bodies in every way, losing her virginity in the backseat of a car was not the romantic first time she had envisioned. So, she brushed her fingers through his hair instead, trying to calm the fire blazing from his over-heated skin, from the need simmering in his eyes.

In an effort to calm her own desires, she took a deep breath and bit down hard on her bottom lip. "I'm sorry. I just feel this sense of urgency." She cupped his jaw. "Everything about my life has been so very controlled, fixed on one goal. Equations with answers. But with you, I'm like...well, like Pi, a never-ending number." She leaned forward and brushed a light kiss on his warm lips. "Everything about you is so raw."

"So I'm raw pie?" Flint chuckled and then kissed her forehead. With a bit of finagling, he reversed their positions and settled her between his legs. "We'll have our "more," but not here. This isn't our place." The husky murmur vibrated more through his chest than his lips.

Violet shifted against him, silent, because she understood taking their "more" would need to happen soon. She nodded and squeezed his hand. "No, this isn't our place." A twinge of sadness stole across her heart. How many remaining moments of stillness did they have? Moments of just reveling in quiet comfort. Of finding peace through the simple joining of their hands.

At times like these, the weight of the spell's burden became almost unbearable. The urge to scream and pull her hair, to fight back with an enchantment of her own, scorched across her damned soul.

Each hand on the clock ticked closer to her final showdown. Centuries ago, her ancestor had written the equation of her life across the chalkboard of time—no X, no Y, just death.

CHAPTER 22

Relaxed, with Violet's sated body lying on his, Flint closed his eyes and imagined losing himself to slumber, but something troubled his redhead. Irritation rose over his continual inability to glean her thoughts. Hadn't he earned a modicum of trust? When would she drop her shield?

Violet swirled a finger across his chest. "What you said earlier...did it mean...I suppose, I'm curious if you've ever wished to become human again?"

"Yes." Flint shifted underneath her.

"Can you?" she whispered.

"What's that?"

She rose on her elbows and met his gaze. "Can you become human again?"

He tucked a stray curl behind her ear. "When an Elemental is finished, he or she is returned by Mother to a human life, and they remember only faint glimpses of their time. This job is not for the weak. Many balk at the constant duties and the unceasing need to perpetuate their life force."

Violet's plumped lips pinched together, and she tapped her bottom lip. "I don't understand. They only recall...what? Explain, please."

"I'm not sure, myself. Perhaps, the condition is similar to recalling certain aspects of your human childhood. Some thoughts are hazy, unclear, while others are lost. Mother actually discourages the transformation. From what I understand, only a few have asked to return to their human form."

Her sex-fluffed head of red hair tilted. "Why have you remained?"

"More sex." He chuckled as he nudged his rigid cock against her. This conversation had turned way too serious.

She pinched his arm. "I believe you've had more than your fair share."

"Oh, now, Red, that's where you're wrong. I'll never have enough." Delving a hand under her skirt, he squeezed her ass.

Violet merely scoffed. "Oh? 60,000 plus times isn't enough?"

"You know what they say, practice makes perfect."

She fought to pinch him again, dissolving into gales of laughter when he tickled her. "Okay, okay, stop. I'm too tired to fight." She sighed, and her body went slack against him.

Too bad, the little tussle only added more fuel to his already rock-solid erection. Flint shook her shoulder. "Violet, we should go. Don't fall asleep."

Darkness had fallen across the visitor parking lot. A lamppost two aisles down provided a faint glow against the fog. They needed to move. Sitting in one place for too long wasn't wise with Schwarz's dogs on the hunt.

After a slight groan of protest, Violet sat up and murmured, "Was it a woman?"

"Woman, women, I'm not picky." He chuckled.

"Enough." Violet swatted his chest. "I am asking if a woman brought about your decision to become human again."

Flint closed his eyes as the pain that came with remembering Eva fired through his chest. He remembered her sure smile, her steady nature. Everything about her so relentlessly determined. He linked his fingers with Violet's. "Eva was a nurse in the Second World War. The first time I saw her, I was standing in a field. Smoke and the copper scent of blood filled the air. I've seen many battlefields over my peri-mortal life, and this carnage was no less savage." Flint stopped for a moment to clear his throat, willing away the sorrow brought forth from recalling those soldiers' cries for death. He often wondered what his swan song would be, or if he'd simply close his eyes and welcome an end with open arms. "So much regret. So much fear. And a quiet cry for grace."

After taking a deep breath, he continued. "Eva stomped around like a little general. In the middle of chaos, she bellowed out orders. And yet, I could see inside her mind. Fear, doubt, and despair swirled through her, but she held everything together. She became my landline. My link to humanity in a world gone mad."

"I'm sorry for all the horrors you've seen." Violet leaned over and kissed his jaw. "There is no blank slate though, is there? You've seen so much darkness. I don't know how you've remained sane."

He huffed out a laugh. "Who says I'm sane? Like I've told Terran, I've fallen off sanity's bridge too many times to count, but somehow, I always fight to the surface. The Elemental call is too strong. So much destruction, but those moments of purity...those selfless acts by mere humans keep me from falling into despair." He shook his head at the thought of times he'd fallen, only to return. "Eva's unceasing determination lit up that field of death."

Flint closed his eyes and pictured Eva's face, her long blonde hair tied up in a bun. Her svelte form, her glare as he approached the first time and flashed his sure grin. "Eva and I worked together. I had this uncanny ability to cauterize wounds."

"Imagine that." Violet smiled, and then trailed a finger down his arm, tracing the veins along his wrist.

"Eva understood I had many secrets I couldn't share. But, I did anyway. Centuries, decades, I'm not even sure, so much time had passed since I had felt real love, and I embraced the foreign emotion in order to ease my solitary existence." He brushed his hand through Violet's hair. Her wild red locks were thicker and less tangled than Eva's.

"I was ready to leave behind the Elemental life. Eva was aware of who I was, and the enormity of the choice I was making. I asked Mother for one more cleansing by fire. To say goodbye, as it were." Absently, Flint ran his fingers across Violet's hand and then heaved a deep sigh. "I left Eva alone...and that was my biggest mistake."

Violet tipped his chin with her finger. "Why? What happened?"

"At the time, the man who was Earth was too long in the Elemental world." Flint shifted in the seat as the pain of betrayal struck anew. "He felt the earth was his, and that humans fouled his sphere with their presence. Eva's knowledge of who we were was strictly forbidden. Earth decided to remedy that situation by erasing Eva's memories of our time together. When I returned, I discovered she didn't know me. I searched her mind for memories of our time together, but nothing remained."

Violet kissed his fingers. "What did you do?"

"Earth is the strongest Elemental—our grounding force. Air, water, fire—we exist in Earth's sphere. But none of that mattered. In that moment, I was a bit like the Earth Queen seeking revenge for her Fire King."

"I'm so sorry." Violet wiped at the tears on her cheeks. "How could he do that to you?" Her indignation made Flint smile.

"Mother and Nodin intervened before I could deal with Earth on my own. She hid him away and removed his gifts. Still, erasing who he was did nothing to negate my loss. They say love conquers all, but not this time. Eva remembered nothing." Flint shook his head. "I believed our love was strong enough to withstand any force of nature. I'd said good-bye to hundreds of years of memories, all for nothing." He released his hand from Violet's grip, and scrubbed both hands over his face. "In an effort to regain what was lost, I frightened Eva with my declarations, my persistent pleading. I no longer saw love in her eyes, but fear and confusion. So, I walked away." Closing his eyes, he felt the old pain, the loss of love sear across his heart. "I walked away."

Violet kissed the tears from his cheeks. "So much has been taken from you. I would not ask—"

A knock came on their window.

"Oh, good gracious." Violet shuffled her skirt over her legs and wadded her seared shirt together over her chest.

"Violet, stay in the car." Lost in the past, in the pain, Flint had let the present sit idle too long, and now he had to deal with the consequences.

"Why? What's wrong?" She searched the floorboards for his shirt.

Another double tap against the window.

"How did they find us?" He glanced at Violet. "Did you use your credit card?" They were sitting ducks, and Schwarz's goons had taken full advantage.

"No, I didn't…Oh, wait…we did use it to buy gas."

He raked his fingers through his hair, trying to decide the best way to proceed. "Stay here." Flint slipped on his pants before stepping out of the car's backseat.

The bounty hunter was costumed in ill-fitting security guard attire. His high-dollar shoes gave him away. One thing Flint did know was fashionable footwear.

The man tapped a baton against his palm. "Sir, you need to move along. The girl, however, will be staying."

Flint leaned against the car door. "You know, if you play at being a bad guy, at least complete the look."

The man arched a brow.

"Those Edward Green shoes don't match the thirteen dollar an hour security-guy ensemble you've thrown together. The last pair of Edward Green's I *borrowed* cost fifteen hundred dollars."

A heavy fog cloaked the air, and tiny drops of mist sizzled upon landing on his skin.

The man drew a gun from the back of his pants and pointed it at Flint. "The girl comes with me. Get her out of the car."

Flint sighed. "You really shouldn't be standing out in the elements with those shoes." He'd already been shot once this month, and he wasn't about to go through that again. But what really irritated was this man's disregard for quality footwear.

"I pulled these shoes off the last guy who stood at the receiving end of this barrel." The man waved his weapon. "So, don't think I won't pull this trigger to get what I want. Your girl is worth a lot of money. So stand aside."

"I know what she's worth." Flint took a step toward the front of the car, just in case the man fired wildly. "Turn around and go home. Forget you were here. Find another line of work." He leaned against the hood. "You kind of suck at this one."

"I want the girl." The faux security guard's hand shook as he glanced at the car pulling up alongside.

A bleached-blonde harridan banged a fist against her clunker's outer driver's-side door. "What's going on? Get her, and let's go."

Flint shook his head. "Sorry, she stays with me. Last warning. Go home."

Two thick-necked simpletons hopped out of the car's backseat and approached him with guns drawn and held cocked to the side.

Was everyone some kind of gangster these days? Flint rolled his eyes. "Sometimes, I miss buckshot, the sound of a slashing sword, even a simple knife fight. Anything would be better than facing down a man who has never fired a gun, let alone learned the proper way to handle the weapon."

"Is she in the backseat? The redhead?" The wild-haired blonde wench shouted from the driver's seat. "Get her."

Flint lifted his clenched fists to his lips and blew a fiery stream across his knuckles. Stepping toward the bug-eyed men, he swiped the guns from their hands, blistering their fingers in the process.

Groaning in pain, they stumbled backward, clutching their burned hands.

"Now who's the one with firepower?" Flint chuckled. "Get back in your car."

The woman fired her gun, hitting the front fender right by Flint's leg.

"What the hell do you think you're doing? You could have hit her." Flint grabbed the fake security guard by the throat and slammed him against the woman's window. *"Who hired you?"*

The man's mind traveled to a bar where he'd answered a payphone. "D-d-d-don't kn-know."

Was Schwarz masking his involvement by anonymously hiring others? Smart move, considering their elemental gleaning powers.

"You will not hunt for Violet again." Flint threw the man against his moaning compatriots, and then turned his gaze on the real mastermind of this little abduction. The woman.

Bracing his hands on the open window, he met her drug-fueled gaze. *"You will not remember tonight's events. Return to your home. Start anew."* Flint turned from her and shot his fiery influence through the frightened men's dark souls, trying to burn out their evil with light and positive purpose. *"This woman is under my protection. Do not hunt for her again."*

Leaving the men scrambling to return to the getaway car, Flint helped Violet out of the back seat.

She ran a hand over his chest. "Are you all right?"

"Yes. But we need to go."

Glancing over his shoulder, he watched the car's taillights swerve and speed through the exit. "Schwarz must be hiring men who don't actually see his face, using head hunter firms as a go-between. We'll need to play smarter. We need Terran." Flint settled Violet in the passenger seat then vaulted over the car's hood and jerked open the driver's door.

"My grandfather will help. He's a very powerful wizard." Violet squeezed his hand.

"Really?" Flint reached into the backseat for his T-shirt. "If he's so powerful, why is he allowing you to travel alone?"

Violet shrugged, tugging at the hem of her skirt. "What does Schwarz want with me?"

"To hold you captive until Quint returns, conducting sick, exploratory tests on your body. He isn't one for moral science practices."

Violet turned quiet, staring out the window.

The poor girl had gone from an ordered world based in scientific fact to complete and utter madness in the span of a week. Hadn't her grandfather prepared her? What was wrong with the man, letting his only grandchild flit about Europe on her own?

She placed a hand on his knee. "Whatever happens between now and the time Quint returns, please know I am grateful you've remained by my side. I know I…I was wrong to fight the truth of my destiny for so long." Her teeth dug into her bottom lip. "Still, don't wear yourself down on my behalf. Do you need to return to the fire? Renew yourself?"

"While I appreciate the concern, I'd rather you focus that analytical mind on working with Terran to defeat Quint. I'm hoping Maya's healed by now, because Pigpen won't leave her side otherwise."

Violet folded both arms across her chest. "My mind is constantly contemplating the resources necessary to contain Quint, but that doesn't mean I'm not concerned about your welfare." She shot him a glance. "Please, do not neglect your care, especially with these continued abduction attempts."

"Attempts are right." He scoffed. "Schwarz is hiring nothing but fools."

"Still, you should remain strong. The higher the number of persons hired by Schwarz, the higher the probability of a worthy foe."

"I'd rather this journey was over. I'll call Nodin."

"No." She clutched his arm. "Don't…please, don't call Nodin. I want…can we just finish this journey together?"

"Violet, you're in danger. That woman could have shot you." He grasped her shoulders. "I won't lose you."

"Please, Flint, it's not that much farther. Please. I need this time. Moments like today…" She shook her head, and then met his gaze, tears pooling in her eyes. "You have the ability to freeze time. What I wouldn't give for that gift. To halt the moment we shared in the stones. Just you and I locked in a fairy tale. I was happy. At peace, and that's rare for me. And with you…I want…please, just let me have more time with you? Just you." Face damp from the tears pouring down her cheeks, she pressed her wet lips to his. "Please."

"It's too dangerous." Her tears had weakened him, and he couldn't deny he wanted more time together. Today had been a golden highlight in his vast elemental life. "Schwarz will send more men."

She wiped her face with her sleeve. "Are you saying you can't protect me?"

"Going for the ego shot? Smooth, Red." Flint tweaked her nose with a finger. "Don't worry. My flicker's just fine."

She rolled her eyes.

"What?" He laughed as he started the car and shifted the car into drive, leaving the mystical stones behind. Though unwise, he'd grant her wish and continue the journey. Who could say no to those pleading violet eyes? Maybe he *should* halt time, lock Violet away, alone and secure. Block every threat to the embers of love building in his heart. Acceptance of that emotion cemented as he clasped her hand in his, linking them together with a mesh of skin on skin.

She met his gaze and flashed a vibrant smile.

Love.

Ah, hell.

CHAPTER 23

Upon arriving in Liverpool during the early morning hours, Flint had delivered a very sleepy Violet to an all-night diner. Now they idled in line for the ferry, ready to cross the Isle of Man. "Hopefully, this crossing won't take more than two-and-a-half hours." Flint glanced at Violet.

"Or have wayward pyro-girls lighting bonfires in your honor." Shooting him a smirk, she straightened from her slouch and punched off the audio book.

Hadn't the woman ever heard of Classic Rock? These banal science musings were enough to put him to sleep, and that was saying something, since he hadn't slept in five hundred plus years. "On the next leg of the journey, I'll take over the radio."

Violet twisted in her seat. "But this research into galaxy formations is groundbreaking. These concepts theorize that the first galaxies formed around clumps of dark matter." Her fingers smashed together in a mock example of particles colliding. "Earlier this year, I attended a conference at Durham University where the professor spoke of Supercomputers using software called Arepo to help recreate a virtual universe. If I can study their work, I may comprehend how Quint evolved."

As he came to a stop on the ferry and turned off the car, Flint grunted. "We've got plenty of time to kill, but I refuse to listen to another physics lesson. Should we stretch our legs?" He shot her a glance. "Snack bar?"

"No." She tossed her bag in the back seat and leaned closer. "I'd like…I want to try something." Biting her bottom lip, she ran her hand up his thigh. "Lean back, please."

"Violet, what are you doing?" He stilled her exploring hand.

Lightly brushing two fingers across his lips, she whispered, "Let me."

Flint scanned the area to make sure no one was watching, but someone could be, and that made this hotter, more dangerous. "Let you what?"

"Let me do this." Tossing him what could only be considered a very wicked grin, she unzipped his pants and burrowed inside for his now-solid cock.

At the feel of her determined fingers, he jerked in the seat, and then shot a glance at the rear view mirror. "We are in the middle of a ferry parking lot, Red."

"Parking lots seem to work for us." Bending over, she circled the exposed tip of his cock with her tongue before shimmying her hand down to his base. With a purr, she traveled up and down with her mouth, suction tight as she took him deep down her throat.

As his balls tightened, he brushed away the fall of red hair blocking his view then settled his hand at the back of her neck. He refrained from arching against her, since this was her first attempt. Eyes closed, he escaped into sensation. The soft smack of her lips, the hums and quiet moans as she worked him over and licked his straining head, created a steamy chorus that vibrated up his body. "Violet, fffuuu…ck me." Flint opened his eyes when she started working him with her hand and mouth simultaneously. "That's right, just like that."

Then, when he rested fully down her throat, she gripped his balls and tugged—and that was the end of life as he knew it. "Violet, pull back."

"You like that, Rurik?" She buzzed against his shaft, nipping the tip with her teeth.

The cheeky witch bobbed down, then back up as she fondled his sack. He hissed out a breath, trying to hold back the pending explosion, reveling in each glide of that sweet mouth.

Moving her tongue in breath-taking swirls around the underside of his sensitive head, Violet kept one hand stroking his cock, and the other bearing down hard on his balls.

"Oh, yeah. That's perfect, Red." His breath turned to smoke as the final waves of ecstasy sizzled through his body, clenching, and then releasing in a crescendo of erratic pulses so intense he shouted in his native tongue, words, expressions, who knew what the fuck poured from his mouth.

She released him with a pop, met his gaze with a cat-wallowing-in-the-cream smile, and then she licked her lips.

Sweet Mother. That simple movement shot another blaze of fire through his loins, jerking his spent cock once again. He yanked her upright from his lap and drove his tongue down her throat. Branding her as she'd just branded him. He raked his hands over her breasts, kneading and tightening his grip. Out of his mind with the need to make her feel his gratitude.

Not quite steady, he pulled back and studied her face. Her cheeks had pinked. Her lips rough red. Her breath panting against her silky lips.

Taking a deep breath, Flint tightened his grip on her neck. "How could you possibly know how to do that?"

Violet shrugged. "A few years ago, I found myself curious about such things after overhearing a co-worker's conversation with a friend, and so…" She cleared her throat. "I…well, I watched videos on-line. I suppose they could be considered pornography clips, but I used them for educational purposes. I found the male-male videos the most instructive, actually."

She spoke as if learning in this way was an everyday occurrence. *Oh pardon me, while I watch various persons suck cock and pump seed down their throats. It's purely for research, though, darling.* And the thought, just the visual of her squirming in her seat as she watched people having sex—fuck, if that didn't make him rock-solid all over again. "So, let me get this straight, my little video voyeur. You watched men give each other—"

"Yes. I found each episode a practical method of study." Violet pulled away and sniffed.

"That is the hottest. The most—" As thoughts of what she'd been watching seared through his mind, he yanked her closer and kissed her again. "So, did watching those men together make you hot?"

She ran a single finger across the leaking head of his reinvigorated, and seriously overly-stimulated, cock, and then placed his hand on her breast. "What if it did?"

"Violet, you're treading into dangerous territory." After giving her a hard kiss, he straightened and pulled away. "Someone's coming." He'd gleaned a couple with children about to pass by the passenger window. While comfortable with his nudity, he balked at full-frontal exposure in front of youngsters.

And then there was the "well-seasoned" wench approaching their door.

Violet settled in her seat, but reached across and squeezed his knee. "I think I'm capable of taking you through a few phases on my own."

He raised a brow. "Is that right?"

A hard double-knock came on the passenger window.

Violet shrieked and scrambled closer.

This knock irritated him the same, if not more, than the idiot pounding against the window last night. He sighed and tugged up the zipper on his pants. *Just when things were getting fun, the human saltshaker shows up.*

Pillar cleared her throat loud enough to be heard through the window. "Steaming up the windows, Violet? And here I thought *you* were the good girl."

CHAPTER 24

Settled in Dublin's finest historic hotel, which overlooked St. Stephen's Green, Violet combed her fingers through her freshly-showered hair.

"No longer the shy-violet, eh? How does it feel to be a shade darker than lily-white?" Pillar sorted through the makeup in Violet's toiletry bag until she found a lipstick, but after checking the color, she grimaced and tossed it back in the bag. "Flint *would* have that kind of influence on a girl. I mean, who can blame you, really?"

Violet thought about the scorching kiss Flint had given her before he'd left for a quick volcanic dip in Mt. Stromboli. "I can't stop myself. I want to feel. I don't have much time, and I want this one thing for myself."

"One *big* thing." Pillar smirked as she held her hands approximately 15 centimeters apart. "No judgments. I'm all about taking what you want, when you want it." She stood and studied her form in the mirror. "No need to justify your actions. Men should be used. And in general, they don't seem to mind." Pillar met her gaze in the mirror.

"Flint isn't like that." Violet picked at her cuticle as she watched Pillar pace about the room. "Are you all right? Where have you been?"

"Violet, don't change the subject." Pillar stopped before the mirror again and ran a finger along her pale brow before pouting her lips. "So, tell me, is Flint as good as he looks?"

"What?" Violet settled on the hotel bed and wrapped a pillow in her arms. "Could you sit still? Why are you so jittery?" She rubbed a hand against her temple. "Flint isn't at all what he seems. That's the trouble."

"Oh, no." Pillar spun around and wagged a finger.

"Oh no, what?"

"Don't fall for him. Violet, dear, that is so cliché." Pillar laughed, throwing back her blonde hair. "He isn't your savior, your knight in shining armor, or even some kind of fairy tale dream-man come to life. Remember this…he is with you because the Elementals need to destroy Quint." She poked Violet's leg with a long, pale finger, nail beds painted pitch black. "You are their key. Don't confuse love with lust. Or lust with killing time."

Violet plumped the pillow at her back, considering her friend's words. "I-I…I haven't. Or, I don't know, maybe I have. So what? Shouldn't I get one chance at love? One instance where I can open my heart? I'm on the last leg of this journey, why not go out with no regrets?" Feeling tears threaten, Violet dug her nails into her palms.

"Why are you saying all these things, Pillar? Don't you want me to be happy?" Her friend's propensity to judge other relationships with the measuring stick of her own failures didn't sit well.

Pillar stopped pacing and wrapped both arms around her slim waist. "Violet, listen to me. Do you really believe you have a future with Flint? He's an Elemental. Peri-mortal. And you, my dear, are human. Mortal." Pillar sat beside her and took her hand. "Enjoy him, yes. This I fully agree with, but do not involve your heart. That path leads to ruin." Pillar stared at their joined hands for a moment, before tracing her finger over the ridges of their joined knuckles. Once more, she whispered, "ruin," before she wrenched away and marched a narrow path in the room again.

Now that Violet had a chance to study Pillar, she noted her friend seemed a bit unkempt. Dirty clothes, no shoes. Odd, as her friend typically dressed in flowing dresses and was quite fastidious about her appearance.

Violet tossed aside the pillow and searched her suitcase for a pair of socks. As Pillar paced, Violet caught sight of the bottom of her feet. The soles were black. Had Pillar not taken the time necessary to rejuvenate her life force—salt? Violet had no understanding of the intricacies of sustaining a life through the use of sodium chloride. However, Pillar had managed to roam this earth even longer than Flint.

Finding a pair of fluffy pink socks, she tossed them toward the end of the bed. "Pillar, put these on. Once Flint returns, why don't you take time to recuperate? You seem a bit on edge."

"And why shouldn't I be?" Pillar threw her hands in the air. "You want to know where I've been?" Pillar jabbed her leg again with a sharp, black nail. "I've been visiting with Nodin and Veimhet Schwarz. That German mouse has plastered your face on Most Wanted posters in every dive across the globe. What if one of those stupid fucks messes up your abduction? What if they accidentally kill you? Where will I be then?" Pillar's voice hit an unearthly high pitch at the end of her litany.

Considering how to answer, Violet sank back against the headboard.

"Fucked! Fucked completely. That's where I'll be."

Stunned by Pillar's bellow, Violet stiffed and studied her distraught friend.

Pillar kicked the hotel's office chair across the room. The black leather missile crashed into and splintered the glass patio door. Chest heaving, eyes pure white, Pillar raked a hand across the desk's table top, knocking everything to the floor. A salty tang coursing through the room.

Violet blinked the salt spray from her eyes and rushed to Pillar's side. "Please, calm down." She wrapped her arms around her friend's waist. "It's going to be okay. Flint will protect me."

"Don't you do that!" Pillar shoved her to the floor. "Don't you dare rely on a man to save you. Have you learned nothing from our time together? I warned you. But now you think you're in love with that flaming asshole. What kind of fool are you? He does not now, nor will he ever, love you. You're not enough."

Violet bit her bottom lip as she tried, and failed, to dismiss Pillar's vitriol from sinking deep and slicing across her heart.

A current of dizziness radiated through her body. She saw the room in a series of waves. Hands clenched into fists at her sides, she bit her bottom lip, her body heating and pulsing with unexpended energy. A white-blue glow emanated from her hands, and her hair stood on end. *No, not again.* She took a deep breath, fighting for control. "Pillar, you need to back off now."

The television sizzled and popped.

The coffee machine buzzed before flames shot out of the socket.

A burnt-wire smell hung in the air.

Pillar stood above her. "He is using you."

Shaking with unspent rage, Violet stood and forced the woman into a corner, more than done with Pillar's intimidation and venom.

Eyes wide, her friend lifted a hand between them. "Violet, I'm sorry. Listen, calm down. I didn't mean it." Sobs tore from her throat and tears poured down her cheeks, leaving a crusty trail. "I didn't mean it. You're right. I can't take this nightmare anymore. And seeing Nodin, working with him again...I...I can't do this. I hurt, Violet." She clawed at her hair. "I hurt."

Violet's entire focus remained floating across those electromagnetic waves. Ready to use any and all energy fields against the threat before her. After taking a deep, steadying breath, she studied Pillar. Shame over her bullying behavior swamped her. But wasn't she on edge, as well? Weren't they all?

Pillar collapsed before the desk and wrapped her arms around Violet's legs. "Forgive me, dear friend. Forgive me."

Violet started to run her fingers through Pillar's hair, but as her hand got close, all the hairs on Pillar's head rose from the remaining static electricity. She clasped her hands together against her chest, praying for calm. "I understand and acknowledge everything you've said, Pillar. I know you worry, and I appreciate your counsel. But I'm past that now. I can only move forward, and I will do so with Flint."

"Don't let him use you," Pillar whispered against her pant leg.

Violet rubbed both hands over her eyes, gathering her thoughts for a moment. "In a sense, I am using him, too. What exists between Flint and I is based on pure need. Long ago, I accepted that forever is not an option." She had a duty to mankind. A mission. Flint would light her path in this darkness for a short time, and she needed that warm glow, that bright spark to light her way until the very end. That beacon holding steady against every shadow and every doubt during the final days.

Pillar nodded against her leg. "I am so far removed from understanding an end. I've lived so long, seen so many things. I-I feel...I'm not sure how much more...never mind...it's nothing. I'll survive. I always pull through. Just a bit melancholy today." Pillar rested her head upon Violet's leg, and several moments passed before she spoke again. "Just guard your heart. Flint has always been a bit of a Lothario. You won't tame him."

"A tame Flint." Violet laughed at that preposterous image. "No, thank you." She patted Pillar's head, but when she pulled away her hand, a large chunk of blonde hair got caught in her fingers. "Pillar, please, once Flint returns, go rejuvenate your life-force, or whatever it is you...um...do." Frowning, she fingered the chunk of hair in her hand. "I'm worried. You're not well."

Pillar laughed—an almost mad cackle, before she stiffened and released Violet's legs. "He's back, Violet. He's back, back, back." Her shoulders bopped side-to-side with each word. "You should—"

A pounding on the door was followed by the sound of the lock clicking open.

Flint sniffed, and then roared, "What the hell is burning?"

CHAPTER 25

Later, after Violet had fiddled with her dinner, they stayed and listened to an Irish band. Flint sang along with the other bar patrons, trying to lighten her mood. No matter the century, O'Donnell's pub featured the same songs.

When he'd entered the hotel earlier, he'd been aware of the heavy thread of unspent energy thrumming through the air. Smoke poured out of a coffee maker, the TV screen was shattered, and the glass patio door destroyed. He joked about missing a catfight, but neither woman had laughed. Irritation still simmered over his inability to glean Violet's mind, and not only that, she blocked him from reading Pillar's, as well. Whatever happened in that room, neither was telling. Pillar had escaped in a swirl of white, leaving them to clean up the mess and pay for the damages—or at least making the hotel manager believe so.

Far away, both physically and mentally, Violet sat across the dimly lit booth and fiddled with the stem of her empty wine glass.

Enough.

He scooted from his side, and then sat beside her in the booth. "What's wrong?" He tipped her chin with a finger. "You've been quiet tonight. No rambling facts about Irish music or dance, no quarks or electrons. What's rattling around in that red head?"

Stalling a bit, she brushed crumbs off the table. She sniffed, and then once more met his gaze. "These past few days, we've been in a bubble, floating along, buoyant, but Pillar reminded me of my future. My purpose." With a single finger, she swirled the condensation on her water glass. "I'm feeling a wee bit blue, and I miss my grandfather." She twisted her fingers in her lap as she continued. "I'll be glad to see the fortified walls of Castle Nemon tomorrow. We shouldn't have dallied here. It's just…when I'm with you, I stop worrying about each passing day, but you were right when you said I should return home. I cannot escape Sorcha's spell, and asking you to prolong this journey wasn't a wise decision."

She met his gaze again, those dark violet eyes seemed to burn with sorrow and regret. "I'm sorry."

The feeling that fired through his chest at her words scorched his already charred heart. Her honesty. Her purity. Her inherent goodness. All struck him at once. This beautiful woman should never feel a moment of sadness. He'd do anything to erase the weariness in her eyes. "I choose to be here, and"—he tugged Violet out of the booth—"I choose to dance you out of your funk."

Once on the dance floor, neither knew the right moves, but together they found a lively rhythm.

She even laughed as he spun her around and around. That raspy sound fueled the embers of his heart.

Other men begged their turn, so he let her go, but only because he'd gleaned no danger. He returned to their table and watched as she dipped and twirled. The bar lights illuminated her flushed cheeks and the sheen of perspiration on her skin. Violet's energetic laugh waved through the room as she tried to follow each dancer's intricate steps.

She caught his eye and smiled, then began an animated conversation with the man standing beside her.

An earnest expression lit her face as she, no doubt, lectured the man on the origins of whiskey, Irish dance, or some such nonsense. He chuckled as the poor man stepped away, shaking his head.

Her merry expression ignited his heart as she made her way across the bar. She stopped and took his hand in hers, squeezing with her dainty fingers—a silent thank you in a room filled with music and dance.

That gentle squeeze not only wrapped around his hand, it tightened around his heart. And once more, he considered the rewards of leaving this life—for her. This radiant redhead at his side who danced with toothless old men, spouted useless trivia, and took the hand of a man who had burned his way through life for far too long.

"Ready to go?" Flint shouted in order to be heard over the pub's natural music—voices, laughter, glasses clinking, clapping hands.

She met his gaze and nodded.

With her hand in his, he weaved through the crowd and out the door. Cool air washed over his body, and he missed the comforting warmth brought by the crammed bodies inside the bar.

Violet stepped next to him. "I had no idea what I was doing out there. Grandfather would have known all the moves. He's quite the dancer. Did you know Castle Nemon held its first *céilí* in—"

Flint shoved her against the building's brick wall and kissed her. What was meant to be a halt to the history lesson quickly turned into a lesson in lust.

She met him with equal fervor, driving against him, her hands frantic as she tugged at the buttons on his shirt.

A pulse of white-hot energy boiled through his body, firing their single flicker of passion into a towering inferno, threatening to burn them both to ash, only to renew them once more.

She coursed her lips over his face, down his neck. "Make love to me, Flint. No more halfway." Each kiss held an edge of urgency.

Restless—as if she were afraid everything would wisp away like paper engulfed in flame. He bent and kissed her again. "Violet, don't let Pillar's dramatic speeches rush you into something you're not ready for."

"I'm ready. I want to feel your light, your heat. Make me burn." She trailed her fingertips along the bulge in his pants, and then tugged on his belt.

Red heat seared along his skin, mixing signals in his brain…this flare wasn't burning in a mix of red and blue, but in a dark trail of bloody black. A miasma so thick you couldn't detect the danger until you were lost in the haze, choking, gasping for your last breath.

A warning he'd almost missed.

Spinning on his heel, Flint studied the area while fighting back red embers of lust still flickering through his body. Senses now on full alert, he stepped away from Violet and gleaned a strange, dark mind. Almost demonic.

Danger. Fury. Pain. Wrath.

Evil emanated from every pore of this human's body.

Blaring music with indistinguishable voices screaming lyrics. Giddiness over the cut of a blade across pale skin. The heavy roar of release found by inflicting pain.

Where was Schwarz finding these warped minds? This demented threat deserved life in prison.

Nodin! Terran!

Flint's elemental gift wouldn't penetrate this encroaching predator's mind with reason, because this man did not rationalize like sane people. This man, who with each step, crept closer, held one of the darkest minds he'd ever gleaned. Women, children, death, hate, mother, brother—this human already had a cacophony of trilling voices in his head. How to break through? How to be the one voice heard over the madness?

Nodin!

Someone had taunted this predator with pictures of Violet, and those images fed him like a starving dog.

He had one goal.

Attainment.

However, the person fueling this man's dark mind failed to register he would kill her. The images flickering across this foul man's mind sickened.

Terran! Maya! Flint shouted across the frequencies for assistance from all three Elementals, although Nodin typically served best at piercing minds and finding the exact area of focus to change a human's intent.

Flint didn't fear this man, but his concern for Violet's safety made him overly cautious. He wouldn't lose her. Couldn't lose her, not now when she'd come so far. "Violet, listen to me. A very dangerous man is approaching. We need to get you to the hotel."

With his arm at her waist, Flint raced down the sidewalk, hoping to get her as close to the hotel as he could before facing off against the man.

"Who is he?" At his side, Violet jogged to keep up, but stumbled on the uneven sidewalk.

Keeping her upright, Flint turned toward the sound of loud music blaring hard-core lyrics through the man's ears, jacking up his nerves, preparing him for the kill.

"Flint. What are—"

"Not now, Violet, please." Flint shook her shoulder and led her closer to the hotel's entrance.

A shuffle down an alley and an increase in the music's volume thrumming from the man's head into his indicated the would-be-abductor was close.

Flint plunked Violet down on a bench in front of the hotel. "Stay here and use your power to radiate anyone who comes close."

"But Flint, I can't hurt—"

"You must." He kissed her. "I'll be right back." He winked then turned and faced the mad creature coming down the street. Flint walked toward the man, and then shifted into smoke, billowing as a dark vapor around the man's face.

Coughing, the man tried removing the wash of smoke from his lungs. He swung wildly with his arms and growled. "Witches' tricks. Witches' tricks. I won't be fooled."

Flint switched to human form and tackled the man to the ground.

The predator snarled, twisted to his feet, and then lunged with a knife.

The blade sliced through Flint's arm, and he winced. A flicker of red flame danced around the wound before it closed. "Thomas Riley. You must stop. I've seen everything."

The man laughed, a deep rumble.

Visions flashed through Flint's mind of this man's mental facility stints. *Confinement, white jackets, white room, little pills, needles, and a male nurse covered in blood.*

Violet's piercing scream scorched through the air.

What the hell?

With no chance to glance over his shoulder, Flint blew smoke into the man's face. "Playtime is over, asshole."

Gasping for breath, the predator dropped to his knees.

Flint held the man's chin at just the right angle and threw a right hook that knocked the man out. He removed all the hunter's weapons and turned to view the living-nightmare of Violet being dragged to a van by a dark-haired Amazon who held a knife to her throat.

Taking long strides, Flint approached, a searing rage rushing through his body.

This woman was no match for his powers.

"Back off, freak." The female abductor waved the knife in his direction. "Who do you think you are, walking the streets stark naked? A shame is what you are. I'm taking the woman, so run along."

Flint easily gleaned the woman's mind and altered her plans. *"Let her go. You will not search for her again. You will not remember me, or your purpose here."*

The woman released Violet and stared at him with a slack jaw.

"Greta!" The get-away van driver yelled. "Get the girl. What are you doing? Let's go." The Amazon's counterpart revved the engine and pointed a gun at Flint's head.

"Yes, Greta. Go." Flint turned to smoke and wrapped around Violet, dragging her to safety beside a copse of trees.

Tires squealed as the van raced back down the street. In a panic, the van's driver didn't see the crumpled human lying unconscious in the middle of the road.

"Stop!" Flint yelled to no avail.

Violet screamed as the van ran over the psychotic bounty hunter with both sets of wheels.

The van halted, and then the large woman ran out to check the victim lying lifeless on the pavement. She yelled something at the driver before rushing back to the passenger seat.

The sound of screeching tires filled the empty space left by the vacuum of death.

Violet pulled away and attempted to rush into the street.

Flint hauled her back to his side. "Where in the hell are you going?"

"That man, he needs our help."

"Violet, that psychopath is dead. And believe me, no one will mourn the loss. If he had you in his clutches, he would have shown you real-life nightmares before he chopped you into small pieces and buried you in his backyard with the rest of the bodies."

Eyes wide, she pointed at the unmoving body. "You don't know that he's dead."

He squeezed her arm until she met his gaze, and when she did, he merely raised a brow. "Don't feel sorry for him, Red."

"We can't leave him in the street." Violet huffed.

Flint saw no reason not to let him rot in the street, but he would handle the matter—for her. She'd been through enough tonight, these sorts of happenings weren't a part of her everyday world and that woman...that Amazon had almost—"Wait a minute...why didn't you burn that woman? Sizzle her skin? Damn it, Violet. You can't be afraid to use your gift. That woman meant you harm. Next time someone comes along and tries to drag you off into a fucking van, *RADIATE THEM!* Blast them with your ray of light, or whatever the hell electro-shit you've got." Narrowing his gaze, he grabbed her shoulders. "I need to know you are willing to protect yourself in battle. You've been given the most powerful gift in this realm so *WHY DIDN'T YOU USE IT?*" Flint paced away. Angry at her. Angry at himself. Angry at the dead man in the street.

Where the hell is Nodin? The least that airy puffball could do was haul that piece of shit off the street.

Violet mumbled something.

Something so insane the words initially failed to register in his over-fried mind. Flint spun and faced her. "I'm sorry, what did you just say?"

Violet shuffled a rock across the pavement with her foot. "I can't hurt humans."

"*I can't hurt humans.* Did you just say, I can't hurt humans?" Flint threw his hands in the air before bracing them against his hips. "I cannot believe those words just came out of your mouth. How in the...how did you expect to...FUCK!" He paced away, not trusting himself due to her ridiculous confession. Was the woman mad? Were her ancestors? Why wasn't her grandfather protecting her, if she couldn't protect herself?

And something else..."Why would you travel across Europe if you can't protect yourself? What were you thinking?" After raking his fingers through his hair, he immediately detected a pungent burnt-hair aroma. *Damn it.*

Violet continued her intense study of her feet. "Just imagine if I had my powers as a child. In anger, I could have hurt so many people. A safety gap was an essential part of the spell."

"Oh, it's a gap, all right. A fucking ravine. A grand, flipping-ass canyon. Are you catching what I'm saying here, Violet? Why the hell would they do this to you?" And why had she never told him? Never prepared him with an understanding of her failings.

"My limitations are safest for the world. I can only hurt non-humans...um...like...you, or the other Elementals and...uh...Quint, of course." She finally met his gaze. "My ancestor understood one person controlling so much power could end in the world's destruction. The spell was cast for a single purpose—destroying Quint."

Flint massaged his temples, trying to soothe the rage searing through his body. How dare they leave her so helpless? "How was this going to go, then? You can't protect yourself. Why would you risk this journey? Did you...hell, did your ancestors not realize someone would eventually find out? Someone smart and ruthless like Veimhet Schwarz. Someone who will stop at nothing to have you. Control you. They left you like a helpless rabbit for a snarling wolf." He slashed his hands between them, and flames sparked from his fingers.

"I know." Violet answered in a small voice.

He heaved a sigh, but he wasn't finished. He'd thought there was a level of trust between them. Apparently, he'd been very wrong. "Why didn't you tell me?" A yellow wave of betrayal scorched across his heart. "I thought we were...that we had—"

"The subject never came up." She shrugged and glanced away.

Taking a moment to swallow that ridiculous justification, Flint studied her bent head for a moment, and then shook his own. "Right. Never came up." He rubbed at the ache in his chest. "Fine. Well, Nodin's almost here. I'll leave you in his care while I clean up this mess and alert the authorities of this dead man's sick practices." He needed to step away from her, from this foreign emotion drilling through his chest. What was this? Anger, betrayal, hurt...feelings. For fuck's sake, this would never do. Briskly scrubbing his hands over his face, he refocused on his priorities and set to simmer his boiling emotions.

As he stepped closer to the vile murderer, whose stench in death matched his stench in life, Flint felt a strong breeze bluster across his overheated skin.

Nodin appeared beside him, and after stepping around the body, he braced a hand against Flint's shoulder. "One good thing did come from this foul creature's death. All those families who've agonized over a missing loved one will soon have answers."

Flint nodded. "Yeah, right. Answers." Jaw clenched, he glanced across the hotel's U-shaped drive.

Violet stood with her arms locked around her body.

He breathed deeply in an effort to clear the flare of pain she'd ignited with her lack of trust.

Hotel employees began milling around outside. Sirens sounded in the distance.

He turned to Nodin. "I'll wrap up things here."

"Are you sure? I can deal with the questions."

Flint squeezed his Elemental friend's shoulder. "I need…"—he ran a hand over his chin—"hell, I don't know what I need." He sighed. "Just do me a favor, and take Violet to Castle Nemon. We were headed there in the morning, but would you mind taking her now?"

"You're troubled, brother." Nodin squeezed his shoulder.

Flint shook his head before scoffing. "Trouble? Oh, you don't know the half of it."

CHAPTER 26

Intricately soldering together two wires on his Hans Berger helmet, Schwarz raised a brow over the sudden halt in the unending cacophony usually sounding from the corridor outside his office.

Damn Irish, probably breaking again for tea.

Catcalls and whistles filled the silence.

Schwarz lifted his safety goggles, tossed down his tools, and opened his office door to determine the cause of the disturbance. Not much was required to distract them from their work. The fools were probably toying with some woman.

Walking down the corridor, he noticed the work area once more went silent. A salty aroma filled his senses. He blinked and scuttled forward, bracing his hand against the wall.

A woman's familiar laugh echoed off the walls and chilled his spine.

An eerie stillness surrounded him as he blinked away the salty sting from his eyes. "Pillar?" Pulling a tissue from his pocket, he wiped his dripping nose and scurried down the hall in the opposite direction. Vision blurred, he trailed a hand along the wall to guide the way. Metal handles bumped against his hand until he stopped at door number three. He stumbled into the room and rinsed out his eyes at an eyewash station mounted against the wall.

The door behind him clicked open.

Schwarz lifted his shirt and dried his face. "I'd be careful of your tricks in this room, dear. Deliquescence isn't a fancy dress designer. With a push of a button, water will pour down from the sprinklers, and you'll simply wash away. Salt and water don't mix." He fingered the remote in his pocket and turned on the misters.

Upon hearing the swish of skirts, he turned and watched Pillar step further into the room. Pulling the device from his pocket, he waved it between them. "I warned you." Schwarz set the sprinklers to full throttle.

Pillar shrieked and covered her head with her arms.

He took a moment to enjoy her wet dress clinging to her thin body. Her nipples peaked from the chill.

"Turn it off, you stupid German mouse," Pillar screamed.

The water level trickled over the tops of his shoes.

"Why should I?" Schwarz shouted over the gushing water. "You knocked out my men, and you thought to come here and terrify me. Threaten me. Who's threatened now?"

Pillar's pale skin faded to deathly white. "Stop." She fell to her knees, shivering and wrapping her arms around her body. "Please, no more."

Schwarz flicked off the switch and opened the floor vents, flushing the water from the room. With another click, air vents blasted warm air, heating his chilled, wet body. "There, now. You like air, don't you? As a matter of fact, I know all about your relationship with that air Elemental, Nodin."

"You know nothing about me," Pillar snarled as she squeezed the water from her dress.

Not quite accurate, but he'd let the matter slide—for now. "Why are you here, Pillar? Come to issue more threats? As you see, I'm prepared, so go alter someone else's mind. I won't succumb to those tricks again."

She studied him for a moment, and then twisted her hair into a bun. Sighing, she leaned against the opposite wall and folded her arms across her chest. "You've studied the Elementals. You believe you know all their secrets?" She pushed away from the wall and paced before him. "Just how many truths did Quint reveal? I need to know." She stilled and met his gaze with pale yellow eyes. "What answers lie between those mousy ears?"

Very peculiar. If he didn't know better, he'd say her questions were more of a plea.

"He told me everything." Quirking a brow, Schwarz waved a hand before him. "He knows everything. He is everywhere. A god among mortal men."

Heisenberg trotted into the room, stopped at his feet, and lapped up water from a leftover puddle.

"Quint is nothing but pure poison." Pillar spat as she poked a finger in his direction. "A virus infecting humans with his foul, dark matter, bent on destroying everything he touches. And don't think he won't turn on you. Everything he touches ends in darkness. He knows no other way."

"I don't have time for your ridiculous speeches, or your interference with my work. Get to the point of this visit, or the sprinklers go back on." He raised a brow, waiting to hear her purpose in invading his sanctuary.

Heisenberg released a throaty growl and then barked.

Schwarz squatted and patted his head, reassuring his pooch there wasn't any danger. "Quiet now, Spitzy." He glanced at Pillar with his thumb hovering over the button.

Pillar's jaw ticked and she glanced away. After a long moment passed, she cleared her throat and sniffed. "You will tell me everything Quint disclosed about the Elementals' transformation process."

Interesting. What was her end game? And why hadn't she turned to the Elementals for answers? "What do I get in exchange?"

"I'll let you live."

"This, coming from a woman who almost dissolved moments ago. You seem a little weak, Pillar. I'd have no trouble overpowering you. You should never enter the lion's den. We tend to bite. And I'd love to bite you."

"I'm clear on what you want, Schwarz. But I'm crystal clear on what *I* want. Always have been. So, let's work this out together, shall we?" Pillar lowered her arms and stepped closer. "My end is coming, but I won't go down without exhausting all options. I haven't survived this long to surrender now."

Her soaked skirts left a trail of water behind her. A briny tang filled the air—a salt-water cocktail that left him drunk with desire. His cock hardened at the thought she just might give him what he'd been waiting for—a chance to lick that salty trail between her thighs. He might disgust her, might not be a handsome man, but he had studied how to please a woman. He reveled in the possibility of showing her exactly who could give her pleasure. In the bedroom, he wasn't a mouse. Not at all.

Her nostrils flared then she glanced at the bulge in his trousers and flashed a wicked grin. She waved a single index finger back and forth between them. "Not yet. First…tell me what you know about Quint and the Elementals. There has to be more. You've been doing all these studies. What have you learned?"

Heisenberg growled when she stepped closer.

She bent level with his quivering pooch. "Boo."

His dog yipped and scurried behind Schwarz's legs.

"What game are you playing, Pillar?"

Straightening, she shrugged. "The only one I've ever played. Survival. Once Quint returns, I'm done. My decision to turn Violet against him will be punished in full measure. Perhaps, if I'm human, I'll no longer interest him. Quint views humans as nothing but vessels. My hope is that he'll forget about me, about revenge, once I'm weak."

"I doubt he's forgotten anything." Schwarz shook his head. "Your duplicity deserves some form of punishment, but I'll leave that to Quint."

"Have you spoken to him?" Eyes wide, she grabbed his shirt in her fists. "Tell me."

Heisenberg barked and nipped at her heels.

"Heisenberg, *nicht!*" He tapped the German Spitz with his foot. "I don't have your answers, Pillar. Only this truth—there are consequences to our actions. I won't help you hide from Quint. You continually preach about how no one is loyal, and yet, you continually deceive. You don't deserve his mercy, and you certainly don't have mine."

"You'll never win. Violet will destroy everything." Pillar drilled his chest with her index finger.

"Will she? I believe there are a few facts about Ms. Levina you don't know. But, why would she trust you? I have a special treat for Violet that just might make her see things my way. Everyone has a weakness. This, you of all people should understand. For centuries, you've made a practice of exploiting people to get what you want."

"That's right, Schwarz. I get what I want, one way or another. And I will find a way to break free from Quint's death-grip. Understand that."

"Stay here or go, Pillar. Either way, start counting the days, because that's all you have left." He turned to leave, his cock still throbbing in his pants, hoping against all hope she would halt his exit. He clutched the wet metal handle, ready to quit the room. Releasing a heated breath, his heart throbbing in his chest, he turned the latch.

Her cool hand covered his. "I'll leave after you reveal this 'supposed' information on Violet."

Schwarz peered over his shoulder, gave her body a thorough once-over, and then brushed his finger down her chilled arm. "What do I get in return?"

Keeping her gaze on his, Pillar slid both dress straps off her shoulders, slowly removing the wet fabric from her skin, revealing her body to her waist. "What do you get in return?" She smiled and trailed a finger down her chest. "Simple man, I'll give you what you've always wanted. Now, *I'm* the one asking this time. Stay here, or go?"

He stayed.

CHAPTER 27

After escaping the chilling horror surrounding the discovery of the dead psychopath's multiple graves, Flint had left behind the madness and fired through the crisp, clean air to Castle Nemon.

Now nestled in the dining hall, Flint shifted in the rigid, high-back wooden chair. He focused on the crackling pops and snaps of the wood burning in the stone hearth. Why hadn't he gleaned the foul creature's sick practices sooner? With his gifts, he should have detected the negative intent pouring from the man ages ago. As it was, he'd been required to employ some ingenious manipulation of the police detectives' minds. That sickening nightmare might be over, but another faced him, one much more deadly.

Clinks against the silverware and the soft murmur of Violet and her grandfather's words did bring a certain level of comfort.

Tapered candles emitted a warm glow as Violet and her maternal grandfather, Eamon, enjoyed a dinner of lamb stew and soda bread. She updated the wizard on their adventures, playing down the danger in a way that did not fool the wise old man sitting at the head of the table. His familiar violet-blue eyes took in every nuance of the discussion, seeing things that hadn't been said, but understanding completely. His bushy, iron-gray brows rose in delight with each tale she told, his indulgence clear in every non-verbal cue. A subtle wave of power exuded from the man. Not seen, nor heard, but surrounding him all the same in a pulse that warned of inherent danger—ready to strike should you errantly cross his path.

While this respite from marauding bounty hunters was welcome,

Flint still needed to rejuvenate for the coming storm. Violet had him on edge with her tales of prophecies and death. So, he shot a mental message across the elemental channels to the one person he knew could offer the necessary comfort to his woman. *"Maya, I need you to stay with Violet. I am in need of a dip in the nearest volcano. Come soon."* Hopefully, the water-girl had healed enough to make the journey.

Nodin had just exited the castle grounds after Flint's not-so-subtle mental nudge that declared leave now, or he wouldn't be responsible for his actions. Prior to dinner, the airy charm oozing from his Elemental brother had cloyed in Flint's nostrils, and had him clenching his jaw so tight he'd worried it would crack under the pressure.

Flint glanced at the vibrant redhead seated across the table and considered how far she'd come. Though still steaming over her lack of disclosure, he understood the purpose behind the spell's limitations. Even if he didn't appreciate those restrictions when a psychotic scientist had hired mercenaries to hunt and capture his woman.

His cock stiffened under the table as she licked a bit of pudding from her spoon. *Sweet Svarog, have mercy.* His bright violet was a vibrant bloom, just waiting to be plucked.

A hard clink of Eamon's coffee cup against the fine china brought Flint back from his musings. The wizard's glare was now steel-blue as he shot out of his chair. "Flint, a walk through the grounds."

Damn. He'd forgotten this particular human had certain gifts.

Violet bolted out of her chair, glancing across the table with wide-eyes. "Grandfather, I'd like to join you. A walk sounds lovely."

"No, my child, stay here. I must speak to Flint alone." As he passed her, he stopped and kissed her cheek.

Violet shifted to face him and narrowed her eyes. "Why?"

He shook his head. "If I wanted you to know, I'd have invited you along. I believe you were anxious to study Sorcha's enchantments, were you not? Leave me to discuss things with Flint, *mo chroí.*"

My heart. Flint believed she was the purpose behind every beat of the old man's heart. How could you not care for a woman who was so innocent, and yet so brave at the same time? Still, during the walk with this old wizard, he'd make clear his displeasure at her inability to protect herself.

"Violet, Maya and Terran may be visiting soon, so you will need to prepare. I'll be fine with your grandfather."

"When will they arrive?"

"I'm not sure they will."

Halting her water glass halfway to her lips, she glared over the rim. "Sometimes I wonder why I speak to you."

"Apparently, you don't." Point made, Flint pushed back in his chair and followed the old wizard out the patio doors. On his way out, he heard Violet's half-growl, half-sigh as she stalked off toward the library.

Once outside, Violet's grandfather walked along the worn dirt path for a while without speaking his purpose.

Long ago, Flint had buried memories of his own grandfather. A burly blacksmith, covered in soot and sweat. As a child, he'd sat at his grandfather's knee and listened to stories of Rurik, a Varangian or Viking, the people of Novgorod had brought over to establish order in chaotic, early Russia. This occurred before the Tartars invaded and destroyed all the major Russian cities.

"The Mongol Yoke."

The man beside him finally deigned to speak. "I'm sorry?" This mind-reading elder would never do, especially when Violet was present. He laughed at the irony. He understood now how everyone else felt, having their every thought gleaned through magic.

"I choose when to delve, Flint. You seemed in a reflective state, so I dared a peek. The Mongol Yoke, the time in Russian history, which lasted 250 years before Prince Dmitry Donskoy turned the tide against the Khan in 1380 at the battle of Kulikovo. Your grandfather was wise to pass on the history of your people."

"I forget how much I miss him." He brushed a hand through his hair. "I should have cherished him more, and yet, there is nothing I can do."

"I understand ties to the past. Brodick Nemon built this castle for his lady, Bridgid. A solid fortress, built with blood, sweat, and tears. Over the centuries, these grounds have known great sadness and great joy." Eamon stopped along the path and faced him. "We both know what this walk is really about, so I'll be blunt. Violet will be treated with the respect she deserves, or I will remove you from this place."

A chill wind broke against Flint's skin. Leaves stirred at his feet, and all the hairs on his body stood on end. "I'm not the one who left her unprotected." An electric sizzle raged across his skin. So, he'd poked the wizard, had he? *Good.* "Why didn't you just bind her powers until she became mentally equipped to handle the intensity? Why leave her to fend for herself? She was driving across Europe on her own, for shit's sake. Why would you let her do that? Are you insane?" Raking his hands through his hair, Flint glared at the old man.

Eamon stomped two paces down the trail then turned back. "Surely you understand the power she holds would never be safe in the human realm? The slightest slip, and the damage she could cause would be catastrophic. As far as not protecting her…well, I believe you relished the role *I* provided."

Being a pawn on this wizard's chessboard did not amuse. "I'm not playing your game, and neither is Veimhet Schwarz. He will stop at nothing to contain Violet." At that thought, heat infused his body, and he jabbed a finger against the old man's chest. "You abandoned her when she needed you most."

An electric jolt fired down his spine and knocked him on his ass.

Eamon stood above him, hands braced on his hips. "I'd be more careful with that tone. Mother Nature and I made sure you were at her side."

"Did you? Pillar and Terran led me where I needed to be, not you."

The man closed his eyes, murmuring incoherent words. After shaking his head, he met Flint's gaze. "This lesson was for Violet, alone. Her entire life has existed in a world of theory. She needed reality. Grit. Hardship. Desperation. Fear. Not analyzing every move and theorizing each outcome, but down-in-the-trenches warfare. I could only guide her so far. If I had journeyed with her, I would have shielded her too much." Eamon offered a hand and helped Flint to his feet. "You led her gently along the path, but let her experience each event as she should."

"Explain that to her." Flint dusted off his pants. "Violet and I are done running through this gauntlet custom-built by you and Mother. The danger to your granddaughter is very real." Anger over these manipulations seared across his mind. His fists lit with flame, ready to strike. "I'll be speaking to Mother about this, as well. Magic doesn't always win. She should know that even better than I. How dare you test Violet like that."

"Would you rather I lose her, then?" The wizard crooked a bushy brow. "Leave her unprepared against Quint? Who better to teach her how to fight than a warrior out of time?"

"Warrior? Really? Your flattery won't placate me, old man." Flint studied the withered creature before him and shook his head. "Don't do that again. Violet trusts you."

"I will handle my granddaughter as I see fit."

Flint scoffed. "You may be her elder, but you're certainly not mine. I've roamed this earth far too long to play by anyone else's rules."

For a moment, Eamon stared back at the castle. "My granddaughter is everything." He wiped a tear from his cheek. "I failed with my daughter, so Violet is my one chance at redemption."

Choosing to let the slight betrayal drop, Flint continued along the dirt trail.

As the sun dipped low on the horizon, a dull gray coated the vibrant green grass sprouting along the side of the path. A light fog cloaked their trail and carried with it a slight chill. Stone ruins peeked out between blankets of mist. These ancient relics stood tall throughout time—slightly crumbling, yet likely to remain even longer than a peri-mortal like him. With that in mind, who was he to cast stones? While he had no regrets, he was quite certain he'd made many questionable decisions during his elemental life. Still, he didn't appreciate being tossed on the playing field without knowing the rules of the game. "What happened with your daughter?"

Eamon braced his hands behind his back. "My Freesia. Her mother had a fondness for the flower." He met Flint's gaze and then cleared his throat. "Freesia excelled at brewing potions. One could always find her experimenting, and the castle kitchen was never the same after she worked her magic." The old man's face glowed with pride, but then he shook his head.

"Where is she now?"

"She succumbed to the euphoria created by other realities, other dimensions. In an effort to further feed her obsession, Freesia delved into black magic. With her gift, she blinded her mother and I to her actions until we were forced to intervene after we realized her hand in harming a local girl." Eamon pressed a fist against his forehead.

"We stripped her of her potion-making abilities, and so she turned to mixing mainstream drugs." The wizard shook his head and wiped at the corner of his eye. "Our punishment for binding one of our own, perhaps."

Flint let the man gather himself for a moment. "I'm sorry."

"Yes, son, so am I. So am I." The wizard patted his shoulder, and stopped to catch his breath before continuing down the path.

Searching for another topic, Flint settled on their initial subject "Do you know much of my history?"

Eamon cleared his throat and nodded. "Some."

"I fully comprehend how the need for escape can overpower everything. Due to my family's connection with the Ipatiev Monastery in Kostroma, I assisted in deciphering the Hypatian Codex. Svarog, the Slavic god of celestial fire and blacksmithing, is mentioned in this text. I became entranced with his gifts, likely due to my family's history as the village "smithy". However, I displayed a more artistic bent, and I began studying the art of glassblowing. One night, after a week of strange dreams, I was sure I was seeing an angel when Mother Nature appeared in my workshop. She asked if I wanted to follow in Svarog's footsteps." Flint shook his head at all that had passed since that fateful day. "The rest, as they say, is history."

With a wave, Eamon gestured toward a faded wooden bench and pulled a large hunk of amethyst from his pocket, working it between his fingers.

The early-evening mist settled around them in a thick fog, and a humming sound came from the wizard beside him.

Eamon suddenly stiffened, and then spoke in a low, deep tone. "Within the white, particles separate. Within the gift, time turns, unyielding."

Flint eased away as the wizard's body pulsed with an eye-searing blue light.

"Within the fire, death gains his due. Within the field, a battle's fought, releasing one spell-bound." White beams joined the blue, pouring from Eamon's mouth and fingers.

His next words reverberated through Flint's mind. *"Within the veil, wind must shift, revealing what cannot be seen. Within vision…"*

Eamon reached out with one hand. "Within vision…" The pulse of light shining from his body flickered in and out until diminishing completely. He stilled and whispered, "She's waiting within…" He clenched his hand, still raised before him, toppled to the side and slid off the bench.

Flint jolted to his feet before kneeling at the wizard's side. "Are you all right?" Had the man meant to speak those words, or was he overtaken by magic?

"Give me a moment, please. These old bones don't spring back like they used to."

Resting his hand upon the old man's shoulder, Flint remained crouched beside him.

"These visions come upon me at times. Much stronger lately, which…does not bode well." Eamon braced a hand against Flint's arm. "Help me back onto the bench, won't you?"

Flint settled Eamon on the seat and sank beside him.

"Mother and I have been studying a girl we believe is of great importance to our cause. Although, the damn tribal shaman blocks our efforts." He scratched at the tuft of white hair above his ear. "This does not discourage us, however, only leads us to believe her gifts are very real. Our studies reveal this gift was passed through a maternal blood line, like Sorcha's gift to Violet."

Flint rested his ankle across his knee and sank back against the age-old wood, but upon hearing a crack, sat forward again. "Mother's never mentioned this girl. What ability does she possess?"

"Vision." Eamon smoothed the amethyst with his fingers again. "Nodin will investigate, but her story shall keep." He patted Flint's hand. "In this moment, your focus must remain on Violet. She may hold the entire electromagnetic spectrum in her hands, but you are her light." He drew his cape tighter around his body and then tucked his purple stone in his front pocket. "Darkness creeps closer and closer. Evolving. Renewing. With each passing day, I become more and more frightened Violet will die." He rubbed his gnarled hands together then whispered, "Have I been blind?"

An icy chill incongruent with his inner-flame surged down Flint's spine. "What do you mean? Blind about what?"

"Mother believes a sacrifice must be made."

"A sacrifice? By who?"

"The prophecy says Violet."

Hearing this, Flint shuddered. "No."

"You must prepare for the possibility—"

"I won't. I'll stop time. I haven't used that gift in decades, but if I'm preparing for anything, it will be using that ability again."

"And is that fair to her?"

"Fair to her?" Flint fired off the bench. "You sit there and ask me if it's fair to her, when you're the one spouting nonsense about her dying? Fuck that." He slapped the edge of the bench, knocking loose a wooden chunk. Fire churned in his belly ready to break free, and rage at his will. He glanced at the wizard sitting so calmly on the bench and shook his head. "What about what's fair to me? Huh? Did you and Mother count that in your little plan?" He paced before the old wizard who remained silent. "As far as my woman is concerned, know this, I'll keep her locked in forever, and everyone else can just kiss my ass. Violet is mine, and that's the end of it. Fuck destiny." He stalked away before he lost control and incinerated everything in his path.

Yet, Eamon's unwelcome words trailed through his mind like roiling smoke. *"Destiny, like death, always finds a way."*

CHAPTER 28

Brushing her fingers against the smooth tan of ancient vellum, likely made from sheep or calf skin, Violet relished the sizzle of energy shooting up her arm. With every turn of faded pages, she experienced the crisp power calling to a place deep within her soul.

Dust motes stained with magic filtered through the air. Each breath splintered the focus of her convictions and tickled her senses with a heady desire for control, for dominance. Criss-crossing voices played a mystic beat in her mind, screaming, *Release your true nature.*

Violet swayed in her chair, and her body shook with pure need. "I won't succumb. I am more than a witch."

Stepping away from temptation, she crossed the room and slanted open a window. Breathing deep of the fresh air, she gasped when she noted the tips of her fingers glowed blue. "Stop." Whirling sharply, she yelled at the inanimate manuscripts, and then stuffed her hands in her pockets. "My purpose is to find a binding spell. If you wish to be of use, then join my cause. I will not be swayed from my purpose. You wish me to speak the spells. Fine, I shall speak my own."

Chest heaving, Violet placed her hands upon the books littering the tabletop. Eyes closed, her entire body shaking, she drew from the power swirling within the tomes. "Hear me now, as I make my vow. I will not fail, nor let the flame burn out. Leave the Elementals be. Use the power within me. Take me far to fulfill my deed. May Sorcha's gift be all I need. Pull not from the elemental tree. As I will, so mote it be. "

A scalding burn, like liquid fire, seared from her throat to her heart, driving the organ to madness, eliciting a deep scream. Unbearable heat blazed in her chest, pulsing with a scorching fire too excruciating for words. Heart exploding, she dug her nails into her chest, attempting to remove the blinding pain.

Time slowed.

Eventually, the pain receded, and in its place, she watched as a warm glow burst from beneath her skin in muted shades of red. Pink light pumped with her heart's steady rhythm and coated her entire body from head to toe. Wave after wave of bliss rushed through her core, and she sank to the floor. Shuddering out a breath, Violet closed her eyes as the glorious feeling left her body. "Unbelievable. No wonder my mother left."

After brushing sweaty hair from her face, Violet sank into a rocking chair and tipped it into motion with the pad of her big toe.

So, that was the power of magic. Pain and pleasure mixed together until you craved them both. "I was right to fight this, to lose myself in science."

Still, she needed both the power and knowledge from the books. Needed to garner their energy in the fight against Quint. Finding the right spell to keep Terran from harm during the process of binding the dark matter menace was crucial. Though, not requiring his aid at all would be her preference.

Would her death come quickly? Would she suffer? Swaying back and forth in her rocking chair, Violet gazed out the window and considered the spell that foreshadowed her end.

"Your mother used to sit in that same chair to take her tea."

Torn from her contemplations, Violet jumped, but smiled at the source of her distraction.

"Good to see you taking an interest in these ancient tomes." The castle cook and beloved caretaker, Enda, spoke from just inside the library's door. "Although, whispering that spell over and over doesn't bode well for you, dear."

"Was I whispering it?" Violet furrowed her brow. "The spell does foretell my end, Enda."

"Does it?"

"*Reaper hold they scythe 'til then? I shall hold thy place for thee?* Sorcha's hold is the only thing keeping death's blade from striking down upon my head. Once we complete her vengeance, we're done."

"I wouldn't be so sure."

Enda was, just as her Irish name suggested, a little bird-like woman who squawked and chirped around the castle, ruling all in her nest. With her piercing blue eyes, sharp nose, and soft-gray hair, she seemed like a swift, one of the fastest-flying birds in Ireland, rarely stopping to rest but always twittering about. She stepped across the room, tea tray held securely in her arms.

"Love has a way of breaking through the deepest of spells." Enda perched her tray on her hip, and then stacked various books on top of each other, making room. Shifting the tray to the now-cleared space, she poured a bit of the steaming black brew into a cup.

"Love? No, I don't believe anything can break this spell." Violet breathed in the soothing aroma of the Irish blend tipped with lavender—Enda's signature tea. "Everything has come true. I'm the 25th daughter. I've joined with four elementals or, as the spell says, petals." She flashed quotes with her fingers. "The light's beam is likely Flint. The shadow is Quint. The white field is my electromagnetic spectrum. Once we destroy Quint, Sorcha and I perish together. She made a deal with death, and I believe I'll pay with my life."

Enda settled in a chair beside her and propped her feet on an embroidered footstool. "All that may be true, but don't give up on love. It *is* magic, my girl." She patted Violet's hand and then sipped her tea.

Steam whirled from the top of her cup. Violet studied the wisp, wishing she could float just as freely—break away from all that bound her to earth. "If that is so, then I do have cause to worry, because Sorcha loved her mother. A daughter's love for her mother can be very strong."

Enda reached over and squeezed her hand. Unspoken understanding filled her simple touch.

Violet scrubbed a hand across her brow. "Why did I let the pain of losing my mother keep me from magic? Now I'm floundering in the dark."

"You were interested once."

"As a child, yes, but after she left, I hated everything about magic. I may have become interested again, may have dabbled a little as a pre-teen. But once I turned sixteen and Grandmother told me the truth, I left it behind. Found answers in fact. Math. Science."

"The answers you needed." Enda nodded.

"Magic took my mother, and when I discovered Sorcha's spell also laid claim to my life, I blocked everything in me that screamed for the power found in those pages." Jaw clenched, Violet rocked back and forth in the chair, and then whispered, "I even blamed Grandmother and Grandfather."

"I know, dear." Enda flicked a finger at her cup. "Drink your tea before it gets cold."

Violet sipped the brew, and as it trickled down her throat, she felt a soothing calm wash over her senses. "I should have known you'd spelled this tea. I've found no other like it."

Smiling, Enda simply winked.

As Violet thought of that young girl, curled in a corner crying when her mother hadn't returned after days and days had passed, she experienced the return of the old ache, throbbing through her heart. "I never understood why she left, Enda. But today, a small glimmer of the why became clear. The power in those books is heady."

"Freesia...your mother...she started too young, had too much power. She couldn't contain all that she was. Your grandmother's blood, mixed with your grandfather's, created the most powerful witch we'd seen in centuries." Enda sniffled in her tissue, tears escaping down her cheeks.

"I'm sorry, Enda. I didn't mean to cause you pain."

"Pain's a dear friend at times. Reminds us of those we've loved and lost. And love Freesia we did, but she...she loved magic more." Enda sighed.

Leaning forward, Violet retrieved the teapot and refilled both their cups. After adjusting her hair in her large clip, she glanced at Enda. "You said my mother used to sit in here. What else did she like?" Being here, understanding just a flicker of what pulled her mother away, had her seeing things from a different perspective.

"Freesia had a fondness for salty over sweet. Not hard to imagine. Ever brewing something in the kitchen, she was." Enda studied her over the rim of her teacup. "You've never asked after her before."

"I guess I'm curious about her now. Maybe because..." Violet shrugged and held back the emotional storm always on the verge of erupting when she thought of her mother. "Because I understand the pull."

"Your mother was an old hand in the kitchen. Couldn't keep her out of these books. I think she even refined a few spells. It's a shame, the way of it."

"I've never been much of a cook. Or a witch." Violet shrugged and sipped her tea.

"If you don't feed the seed, it won't flourish." Enda clasped her hand. "Enough of the past, tell me about this fella, young Flint. He seems to have woven a spell of his own. Handsome lad, he is." She chuckled and slapped her knee.

Violet refrained from smiling at Flint being referred to as a lad.

"I see your little smirk, miss." Enda waved a finger. "You think I didn't love a time or two in my day. Enjoy the attentions of a brawny man? Well, I've many pleasant memories." She huffed out a sigh and sipped her tea.

Violet smiled and grabbed a biscuit from the tray. Lemon, powdered sugar, and buttery goodness melted across her tongue. She grabbed another. "My mother cooked? I know you'd rather change the subject, but I'm curious. Just for today, would you indulge me?"

"Your mother was a free spirit, and when your grandparents tightened the reins, she rebelled." She sighed and shook her head. "They had to do something, or she would have injured someone worse than she did."

Interesting. "Tell me the truth, Enda, what did she do? What caused the rift? Why did she leave?"

"I shouldn't say." Enda bit her lip and dug a small flask from within her skirts. She winked before tipping a bit of the amber liquid into her tea. "A drop brings heat to these old, hollow bones."

"Enda, please. I'm no longer a child."

The cook took a sip and smacked her lips. "I suppose not. Tilt your cup this way, then." She tipped a few drops from the flask into Violet's tea. "Your mother was a trifle jealous of the McAfferty girl. So she conjured a spell that was meant to distort her features." Enda heaved a ragged breath. "McAfferty was driving when Freesia spoke the spell. She lost control of her car. Her face and chest were sliced open, leaving dark pink scars. Horrific tragedy. No one understood what truly happened. The roads were clear, not a cloud in the sky. But your grandfather knew." She tapped her temple.

Violet's stomach churned. "Poor grandfather. To see that vision in his own daughter's mind." Sighing, she ran a finger along the rim of her teacup. "But, my mother is capable of more than just brewing spells, right?"

"Those are questions for your grandfather, dear." Enda tugged on Violet's hair. "Come, sit like you used to, lass."

Violet stood then settled between Enda's knobby knees.

She removed the clip from Violet's hair and combed through the strands. "The choice your grandparents made was out of love. Freesia was furious, fought to break through their spell, but to no end. She was able to create many spells through words, but her potions, her brewing gift was erased. So, she sought her high elsewhere. As she experimented with each drug, she became lost to addiction. Once more, your grandparents sought to intervene, but Freesia's need for escape overwhelmed all." Enda twisted Violet's hair into a braid. "Your grandmother never gave up. She'd find your mother and beg her to return, but each time she'd come home alone. Each time, I'd wait for her, and comfort as best I knew how, but nothing ever repaired that ragged edge of your grandmother's heart. When your grandmother died, the final words on her lips were of her and of you. There is no stronger force than love, my girl." She smoothed her shoulder and leaned close to whisper. "In your darkest times, remember that, and only that."

Violet closed her eyes, and let Enda mother her. Let her tug and twist her hair as she'd done when she was a child. She wiped at the tears trickling down her cheek. Sadness evoked by the pain her mother had caused so many people. She was grateful Enda had provided more answers, especially since she'd never known her father. Before she was born, her mother had disappeared for a time, and then returned to the castle with a newborn babe in her arms. Freesia had stayed for seven years, but eventually left again.

Where was her mother now?

There is no force stronger than love.

Violet studied a strand of hair that had fallen on her arm. In Sorcha's case, that was true. Her love for her mother had spanned the ages, had through the passage of time only grown stronger.

Love *was* destined to defeat Quint's unending darkness—only not through a bright beat of a red heart, but delivered by the black stroke of a merciless enchantment.

White field from my future line. Clasp your golden hand in mine. Together, vengeance we shall see. I shall hold thy place for thee.

CHAPTER 29

After spending the next day combing through rituals, enchantments, and Celtic lore, Flint stretched and studied the determined red head at his side. Her riot of curls were secured in a clip, yet most had chosen to break free from their confinement. Her nose was tipped bright pink, as she'd spent half the day sneezing from the dust-lined tomes.

"Let's get some fresh air."

At first, she didn't hear him. Her lips continuing to move silently as she read through the brick of a book on the library table. Her tea long forgotten at her side, along with the scraps of her barely-touched dinner.

He stood and rounded the table. "Violet."

"Yes, just let me finish this passage."

Sighing, he paced at her side.

She turned and glared. "It's hard to concentrate with you making all that noise."

"What noise?"

"The walking and sighing." She shook her head, and the clip in her hair broke loose.

He pulled it free and massaged her scalp.

Violet arched back. "Oh, that feels nice."

Her low moan shot straight to his groin. Too much time had passed since he'd touched her. This stopover under her grandfather's watchful eye was straining his already frayed patience.

Tipping backward, she flashed an upside-down smile. "You

must have absorbed some of the magic into your fingers. That feels amazing."

He bent and spoke beside her ear. "Once I get my hands on you, you'll know amazing."

Violet didn't laugh or chide him for his words, only stood and locked her hand in his. "Let's take that walk."

"When you say walk, are you implying something more?" He tweaked her nose.

She arched a brow. "Come along and see."

Heat flared at her words, and for the first time in what had truly been forever, he was at a loss for how to respond. Last night, after his walk with Eamon, he'd considered all the possible outcomes of Violet's face-off with Quint. An icy shiver tore down his spine—an unusual feeling for a man who lived by fire. Yet, the thought of losing her brought an arctic breeze to his flame-filled veins.

"You are quite sedate this evening." Flint squeezed her hand as they walked through the grounds.

"I'm sorry. I was lost in magic spells and incantations. I may have found a couple binding spells that could work."

"Good."

They continued along the path for a moment. The cool autumn breeze rippled through the air. Leaves tumbled along the path. Though, the crisp green grass remained constant through the changing seasons.

"These grounds have been in my family for centuries. I wonder if my ancestors ever discussed the 25th daughter? Did they consider the price of each girl born? Or were they just grateful the burden had passed them by?" Violet shook her head. "Has vengeance ever brought peace?"

"For some, it may." Flint shrugged. With her grandfather's warning searing through his mind, he tightened his hold on her dainty hand, not willing to let her go. Death would have to wait. His future would not be disrupted, not this time.

Walking farther along the path, their shadows meshed as the sun rested on the horizon in deep red and amber, laced with gold.

A desire to blend with Violet in more than just shadow had him halting on the path and drawing her closer. He reveled in her slight gasp before he blazed down upon her lips. Coaxing open her mouth, molding her against him, focusing on every nuance, every scent so that he would remember.

Visions of red-haired children danced through his mind. Violet's children. His children. A clear glimpse of his human death after years by her side. After leaving behind their legacy. A picture so vivid—he would see it to the end.

As she swiped her tongue across his, he moaned, caught up in the sweet cocktail they created together.

Flint had a lot to discuss with Mother Nature the next time he saw her. For now, he clasped Violet's face in his hands and broke away from their kiss.

Her cheeks flared pink, and her breath puffed in warm bursts against his lips.

He ran his thumbs along her red-tipped brows. "Violet, such a rare bloom. To me, you are every shade of the spectrum. I've searched for the flame, let it pour over my skin for so many years, and yet, it was here all along. You are my hearth. My vision of home. I've found you at last."

She tilted her head as she met his gaze. "I only wish I could offer you the same comforts. My heart is breaking at your words, because I know you'll be sitting before that hearth alone."

"No." He wrapped her in his arms. "You're shaking. Come, I'll build a fire in the ruins ahead."

Pulling her farther down the path, he escaped from reality into a scene straight from the past. Stones peeked from behind tufts of grass, still standing tall after hundreds of years. In this place, surrounded by the past, they would forge their future in a clash of heat through tangled limbs and gasping cries.

Approaching the half-buried, ancient stones, humming with past passions and whispered dreams, Flint envisioned painted blue bodies dancing around a pit of swirling orange flames.

Violet stopped beside him, studied the ruins, and then bent her head. "I'm sorry I didn't tell you about my inability to use my curse against humans." She tapped the top of his shoe with the tip of her own. "You were right. I shouldn't have taken the journey to Ireland alone. I'm grateful you were with me." Placing her hand upon his chest, she met his gaze. "I may say I'm ready to fulfill my destiny, but deep within, I secretly fight this burden. Have fought for years, by studying science, focusing on the facts of this world." She stepped away and ran her hand along a pillar. "If I could come here and burn away my fate, dance among these ancient stones and call upon some god to purge me through fire, I would."

He backed her against the stone. "You want to burn, dance among the flames? Then we will, right here, right now. *I* am your fire god." He dropped a scorching kiss upon her lips, and then blazed a trail down her neck to her pulse-point, pounding with a beat, a thrumming violet vein, which called to his primal nature.

Violet ran her hand along his chest, and then traveled through his hair before locking her fingers at the back of his neck. "I thought I'd find answers to defeating Quint without using magic. But after being with you, I've come to understand there are some things science can't explain."

A slight breeze stirred her hair. The red whips carried across the wind, breaking away from her face. "I understand now. You have to go with your heart. With love." She placed her hand above his heart. "Show me the light in the darkness. Burn me with memories of pleasure." She tipped his chin downward and kissed him solidly on the lips. "Make love to me, here among the magical stones. Where spells were forged and lovers bound. Mark me as your own."

Holding back his natural reaction to take, to pillage, Flint wrapped his arms around her waist. "Beautiful girl, your first time should be under the stars. Stars your ancestors have wished upon for centuries. Stars whose light has led many weary travelers back home. And together, we are home."

"Don't say that." Violet closed her eyes. "Not here. I'll give you everything, but I can only live in the now."

He cupped her face in his hands. "You are like a rare piece of glass, forged by fire, yet delicate, so fragile and easily shattered. So, I'll be careful and won't let you break without shattering to pieces with you."

Her features were barely visible as the sky turned gray. Her unwillingness to hope for more, to fight for what flared between them, created an unease, a sense of urgency to take her in this moment, and forget all else. "Here, in this otherworldly place, we'll join at the center, where there's no beginning or end." Flint tore off his shirt and laid it on the grass in the center of the stones, then followed her down to the cool, damp earth.

Violet brushed a shaky thumb across his bottom lip. "No matter what happens in the coming days, this moment will remain, swirling between these stones, creating a wave of hope and happiness for all who pass. May future travelers feel this link between us as they stand in this very circle. An aura of love found and celebrated, left for all time."

At her words, his heart flared bright blue in his chest, flickering in excitement over the spoken enchantment. Her words were a spell, something inherent in her person, now rising to the forefront without her realizing. A cloud of unspent energy settled around them.

He kissed the tip of her nose. "Seems you're a witch, after all."

"Then let me cast a spell over you." Peering from beneath her lashes, Violet unbuttoned her shirt.

A wall of flames erupted along the outer edge of the circle, heating them while shielding them from outside view.

Settled above her, he trailed a finger down her neck, across her shoulder, and nudged her bra strap down her arm. He scattered kisses along the same path, and then drew her peaked nipple between his lips.

Violet arched and clung to his shoulders.

He tugged and lashed the tip with his tongue, nipping softly before proceeding to the next.

Violet shivered. "I wish I could lock us in time."

"No need. I can stop time, but I won't need to, because this won't end." Flint stoked the embers with slight kisses before delving deep and fanning the inferno between them until she frantically clawed at his back and panted for air.

He rose above her and shimmied her pants down over her thighs, bending to pay homage to her breasts once more, while sliding his fingers over her soft mound and through her slick folds.

She clutched his head in her hands and drew him up for a simmering kiss—tongues dueling, lips grinding, piercing, claiming.

With the slick glide of his finger, he circled her closer to the edge, then shifted and slid one finger inside her wet heat. "Oh, that's custom made just for me."

A soft whimper broke against his lips.

Kissing his way down her chest and over her flat belly, he hovered over her core. "Let's see just how sweet this violet tastes." He flicked the tip of his tongue over her pink bud.

"Don't tease, please."

"You tease me all the time, walking around with that prude little nose in the air. You should know that only drives me to corrupt you in the most wicked ways." He tortured her with single swipes of his tongue.

Violet thrashed and twisted.

Flint braced his hands on her thighs and lifted his head to meet her gaze. "Touch yourself."

She bit her lip, but lifted her hand, slowly brushing her thumb over her nipple.

With a groan, he fought to ignore the overheated cock in his pants. "That's my Red. Uninhibited. Open. Experience all the pleasure this moment can bring." He kissed her hip. "Now, keep that up and watch me."

With care for her innocence, he gently slid two fingers in her drenched center, and then buried his tongue along with each thrust. He glanced up and caught her pinching her nipples, and his steel cock went from almost-there to almost-done.

Her deep-blue gaze caught his as she clutched and squeezed her breasts.

Increasing the pace of his fingers' steady plunge, he shifted up her body and kissed her, lost to mindless passion.

An electric hum buzzed through the air.

Panting, her skin slick with sweat, she stiffened and buried her teeth in his neck as she came against his hand.

"That's right. Ride out that orgasmic phase." Flint slowed the pace before removing his drenched fingers.

Red and gold from the outer circle of flames flickered in her eyes as she fought to catch her breath. "I thought you were going to shatter with me."

"Those were mere splinters in the glass, now I'm going to break through." He stood, tugged off his pants, and gripped his solid cock in his hand. "Think this'll do the job, Red?"

She rose up on her knees and braced her hands against his thighs. Drawing her tongue along his length, she circled the head with her tongue. "Seems adequate enough."

He sank down beside her and tugged back on her neck. "Adequate? Perhaps you should do a check and balance report?"

"How's that?" Violet murmured against his lips.

"Check." He captured her hand, drew it between his legs to cup his sac, and guided her other hand along his length. "Balance."

"I think you might have those backwards." She quirked a half-smile.

"Backwards is right. I've been in a tailspin since I met you, but that ends tonight. I've landed right where I belong." Flint groaned at her tightened grip on his cock. "I'm spellbound." He nudged her back to the ground, and then settled himself at her wet center.

"Take this gift." Violet arched beneath him. "Bind my body, my heart to you for all time."

Easing gently forward with a slight rock of his hips, mind dizzy with lust and the spell she wove around them, Flint bent and kissed her, softening her for the final breach. "It's time to take me. All of me." He plunged forward and then stilled.

Flinching, Violet hissed out a long breath.

Though his body fought his mind, he kept from sliding, taking. He bent and sucked her rouged nipple in his mouth, tonguing the tip, before rising above her and kissing his way up her neck to her mouth.

"Move." Violet slid sharp nails down his back. "Mesh our bodies with blood. Complete the spell."

"There may be blood, but there's also fire." Flint withdrew, and then plunged again. Lost in the tight grip of her body. Lost in the knowledge that by taking her innocence, he'd found his own.

The wall of flames surrounding their undulating bodies flickered, higher and hotter.

Under the stars, their raw connection sealed for all time with each slick glide.

Stunned by the sheer pleasure searing through his body, Flint drew back from their rhythmic kiss.

Her gaze burned with ultraviolet intensity. Her body lit by a white-blue glow. Her mouth open with gasping cries as she took each deep thrust into her core.

They melted together.

The tip of the flame beckoned and, with each heated gasp against his skin, they drew closer to the white-heat at the fire's center.

Bending, he forged deeper, licking and nipping at her mouth, capturing the cries of her surrender. Driving her closer to the heat, until she arched against him.

Pushing for her pleasure, he twirled the tip of her flushed nipple with his rough tongue. Beyond the melting point, sweat pouring over his skin, he kept up the relentless pace, reveling in each stroke and plunge.

"Flint." Violet shuddered and bit her bottom lip. Sighs and gasps broke against her plump, wet lips as she found release.

Driving his tongue deeper into her mouth, he devoured her gasps and swallowed her pleasure. Unrelenting, he reached between them and combed his fingers over her tight bud.

She cried out a curse and rode a second wave to oblivion.

At her bliss-filled cry, he charged through the fire, reveled in the heat, and emptied everything he had within her.

The culmination of this joining, the spell created by their combined magic, turned the outer flames to a white-hot blue as he sparked through the final glory.

Illuminating his searing joy found by firing past the pinnacle of pleasure with this woman.

In this age-old dance, he'd always held the reins, yet in this moment, he discovered he still had much to learn.

Overcome by that most elemental high, he rested his head upon her heaving chest and accepted the searing truth—he wasn't the one lighting the candle in the darkness.

Violet was.

CHAPTER 30

A faint cry of a Yellowhammer "sri, sri, sri, zu" broadcasted across the night, followed by the screeching screams of a barn owl. Embers flickered in the green grass, creating swirls of earth-scented smoke across the stony relics.

Sated and relaxed, Violet shifted as the grass tickled along the curve of her back. Nothing about this moment could be more elemental. Innocence lost, blood spilled upon the land of her ancestors, and her sweat mixing with the dirt in this ancient place of worship.

The sizzles and crackles of the diminished fire drowned out the outside world. As she looked up at the star-filled sky, she reveled in this moment of peace and pleasure. For so many years, she'd held back her heart, but now it flowed, unstoppable, coursing in a river of deep red for this unearthly man above her. He'd given her so much in their short time together. And she wanted more. She understood her mother a bit better now. Flint could easily become her drug. Wasn't she already addicted?

Why me? Why had this prophecy gone down the line to end with her? She'd shouldered the burden for so long, but now it seemed too heavy to bear. Still, there was no choice, so she'd glory in the present, in each moment with Flint.

"I don't know how much time I have left. I don't know how to play coy, and I've held back deeper emotions for far too long." She nudged him onto his back, settled above him, and then braced her elbows against his chest. "I love you, Flint."

He shook his head. "Don't—"

Violet pressed two fingers against his lips. "No, don't tell me it's too soon, or that I'm caught up in the moment. This is love. Like a solitary snowflake shimmering in the sun. Just as precious. Just as fragile." She placed a kiss upon his chest, right above his heart. "Our future may be uncertain, but my love for you is not. This moment under the stars, on my ancestor's land, sealed our connection. My blood spilled between these ancient stones binds our hearts forever."

Violet's body thrummed as a powerful spell coursed through her mind. Reality dimmed, and she fought to stay conscious. A voice she wasn't sure was her own poured forth. *"Through my blood I bind you. Through my heart I tie. Though I may be miles from you, nowhere shall you hide. Blood spilled across your skin links our very souls. This sacrifice I give to you. This tie I own."*

The wave of dizziness passed, and she opened her eyes to see her body glowing like a 1,000 watt light bulb and floating—ten feet off the ground. "Wahhhh…" Violet tumbled back to earth. "How did I do that?" She rose to her knees at Flint's side, tamping down her hair, which flared in all directions around her head, crackling with static electricity.

"Blood will out." Shaking his head, Flint sat up and helped her brush her hair behind her ears. "Was that trick your witch blood, or part of your spectrum?"

"I'm not sure, but that was amazing." She settled against his side, calling on her scientific nature to explain the unexplainable. Waves of light passed from his skin to hers in bright streams of red and blue, linking their bodies in an unearthly way. "Are you doing this?"

Brows raised, Flint glanced over. "No, that's all you, Red."

"I wonder if I could fly?" She shook her head, fighting for a modicum of reality in this moment out of time. "I read a book recently that suggested witches used ointment, which was best absorbed through mucous membranes, when inserting an object or "broomstick" into the vagina, thus resulting in hallucinations that could be interpreted as flying."

"I'm not sure where in the hell that information came from, or why it's relevant." Flint chuckled, the sound vibrating through his chest. "I sure as hell didn't coat my dick in henbane or hemlock. Any flying was all you, all pleasure." He dropped a kiss against her forehead.

Violet ran a hand through the dark hair on his chest. "If I am a witch, then I'll cast a spell over you. I want more. Take me again." Her body hummed with energy. That potent flow no longer corked, but flowing free from her body. She was drunk with bliss, heady with tiny impulses firing along her skin, creating this inner heat, this unceasing need for a connection, for love.

Flint ran a hand over her bottom and squeezed her fleshy mound. "Violet, making love again, especially since this was your first time, isn't a wise decision." He belied his denial when he arched against her.

At the brush of his hard cock against her stomach, she swirled her tongue along his ear and bit his lobe. "Pain mingled with pleasure is how we know we're alive."

In retaliation, he nipped her lower lip. "I can't deny you. Once more, my sweet Violet, but that is all. No matter how much you've spelled me."

Once more, they reveled in the flame. Bodies arching. Burning. Searing. Meshing into one form. One shadow—illuminated by the moonlight and dancing across the night. Together, they found that ancient rhythm and created a melody across the stones with a symphony of sighs and moans. The final scream of release became the crescendo to the musical piece they could only create when connected by their very souls.

After the music died out, Violet rested her head against his heaving chest. *"Have I touched your heart?"*

"Ah, finally letting me glean inside that red head?"

"Should there be boundaries in love?"

"No, no boundaries." Flint drew her up to meet his gaze, and then kissed her, but left her initial question unanswered.

She shivered, though not from cold, but from concern over their future direction. If she asked, would he freeze this moment in time? She bit her lip against speaking the desire to halt it all. To hold back the coming tide, and just drift.

"We should head back, you're cold." Flint shuffled around and groped for his pants.

As she was slipping her shirt over her head, she felt warm kisses against the top of her breasts. "Stop. I can't see."

Flint lowered her shirt and then clasped her head in his hands. Kissing her with a softness, a reverence. Kiss after kiss, brushed against her lips. His tongue softly stroking through her mouth, held a tinge of sweetness, especially for a man whose words generally ran more salty.

Pulling back, he took her hand. "Violet, I've roamed this earth a long time. Finding you made the wait worthwhile."

A single tear slipped down her cheek. "Why am I the lucky girl who ended up with a brawny blacksmith in her bed?" She chuckled and glanced at the flattened grass. "Or field. Whichever."

He wrapped her in his arms and breathed a hot whisper in her ear. "We'll get to the bed soon enough." He released a shaky breath, and then dropped to his knees before her. Clasping her left hand, he kissed her wrist. "For so long, I've searched for a stopping point. This Elemental life, it..." he sighed heavily and turned away. "It's solitary, but I've found my place, beside you." In the darkness, he handed her what felt like a piece of glass.

"I can't see. What is it?" The piece was still warm from his touch.

"Need me to shine a little light on the subject?" Flint chuckled, then raised his hand beside hers, and lit a small flame in his palm.

The light flickered across the glass and illuminated his gift.

A vibrant purple flower.

"It's a violet." Violet brushed her finger across the smooth glass petals.

"No, it's more than that. Look closer." Flint held the flame over the flower.

And she saw it—a heart bursting with every shade of red sparkled within the flower's glass core. "Oh, Flint. It's beautiful. So precious. However did you get that heart inside?"

"You tell me." Rising, he tipped her chin to meet his gaze. "Because my heart is locked deep inside a violet, and I never want to break free." He wrapped his hand around hers, locking the glass violet in her palm as he kissed her.

"I love you, too, Violet."

She smiled against his lips, holding the glass gift against her heart. *"And I you, Rurik."*

CHAPTER 31

During the middle of a very tense breakfast filled with stern glances from her grandfather, Violet started when an alarm blared, signaling an intruder on the castle grounds.

The too-wise wizard closed his eyes and muttered a quiet spell.

The alarm's piercing shrill immediately halted.

He gestured with his teacup. "Your friend, Pillar, approaches."

"Oh, well good." Violet cleared her throat, avoiding his knowing gaze. "I'll just go greet her then." Swallowing the dregs of her tea and chewing the final piece of her toast, Violet seized the moment to escape. She rounded the table and headed for the carved wood front door. After yanking on the faded metal handle, she waited in the entryway.

Pillar's dress billowed around her legs as she made her way up the stairs. The hem was ripped and covered with dirt.

"I'm so glad you're here." Violet wrapped her friend's frail, chilled body in an embrace.

"Violet, good to see you, too."

Pillar's voice seemed scratchier than usual. As Violet led her friend up to her bedroom, she further noted Pillar's appearance— stringy blonde hair, pale purple bruising under her eyes, and she kept clearing her throat as if something were stuck. Violet was just about to ask Pillar what was wrong when Enda appeared.

"Would you girls like some tea?"

Pillar shifted over to the window, mumbling incoherently the entire time.

Enda followed her motion and raised a brow at Violet.

"Yes, Enda, tea would be helpful. Strong black tea, I think." Violet searched through her clothes for something Pillar could wear, something comfortable.

"Shall I brew a tonic?" Enda had stopped in the doorway.

"I'm not sure. I believe Pillar has a restrictive diet." She watched Enda leave, pulling the door closed, and then turned her focus toward her friend.

Pillar continued pacing before the window. "So, you made it here safe and sound. Good. Good. That's good."

"What is troubling you? Come sit beside me." Violet tapped the bedspread.

Pillar raked her fingers through her hair and whispered what sounded like, "Too late."

"I'm sorry. Did you say something?"

"Nothing." Pillar fiddled with the lotions and pens littering the top of Violet's dresser, and then thumbed through her book-marked romance novel. "You read these?"

"Yes, that's a brilliant series."

"This is what love is to you?" Pillar met her gaze, a slight tilt to her head.

"Perhaps in the past, but Flint is my representation of love now. With those books, I enjoy the drama, the suspense, and in the end, when the couple finds love, well, that's an added bonus."

Enda knocked, then entered with the tea tray.

"Thank you." Violet rose and took the tray, then kissed Enda's cheek.

"Is everything well, girls?" Enda glanced at Violet before frowning at Pillar.

"We're fine. Thank you." Violet understood her caregiver's reticence over leaving her with such an unbalanced woman.

With a slight nod, Enda left them.

"I'm so glad you're here, Pillar." She poured tea into her cup. "I've needed to speak to another woman. I'm bursting to tell someone."

Pillar turned and raised a white-blonde brow. "I'm sure I can guess, but tell me anyway."

"Flint and I finally made love." As Violet got caught up in memories, she overfilled her teacup. "Oh, shoot." She flicked the excess water from her fingers and sucked her burning thumb.

Pillar giggled, but her laughter dissolved into a hacking cough. "So you finally understand the fuss? Eager to go again, are you?" She smiled, but it didn't reach her eyes—pale yellow eyes, flashing with specks of black. "Men are deceitful creatures. They say they love you, and then marry another for ridiculous reasons like honor and duty. Speaking of duty, has Mother Nature even met you? Contacted you? You, their supposed savior." Pillar flashed air quotes with her fingers at the word supposed. "Nodin and I were in love once, but the saintly Mother Nature led him away. She'll do the same with Flint. Mark my words." She poked a jagged fingernail against Violet's chest.

Flinching from the violent poke, she frowned. "Did you not have a chance to rejuvenate? Can I get you something? You seem…well…it's just…are you feeling all right?" How had Violet's happiness over finally finding love turned into talk about Pillar's despair over losing Nodin?

Pillar continued on the same subject. "Mother changed Maya and Nodin without their permission, basically did the same thing to Terran. She'll stop at nothing." She slammed her fist against her open palm, floating around the room, pacing in a swish of skirts. "She glides around controlling everyone's lives, but doesn't stop to lend a hand when you need her. That stick-figure bitch is nothing but a selfish dictator."

Violet sat on the end of the bed. Her gift hummed under her skin and then rocketed to the forefront, ready to protect should Pillar's increasingly bizarre behavior take a violent turn. She took a long sip of her tea then placed the dainty cup on the tray, biding time, hoping Pillar would calm with a moment of quiet. "I don't know why I've never met Mother Nature." Violet fiddled with a broken sugar cube. "I do know she spends time with Grandfather. Perhaps he's asked her to leave me be."

Pillar arched a brow. "Is that what you believe? Where is Flint now, Violet?" She wrapped both arms across her chest. "He takes your innocence and just leaves you?"

"He said he had to meet with Mother."

"Exactly." Pillar shrieked, as she poked a finger in her direction. "He's filling her in, reporting to her highness that he has your trust now." She lifted her hands before her eyes, folding her fingers together over and over.

Her friend seemed mesmerized by the action. Violet raised a brow. "Pillar?"

"Yes, yes." She blinked, cleared her throat, and then dropped her hands to her sides. "Now, he has you. Now, he has you. Wrapped around his finger. Wrapped around his finger." The words came out like a song as she twirled around the room, before stopping and sinking to her knees before Violet. "You'll do anything for him, won't you?" Pillar reached up and grabbed her jaw. "Look at me. You are weak. That is what love does. It blinds you to the truth. You are smarter than this. Figure it out. Use a math equation. The Elementals need Quint destroyed. Plus, you alone have the ability. Add in a bit of your heart, using the Flint "factor" to draw you in, then *BANG*." She clapped her hands together inches from Violet's nose. "Problem solved. Fucking for the team." Pillar waved her hand toward the bed. "That's all this is to Flint. And like a good girl, you fell for it. Hook, line, and sinker." She grasped the bed's quilt in a death grip. "Hook, line, and sinker. You're drowning in it now!"

"Stop, Pillar, please." Violet reached out to comfort her friend. "I only know—"

"You know nothing." Glaring, Pillar slapped her hand away. "You are blind. Lost. Flint has you in his grip. Seared your naive little heart. But I know better." She erupted into a deep cackle, which ended in a racking cough.

"That's enough." Violet shot off the bed and knocked Pillar to the ground. "If Flint is using me, then so be it. If I mean nothing to him, then he will not mourn when I'm gone. But I won't listen to you speak like this anymore. I love him." Her whole body vibrated with anger, and sparks flew from her fingertips.

Yet, Pillar's words had seeped through, digging into her mind. *No.* No! What she had with Flint was real. She had to believe. Nothing else had ever felt like this, and she'd made a vow. A witch's vow. An unbreakable bond.

Violet closed her eyes and attempted to calm the fury rising like a crashing wave through her body, electrifying her. *"Hurt her."* A harsh female voice seared through her mind. Was this Sorcha? Was the ancient witch alive in her consciousness?

"Make her pay for questioning who we are. Use her to sharpen your blade."

The room blurred, familiar objects hazed with red. Violet bit her lip, focusing on the pain, on what was real. Concentrated on her mother, and the tragic results that came when a witch lost control.

"Don't let the gift rule you," a softer voice warned. A different voice.

A familiar voice.

"Grandmother, is that you?" Violet's heart drummed a song filled with hope. Was she merely projecting her grandmother's words, or was her grandmother somehow breaking through death's veil?

"Finish this. She's betrayed you."

Violet flinched at the unforgiving scream in her mind. Too many voices fought against her reason, her will. "No. Get out." Shaking her head, she wobbled and fell to her knees.

Digging her nails into her palms, Violet fought back the heady desire to inflict pain upon another. "Get out, Pillar. I let you speak to me this way once. Not again. Leave. Sorcha…she's…she's trying to break through."

Pillar's hair stood on end, her entire body shaking as she slowly got to her feet. She raised her hands, palms up. "Calm down, Violet. This is what happens when you allow emotions to rule. You lose control and focus. I'm sorry to hurt you, but these are truths you need to hear. I've never had a sister, yet I feel like a big sister to you. Isn't this what human sisters do? Pass down advice?"

"I wouldn't know." Violet sniffed, still furious with Pillar's odd behavior and her condescending attitude. "I don't have any sisters." She closed her eyes and focused her thoughts on Flint, on his inner fire and strength, and drew from his flame to calm her pounding heart and to silence the voice invading her mind.

"No sister, no mother, just like me. But I've lived a lot longer than you, so let me offer a word of caution." Pillar stepped closer and then knelt beside her. "Be aware of underlying motives. We need you strong in this fight against Quint, not weak with heartbreak. Step back and look at this from another perspective. Don't open your heart to someone whose only goal is controlling you. Flint is ruthless, burning a path through anything in his way. Relentless. He's had years to perfect the art of seduction."

"It's too late, Pillar. I've bound myself to Flint in every way. I cast a spell too strong to be broken. I will die loving him. He is my guiding light now." But how much light was at the end of the tunnel? Her heart skipped a beat as she considered her reckless fall into love. Was she seeing a mirage? After all, what future could they have? Not a bright-shining beacon, but a candle dimming with each passing day as the flame melted away the wax.

Pillar clasped her hand, her nails still that odd pitch black. "Violet, there is something I need to tell you, but I'm frightened of your reaction."

"What?" Her heartbeat sped once more.

Pillar led her back to the bed, and then knelt between her legs. She cleared her throat before speaking. "I've located your mother."

Violet's world tumbled. Her wildly beating heart took flight and crashed into her stomach. "I never asked you to find her, Pillar." Hand shaking, she sipped her now-cold tea, wetting her suddenly dry mouth. "I gave up on locating my mother a long time ago."

"She says the story your grandparents have told you is a lie. She was forced to abandon you as a…sacrifice." Pillar waved a hand in the air. "Freesia wanted you to have a different life. Didn't want you to exist only to fulfill their ridiculous prophecy, so they ran her off. Even stripped her gift for magic potions. Tell me you'd like to visit her, to hear the truth, and I'll take you. She wishes to see you, but she is frightened of your grandfather."

"I don't know." Violet wished Enda had brought peppermint tea, which would calm her rioting stomach. Although, at this point, she'd be better off chewing raw ginger root. Why was she so frightened? Hadn't she always dreamed of this day? The day she'd find out why? Why? So many times that single word had circled through her adolescent mind, and though buried, that single question had followed her into adulthood. With the answer potentially before her, why hesitate? "Where is she?"

"She's staying at a facility, just two towns north of here, in Durrow. Shall we go?" Pillar took her hand.

"I'm not sure." Violet studied their linked fingers, biting her lip to hold back tears. Two towns away? How was that even possible? Had her grandfather known all this time his daughter lived so close? And if so, why hide the truth?

Pillar squeezed her hand. "Shouldn't you let your mother have her say before this ends? Everything was taken from her, too. She has pictures of you in a scrapbook." Pillar cleared her throat. "Give her a chance to explain. There are two sides to every story."

"I shouldn't leave the castle grounds while Flint is recuperating. Can we wait until he comes back, and we'll all go together?" Her hands shook as she pulled away from Pillar's grip. Was her friend's story true? Had her mother truly had no choice? After all these years, had Violet been living a lie? Why was distinguishing the truth so hard? Was her mother even capable of telling the truth? Was Pillar?

"Do not fear." Pillar tugged Violet's hand. "I will protect you. All must be revealed. There has to be something else, another way. I have to take this path, and I want you to follow. Do this for me. I wouldn't lead you astray. You've only been shown one path, but others exist."

Violet broke free from Pillar's grip.

"Come with me, Violet." Pillar stepped across the room and stopped beside the bedroom's French doors.

As alternate beliefs clashed in her mind, Violet wavered. What if her mother had not left of her own accord? She knew how important destroying Quint was to her family. Had they removed her mother from the equation so they could have their victory? Was that why Freesia had turned to drugs? Using that haze as a coping mechanism for losing her family?

Trusting Pillar when her behavior was so sketchy of late seemed quite unreasonable, as well. Still, if they just went for a short visit, maybe Violet could get answers to all those questions locked in the shadows of her mind. Didn't that little girl who'd shed so many tears over her mother's loss, who'd spent so many sleepless nights wondering what she'd done wrong, deserve answers?

All rational thought fled as she stepped across the room, clasped Pillar's hand, and flipped open the door's lock. "Let's go."

CHAPTER 32

Since the tableau playing out before him made no sense, Flint watched Pillar lead Violet along the outer edge of the castle grounds. Anxious to return, he'd quickly wrapped up his visit with Mother Nature and barely dipped a toe in Mt. Stromboli before drifting across the sky in a whirl of gray smoke. A giddy feeling had simmered under his skin the entire time he'd been away. A result of Violet's spell, perhaps? He'd hate to think being in love had turned him into a cheery sap.

"I'm not sure about this, Pillar." He heard Violet murmur, her voice and reticence carrying on the chill morning breeze.

Pillar halted, stood stock still, and only her head turned like a sneaky owl as she looked in his direction. "Too late. Run."

A burst of cool air whipped past his overheated body a moment before Nodin appeared beside Pillar.

"Where do you think you're going?" Nodin stood his ground before the salty fiend.

Echoing his friend's irritation, Flint stomped across the damp grass to Violet. The blades sizzled and wilted under each heated step. Harsh words tumbled in his head as he prepared to read her the riot act for leaving the safety of the castle grounds.

Pillar flipped her hair over her shoulder, as she struggled to free her arm from Nodin's steely grasp. "Release me."

Halfway across the field, Flint flinched when a loud crack fired across the meadow. A burning sting erupted in his chest, blossoming into a feeling of fullness. At the bullet's rupture point, he felt as if icy air pillows were expanding under his skin. He tore open his shirt. The wound foamed and turned white, swelling outward from the point of impact.

Another crack from the woods had him racing toward Violet. "Get down."

His vision blurred as he watched Violet run toward him, with Pillar running alongside.

Nodin remained still, studying the forest around the castle like a mountain lion before the strike.

"Nodin," Flint shouted. "Spin. Get the women to safety."

Squinting, Nodin kept his gaze on the forest. *"One shooter. Ukrainian. His weapon…I've never seen anything like it."*

"Then move. Turn into a fucking funnel. Do something."

Fear gripped Flint's heart, for Violet, but also due to the bullets excruciating burn, unlike anything he'd ever felt.

His chest blazed ice cold, yet seared with pain, and the balloon still stretched. A hiss poured from the wound, along with a steady stream of white vapor. What kind of bullet was lodged in his chest? And how much longer could he survive?

"Get her, Nodin…get Violet." Flint stumbled to his knees as what seemed like razor-sharp ice crystals pierced through his body. He fought to catch his breath. He could only observe, locked frozen in place, as Nodin wrapped the women in his arms.

"Go," Nodin yelled. *"I've got this."* He transformed and lifted the girls in a swirling wind.

Flint braced a fist against the ground as the strong current stirred around his body. Once he saw them reach the castle walls, he struggled to stand.

The nightmare intensified as another bullet ripped through his shoulder.

Lost to the agony sizzling and spreading through his body, he transformed to smoke, traveling to fire before he ceased to exist. What was in those bullets? Where had the damn fool redhead been going? Had Pillar led Violet outside intentionally? Were the bullets meant for her?

"Nodin, find out...find out...what happened. Keep her...safe."

"Rejuvenate, brother. I will care for Violet."

Flint gleaned waving discrepancies in Violet's mind and something about visiting her mother. Then another's thoughts rushed through his mind—a dissatisfied shooter. What had Nodin said about a Ukrainian?

Anger coursed and burned along the trail of white vapor. If he had any strength to spare, he'd strangle the bounty hunter with his bare hands.

Yet, due to the nature of these odd wounds, he had no choice but to trust Nodin. His injuries were unlike anything he'd ever felt before, and for the first time in over five hundred years, he had a fleeting worry that this time, he might not survive.

#

Wrapped in a funnel of swirling air, Violet could only watch in horror as Flint's body once more jarred forward from a bullet. She screamed for release, but Nodin kept spinning. Emotions out of her control unleashed her gift, and her entire body blared bright white. A raw need for revenge roared through her system. *"Let me go!"*

Through their link, Violet gleaned Flint's pain and terror over his debilitating injuries. Because of her, he'd been shot—again. What was she thinking, leaving the safety of the grounds? She should have waited, and now, Flint suffered the consequences of her impatience.

"Violet, stop. I have to get you to safety." Nodin's voice couldn't break though her need to save Flint.

Waves of energy pulsed from her body, and she broke from Nodin's grip, falling back to earth.

Too late. She watched in horror as Flint's body turned to smoke and disappeared in a trail of gray.

"No. Wait. What is he doing?" Violet raced across the back patio, attempting to capture the fading trail.

Another loud pop echoed from the forest.

Flinching, she waited for the bullet's impact, and then allowed the fall when she was tackled from behind.

"Violet, stay down," Pillar growled. "Are you trying to get yourself killed?"

Face down on the pavement, Violet fought to catch her breath.

"Are you all right?" Nodin crouched beside her and tugged on her arm. "Pillar, let's help her to her feet. We must get inside."

Pillar maintained her protective stance, smothering her against the patio stones. "But Nodin, the shooter—"

"Is gone." He helped Pillar to her feet. "I'll find him, though. He seemed to have something...I can't explain it, but there was something off about his mind. Dark, as if a seed of..." He cleared his throat. "We'll discuss this later, right now, let's get Violet inside."

Violet drew up on her knees. Her hands and elbows burned from where she'd fallen on the patio stones. Bits of salt stung in her wounds. She glanced at Pillar and gasped. "Oh no, your arm."

Pillar's arm had shattered. Pale yellow shards glistened in the morning sun from where her limb had once been.

"Violet, it's all right. She'll heal. Come." Nodin lifted Pillar in his arms and carried her to the double doors.

Violet flitted around them. "Please, Pillar, you must go. Wherever, however, and fix your body. Please." Wide-eyed, she shook Nodin's arm. "Take her away. She's been neglecting her care. And, Flint, where is he? Is he all right? Why were those people shooting at us?"

She gasped when she noticed the blood smears she'd left on Nodin's bare skin. "Where's this blood—" Her palms were bleeding and spattered with dirt. No, not dirt, but red and purple glass. Broken shards embedded in her hands and wrist.

Bits of glass.

Red and purple glass.

She clutched for the glass emblem at her chest, but found nothing but empty leather twine. "Where is it?" Frantic, Violet raced back outside and dropped to her knees on the patio, searching. "It didn't break. The heart's still mine. I'll find it."

Nodin yelled for her to return, but she blocked him out.

Air swirled through her hair and around her body.

"No. Stay back." Energy surged at her core, and she rejected Nodin's elemental sway.

At the edge of the patio, she caught a glimmer of red and scrambled over. Picking up each jagged piece, she gathered the broken glass shards in her bloodstained hand. In agony over the loss of her treasure, she ran her thumb along the edge and sliced open her finger. Lost in the drip, drip, drip of her life force, she swayed when arms wrapped around her waist and carried her back to the house.

Voices murmured, but her gaze remained trained on each bright red drop escaping down her finger and spilling onto the violet now splintered in two.

CHAPTER 33

After an endless day of waiting for Flint's return, Violet paced across the worn, wooden floors of her bedroom.

As the evening drew closer, she'd started a fire, a call for Flint to come home. Searing with a need for revenge, her grandfather and Nodin had barely kept her from hunting down the shooter. They'd assured her they would achieve justice for the attack. The two men had huddled together in the library, debating the potential reasons and outcomes until, flustered by the inactivity, Violet sought refuge in her room.

Regardless of whether her eyes were open or shut, she could still picture the stunned look on Flint's face, the absolute terror and shock, when the bullet hit. If that scientist Schwarz was behind this, he'd pay. She'd find him and let her inner witch free.

Violet studied the bandage Enda had put on her thumb, still furious over the cause. That bounty hunter had destroyed her violet, split the glass symbolization of her love in two. Perhaps the time *had* come to delve a little deeper into those dark magic books. Though inhibited in using her electromagnetic gifts against humans, she believed the spells written within those dusty tomes would work just fine.

Violet shook her head. What was she thinking? A shadow sat on the verge of her soul, trying to cover her light with gray, with black.

Were these thoughts really her own?

A scratchy cough drew her attention to her friend. Shivering and pale, Pillar sat wrapped in a blanket, rocking in a chair beside the bed. Her voice nothing but a crackle. "Do you see what you've done?"

"What?" Violet snapped around, ready to lash and release all this anger and frustration.

"You put Flint in danger."

"What are you saying, Pillar? Not so long ago you asked me to seek the Elementals' help." Violet glared at her friend. "Why are you still here, anyway? You should go. For pity's sake, you're crumbling to pieces."

"No, I must see this through. You have no idea the sacrifices I've made. I won't leave now."

"What sacrifices?"

Pillar turned away from her gaze and stared into the flames. "I see now they can't protect you. If you truly care for Flint, you won't watch him die while defending you. He may be peri-mortal, but his life force can end."

"I know this. Peri means perpetual. Round and round, he must renew in fire, and if he doesn't, then…" Violet scrubbed her fingers through her hair and resumed her pacing as she fingered the broken violet pieces in her pocket.

"He may not recuperate from his injuries." With her words, Pillar added fuel to the fire.

Unwilling to rise to whatever bait Pillar was casting, Violet shook her head. "He will survive. I can still feel his life force. It's faint, but it's there."

"But for how long?" Pillar shot out of the chair and grasped her shoulder. "This man you are up against. This Schwarz, he knows everything about the Elementals, knows how to use science against them. I wouldn't be surprised if that sniper had some sort of specially-crafted cartridge. Give up this ridiculous notion you can have a normal human life. Love, constancy, friendship, all lies." Pillar jabbed a brittle finger against Violet's chest. "The only thing waiting for you is Quint, and after what you did to him, he's coming, guns blazing."

True she had blasted a hole through Quint's chest during their initial meeting, and right now she wondered if Pillar was trying to do the same with all her pokes and prods. "I suggest you stow that pointy finger. I've tolerated enough of your physical *and* verbal jabs. As to that, in your worry over Quint's return, are you more concerned about me, or yourself?"

Pillar merely raised a pale-blonde brow. "I see Flint's sass has rubbed off." She shrugged her good shoulder, and then sank back into the rocker. "It's a simple equation, Violet. You facing Quint alone equals no pain for Flint. It's time to leave these Elementals behind. I'm sickened by all this talk of love and Flint. Stand on your own. Don't expect a man to fight your battles, because you'll always lose."

"Pillar, that's enough," Nodin stated as he entered the room. "I won't have you lashing Violet with your salty tongue."

"You used to like my salty tongue," Pillar quipped.

Nodin glared, his jaw tight. "Where were you leading her anyway? You know she's not safe outside the castle walls." He stepped closer and locked his hands against the rocker arms, pinning her in. "What exactly have you done?"

Pillar shoved against his chest. "Get out of my personal space. You gave up that right years ago."

Violet sighed, not in the mood to watch these two dredge through the past again. "Pillar, perhaps you should—"

"No, Violet. I've had enough of others believing they know me. Thinking they know best." Pillar drummed her nails upon the rocker arm, sprinkling salt onto the floor. "Violet and I owe you nothing, Nodin. Our purpose had nothing to do with you. I trust you can comprehend my reticence, since explanations were never your strong suit."

"Must you twist everything back to that?" Nodin shoved down against the rocker, causing it to madly sway back and forth. He raked a hand through his raven-colored hair. "My elemental brother is lying injured in a pool of magma. He barely escaped in time to renew his life force because *you* led Violet astray. What's the scheme this time?" He locked a hand around Pillar's neck, tugging back on her hair. "Flint trusts me to look after his woman. He'll be very displeased if I let you place her in danger."

"Aren't you the noble one, always sacrificing for others?" Her pale lips drew back in a snarl. "Doesn't it wear on you to always be the good guy? To do the right thing?"

"I can't make excuses for you anymore." Nodin shook his head. "I want you to leave."

"I've never cared what *you* want." Pillar shoved him away. "And I'm not going anywhere."

Nodin opened his fist, and a hunk of blonde hair fell to the floor. "What is this?" He stirred the fallen locks with the tip of his bare toe. "You are in worse condition than I thought. Why are you neglecting your care?"

Pillar stood toe to toe in front of him. "As if you've ever cared. You'll destroy Violet, just as you've destroyed me." She huffed out a laugh, which quickly dissolved into a coughing fit. Composed once more, she glared at Nodin. "You high-and-mighty Elementals have it so easy, but one thing you constantly overlook when dispensing all that *supposed* justice…one thing you seem to forget: there are consequences." After gritting out each word, she shifted over to the window. "Not everyone appreciates your 'gleaning'." She glanced at Nodin over her shoulder. "Some of us prefer the dark. I've been wallowing there since you pushed me into that unending abyss."

"An abyss? That is a lie of your own making. I've tried." Nodin grabbed her shoulder and spun her around. "Tried, over and over. For years, I've struggled for your forgiveness, but to no avail. But, no more. What we had"—he waved a hand between them—"neither of us fought to keep, so what does that mean? You didn't love me any more than I loved you."

Speechless, Violet could only watch, as Pillar slapped Nodin across the face.

"Don't tell me what I felt, you self-righteous bastard."

Salt filled the air as Pillar roared, then transformed into a salty funnel and knocked against Nodin.

Tiny, square particles battered through the room, stinging Violet's skin. Eyes watering, she coughed, trying to catch her breath past the endless battering of salt flowing through her throat and nostrils. "Pillar, stop."

The spinning swirl stopped, and Pillar fell to her knees.

Nodin clutched Violet's shoulder. "Violet, please tell me. Where was she taking you? What were her plans?"

Violet blinked away the stinging salt. "She said...she was taking me to my mother." After rubbing her eyes, she searched the room for her tissue box. "The decision to leave wasn't all her fault, Nodin. I chose to go. Pillar was helping me. I... I just..." She shook a tissue from the box and blew her nose, taking a moment before revealing the desperation of a seven-year-old girl. "I was searching for resolution to a painful part of my past. I'm not sure what to believe anymore." She drew another tissue from the box and wiped her itchy eyes. "I wish...I would hope Pillar would not betray our friendship in such a way, but she is not well. I'm so sorry. I just wanted to...to meet my mother. Foolish, I know."

Nodin wrapped his arms around her. "No, not foolish at all."

Pillar sniffed from her crouch by the door.

Violet shifted in Nodin's arms and met her friend's gaze. Pale-yellow eyes pleaded for something—forgiveness, sympathy. Violet had no understanding of the history between Nodin and Pillar, yet the emotion bristling between them was palpable. Was this what happened when love turned to hate?

A heady mist filled the room, clearing the lingering salt haze from the air.

Violet stepped away from Nodin, and then jumped when a beautiful, but quite naked, blonde suddenly appeared between the bedroom's open French doors. Her voice carried across the room like a delicate bubble. "Good evening. May I borrow some clothes?"

"Maya." Nodin greeted the water Elemental. "Glad to see you're well."

Violet snapped out of her stupor. "Clothes, right, sorry. My closet is over here."

Why had Maya come? Their last encounter had occurred when, at her grandfather's directive, she'd watched over the water-girl's recuperation.

Pillar may believe the two of them were at the top of Quint's hit list, but Violet believed they were in line behind the Earth elemental, Terran.

After Violet produced sweats too short for Maya's tall frame, and a large, faded concert T-shirt, she was encompassed in a comforting embrace.

"I'm very happy to see you again, Violet, but I regret to be the bearer of troubling news." Before dropping her arms, Maya added a quick squeeze.

As she pulled away, Violet blinked when the water-girl's eyes turned from clear-sky aqua to stormy blue.

"Perhaps you should sit?" Maya led her to the rocking chair Pillar had recently vacated. "You've had a horrid night. I'm sure you're tired. Do not worry over Flint. He's survived too long to let something like this snuff his life force." She rolled her eyes. "Lord above, I'll bet he's raging mad."

Nodin barked out a laugh. "That's putting it mildly."

On the floor beside him, Pillar rocked back and forth with her single arm wrapped around her bent legs.

Maya sat on the rocker's footstool and clasped Violet's hand. "I overheard the reason you left last night. You wish to see your mother."

Holding back tears, Violet nodded.

"I can't imagine your feelings. Too many years have passed since I've had a human mother, but we all crave that connection in the end, don't we?"

Violet glanced behind her, wishing she had her box of tissues.

Maya smiled and massaged her hand. "I'm sorry to tell you this, but…your mother is being kept by Veimhet Schwarz. *That* is where Pillar was taking you."

Nodin hissed out a breath.

Pillar screeched and shot forward like a bolt, attacking Maya, knocking her to the ground.

Violet scuttled out of her chair. "Stop." She'd had enough violence today, and now with the added punch of Pillar's betrayal, along with the knowledge that Schwarz, of all people, had her mother, everything became too much to bear. "Please, stop."

Maya mounted Pillar in some kind of slick jiu-jitsu move, holding her steady. "Terran's taught me to take the fight to the mat, Pillar. I've learned a few moves since our last…altercation." From her raised hand, she dripped drop after drop of water onto Pillar's forehead.

Pillar struggled for release, and a wash of salt coursed through the air.

Maya released a torrent of water over her trapped prey.

Pillar sputtered, lighting up the room with colorful verbal descriptors of Maya's person.

"Enough." Violet braced a hand on the water-girl's shoulder. "Maya, please. Let her go."

Maya mumbled something that sounded like, *Salty Schickster,* but she released Pillar.

"I trusted you." Violet turned to Pillar, who was squeezing water from her clothes.

"As you should," Pillar scoffed. "They lie. Your mother holds the truth, but now you'll never know, because you've chosen to stay with these fools."

Violet studied the woman she'd believed was her friend. So many people wanted so many things from her. Could she trust her instincts enough to know who was sincere and who wasn't? For now, she only had the fact that Pillar had led her outside, and because of that, Flint was injured. Potentially lost to her for days, weeks, as he recuperated. With a heavy heart, she made the only decision that seemed right. "I think you should leave."

"Violet, don't." Pillar shook her head. "This world they live in…it's not…it isn't real. If you let them, they'll—"

"No. Stop the manipulations." Violet swiped a hand through the air. "It's best if you go. I'm sorry, but I need some time."

"You'll regret this." Pillar shot a glare at Nodin and Maya. "I'm the only one who sees the truth." She jabbed a finger against her own chest. "I won't filter your reality through rose-colored glasses like this stupid water-bitch. Quint will come back and destroy everything. Maya's skills are worthless, and all her molly-coddling won't help."

Violet's hand shook as she wiped a tear from her eye. "No, what doesn't help is this fighting. This doubt. All the lies I can no longer weave through. Please, just leave, Pillar."

A sharp crackle was the only sound indicating Pillar's departure. A snap that reverberated across her heart, as the friend she'd trusted vacated her life.

Unable to hold back the tears of confusion, of betrayal, of uncertainty, of fear, Violet covered her face with her hands and succumbed to the pain.

Too much.

She missed her lab instruments, where if you input a sample, raw data would result. A world clearly established in solid fact, with no emotional turmoil.

Maya approached and murmured that things would be all right, and then scooted her into a chair by the fireplace.

Violet rocked and studied each red-orange flicker. Who had her best interest at heart? Did her mother truly hold any answers? Had Pillar really been leading her to Schwarz? How much danger were the Elementals in by merely being in her presence? And where was her grandfather? Mother Nature? Why did they leave her to face these questions alone?

Wood popped and sizzled in the fireplace, drawing her attention once more to the dancing flames, but she drew no comfort from its warmth.

She sniffed and fought to keep her eyes open as she fingered the broken shards in her pocket.

Had she let the flame burn out?

CHAPTER 34

Drifting in a volcanic tub of magma, Flint seethed and plotted revenge while recovering in a bubbling mass of amber and gold. Flares rose and landed on his skin, feeding his inner fire—a blaze that didn't require further fuel, due to his edge-of-madness rage.

What kind of game was that salty deviant playing? Why would Violet willingly leave the castle grounds?

They had so little time together, and this recent spotlight on Violet's mortality wasn't diminishing his roaring fury.

What was Schwarz up to? Clearly, those specially-devised cartridges came from no other source. Once the bullet had entered his form, a gas expanded in his chest, depleting his life force as it ballooned through his body. What other science fair projects did Schwarz have awaiting an Elemental test subject?

More than done with all these pointless musings, Flint held back the overwhelming urge to break free of this volcano and return to Violet prior to being fully healed. Were the Elementals keeping her safe? Had they captured the shooter?

"Once I get my hands on that son of a bitch, I'll toast his ass." Flint rubbed more magma over his shoulder wound. "Recess is over." He huffed out a laugh. "You wanted Rurik, Violet, well, he's back. If she thought I was an overbearing ass before, she hasn't seen anything yet. After I fuck that woman into submission, leave her sated in her bed so she won't even consider leaving the castle grounds, I'll hunt down that sick scientist and erase his life in a fiery blaze."

No more fawning romantic, nor flirting fool.

If Schwarz wanted to fight dirty, well then, Flint would accommodate.

He'd held back the burn. Contained the raw wrath of his warrior nature for far too long.

The first volley had crossed the battlefield, been accepted, and now he considered the course of retaliation. Hands clenched into fists, Flint roared out a battle cry, anticipating the moment he'd glory in the spoils of war.

And this was war.

By placing Violet in danger, Schwarz had signed his death warrant.

First move, bring in Terran. The earth Elemental would have a theory as to what kind of bullet had caused his injuries. Plus, by utilizing Terran's rational mind, they would establish a logical strategy for breaching Schwarz's lair.

Reason and mercy no longer simmered in his brain, only an elemental call for revenge existed.

"Terran, you have one day to prepare. Meet me at Castle Nemon. We're going to war."

CHAPTER 35

"I need it. Give it to me." The foul-smelling woman cried out between clenched, yellow teeth.

"We have a job for you first." Between his fingers, Schwarz rocked a bag full of specially mixed drugs.

"This isn't going to work. She's in no condition to cast magic strong enough to breach those castle walls." Pillar leaned against the door, drinking a super-saturated solution of salt water.

"You underestimate her. I do not. I've studied enough de Meath and Levina history to know Freesia, here, is one of the strongest witches ever conceived, second only to Violet."

"I won't go near him. I hate him." Freesia sneered from her perch on the sweat-stained cot. "My father took everything. I refuse to go back."

Schwarz raised a brow. "Don't you wish for revenge? Wouldn't sneaking past the old wizard's guard be a grand glory? Weave your magic and pull your daughter right out from under his nose? I believe I've found a spell that can help you."

Pillar shook her head. "Don't be a fool. The Elementals will have the castle well-guarded. They'll glean Freesia's intent in a matter of seconds. Hell, her wizard father is probably on his way now."

"Let them come. I'm more than prepared. I've had two teams working non-stop this past week. We're almost finished. Besides..."

he waved a hand at Freesia. "She wants what I can give her." Schwarz kicked Freesia's cot. "Time is short. I need Violet here, and you will comply."

"Why do you say that?" Pillar shoved away from the door. "Time is short? What do you mean? Have you heard from Quint?" She gripped his chin in pale fingers. "Don't forget your promise."

"You speak to me of promises?" Schwarz scoffed. "I believe you promised I'd have a certain flower here now, but as always, I have to handle these matters on my own."

Pillar shrugged. "Your Ukrainian dog should have kept shooting. Two bullets won't deter Flint for long."

Freesia shrieked. "Stop talking. Just stop." She clasped her hands over her ears. "I won't search out that girl. I won't. But if you just give me a little, just a taste, I promise I'll think of another way."

Heisenberg barked and growled at the wasted excuse for a human wrapped up in a ball on her bed.

"I don't believe her either, Spitzy." Schwarz leaned against the metal cabinet serving as this woman's dresser. "There is no other way."

Glassy violet eyes glared from under Freesia's red-rims. Lost in need for the next hit, her entire body shook against the cot.

"Apparently, I haven't made myself clear." Schwarz drummed his fingers on the dresser. "You're being far too uncooperative tonight." He stuffed the drugs in his lab coat's front pocket. "Come, Heisenberg."

"Who is that woman? Why is she here?" Violet's mother shrieked and pointed at Pillar.

She shot Freesia an icy-glare. "I'm your daughter's friend. She'd like to see you."

"Why should that girl wish to see me?" The woman scratched at her neck and arms, which were bruised with track marks.

"Because you're her mother." Pillar tilted her head and folded her recently-healed arm across her body.

Freesia laughed. "I don't want anything to do with that freak."

In a flash so quick Schwarz didn't see her move, Pillar slapped Freesia across the face.

"You fuck anything that walks for drugs, pick through garbage for food, and yet you have the audacity to call Violet names?" Pillar backhanded the simpering redhead.

Clutching her blotched cheek in her hand, Freesia huddled in the corner.

Pillar stood over her prone form. "Violet is ten times the person you will ever be. I'm sickened that such a strong girl came from such a weak, disgusting creature. Now get up and do one useful thing in your wasted life." She nudged her with her foot. "You *will* bring her here."

"No. My father won't let me pass. But if you…if you give me what I need, it'll work better, I promise. It's the only way."

Pillar wrenched the woman up by her hair, her eyes flashing pure black and a wicked smile darkening her features. "There is only one way. My way."

Schwarz remained immobile, realizing he'd misjudged Pillar's nature. The salty creature was half-feral. A rush of lust shot to his loins. He'd found his match—finally. Heisenberg circled and yipped at Pillar's feet, as caught up in the violence of the moment as he.

With her face inches from Freesia's, her hand locked around the addict's neck, Pillar spat out, "Do you think I haven't seen thousands of women like you? I know exactly what you are. You want your poison? You pay. If I have to beat compliance out of you, I'll gladly deliver each blow."

"Pillar." Schwarz adjusted his cock in his trousers. While this display of dominance was arousing, he'd prefer to be the creature under Pillar's hand.

"Stay out of this, Schwarz." Pillar kept her hold on Freesia's neck, bracing her against the wall.

The woman struggled against the iron-hold, her face turning red as she gasped for breath.

He shuffled closer and clasped Pillar's shoulder. "She's been without drugs for three days now, so she'll do as we ask." He shot a glance at Freesia. "Won't you?"

She glared, and then finally complied with a single nod.

Pillar released her and stepped back.

Freesia crumpled to the floor, clutching her neck, coughing and gasping for air.

Heisenberg barked and circled around her wheezing form.

Schwarz waved the bag before Freesia's dazed eyes. "Pillar, doll her up, give her a small taste, and then bring her to Room 4. I have what I believe is the right spell and the necessary supplies. Let's hope my theory is correct, and she's strong enough to break through whatever magical barrier surrounds that castle. With the enchantment I found, Freesia should have the power to slip into Violet's subconscious and lead her away without sounding any alarms." After giving that ridiculous speech, he rolled his eyes at his actual belief in supernatural security systems.

Pillar wet her finger, and then dipped it into the bag. "A small taste. Is that what you want too, Schwarz?" She ran her powdered finger along his lips.

He yanked back on her hair and nipped along her neck. "I'm up for a change of plan. I've yet to show you the new equipment I purchased for Room 5. You're familiar with Edgeplay?"

"I invented it." Pillar bit down hard on his bottom lip and shifted toward the door. She glanced over her shoulder. "Bring the bag."

CHAPTER 36

Faint strains of an old Irish lullaby filled the room. Startled, Violet opened her eyes. Yet, her vision remained blocked by the darkness cloaking her bedchamber. Breathing deeply, she rasped in air tinted with a sweet, floral essence that burned as it traveled down her throat. Violet blinked, yet, her vision remained obscured.

A blinding white light pierced through the veil of black.

At the light's core, a woman with features similar to her own materialized and beckoned. The vision's head tilted as she quirked a half-smile. *"Come."* The word didn't pass through her lips, but echoed inside Violet's head over and over. *"Come."*

"What do you want?" With her forearm, Violet covered her eyes, blocking the glaring white beam.

"Come."

A strong energy vibrated between her and the unearthly figure standing beside her bed. A connection. A feeling of welcome that could only be found in a mother's arms. A soothing calm she'd never felt before. Something she'd craved since she was a scared and confused little girl. Acceptance. Maternal love.

The glowing white figure shifted across the room toward the French doors.

"No." Sorcha's raw scream fought to break through the mist shrouding Violet's mind.

Slight murmurs from Maya and Nodin in the next room mixed and churned with this odd dream.

Is this a dream? What was real?

Violet scooted off her bed and padded across the room, aching to retain that heady feeling, that bond with the beautiful woman. "Mother?" Her words were spoken out loud, but she remained unsure if they came from her lips.

The air seemed heavy and damp against her skin. A vibration hummed between her and the ghostly figure—a pull at the core of her heart she didn't wish to deny. Her greatest wish finally granted—her mother had returned.

"Yes, my sweet child, you must come. The truth lies with me." Her mother's red hair billowed around her face. She smiled and held out her arms. *"Come."*

Violet followed her outside, but pain seared through her mind as Sorcha fought to break through. *"No. She's a deceiver."*

"Let me go to her, just once, please." Violet stilled in the doorway as the cool evening air struck her skin.

"Come, Violet. Let me reveal the truth." Her mother's eyes flashed black, and then sparkled a vibrant blue. A familiar shade. A link between them.

Yet, after two steps forward, Violet froze, unable to continue.

Soft arms enveloped her in an embrace, and all was lost as she rejected every rational thought for the comfort found in her mother's arms.

Violet drifted across wet grass in a swaying motion, dancing through the night. *"Where are we going?"*

Freesia clutched her shoulders and smiled, though her face seemed to blur. *"Just a little further, girl."*

Lost in a nether world of dreams, Violet tried once more to shake awake, but she was caught up in fantasies laid in place by an abandoned seven-year-old girl.

Her mother's form, like a shimmering blue wraith, skipped across the castle grounds, laughing and beckoning. Her red hair dancing in waves around her shoulders. *"Come. Come."*

Violet glanced down at her feet, which were magically moving forward of their own volition. Unhindered by Sorcha's muffled screams.

With her hands linked at her waist, Freesia stood along the forest's edge.

Her image faded in and out, like losing reception on a TV screen. *"Wait, mother. It's not safe."* A sense of foreboding wrapped around Violet's heart, yet hadn't deterred her forward motion across the early-morning dew and multicolored leaves, which sparkled with the first rays of dawn. Feet dry, Violet floated farther and farther from the safety of the castle, but closer to her mother, who had drifted behind the trees.

Violet rounded an ancient stone relic protruding from the grass. *"Mother? Mother, where are you?"* As her hand pressed against the cold stone, she jolted as a buzz of energy zapped through her hand and across her heart, breaking her trance-like state.

Where am I?

She blinked and shook her head. A wash of heat sizzled down her spine as she realized she'd wandered into the stones where she and Flint had sealed their bond. Still somewhat dazed, Violet shivered and wrapped both arms around her body as the reality of her situation broke through what she could only deduce was some kind of dream spell.

A rustle sounded in the grass behind her. If she turned, would she see her mother? Or was some grim fate awaiting her? Fear gripping her heart, she glanced over her shoulder.

A huge man wearing all black rushed her.

Terror blocked her scream as she whirled to escape but tripped over a jutting stone. Hands covered with wet grass, she scrambled to her feet.

Where was her mother?

Would Flint feel her fear?

Footsteps and a string of foul words erupted to her left.

Braced to run…she wrenched forward.

A strong hand wrapped around her hair and yanked her backward.

Arms flailing, Violet kicked and screamed. A grunt sounded when her elbow connected with hard flesh. "No. Let me go."

"Flint." Knowing he would save her, Violet used their bond, spoken in this very place, to call for help. *"Flint."*

A pinch stung against her neck then singed a fiery trail to her heart. Her overworked organ pounded a techno-bass beat as the drug poured through her blood stream. She doubled over with laughter, euphoria cycling through her veins. A spinning disco ball colored her world in rainbow-filled bliss.

A coarse laugh filtered though the haze, and then a wash of salt crossed her tongue.

"Pillar?" Violet turned and saw her friend emerging from behind a mirrored column. "Dance with me." She wrapped her arms around the pale woman and spun in a circle, trying to escape into the sky.

Arms suddenly empty, Violet stared off into the sparkling forest. Greens and browns beckoned with shimmering waves. "Where did she go? I want her back."

Harsh words spoken around her tried to break through her search for her mother.

"Give her another shot, now."

Pillar's words struck like a bullet through her heart. "But Pillar, we're dancing now. We have to find my mother." Violet stepped closer to the magical forest where the wall of fanciful trees swayed.

Strong arms wrapped around her shoulders, and she felt another pinch sting her inner arm.

No! Violet glanced at her captor's face and saw a black-eyed monster with snarling lips and misshapen ears. She screamed and broke free, running toward the forest. Yellow cautions signs flashed before her eyes. Screeching red birds swooped in from all sides. Tree branches dripping with black sludge stretched and tore at her body, tugging her down, down, down into…oblivion.

CHAPTER 37

Once more, blinding light pierced her retinas. Violet moaned as she squinted against the glare, only this time she knew she was awake because the pain was all too real.

"Wonderful, you're awake. You have no idea how much I've wanted to meet you."

Shivering, Violet opened her mouth and tried to breathe, fighting back the rise of nausea. "I-I'm going to be sick."

"Oh, forgive me. This should help."

A tug on her wrist, and then a finger thumped against her inner elbow before a pinch as a needle slid home.

"No, please, not again." Violet tried wetting her very dry mouth as fear of another drug-induced haze surfaced in her foggy mind. Her body clenched in anticipation of the rush, but none came. As the nausea began to subside, she became more aware of her foreign surroundings. Everything was very white, clinical, and she seemed to be resting against a flat, hard surface.

"No need to fear this drug, dear," the voice proclaimed. "It's a quick fix for stomach ailments. A little something I developed."

A male voice. One she didn't recognize.

"Oh, but I'm a bit ahead of myself. So exciting to have someone as powerful as you in my presence. I am Veimhet Schwarz."

Jaw clenched against the pounding behind her eyes, Violet

blinked and stared at the man who reminded her of a bald mouse. She licked her dry lips. "Where…where am I?"

"Where you belong." The man smiled and pawed her hand. "Reunited with your long lost mother."

Violet sucked in a shaky breath. "Where is she?" Even though the slight turn of her head felt like a vice tightened on her temples, she shifted against the table to search the room.

A hollow woman with unkempt red hair stood beside a table covered with beakers and various pieces of lab equipment.

This was her mother? This pale, emaciated creature dressed in tight jeans and a black T-shirt, track marks up and down her bruised arms? Not the beauty she'd seen in her magical dream, but a faded relic of what had once been.

"Give it to me." Her mother snarled at the mousy-man. "I got her here. You promised."

"What have you done to her?" Violet slowly rose, biting her lip against the aches making themselves known from every corner of her body. After taking a deep breath, she drew her legs to the side of the table, and then stood. Dizziness wouldn't keep her from this reunion.

Unsteady on her feet, she braced a hand against Schwarz for a moment, and then crept closer to her mother. *Her mother.* And yet, who was this empty creature?

"Violet, please sit and get some rest." Schwarz wrapped an arm around her waist and tried to lead her back to her bed. "No need to worry yourself. I've taken every care with your mother, fed her, and slowly weaned her from her addictions. In all honesty, I'm the best thing that's ever happened to her."

Violet let him walk her backwards, and she leaned against the bed, her gaze never wavering from her mother.

"I'll get you some tea and toast." Schwarz brushed her hair behind her ear.

And with the motion, that touch, everything became very real. "Wait, wait, this isn't right. I can't be here. I don't know what you've done to me, to my mother, but we need to leave."

"Oh, I don't think so." Schwarz sniffed. "You'll be enjoying my hospitality for some time to come." He stepped closer to her mother, pulled a needle from his pocket, and then stabbed her mother in the neck.

"No," Violet screamed and wrenched forward. "What are you doing?"

Her mother wobbled and then slumped to the ground. The glass vials on the tabletop clanked together as she fell.

Schwarz dusted his hands together. "I'm finished with her now."

"Finished?" A cold sweat broke over Violet's skin, and she bent over and purged what felt like everything she'd eaten in the past month. Eyes watering, the stench of vomit cloying in her nostrils, she fought to catch her breath. "Did you kill her?" The words were whispered past the acid tang still heavy in her mouth.

"Merely a painless unconsciousness." Schwarz waved at the woman at his feet. "I've been perfecting the formula for days. I'd say the drug did a nice job, wouldn't you? The whole dramatic crash to the ground really added to the scene, don't you think?"

Overcome by rage, Violet launched herself at his throat.

A fluffy black dog growled, barked madly, and nipped at her ankles.

"Violet, let him go."

Her nightmare world went from hazy gray to flaring red as Pillar wrenched her fingers from their lock around Schwarz's throat.

Why was her friend holding her back? How long had she been watching? Her stomach roiled again as she glared at Pillar. "What are you doing here? Don't you know who this man is?" Anger at this blatant betrayal swirled to life the energy dormant within. Without conscious thought, Violet released an energy pulse that knocked Pillar to the ground. "How could you, Pillar? Were you always on Schwarz's side?" Body shaking with anger, hands glowing bright white, she knelt over Pillar.

The black dog barked and sank his teeth into her leg.

Oblivious to the beast's nip, Violet allowed her gift free rein. She glared at her salty friend. "I believed in you. You wanted me to trust you, to follow you, well here I am. Understand this, you'll finally get to experience the full spectrum of my powers." Blue arcs crackling between her fingers, Violet reached for Pillar's face.

Schwarz shoved her aside and backhanded her.

Violet fell against the table. Glass shattered as she tumbled to the tile floor.

Schwarz kicked her side, and then locked his brown loafer against her neck.

The snarling black dog growled beside her ear.

"Heisenberg, heel." Schwarz tilted his head and studied her. "Why aren't you using your powers against me, girl?"

Violet struggled against his hold. Her powers faded in the presence of a human, yet she still had one ace up her sleeve. "Flint will burn you to ash."

He laughed and kicked her side again.

Piercing pain shot through her body. *Had he cracked a rib?* Scrunching into a ball, she coughed and struggled to breathe.

"Flint will burn me, as you cannot. Isn't that the way of it?" He locked his foot against her throat again. "Quint informed me of many things."

"Is it true, Violet?" Pillar shuffled to her feet. "You can't hurt humans?"

Violet glared at her dear old friend and then purposefully turned away. After this duplicity, she deserved no such courtesy.

Schwarz dug around in his pocket and pulled free a pocketknife.

Unclear of his intentions, Violet squirmed under his foot, seeking leverage with her hands.

"Stay still." He smashed his shoe against her face.

Pain shot through her nose, trailed by the scent of copper. She choked as blood trickled down her throat. Twisting to her side, she came face to face with her mother.

Had Schwarz lied? Was her mother actually dead?

Though she had no idea why, especially in this moment when physical pain should override any other feeling, she experienced a wave of pity for the woman, just as she would some stranger on the street. But, some deep part of her still felt a connection, and needed to feel her mother's pulse, just once, to know her heart still beat. So close, and yet, she couldn't establish even the smallest bond.

Deciding one tiny touch was worth the risk, Violet's hand shook as she reached across the floor.

Schwarz's foot slammed down on her fingers.

She gasped against the searing pain shooting up her arm.

"Schwarz, that's enough."

Pillar's voice broke through her cloak of agony. *How kind.* Her friend had finally decided to stick up for her.

"No, my salty lover, it isn't."

Violet could only watch in horror as Schwarz dropped to his knees and drove the pocketknife's blade into her shoulder.

An unearthly scream ripped from her throat as what felt like blazing white-hot ice shot down her arm.

The black dog barked and circled in excitement.

"Schwarz, what are you doing?" Pillar pushed him away.

"She injured you, my pet. Violet will not harm what is mine. Plus, this was a fun way to get a blood sample."

Violet flinched when Schwarz flashed the blade before her eyes.

Her blood stained the silver in a wash of dark red.

Waving the dripping blade, he lifted a gray-tipped, black brow. "Are you going to leave Pillar alone, or shall I cut you again?"

"Enough, Schwarz, she wasn't to be harmed. What are you doing? Quint wouldn't want her damaged."

Violet gasped. No longer focused on the fire shooting across her shoulder, she fixated on the terrifying truth of Pillar's statement. "Why would you help him? We were a team. I would have given you my protection."

"Violet, you cannot understand...you don't know Quint like I do...I must take measures to ensure my survival." Pillar crouched at her side. "I cannot rely on anyone to save me, not even you."

Schwarz nudged Pillar's shoulder with his knee. "Enough of this heart-to-heart. Get her up, and take her down the hall."

Ignoring the danger, Violet snorted. "Taking orders from a man, Pillar? I thought you were better than that. And to think, I looked up to you."

Pillar grabbed her injured arm and wrenched her to her feet. "You're the one who abandoned me."

Wincing from the pain, she bit down hard on her bottom lip and met Pillar's gaze. "I've been a fool. Here I was concerned you'd lost your mind, and all along I was the crazy one for believing you." Violet released a bitter laugh. "I mean, you did warn me. Now, let me do the same." Shoving free of Pillar's grip, her body thrumming with the need for retaliation, she shot Pillar across the room. Standing above her target, she halted when she heard the distinct sound of a gun click.

"I'm accurate enough to hit you in areas that will make you bleed, but keep you alive. Or maybe I'll just finish off your mother."

Violet glanced over her shoulder. How had Freesia come to be here? As to that, how had she? She traced her gaze back to Schwarz. "How did I get here?"

Pillar scrambled to her feet, flipping wisps of her hair from her face. "Magic, Violet. Your mother easily scaled past those barriers your grandfather put in place. I laughed for hours, thinking how those Elementals were fooled by a simple witch's spell."

Violet huffed out a laugh. "Of course, you did."

Pillar circled around her. "Oh, are you going to cry, little girl? Sad your wittle mummy didn't weally want you?" Her lower lip bent as she flashed a mock pout. "Spare me."

Violet clutched her bleeding shoulder in one hand and wrapped her arm around her bruised body with the other. She took a deep breath, fighting back all the pain and revelations of the day before meeting her old friend's gaze. "I may have spared you once, but I no longer have a say in the matter."

Schwarz wedged between them. "While I hate to interrupt, I must prepare for the arrival of a certain band of Elementals."

"What are you going to do?" Protective instincts kicking in gear, Violet lunged.

Schwarz thwarted her efforts by punching her shoulder.

Black spots danced before her eyes. Her legs wobbled as she fought to surface from the shooting pain. She would not be defeated, would not let the flame burn out. "Flint will destroy everything."

"Let him try." Schwarz raised the gun between them and flicked his wrist. "Take her to her room, Pillar."

Pillar narrowed her eyes but obeyed, and pulled her out the door.

Walking along the corridor, Violet wadded the fabric of her shirt against her shoulder, trying to stem the blood leaking down her arm. "I need stitches."

"Shut up." Schwarz nudged her back with the gun's barrel. "This one." He unlocked the door and shoved her into the room.

Pillar followed her in and stood by the bed. "Not so bad, now is it?"

The door clicked shut.

Pillar gasped and whipped across the room to the door, pulling on the latch. "Schwarz, let me out of here."

"Remember what you said about men changing allegiances, love?" His voice, more heavily accented now, came through speakers lining the ceiling. "Well, you were right."

Pillar screamed, climbed up on the bed, and banged her fist against the speaker.

Flinching from the jarring shout surging across her overburdened brain, Violet clenched her jaw. "Will you please stop?" She closed her eyes and dropped to the floor. On a thin edge, she focused all her mental energy on contacting Flint. Sending mental frequencies across their connection.

"I know what you're doing." Pillar spoke from beside her. "Calling Flint, right?"

Keeping her eyes closed, Violet ignored the buzzing traitor.

"He'll come blazing in here and get himself killed. For real, this time."

Violet refused to comment, just concentrated on building a flame in her mind. Coloring each layer, starting with white, building to blue, then yellow, orange, and finally red. Using this form of meditation to escape the unending pain fighting for dominion over her body. *Terran is the white flame, Maya is the blue flame, Nodin is the yellow flame, Grandfather is the orange flame, Flint is the red flame.* Over and over, she repeated that mantra. Using the rationalization that a spell getting her into this place meant a spell could get her out.

Violet jolted from her mental chant when Pillar started banging against the metal door.

"I want out." Pillar shrieked and pulled out clumps of her hair. "He promised. I have to know. How do they do it? How do they become human? I want out! Out!" Her cries turned into a crazed laughter. She scratched and clawed at her face with jagged nails, leaving gouges on her crumbling skin.

Sliding down the door, Pillar sat cross-legged, and was quiet for a long moment before her entire body started shaking.

Unease slid down Violet's spine as she met the blonde's unblinking black gaze.

"You like Nodin's quotes, my little violet, well how about this one from Dr. Steve Maraboli? 'Every great tragedy forms a fertile soil in which a great recovery can take root and blossom…but only if you plant the seeds.'" A harsh laugh tore from Pillar's throat. "Believe me, my glorious Gamma-girl, I've planted many, many seeds."

Violet's heart froze in her chest as she wondered who else was in the room with them?

CHAPTER 38

"That fire Elemental destroyed everything, Heisenberg. He burned to ash all the research I'd completed at Aether Pharmaceuticals. I stood outside that burning building and watched everything I'd accomplished go up in smoke. But this time, I'm ready." Swiping a glob of toothpaste on his toothbrush, Schwarz smirked into the mirror. "Think Flint's ever taken a Halon shower, Spitzy?"

The fluffy black bundle yipped and danced around his feet.

When the track lights above his sink flickered and the center globe popped and sizzled out, Schwarz felt the hairs on the back of his neck stand at attention.

Chewing on his toothbrush, he glanced over his shoulder. Had the Elementals arrived? Were they attempting to knock out his electricity? Was Violet? "No worries," he gurgled around the toothpaste in his mouth. "Where was I? Oh yes, I do wish I'd seen those bullets rip through—"

A bitter odor like welded steel slithered up his nostrils.

Heisenberg sneezed then growled.

After a quick glance in the mirror to determine if anyone stood behind him, Schwarz noted the whites of his eyes were streaked with black. He scuttled away from the sink. Toothpaste lodged in his windpipe, he doubled over in a coughing fit. Eyes watering, he clutched the hand towel and wiped his mouth. "What's going on?" A slight vibration tickled his throat, and then settled with a buzz right above his Adam's apple.

The remaining lights flickered before sizzling to darkness.

A voice reverberated through his head. *"I see you've completed my mission."*

The chalky mint taste still coating his mouth, Schwarz gagged and then fumbled for the water cup on the sink's counter.

Heisenberg whimpered and huddled between his feet.

Even after downing cup after cup of water, coughing and hacking, Schwarz couldn't budge the lump. Clearing his throat, he whispered, "Quint. Is that you?" He gazed at his reflection, lit only by the light streaming in from under the bathroom door. Without his direction, his lips curled into a sneer.

"I've developed what you might call a split-personality." A booming laugh echoed through the small room. *"Not putting all my eggs in one basket, as you humans would say. Tonight, I'm allowing you a small taste of what it's like to be owned by me."*

A vice tightened Schwarz's chest, as if a dark hand were squeezing his heart. As blood trickled from his nose, he tasted a hint of copper on his lips.

"Knock, knock. Let me in, Schwarzy."

Body shivering uncontrollably, Schwarz screamed when beyond his control, his head snapped back and his mouth opened wide. A glob, similar to cold pudding, slithered across his tongue and forced its way down his throat.

Gasping for air, Schwarz clutched his neck.

The foul, bitter sludge gave no quarter, but continued its slow glide into his body.

Icy pain shot through his chest, yet his heart raced a hot beat. "I c-can't...b-breathe," he gasped and then fell to his knees.

The solid lump landed in his stomach.

The sound of Heisenberg scratching and clawing at the door filled the sudden silence.

His stomach churned, but he could finally breathe.

"Oh, you didn't think it would be that easy, did you, Schwarzy?"

"No, please. I'll—" His words were swallowed by the gurgling at his core.

Shards of biting pain pierced from his center and spread to every corner of his body. Arching his spine, Schwarz clawed against his stomach, leaving deep gouges on his skin. "Please, no more."

A cold sweat covered his skin, and he shivered against the chilled tile floor. Clutching the toilet rim, he gagged and dry-heaved until he was sure his eyes had bugged out of their sockets.

His spine stiffened and, without his direction, he stood. His arms and legs locked tight, like a soldier standing at attention. Breath coming in short pants, his eyes closed, he fought to break free of the overriding creature now immobilizing his body.

"Stop fighting, you stupid fuck."

Heisenberg whined and cowered by the door.

"It's okay, Spitzy." His voice sounded grated, as if shredded by glass.

Bracing his hand against the sink, Schwarz studied his face in the mirror. His eyes fully black. Inky rivulets coursing under his pale, clammy skin.

"You should be grateful for my presence. Bow in gratitude over receiving just a portion of what I am. It's a heady brew. Much better than that German shit you drink." Quint's derisive laugh echoed through his head.

Clenching his fists, Schwarz tried to comprehend the idea of two people sharing his mind. With a slight shiver, he accepted Quint's gift and the pain still coursing through his body. He met the gaze of the creature in the mirror and gave a simple nod. "I am your willing vessel."

His eyes slowly faded back to brown, and a tooth-bearing grin spread across his face. Overcome by the situation, he laughed, reveling in the dark energy now residing in his body.

"What a naughty boy you've been. Taking advantage of that salty whore, Pillar."

"She's been of use in our cause." Schwarz rubbed a hand over his cock, squeezing the turgid head.

His fist suddenly flew into the mirror, smashing the glass into a thousand pieces. *"She betrayed me. You should have strangled her when you had her bound and gagged in your bed."*

Pain seared down Schwarz's hand, his knuckles bleeding, slivers of glass embedded in his fingers.

"No matter. We'll finish Pillar soon. Right now, I'm more interested in a certain redhead. Take me to her."

Legs wobbly, Schwarz shuffled to the door, waves of dizziness shaking his resolve to serve his master. Clasping the handle, he stumbled and collapsed into the hall, his entire body weak and overcome by Quint's unforgiving presence. "I can't. I'm sorry. The pain is too much." Schwarz clutched his head in his hands. "Too much."

Heisenberg sniffed his ear before growling and skittering away.

"I should have known better than to think you could handle all that I am. Get up."

Schwarz crawled along the hall, shaking and covered in sweat, his body fighting this foreign invasion.

"Stop fighting. Give me control and together we'll show those Elementals what it means to fuck with me. That Earth elemental is first on my list. Then I'll pluck that innocent Violet and destroy everything she holds dear."

Quint's joyous laughter flowed through Schwarz's mind. *"Oh, I'll enjoy watching them fall. One by one…one by one."*

Schwarz scraped the shards of glass from his knuckles, mesmerized by the blood pouring from his hand. Lost to the dark cloak of madness, his mind overwhelmed by Quint's black presence, he crouched into a ball and sang, "The itsy-bitsy spider crawled up the water spout, down came the rain and washed the spider out. Out comes the sun and dries up all the rain, and the itsy-bitsy spider went up the spout again."

CHAPTER 39

Standing within the cobblestone ruins, Flint slammed Nodin against a moss-covered stone. "I trusted you to protect her."

"Flint, let him go." Eamon nudged a hand between them. "As I explained, her mother's magic is stronger than mine."

"Still think this is a game, old man?" An uncontained fury blazed in Flint's veins. He'd arrived back at the castle to find his woman gone and his elemental partners scouring the outer fields.

"That's enough." Terran clutched his arm, standing between him and the old wizard.

"Is it? Would it be enough if Maya were the one in danger?" He slapped away Terran's hand and glared at Eamon. "Where is she, magic man? Can you at least give me that?"

Violet's grandfather nodded. "I traced the path of magic. My daughter is in an abandoned hospital on the outskirts of Durrow."

"Flint." Terran grasped his shoulders. "Listen to me, just because her mother is there, doesn't mean Violet is. We need to—"

"No. We go now." Flint started to transform.

"Stop." With a sweep of his leg, Terran knocked him to the ground. "We have to think this through. If Schwarz was capable of putting that bullet in your chest, he could have other defenses waiting. Ones we don't know about."

Done with all the talk, infuriated over what sick experiments

Violet might be suffering, Flint stood and dusted off his backside. "You want to know what other tricks Schwarz has up his sick-ass sleeve?"

Nodin stepped forward. "Flint, don't do it."

"Let's find out." Ignoring his friends' pleas, he erupted into smoke and fired across the sky, unconcerned about the dangers that lie ahead.

"Flint. Stop. Don't go charging in without a game plan." Terran's command swept through his mind.

"He knows you're coming, you flaming idiot."

Nodin's warning did nothing to penetrate his steely resolve. A flare of heat erupted at his side as Terran joined him in flight. The Earthman had received each elemental gift, so he had no trouble keeping up.

"Turn around. You're not thinking clearly, and that could put Violet in even more danger."

Flint scanned the area, searching for a large building on the outskirts of the city.

There.

Trucks and cranes filled the otherwise-empty parking lot. The upper windows were cracked, and graffiti littered the walls.

He swirled as a gray cloud for a moment, searching for the best entry point, and then barreled for the building.

"Damn it, Flint. Schwarz has to know we're coming." Terran landed behind a dump truck.

Flint transformed beside him and peered around the front of the vehicle. "I'm going in. Are you with me or not?"

A gust of wind heralded Nodin's landing. "'One moment of patience may ward off great disaster. One moment of impatience can beckon life's great disaster.' That's one Chinese proverb you should consider."

"My woman is in there. That's all I'm considering. Take your philosophical shit and shove it up your ass."

Terran gripped and shook Flint's shoulder. "That was uncalled for. Nodin's right. Schwarz is banking on that hot-head of yours to come charging in. He's ready and knows our weaknesses. He hit you once, don't give him another shot."

Flint paced away, fingers stabbing through his hair. "Look at that building. He has workers in there right now. Whatever he's preparing isn't completed." Why wait? Each second that ticked by was another Violet remained alone and in danger. "I'm going in."

"I don't like this." Terran shook his head.

A static sound, like a fading radio signal, waved across his mind. Faint, so faint, that he barely caught each word. *"Fl...t...help me...come."*

Violet's voice.

"That's it." Flint charged around the truck and headed for the entrance, intent solidifying with each step.

On his way to the double doors, he caught a flash of blonde hair off to the side.

Pyro-girl stepped around a rusty blue pick-up truck.

"What are you doing here?" A chill shot through his body.

She waved and lifted something in her hand. Something plastic and black, with an antennae sticking out the top.

"The dark shadow said you'd come. I've been waiting. He'll be angry, but I must show you. I must." She giggled then her voice changed and she sounded like a scolding mother. "Bad girl. Bad girl! Always starting fires." Then her tone turned childish. "But, I like watching the bursting flames, Mama."

Oh shit! "Don't do it. I believe you. I do. You don't have to prove anything to me." Flint stepped to the side and bumped into Terran.

"No. No." She shook her head. "I did this for you. He said you'll be mine. I'll show you I can make fire too."

He shoved against Terran's chest. "Get away from the building."

"Sorry, dark shadow, but I love the fire man. I must show him. You'll see." Smiling, she spun in a circle and released a crazed laugh that echoed through the lot right before an explosion blasted apart the front of the building.

The force shot Flint like a rocket against Nodin and Terran.

Blinking away the dust, he shuffled to his feet, ignoring the huge gash along his side where he'd slammed into the metal tines of a tractor scoop.

Through a break in the smoke, he watched Maya pour water over the building. When had she arrived?

She.

Violet.

Violet!

Blasting past a smoking beam and crawling over cement bricks, Flint charged through what remained of the entrance.

White powder hissed and poured from half-destroyed nozzles lining what was left of the ceiling.

Terran shouted from behind him, "Flint, stop."

One goal in mind, he stepped forward.

The powder covered his skin.

Air died in his throat. He couldn't move, couldn't scream. More and more powder blanketed his skin, squelching his life force.

"I think it might be Halon." Terran's voice wobbled through his white-washed mind.

His skin shriveled around his bones like dried meat. His inner flame dissolved from roaring fire to smoking tinder.

A cool wash of Maya's healing waters poured over his body again and again, but couldn't penetrate his evaporating skin.

Shouts turned to murmurs as his vision bleached white.

Weightlessness.

Air sweeping over and through his body.

Wavering between life and the end of his existence, Flint shivered as a single vision penetrated the avalanche of oblivion—Violet, frightened and alone, clutching a shattered glass violet in her hand.

CHAPTER 40

On her knees, bent at the waist, arms folded over her head, Violet remained on the floor. Had the rumble that rocked their room been part of Flint's rescue attempt? Why would he do something so dangerous?

Sirens blared through the chamber, and water escaped from the sprinklers in jagged spurts as if the entire system had malfunctioned.

Across the room, Pillar lay on her back, nervous laughter escaping every few minutes.

After Pillar's odd seed quote earlier, which Violet believed stemmed from some sort of Quint possession, her old friend hadn't moved from her position.

Very leery, she'd stayed far away, unsure what had happened and if Quint would reappear. Although, her fingers weren't twitching which seemed a good sign.

"We're going to die in here. All these years facing disasters, and it's a crumbling building and dripping water that finishes me."

Violet sighed, exasperated by her ex-friend's psychotic ramblings. "I thought you wanted to die."

Again, Pillar burst into laughter. "I want out." She rocked her head back and forth on the soot-lined floor. "Schwarz said he could make me human again."

Taking the chance that danger was over for the moment, Violet sat against the wall and rested her arms on her drawn-up knees. She glanced at her friend, still lying prone on the floor, and though she knew debate was a fruitless endeavor, she still felt compelled to argue rationally. "You can't believe that's possible."

"What's possible about any part of my life? I'm made of salt, Violet. What is that about? What was my purpose?" She huffed out a sigh. "Schwarz said he could transform me, and he will."

"Is there anything logical left in your demented mind? All this time, surviving by your wits alone, and yet you believe this nonsense?"

"I'm not the only one who believes in magic." Pillar sat up and leaned against the wall, one leg drawn up. "You're one to talk, walking around spouting ridiculous prophecies like they mean anything."

Violet shook her head. If only the woman knew how hard she fought, even now, to keep the voices in her mind from taking over and destroying those who opposed her. Maybe then, Pillar would appreciate magic. "Sorcha's spell is very real. I've felt her fighting for control. Been tested by her many times, so don't tell *me* what's ridiculous."

"As if you know anything. Simple, human girl." Pillar opened her palm and tossed salt against Violet's chest.

"Every slight you believe you've suffered was self-inflicted. You're the one who remains mired in the muck." Violet flicked the salt from her body. "There were so many paths you could have chosen, and in my *simple, human girl* opinion, you've always chosen wrong."

"Have I?" Pillar shifted to face her. "What do you really know of me? I've had no mother, no father, no guidance. Free to roam as I will." She clenched her hands into white-knuckled fists in her lap. "Shouldn't someone have cared enough to teach me right from wrong? Where the hell was my Mother Nature?" Her jaw clenched, and then she blew out a shaky breath. "I had no one, so I took what I could. Grasped life by the fucking balls and lived. I'll make no apologies for that. But I am done. No way will I stay here while that dark menace, Quint, returns. I'll get out one way or another, and if I have to do so by forging alliances with people like Schwarz, I will."

Violet scoffed and waved a hand toward the room's brick walls. "Look where that got you."

"Don't you dare judge me, little girl." Pillar glared, and a hint of salt tinged the air. "Have you traveled this vacant earth for—" She stopped and stared at the wall behind them. "What is that?"

Violet heard a scraping against the wall, like a mouse trapped within and scratching to break free.

Pillar stood and dusted off her hands. "Well, looks like your rescue crew took to tunneling." She held out her hand. "I'd back away if I were you."

As she took Pillar's hand, Violet heard the scratching grow louder. A whooshing sound like the crash of ocean waves occurred over and over until a large crack split down the wall.

Water beaded, and then trickled through the opening.

"Great, we get to deal with high-and-mighty Blondie and her perfect little Ken doll." Pillar shifted to the other side of the room.

Violet kept her gaze on the crack, and then jumped back as water poured into the room, and concrete blocks tumbled at her feet.

"I told you the blast was too strong," Maya chastised, seconds before her head peeped through the opening in the wall.

"I'm only trying to help," Terran answered.

Heart already pounding over the daring rescue, her over-burdened vessel just about burst from her chest when the knob jostled on their chamber door.

Violet glanced at Pillar, who also stared at the door. Why wasn't the person just coming in? Had the earlier rumble locked down the building somehow?

Loud thumps continued to batter against the metal door.

"Just because you can control the water element doesn't mean you can take over all the time." Maya's voice broke through Violet's terror at what waited on the other side. Schwarz? Quint? Her entire body began to hum with energy, crackling to life under her skin.

Someone was calling forth her power.

The knocking on the door turned to unceasing tings as if metal were striking metal.

"You like it when I take over," Terran flirted back.

"Maybe, why don't you—"

Pillar cleared her throat. "Sweet Jesus, will you two shut up and get us out of here before Schwarz breaks down that door?"

Violet scrambled past the concrete chunks on the floor and tugged on the torn portion of the wall, trying to create a larger opening. "Thank you for coming, but Pillar's right, we need to go." A second wind rejuvenated her spirit now that the elemental rescue team had arrived. "Is Flint with you?"

"Step back, please," Terran warned from the other side of the wall.

Pillar shifted side to side. "Hurry. He's coming."

An axe blade somehow pierced the room's steel door.

With his shoulder, Terran shoved against the concrete wall and knocked open a hole big enough for them to slip through. He reached out. "Come on."

Pillar transformed into a funnel of salt and escaped.

The door handle rattled. "Knock, knock, Violet. Let me in."

Eyes widening, Maya gasped and tugged on Violet's arm. "Let's go."

Violet stepped into the underground tunnel just as the door burst open.

Schwarz entered the room, eyes and hair full black, veins of darkness coursing just under his skin.

"Get back." Terran shoved forward, facing off against the threat. "It's Quint."

"It is, indeed." Schwarz smirked.

Violet closed her eyes, calling on Sorcha, on magic—on vengeance. A smile broke across her face as heady power waved and electrified her body. Time to exterminate that dark matter parasite once and for all.

"Make this easier on everyone," Schwarz's voice echoed through her mind. *"Stay with me. I will spare the Elementals, except for Terran."* He winked at the Earth elemental. *"He will die quite painfully, but the others I will leave in peace. The choice is yours."*

"I've never had any choice, Quint." Violet laughed, exulting in the power radiating under her skin, primed and ready to strike.

Terran waved his arm, creating a wall of fire between them.

The flames faded to black and burst into tiny particles before tinkling to the floor.

"I destroyed you once. I will do so, again." Terran stood at her side with one hand holding Maya back.

Schwarz shifted farther into the room. "You have no idea how happy I am to see you, Earthman. You know what they say, ashes to ashes and dust to dust." He flicked his wrist and hundreds of black arrows shot from his hand.

Seconds before they struck Terran's face, Violet erected a white wall, knocking them to the ground. "Enough." She took a deep breath and shot a high-energy magnetic beam at Quint. Unrelenting, she gave her gift free rein, pouring forth all layers of the electromagnetic spectrum against him.

"I knew you'd see things my way." Schwarz's voice broke through her resolve. *"Destroy this weak, human vessel, I care not. I've planted other seeds."* Manic laughter pierced Violet's mind.

What did he mean? Other seeds? She blinked and glanced at her elemental friends.

Red blisters and open sores like burns marred their skin. Their clothes had melted away, as if…as if…oh no…

"Violet." Terran clutched her arm, his eyes red-rimmed with tears leaking down his blotchy face. "We'll survive your radiation onslaught. Destroy him."

Sorcha's voice fought to surface, to scream out her order to destroy Quint and damn the consequences. Violet shook her head, breaking free from her ancestor's narrow-minded intent. "I'm not as sure of your survival, Terran. But, I can damage him." She glanced over her shoulder.

Schwarz had wilted under her rays, his skin boiling and oozing gray sludge. Black lips snarled, and he lifted a ragged, bony finger. *"Like sprigs of wild violets, sprouting along a hill, I've scattered my seed across the land. Destroying this bloom is nothing. Divide and conquer."* Dark matter swirled around the fingertip, and then funneled in their direction. *"I'm ever evolving."*

Violet pulled everything to her core and shot one final blast at Schwarz.

An agonized cry screamed through the room.

Hands over her ears, she watched in horror as Schwarz tumbled over, his body vibrating, and black ooze pouring from his mouth and ears.

"Oh my God, I killed him." Violet stared at her pulsing white hands.

Terran stood before her, blocking her view of the bubbling carnage. "No, Violet. He was dead the minute Quint entered his body." He braced his hands on both sides of her face. "Focus on the facts. Schwarz chose Quint's side months ago."

Violet nodded, though guilt remained deep within her heart.

"We must go." Terran pulled her through the opening. Then after taking three steps, he fell to the ground.

Maya sank beside him and dug her fingers into the clay. As she absorbed the groundwater, she healed her blisters. The earth around her shriveled and turned to dust. Glancing at Terran, she shifted, placed her hands on the sides of the tunnel, and then slathered wet clay on Terran's body. When she finished coating him with mud, she leaned over and kissed him.

Violet stood fascinated as Terran kissed Maya back. His wounds instantly healed by drinking Maya's special gift, flowing from her mouth to his.

Wounds inflicted by Gamma rays, an ionizing form of radiation, which damaged on a cellular level, causing cancer and genetic damage. Rays she had no control over.

"Don't think that, Violet." Maya stood and pulled Terran to his feet.

"I guess all my shields are down." Violet glanced over her shoulder, concerned the dark wash of Quint sludge was sure to follow.

Terran kissed Maya once more. "Thanks for the drink. Maya flavored Kool-Aid is always…rejuvenating." He tweaked her nose and then tugged his water-girl down the tunnel.

Surrounded on all sides by Irish clay, they slogged through the slippery tunnel. At one point, Violet lost her shoe to the muck. "Is Flint waiting?"

Maya sniffed, and then cleared her throat. "I imagine so."

At Maya's vague answer, unease shivered along Violet's spine, or maybe she was dizzy due to blood loss from her knife wound. She glanced down at her rusty-red coated shoulder, and then slipped when she slammed into Maya's back. "Whoa! Why'd you stop?" Violet clutched Maya's arm to avoid falling.

"Knife wound?" Maya gave her a quick once-over. "Where?"

"It's nothing." This Elemental ability to glean her thoughts was quite unwelcome. Violet shrugged. "Can we keep moving, please?"

"There is no reason for you to be in pain." Once more, Maya stuck her hand on the tunnel wall for a moment. Then she placed her hand against Violet's shoulder, wetting the dried, bloody fabric.

Violet hissed as Maya peeled away her shirt.

Red and black bits trickled within the water pouring down her arm.

"Will you let me heal you?" Maya tipped her chin with a finger.

"Ah…sure, I thought you were."

"My gift works faster if delivered directly." Maya leaned closer.

Is she planning to kiss me? Violet jerked back. "Wait, wh- what…what are you doing?"

Terran's chuckle sounded from behind her.

"You're injured." Maya rolled her eyes. "The fastest way to heal you is to take water directly from my mouth."

"It will work," Terran assured. "Better than stitches."

Violet once more faced Maya, yet remained too embarrassed to meet the woman's aqua gaze. "All right." She mumbled, but hesitated a moment before opening her mouth and jutting out her bottom lip.

Maya placed her mouth just close enough so their lips brushed together.

"Poor Flint." Terran laughed. "He's missing out on some prime girl-on-girl action."

Violet felt a smile quirk Maya's lips before a cool rush of water dribbled over her tongue. Thirsty after her imprisonment, she eagerly swallowed, greedy for each drop.

After a minute or two had passed, Maya pulled away and brushed a thumb over Violet's shoulder. "See, all better."

Violet gaped at the now-closed wound. The dull throbbing had ceased, and the only evidence remaining was a light pink mark. "Amazing."

Terran wrapped his arms around Maya from behind and buried his face in her blonde hair. "She is, isn't she?"

"Oh, my God, can you just get Violet out of this disgusting clay-pit without having to fawn over everything Blondie does?" Pillar grumbled from the end of the tunnel.

Violet shook her head at Pillar's attitude. Of course, she had no appreciation for Maya's abilities.

Still, the burning love evident between these two Elementals brought a much-needed glimmer to Violet's heart. Feeling rejuvenated from Maya's healing waters, she spun on her heel and rushed for the entrance.

Hands gripped under her arms and pulled her out of the tunnel.

Her grandfather wrapped her in his arms. "Thank the goddess, you're all right."

Violet rose on tiptoes and glanced over his shoulder. "Where's Flint?"

CHAPTER 41

Three days had passed, and in order to free her mind from worry over Flint's condition, lack of control over her spectrum, Schwarz's death, Pillar's betrayal, and Quint's return, Violet spent hours reading spell books. Locked in the library with Maya and Terran, she fought to stay focused as the letters on the page blurred together. Hours ago, she and Terran had tossed around theories as to how Quint had come to exist and how he kept perpetuating.

She'd asked her Grandfather to keep Pillar imprisoned in a separate portion of the castle, for fear her gift would erupt in some manner. Every horrid event could be laid at Pillar's doorstep—her abduction, Schwarz's death, Flint's injuries.

Violet sighed and studied the doodled heart she'd drawn on a notepad. *Bloody hell.* Her world sat on a precipice, and she was acting like a lovesick secondary school student. Rolling her eyes, she flipped the notepad over.

She sipped her tepid tea. Not even Enda's special ginger-brew soothed the sour ache in her stomach.

Bare feet propped on the library table, Maya brushed her fingers through her wavy hair. "So, to be clear, you can't use your powers on humans?"

"No," Violet smiled at the curious water-girl. "I explained that earlier."

"Then if you were to release, say an electromagnetic pulse, would it damage all the electronics in the area?"

"Yes."

Maya huffed out a breath. "That makes no sense."

"I suppose the best way to explain my…magic, for lack of a better term, is that the gift presents around supernatural beings. The spell's main purpose is to destroy Quint." Violet tapped a pen against her lip. "That's why I studied so hard, because regardless of this ability, I still need to understand how the electromagnetic spectrum could destroy dark matter."

"Studying hard? Is that what you call it?" Maya's voice waved across her mind. *"I know what you're really doing, Violet. You're searching for alternate dimension spells."*

Violet held back a gasp. She glanced at Terran. He seemed undisturbed by Maya's accusations. Perhaps, he wasn't tuned in to Maya's frequency. She returned her gaze to Maya. *"I must discover a way to fight Quint on another plane. I won't harm you or Terran again."*

"He does like to help." Maya picked at the chipped teal polish on her thumbnail. *"Bit of a boy scout, my Earthman. Flint won't let you face this fight alone. He's still in a tizzy about missing Terran's battle with Quint."*

"I must find an alternative. Please clear your mind of these thoughts. It's crucial everyone remains unaware of my plan."

"I'll do what I must."

Heart pounding, Violet willed Maya to meet her gaze, unsure of the water-girl's intent.

The blonde finally looked her way and winked.

"I'm so glad you didn't meet Terran before I did." Maya sipped from her water glass. "You two are perfect for each other with all your science talk."

Tearing his attention from his book, Terran cleared his throat and frowned. "Maya, really." His cheeks pinked. "So…moving along, what's this binding spell you've discovered?"

Violet eased back in her chair, grateful Terran gave no indication he'd gleaned their conversation.

Maya huffed out a laugh. "Oh, baby, I'm sorry. Did I embarrass you?" She scooted around the table, hopped onto his lap, and then placed smacking kisses all over his face.

Terran trapped her cheeks between his hands and kissed her for real before pulling away. "There's never been anyone else. Just you, Shoeless Girl."

"You two are so perfect together." Violet wiped away a tear at his sweet admission.

Terran reached across the table and squeezed her hand. "Thank you. Now, you were saying?"

"Um…right, the binding spell." Violet opened the leather-bound book and cleared her throat. "It says,

"Goddess Isis guide my hand

As I pierce through needle's eye

Our threads align and knot together

While I weave this binding spell

Tie the feet and hold him steady

Secure the hands against his sides

Free our minds from spider's web

Hold dark creature within our shield

May each stitch hold strong and true

Until all snares of evil yield

By the power within me

Led by Earth, Fire, Air, and Sea

No harm shall return to me.

As I will so mote it be."

After speaking the spell's words, Violet blinked as the room blurred. She gasped as her arms glowed white and her fingertips pulsed blue. "Oh, no." She glanced at her friends to make sure she hadn't damaged them.

Maya's hair had wrapped in tight buns around her head. "What do you think, Terran?"

Terran slowly opened his mouth and worked his jaw back and forth before answering. "Well, since I can't move my hands, I'd say it worked."

"I'm so sorry." Violet slammed shut the spell book. "Let me get my grandfather."

"No need." Terran lifted his arms onto the table and clenched his fists over and over.

Maya kissed his cheek. "Are you all right, now?"

"Yes. Good job, Violet." He flashed a grin that lit up his soft brown eyes. "If Violet wishes to use this spell, I will agree, but I also believe I can hold Quint with my Elemental gifts, as well. Two against one." He shrugged. "Better odds."

"Obviously, the magic works." Maya worked at untwisting her hair. "I mean, look at the spell cast by her mother. Freesia led Violet out of the house, and Nodin and I had no idea what was happening in the next room."

"Still sore over those events, water-girl?"

"Extremely." Maya folded her arms across her chest.

Though Violet had tried reassuring Maya many times, the Elemental remained chafed over the magic's trickery. That thought sparked another, which until now had only simmered in the back of her mind. "Who was behind the explosion at Schwarz's compound?"

Terran and Maya shared a glance.

Violet huffed out a laugh. "Don't think to shield me from the truth. I was in that building, after all."

"She's a nineteen-year-old girl with a history of pyromania." A lyrical voice chimed from behind her. "Originally from England, but her parents sent her to a special clinic in Switzerland. She escaped and somehow found a link to Flint."

A tall woman, shimmering with brown, greens, and yellows, entered the castle's library. Her red-gold hair fell in waves over her shoulders and down her back. "Violet, allow me to apologize for the delay in our introduction." Mother Nature glided forward, extending a thin hand with branch-like fingers.

Entranced, Violet remained frozen in place. "You're so beautiful."

Mother smiled and released a musical laugh, which rang around the room like a wind chime on a brisk day. "Thank you, child."

Violet couldn't take her gaze from the glorious, golden creature. Mesmerized by Mother's melodic voice, she momentarily lost track of the conversation's flow. She dialed back in as Terran discussed Nodin's investigations into Schwarz's building.

"Nodin gleaned the workers' minds." Terran stood behind Maya, his hands kneading her shoulders. "He determined what they observed coming in and out of the building, and how the rooms were constructed. However, one room existed that only Schwarz could access." He scrubbed a hand over his chin and settled onto the wooden chair beside Maya. "Due to the explosion, Nodin was able to collect some of the drugs found in the secret room. After testing samples in the mass spec and NMR for their molecular weight and structure, I found molecules generally used in muscle enhancement drugs."

Mother smiled. "I may not understand the intricacies of the science instruments you are using, Terran, but I agree this is very useful information. Perhaps Schwarz has reestablished his super-soldier program."

"Based on the enhanced weaponry I found in a separate room, I'd say Schwarz was preparing an army." Nodin entered and crossed the room to Mother's side. "Welcome." He kissed her cheek. "We have much to discuss."

"Let us sit." Mother waved a hand toward the long library table.

As they discussed all prior events and future plans, Enda entered and flitted about Mother. The afternoon continued with tales of Flint's various Elemental deeds. Laughter and friendship filled the library, and for a short time, Violet buried all thought of the future and simply enjoyed the present. These supernatural beings were beautiful both inside and out. Though she hated to put a damper on their day there was one topic they hadn't yet discussed.

"What will happen to Pillar, Mother?"

Smiling, Mother took her hand. "Your grandfather has agreed to lead her on a better path."

A swift breeze stirred the spell book's pages.

"Reforming her?" Nodin piped up. "A little late for that."

"No, my son." Mother shook her head. "Offering peace, redemption, and renewal is always a worthy task. Eamon will do what he can. Fail or succeed, he feels he should try. He has never given up on his daughter, and she's hurt him more than anyone ever has or ever will."

Violet wiped at the tears spilling down her cheek. "There are kernels of good in Pillar." Finding forgiveness for her friend's deeds would take time. Though, with the imminent arrival of her prophesized death, perhaps she should leave this sphere with an unburdened heart. "I will need some time...some distance...but perhaps, I can assist my grandfather in her rehabilitation. In truth, she's had no guidance."

Mother squeezed her hand. "Good girl."

"There was a moment..." Violet shifted in her chair and glanced at Nodin. "A moment when I believe Pillar was...that a small seed of Quint infected her."

Nodin straightened in his chair. "Why do you say this?"

"For months, she's neglected her care, and when we were locked in Schwarz's chamber, I believe she was briefly overtaken by another's presence."

Maya shot to her feet. "Let's go."

"Wait." Nodin blocked her. "I'm coming with you."

"I don't know that she's possessed now." Violet stood and braced a hand on Nodin's shoulder. "Please, don't charge in and accuse her of some dark deed. Based on my observations, ever since we left Switzerland, she hasn't been herself."

"Oh, believe me, she's herself." Maya scoffed.

"I only know what I observed in that room. Quint implanted something in her, and for a moment he presented and nattered on about seeds, or planting seeds. Quint has returned and—"

"So have I." Flint leaned against the library doors. His amber gaze locked on hers as he entered the room. "Why so blue, Red?" He glanced at Maya, then his gaze fired back to hers. "Well now, what's this I'm gleaning about a girl-on-girl kiss?"

CHAPTER 42

Violet arched against Flint as he kissed her until she couldn't breathe. After shrieks of welcome all around, he'd hauled her over his shoulder, carried her to her bedroom, and dumped her on the bed.

Angling back from their kiss, Flint clasped her chin in his hand. "You, young lady, are in deep trouble." He shifted to sit on the side of the bed, then tugged her over, and settled her on his knee.

She yelped and squirmed on his lap. "What are you doing?"

He swatted her bum. "Punishing you." And another swat. "What in the hell were you thinking? Didn't you learn anything from the last time you left the castle grounds?" This time the swat ended in a carnal caress.

Slightly unsure of his mood, but too giddy to care, Violet pressed back. "Understand this, Flint. If you punish me, I will return the favor. What were *you* thinking, charging into a building armed by a mad scientist?"

He twisted her upright and held her tight in his arms. "I was thinking, I'll not lose her. Not after all this time." He ran his hands through her hair and kissed her temple. "I'll not lose her."

Too many thoughts swirled in her head, too much to discuss— her mother, Quint, Schwarz, and Pillar. Still, she calmed her mind and just settled into the warmth exuding from his body and reveled in his words.

She tilted her head and met his amber gaze. "Time is short. I can feel it. A darkness thrumming along my skin, like a bloodstain you'll never wipe clean. I'm frightened. For you. For me."

Flint locked his thumb and forefinger under her chin. "I have had more than my fair share of this life. If my time is now, if my elemental life ends at your side, then understand, I'll go in peace."

"No." Violet gripped his shoulders, tumbled backward, and tugged him over her body.

"You been missing something, Red?" Bracing his elbows at her sides, he bent and kissed her. "Something only I can give you?" He nudged his hips against her.

"Yes." She lifted her shirt over her head. "You."

Frightened by the sound of the ticking clock, unceasing, moving forward without any concern for those knocked aside by the moving hands, Violet raked her fingers through his hair and drew him closer. Urgent to feel him rising above her, breathing fire through her veins as they connected in the most elemental way possible.

"It's okay, baby." Flint kissed his way down her jaw. "Slow down."

"We have no time for slow." She tugged at the button on his pants. "I want hard and fast. I want you to take me every way you know how. I've studied all the positions." She ticked them off with her fingers. "There's missionary, the spoon, the dragon, the sultry saddle, the squat, scissors, the spider, upright doggy…"

Caught up in laughter, Flint rolled to her side, amber glints lighting his eyes. "Saddle squat? How does that work? Have you been watching videos again?"

#

Idling in a pilfered van on the outskirts of the castle's property, Quint surged with the power found in the drug-enhanced Ukrainian's body. Cloaked as the bounty hunter, Demyan, Quint sat in the empty back with Freesia and the ragged blonde pyro-girl. Planting his tiny black seed into the girl had served him well, though he'd made clear his displeasure over her ill-timed eruption of Schwarz's building.

He still hadn't perfected the right amount of dark matter to release in each human. Splitting his form into a vast number of shells was the next step in his evolutionary process.

Freesia blinked free from her witchy trance. "Violet's inside the castle, but so is my father."

Quint squeezed the blonde girl's shoulder. "You're up, my little pyro. Are you wearing it?"

"Yes." Pyro-girl smiled and rubbed against his leg.

Though this sacrifice was necessary, Quint did regret losing such a wicked mind. "Your soul will forever be a raging inferno." He brushed a stray hair over her ear.

She nodded, her gaze pitch black. "I am fire."

Quint opened the back door, hopped out, and then tugged the blonde to his side. He pulled a dime bag from his pocket and waved it in front of Freesia's face. "Join us, witch."

Standing on the road with them, Freesia tried grabbing the bag from his hand.

"Not so fast." Quint enfolded the drugs into his palm. "Speak the enchantment first, and then you'll have your treat. You're like a starving bitch. The lack of respect you have for your ancestor's gift disgusts me, and very little repels me, so that's saying quite a lot." He sniffed then stepped away from the rabid creature.

Freesia kept her gaze on his fist. "Fine. Give me the spell, a lock of the blonde's hair, and her lighter."

Pyro-girl shrieked when he yanked a chunk of hair from her head.

"Stop your whimpering and hand over your lighter." After unfolding a yellow-edged paper from his pocket, Quint handed Freesia the spell used to cloak detection.

Freesia wrapped the girl's blonde strands around her fingers and massaged the silver lighter in her hand. "Charm follow as my guide, see within its owner's eyes." Her eyes flashed white, before turning light blue. Her body swayed, and she sang in a childlike voice—pyro-girl's voice, *"Fire, Fire, I am fire."*

"It is time, child."

The blonde simply nodded, turned on her heel, and walked toward the castle.

Quint smiled as the blonde girl danced with the swaying green grass along the castle grounds.

The melody of Freesia murmuring the cloaking spell provided the music. Though, a heavy-metal tune would better suit this moment. Something with blaring guitars and pounding drums to match the hard-core explosives strapped to the figure fading from view.

A figure that would silently creep onto the castle grounds and provide a blast of entertainment.

# # #

Eyes closed, lying sated beneath Flint, Violet decided the only positions left were the ones they'd create together. She sighed and braced her forearm over her eyes. "I think I liked the sultry saddle best."

"Oh?" Flint tickled her sides. "I liked the saddle squat better. Seeing you rise and fall above me. Those fantastic, bouncing ti—"

"Shut it." She pinched shut his lips. "Has anyone ever told you that you talk too much?"

"*I* talk too much? Are you serious?"

She went to pinch him again, but he caught her wrist.

"I can think of lots of ways to shut you up." Flint drew her up on her knees, settled himself behind her, and kissed a searing path from her shoulder to her neck. "Shall I explain each one? Tell you exactly what to do with that sweet mouth?"

All thought stopped as he ran his thumbs over her breasts and brushed against the peaked tips. "How to use the tip of your tongue over every inch of my body." He trailed a hand down her flat stomach, and then brushed his fingers through her wet folds.

"Should I tell you how to kiss the tip of my seeping cock before taking me deep down your throat?"

His breath was a heavy rasp against her ear, as he trailed a finger over her throat and into her mouth.

"Would you suck and lave me with your tongue?" He drew his finger in and out of her mouth then brushed the wetness over her lips. "Would you let me thrust against you, grip your hair in my fist until I came, and you sucked dry every last drop from my tip?"

She turned in his arms, and shoved him back on the bed. "Why don't *you* shut up, and we'll see?"

"Red, you do all that, and I promise, my lips are sealed."

Violet bent and lashed their tongues together in a flagrant kiss that held nothing back. Her need. Her desire. Her unencumbered passion. She tugged his bottom lip between her teeth, before kissing along his neck, nipping his ear, and trailing more bites down his chest.

"Mmm...what have we here?" Overcome by her need to answer his every question, Violet held his solid member in her hand, stroking and teasing before drawing him into her mouth. "Is this a suitable reply?" She grabbed his hand and brought it to the back of her head. "Lead me. Guide me until you come."

With a hiss, he arched against her then drove deep.

Moaning, she drew back and circled his heavy head with her tongue, then followed his gentle nudge against her neck, taking him over and over.

Drawing power and satisfaction from his pleas and moans, each murmur electrifying her insatiable sexual appetite. She would get her fill once she showed him how well she could take direction.

Lost in the heat of the moment, in each incoherent shout of Flint's bliss, in his tight grip in her hair, Violet shivered when he came, shouting and begging her to take all he offered.

And she did.

She eased away from the heat, the sweat lining their bodies, and experienced another shiver.

An icy blast from deep within her soul.

A warning.

The cool chill didn't come from pleasure, but from malice, an outside presence she had almost blocked while adrift in the throes of love. She stiffened, then shot off the bed. "Flint, something isn't right."

Likely gleaning her fear, Flint flipped his legs to the side of the bed, stood, and clasped her shoulders. "What is it? Did I hurt you? I was just going with it, I'm sorry if I got caught up."

"No, that's not it." Violet slapped away his hands, her heart pounding a fear-filled beat. "Get dressed. I think…for some reason…my mother's here."

# # #

Whipping on her clothes, Violet ignored Flint's protests as she raced out of her room and leaned over the balcony.

Like a horror film playing out before her eyes, Violet screamed when she saw Enda standing at the front door beside the blonde pyro-girl.

A blast of smoke tore down the stairwell.

Violet heard the girl speak. "Um, you see my car broke down. May I use your phone?"

"No!" Violet screamed. "Enda, back away. Don't let her in. It's my mother. She's been spelled by Freesia."

At Enda's side, Flint transformed from smoke to man, and then shot her a glance. "Violet, get back in your room."

Questions raced through her mind. *What was the blonde planning? Where was her mother? Why did she feel her presence? Was Quint near? And could Flint save Enda? Would he need to?*

Standing just inside the doorway, Pyro-girl's eyes clouded from blue to black as she met Violet's gaze. "I am *not* Freesia. I am fire." She flung her arms wide.

Violet could only stare in horror as the girl pressed down on what looked like a trigger held tight in her fist.

Flint roared.

A blinding light flashed as a massive explosion ripped through the castle.

Aware of the danger, Violet's spectrum engaged, generating a white shield around her body as she tumbled through the air and prayed Flint and Enda had escaped.

# # #

Quint merely raised a brow when Freesia collapsed against the gravel-lined road.

She lay still for a moment, but then her body started to shake with laughter. "Oh, to see his face. It is done. Let's go see his precious castle now." She jumped up and ran toward the smoke billowing from the burning castle.

Pyro-girl had obviously completed her mission.

Though the diversion could be considered unnecessary, Quint wasn't fully recharged, especially after Violet's last death ray. No matter, perhaps she'd been damaged in the explosion, too weak to fight him off. Hopefully, the Elementals were all lying under piles of rubble, as well.

He followed Freesia up the long drive, waving away the smoke rolling from the demolished castle. He didn't care what the witch planned for her father. His thoughts were focused on punishing a certain Earth elemental and capturing his Violet, though he hoped to see Pillar again. She'd be a tasty appetizer before serving the full course of pain.

Quint smiled as he caught a glimpse of Pillar racing across the castle's back patio.

Well, well, the universe was on his side after all. "Freesia. Stop."

The witch halted and glanced over her shoulder. "Oh, that's right, you owe me." She returned to his side and stuck out her hand. "I got the girl on the grounds. Now give it to me."

These humans, did they ever listen to themselves? They really should be more specific about what they wanted. The vague "it" could mean so many things. He had no trouble being quite precise at all times. And in this moment, he was very clear about what he required from Freesia.

Quint grabbed Freesia's wrist and pulled her against his body. He held her head in place with both hands and kissed her, transferring a seed of his dark matter into her body.

With futile pushes, Freesia shoved against his chest.

He just held tight and drove his tongue deeper down her throat, then gripped her hair in his fist and wrenched back her neck. "You are the foulest wench I've ever tasted. What have you done to yourself, woman?" He released his grip. "Though I hate polluting even the slightest portion of my matter, I'm still gifting you with a small seed. Use it wisely."

Stepping away from the gagging creature, he scanned the area for Pillar. "Of course, that salty-bitch would flee without rescuing anyone. Always such a selfish creature. Shall we keep her, Freesia?" Quint smacked the witch on the back a few times as she fought to catch her breath. "Pillar *is* quite entertaining." He rubbed his raging hard cock. Destruction and revenge were apparently quite the aphrodisiacs. "I suppose I am in need of a woman since that Earth elemental set me back a pace or two. But no matter, I'll rectify that slight soon enough."

Quint stepped off the castle drive and headed across the grass, ignoring Freesia's crazed laughter as she ran toward the crumbled stone remnants of the castle. Overlooking the flames pouring out windows, having no regard for the smoke-filled air flickering with bits of ash, and completely discounting the bloody carnage of the dead pyro-girl, Quint continued toward his prey.

Pillar halted in her flight, and she slowly turned her head. "No." She scuttled backward and fell against the grass. "No."

He stopped in front of her and offered his hand.

She didn't move.

"What, my salty-wench? Didn't you miss me?"

CHAPTER 43

Eyes watering from smoke, Enda patted Flint's hand. "Leave me here, son." She sneezed then drew a tissue from under her shirtsleeve. "Your friend saved my life. I just need a moment to regroup, and I'll be all right."

Surrounded by Sessile oak trees lining the castle's drive, Nodin turned and met his gaze. *"Go. Find Violet. I'll stay with Enda."*

Flint could only nod, unable to speak. What if Violet was buried in the rubble? A wash of regret coated his heart and churned in his stomach. He should have dealt with pyro-girl on the ferry. Then this horrific event wouldn't have occurred, and Violet wouldn't be…she wouldn't be…

"Flint." Enda squeezed his hand. "Go find my girl."

He nodded and left her with Nodin. Seconds before the blast, Nodin had whisked Enda away and down the drive. Flint could only hope Violet had also found shelter.

Heading back up the front drive, he shook his head at the destruction to the entire front half of the castle. The stone fortress was nothing but tumbled bricks. Flint shook his head. Neither storm, nor marauder, nor time had breached these walls. Yet in an instant, a tiny blonde pyromaniac brought low a safe haven that had stood for centuries.

"Violet!" Flint searched through the rubble, coughing as dust coated his throat. He sent out a mental message, trying to connect to their link. *"Violet. Answer me."*

Alarmed by no feedback, he turned to smoke and drifted upstairs, absorbing small fires along the way. Since the castle was made of stone, there wasn't much burning.

Terran appeared as mist at his side. *"She fell into the library."*

Firing down the partially-destroyed steps, Flint transformed back into his human shape, before kicking open the library doors.

Each taking a pair of sweats from Maya, he and Terran tugged them on and stood with her just inside the door.

"Nice of you to join us, Flint." A burly man with a Ukrainian accent stood on a stack of smoldering books.

Flint stepped farther into the room and noted the man held an odd-looking gun to Violet's head. "Quint." He nodded, fighting to keep his voice calm. At his back, he sensed Maya and Terran shifting closer to the patio doors. "Not the usual get-up. I figured you more for hiring bounty hunters, not becoming one." Flint leaned against the antique wood table. "Violet, are you all right?"

Violet had momentarily perked up from her slump when he'd spoken, but in response to his question, she shook her head and continued sobbing.

Not good. The most powerful person in the room seemed to be suffering from shock.

"Isn't this a lovely reunion?" Quint stroked Pillar's head.

Jerking away from his touch, Pillar glared from her perch at this side.

"So nice to have the Elementals together, especially you, Terran. There are no words to express how grateful I am to see you." Quint sneered. "Do you have any idea how cold space is? Oh, I'm sure in that huge brain of yours you have some sort of calculation, but you've never felt it, the icy emptiness, the yawning darkness, but you will…when Maya's dead."

"You belong in the endless vacuum of space. Minus 454.81 degrees Fahrenheit is too warm for the likes of you." Terran braced a hand on Maya's shoulder, stalling her forward motion. "If there were a hell, I'd hope it's laced with ice, because then you'd be immobile, frozen in time. And just so we're clear, I'm glad to see you too, because this time, Violet and I will finish the job I started months ago." He stepped forward.

"Back off." Quint pointed the gun at Terran and fired a round in his chest.

Maya screamed and lurched forward.

Once more, Quint jabbed the barrel against Violet's head. "I'd stop right there, water-girl. I thought I'd give your Earthman an up-close appreciation of this weapon. He, of all people, should appreciate Schwarz's little science experiment."

Furious at this turn of events, Flint let his elemental fire surge through his body. His fingers flickered with flames, ready to strike. *"Violet, listen to me. I know you've received a blow, but it is time to stand strong. Get up and fight back."*

Maya knelt beside Terran, pouring water over his wound.

Breezing through the patio doors, Nodin knelt at Terran's side. "He'll heal, Maya." He stood and met Flint's gaze. "We need Violet to do her duty."

Quint huffed out a laugh. "What, no ridiculous quote about war and peace? Come on, Air-bag, dig deep and give us something good."

Flint sent another mental message to Violet. *"Come on, Red. I believe in you. Time to stand strong."*

"Don't think I can't hear your pleas, Flint." Pawing through *his* redhead's hair, Quint flashed him a wink. "Violet and I will be leaving as soon as I'm finished here, and since Nodin ignored my request, I suppose I'll provide the entertainment." Quint cocked the gun then fired a round through Pillar's chest. "Hoh, ho, now this gun is fun." He laughed and nudged her side with his boot.

Maya shot to her feet, water dripping from her hands.

Nodin held her back. *"We need Violet, Flint."*

Flint focused on his connection with Violet. A bond she had created. *"Violet, I need you. Time to get to work, babe."*

With red-rimmed eyes, Violet met his gaze and nodded. *"I'm sorry, Flint. I'm ready now."* Straightening, she wiped her nose with her sleeve and glared at Quint.

"I'm right here with you, love. We'll finish this together." After sending that mental message, Flint glanced at Quint. "I'm just about done with that fucked-up Nerf gun you're using. Dispense with the toys, dark man, or are you afraid you'll lose?"

"Not even a tad curious about what's in these bullets?" Quint arched a brow. "Especially since Schwarz custom-designed them for you, Fire-ball. They're compressed CO2, or dry ice. The special cartridge is covered in a thin polymer film to keep it from exploding in the gun. Once it strikes, the elemental heat in your body, in Terran's body, causes it to sublime, expanding from solid to gas."

Ignoring Quint's science lecture, Flint mentally reached out to Violet again. *"Red, it's time to unleash that spectrum."*

Dark blue eyes filled with sorrow lifted and met his gaze. *"Enda?"*

"She's fine."

Violet visibly took a deep breath and closed her eyes.

"Kick his ass, Red."

Violet stood and stretched her arms above her head. She rose on her tiptoes and then slowly lowered her arms back to her sides.

"Yes, dear Violet. Unleash all that radiation. Every wave of that electromagnetic spectrum." Quint rubbed his hands together. "Let's see how long your Elemental friends can withstand the onslaught."

Flint stepped forward and shot a wall of flame between Violet and Quint. *"I love you, Gamma-girl. Now let's see what you got under all that red-fluff."*

Eyes filled with tears, Violet shook her head. "You must leave. My power...you won't survive all that I am...and I...I refuse to let your flame die out." No mental messages from his woman. Though softly delivered at first, her declaration ended strong and true. "I promised the Fire King and Earth Queen that day at Stonehenge." Her gaze dropped to the floor, and she whispered, "I promised."

"Oh, are we at that climactic moment where the hero and heroine say good-bye?" Quint mocked, his ebony gaze dancing between the two. "Should I get the popcorn?"

"It's okay, Red." Though Flint had no idea what promise Violet was talking about, he nodded his understanding. "If you made a promise, then keep it."

"Enough talk. That's all you Elementals do." Pillar shuffled to her feet, holding a hand against her crumbling side. She stepped in front of Quint and held the gun's barrel against her chest. "Take me. Live in me. You'll never control Violet. She's too strong. She'll destroy all that you are." Pillar ran a shaky hand through Quint's hair. "Let's go, just the two of us. We can travel far away from this place."

Nodin locked his hands on his hips. "Pillar, what are you doing?"

"I'm leaving." She glanced over her shoulder, but didn't meet Nodin's gaze. "Quint and I don't belong here." She turned back to Quint. "Just take me. I can give you a perpetuating life. Please, leave Violet be."

"How noble." Quint raised a dark brow. "Pillar, the most selfish bitch I've ever encountered, now sacrifices herself for another? Hmmm...just how close did you and Violet become in my absence?" He sneered. "I *will* deal with you, my pet...*after* I have my revenge."

Pillar clasped his head between her hands and kissed him. Hard. "Fine. You want revenge? We'll do revenge."

"Pillar, don't." Nodin shouted. A gust of air whipped through the room, billowing against her dress.

Pillar laughed, and then spun into a salty funnel surrounding Quint and Violet.

A ferocious gale joined the spinning salt and forced the swirling particles into a narrow vortex.

Salt particles fired through the air as Pillar reformed.

Blinking the burn from his eyes, Flint wiped at his salty tears and beheld Pillar now holding the gun.

She fired two shots into Quint's chest then lodged the barrel under Violet's chin. "I'll kill her before I let you control her."

With a laugh, Quint dusted himself off and braced an elbow against the floor. "You think you're the hero of this tale, Pillar? I've owned you since day one. As a matter of fact, since you're so unappreciative, I believe I'll take back my seed."

Pillar's entire body started to shake, and she coughed and gagged.

A bubbling mass of black poured from her mouth and crept toward Violet.

"No, I won't let you have her." Pillar shifted her aim and shot Quint, over and over. She fired into his chest until the only sound in the room was the clicking of her pulling the trigger on an empty gun. "Violet, what are you waiting for? Destroy him." Pillar spat out.

Flames formed in Flint's hands. *"Violet, you can do this."*

Pillar's neck bent back in an unnatural manner. Her open mouth hissed and gurgled as more dark tar dripped from her lips.

"Enough!" Violet shoved away from Pillar.

With a sizzle of air, affecting only Violet, Flint watched as her hair lifted and swirled around her face. Then, her whole body started to shake.

All the hair on Flint's body stood on end as an electric current scored across his skin.

Every metal object in the room circled around them, locked in a magnetic field. *"Flint, go now."* Her glorious red mane became streaked with purple highlights, and when she met his gaze, her eyes flickered white. *"Take the Elementals and leave."*

Pillar dropped to her knees.

The gun tumbled from her hand and joined the objects surrounding them in a mad rotation around the room.

Violet knelt and held Pillar's crumbling body in her arms. "My tormented friend, in the end, you *did* make the right choice."

The dark matter spilling from Pillar brushed against Violet's wall of white, and simply vanished.

Now they were getting somewhere, but somehow, Flint didn't

believe the fight would end so easily. "Terran," he glanced at his Elemental friend.

Terran stepped away from Maya. "I'm ready."

Quint laughed. "You think to destroy me." He raised both arms out at his side. "I am everywhere. I am increasing, growing, sharing my seed with so many. You'll never destroy them all." He waved a hand down his body. "Eliminate this vessel, I care not, there are plenty others." He narrowed his gaze at Terran. "But first, I'll have a little payback." He lifted a finger at Terran.

"No.'" Maya screamed and stepped in front of Terran.

A dark matter blast knocked her across the room.

Quint laughed and blew across the tip of his finger. "One down."

Terran roared and charged forth.

Flint erected a wall of flame between Terran and Quint. "No, Terran, speak the spell."

Quint stepped through the flames and lifted Terran up by the neck.

A gust of wind knocked them down.

Terran scurried to his feet and rushed to Maya's side.

Maya moaned and wrapped him in her arms.

He clutched Terran's shoulder. "You must help Violet." Flint didn't know the true extent of Violet's power, but he trusted Terran to fulfill their plan.

A plan he would follow to the end. He wouldn't abandon her now. Plus, he wanted front row seats to that dark blights destruction. Flint swayed as the room pulsed in and out of existence.

Blinding white lights flashed at various points in the room.

He braced his forearm over his eyes, blinking as the beams intensified for longer intervals.

Then each ray focused on Violet. She jerked, and her neck snapped back as a floor-to-ceiling light beam radiated from her body.

Quint jumped on the table and kicked books off the top. "Yes, yes, release your gift. Show me your power."

Flint ducked as books, and every other object in the room, shot through the air.

Then suddenly, the fire crackling in the hearth snuffed out.

He shivered as an icy blast washed over his skin. A wash of misery and sorrow flashed through his mind, so intense, he fell to his knees.

All went still.

Books and candlesticks crashed to the floor.

The room faded from bright white to hopeless gray.

The floor trembled when, from out of nowhere, a giant of a man, ten foot tall, at least, appeared beside Violet.

Flint stopped breathing, stopped moving. *"Should I halt time?*

"Won't matter." Nodin responded. *"He's come."*

Every living, breathing creature's deepest fear stood in the room.

Death had arrived.

Only one question pierced through Flint's terror—for who?

Hidden within a ragged black cloak, which billowed behind him from some breeze likely existing on another plane, Death shifted closer to Violet. One muscle-clad thigh broke through the rippling black fabric. "Payment is due." He spoke, his voice a deep baritone, smooth like the wash of an aged whisky down your throat, yet there was still a slight burn.

"No. Please, wait."

Violet, his brave, reckless flower, stepped forward and placed her fingers upon Death's hand.

"Violet, No!" Flint screamed his mental warning.

Death hissed at the contact.

No longer able to stand by while his woman was in danger—real danger, final danger—Flint fired through the air to Violet's side.

He dared a glance under the hood and encountered the most handsome face he'd ever seen. He was man enough to admit when a figure of true splendor stood in his presence. Death's eyes were like a well-aged burgundy. Pitch-black hair flowed around his shoulders, cut jaw, full lips. Yet, wasn't death, at times, a thing of grace, of beauty? A soft landing in a world filled with pain.

"You dare to touch Death, little girl."

Violet gasped and withdrew, her fingertips slightly shriveled.

No one moved. No one spoke. All seemingly in awe of this giant.

Death adjusted his hood closer around his face, and then whipped the dark folds of his cloak around Pillar's body.

Violet clutched Flint's hand.

Salt began trickling from beneath the cloak.

"Is she…is she dead?" Violet bit her bottom lip.

Flint yanked her away. Unclear of Death's intent, but very clear Violet wouldn't be next on the hit list. Not now, not ever.

Unhindered by the earlier gunshot wounds, Quint remained standing on the table, tapping a finger against his bottom lip. "Do they offer that cloak in smaller sizes?"

Nodin narrowed his gaze at Quint.

Then a gust of wind knocked the dark matter creature across the room.

With tears pouring down her cheeks, Violet knelt beside the mound of salt and ran her hand through the fine granules. "I shall mourn you, my friend. A pale beauty that spanned time. I hope you've found peace at last."

"The salt-creature is free of the black stain. I have provided respite from her pain." Death's cloak shifted closer to Violet. "I'm owed two witches this day."

"You'll not have her." Flint drew Violet upright and shoved her behind him.

Death merely raised a coal-black brow.

Nodin stepped beside him. "Not today, Death. There is another who shall take her place."

"Is that what you believe, future-seer? I've allowed Sorcha this foolishness long enough. Her enchantment ends today." An ominous purr poured from his throat, and the tip of his scythe glimmered in the opening of his cloak.

"So, this is the much-feared Death." Quint circled the large man.

Death shifted his gaze. "You will know fear soon enough, dark creature."

"Huh." Quint tilted his head. "I figured you'd be taller."

Death's scythe slashed through the air, stopping an inch from Quint's nose. "Yes, pity. Then my arm might be one inch longer."

"The duty is mine." Violet stepped into the fray. "I will deliver him to you."

The blade retracted back into the cloak, and all was silent for a moment as they awaited Death's decision. "As the witch says, the duty is not mine." Death whipped his cloak around and then disappeared with a crackle.

"Well, that was entertaining," Quint quipped.

"You want entertainment, Quint?" Flint shot him a glare. Holes from where the bullets had struck were still evident on his white dress shirt. Tiny bits of dark matter seeped from the wounds. "I believe Terran and Violet have prepared your swan song. Would you like to hear it?" He reached for Violet.

"No." She moved to stand away from them all, waving both hands in front of her. "You must leave. My spectrum is too strong."

Flint shook his head. "We do this together. Stick with the plan."

"Violet, take my hand." Terran stepped across the room.

"No, Terran. There is another way." Violet shook her head, and seemed to be chewing a hole through her bottom lip.

Maya nodded. "I understand, Violet."

"Understand what?" Flint frowned at Maya. "What do you mean?" He refused to lose Violet. He had no concept of what was happening. What choice was Violet making? And why did only Maya understand? Women's intuition?

Violet stepped toward Quint.

"Violet," Flint growled out a warning.

Then the woman pushed him over the edge by generating a

white wall between them.

Maya grabbed his wrist. "She must go, Flint. You knew this day would come."

"Violet, what are you doing?" Flint pounded against the wall.

"She cannot destroy Quint on this plane, she must journey to another."

"Sorcha is calling." From the other side of the barrier, with eyes glowing white, hair stained full purple, Violet met his gaze. *"I love you, Rurik Skuratova. I have fulfilled my promise. Your flame remains eternal."*

A small smile lit her lips before her eyes went neon blue. Her entire body burst like a mega watt light bulb, blinding him.

"Violet." He blinked and shoved against the wall, released wave after wave of fire against its exterior, but nothing penetrated. "Damn it, woman. This wasn't the plan. Don't do this alone."

Panic tore down his spine as the wall narrowed into a tiny pinprick then, like some stellar supernova, the tiny circle exploded in a burst of energy, knocking him across the room.

In a daze, Flint scuttled to his feet, limping to where Violet once stood. Yet, nothing remained.

No Quint.

No Violet.

No hope.

CHAPTER 44

"Fáilte, mo leanbh. Céad míle fáilte."

Violet turned toward the female voice welcoming her in an ancient Gaelic tongue. To escape with Quint, Violet had whispered an alternate-dimension spell she'd secretly found among the magic books. Though her heart had ripped in two as she spoke the spell, she understood her sacrifice would save the man she loved. She'd promised, after all, and for once in her life, *she* had made the choice.

"And you've made the right choice, girl." The lilting Irish voice spoke once more.

"Grandmother, is that you?" Though shards of Violet's heart remained scattered on the library floor with Flint, the rosy-red organ gave a tiny thump at the thought of seeing her grandmother again.

"No, though we look alike, she and I." A woman dressed in a black peasant dress appeared out of the emptiness.

"Sorcha?"

"Of course. Who else would be at your side to complete your destiny?" Her ancestor stepped closer and circled her. "You've done well, my child."

Sorcha touched her face, eliciting a slight shock, like she'd worn slippers across a fluffy carpet. "So young. So innocent." Sorcha locked their hands together, and then lifted them out at her sides. She pursed her lips while giving Violet a thorough once-over. "You've prepared for this moment, yet still, deep in your soul, you wonder why."

Violet met her ancestor's gaze. "My mind is overwhelmed with questions at the moment, but the most pressing is, what have you done with Quint?"

"Momentarily locked away. I can only hold him back for so long, but I felt it prudent as we make our introductions." Sorcha smiled, but it didn't reach her eyes.

She released Violet's hands and paced before her. "Do you know the horrors Quint inflicted upon my mother? How he made her suffer? I would catch faint glimpses of her true spirit when she'd try to break free, but her efforts were always in vain." Sorcha clenched her jaw, and she jabbed a finger against Violet's chest. "I changed that. Gave you the power to destroy the dark beast, but he's grown smarter, stronger." She stalked away. "Spread his seed. We must contain him. Obliterate all that he is...together."

"I'm ready."

"Are you?" Sorcha flipped her hair over her shoulder. "Such a short life you've lived. I find I'm quite jealous of your existence. I've been waiting for so long. My human life was spent creating who and what you are. Shouldn't I get to have more? A real chance to live? I, alone, created you. Steeped in dark magic, I gave my all to avenge my mother, and what do I get in return, but death? No, I think not."

"I'm not sure what you mean. *You* spoke the words, the spell says, *Reaper hold thy scythe 'til then, White field from my future line, Clasp your golden hand in mine, Together, vengeance we shall see, I shall hold thy place for thee.* Those are your words, so you *must* do your part." Violet studied the woman before her. Deep within, a long-buried anger simmered to life at all this woman had taken from her, yet now felt *she* deserved. "I came here to destroy Quint on my own, but since you're with me, we'll follow your prophetic spell. As *you* said, we are meant to stand together." Violet stuck out her hand. "Do it, Sorcha. Clasp your golden hand in mine."

Sorcha glared, and then slapped away Violet's hand. "I will give

Death his due, but I will have my more."

Furious over Sorcha's selfish whims, Violet grabbed her ancestor's arm and wrenched her close. She glared into violet eyes so similar to her own. "You want more? You?" Violet scoffed. "You think I didn't want more? That I haven't despised this curse chained to my existence? I didn't ask for this, but I will finish it. Quint *will* end today, and you *will* see your words through."

"Will I?" Sorcha shoved her back. "You think to order me, girl?"

"I am what you made me, but my will, my heart, was forged in elemental fire. So yes, I do order you."

"*Violet.*" A familiar voice shimmered in her subconscious.

Violet's heart skipped a beat. It couldn't be. She'd already wished for that voice, that comfort, only to find another standing in her stead, still...Sorcha hadn't spoken, so who did? "Grandmother? Is that you?"

"What? Where?" Sorcha spun in a circle. "Wh-what…Why are you here?"

Her grandmother's form flickered in and out. Her violet eyes crinkled with an understanding smile. A sweet grin that epitomized purity and solace.

An inner peace erupted in Violet's soul as she took in every nuance of the one person who had represented comfort. She clenched her jaw against the scream barreling through her chest. A scream for freedom, for release from this duty, for a loving hand to brush away all the pain. But no, she must remain strong, because her grandmother had raised her to use her mind and heart for the greater good. She would not falter now.

Her grandmother's red curls, streaked with delicate wisps of white, swirled around her head. Her arms spread wide, and her body pulsed in various shades of red.

The barren white field surrounding them wobbled and ebbed, adjusting to another power within their plane.

"Why are you here? Can you stay?" Violet trembled as a wash of pleasure warmed her ice-cold skin. "Grandmother, I made it. I'm ready." She bit her lip to hold back a sob. None of this made any sense. Had Grandmother come to take her away? Or would they stay together? Fight together?

All thoughts of her future, of her love for Flint, remained locked behind the opaque cloak of her destiny. She'd made her choice, and she would not regret the decision. "Grandmother, I must fulfill my duty. I will not leave the Elementals…will not leave…him…to finish what is within my power to complete. I will not abandon my purpose, even when all I am is dying to fall at your feet and beg deliverance from this burden." Violet clenched her hands at her sides. "I accept my path. Do not interfere."

"You are so much more than I ever dreamed. So beautiful, inside and out. I come only to spare you, while at the same time delivering another from her pain. I neglected my duty in life, but not in death. Remain strong, my dearest love. I am with you, always."

Hands jammed on her hips, Sorcha stepped between them. "What are you doing, witch? Violet is mine."

"She belongs to no one. A wildflower growing on an open plain. Fighting against all the elements, her petals will bloom. She is purity, sacrifice, and above all, love." Her grandmother met her gaze. *"So much love. I am so very proud of you, my child."*

The room around them erupted from white to all shades of red.

Her grandmother drifted closer, took Violet's face in her hands, and wove a spell.

"Violet live another day
Death not take her life away
Halt to time as she is bound
Until darkness within found
A wary girl seeking light
An airy venture she will take
The elementals, plus two make
And end to this dark matter foe
As I will it is so

Air, earth, fire, and sea
I ask once more a gift of thee.
As I will, so mote it be."

Her grandmother smiled, and her sweet, calming voice once more fluttered through Violet's mind. *"Love binds, Violet. Remember that above all else."* She flashed in and out, and then disappeared completely.

Violet stumbled to her knees, wiping tears from her cheeks. "No, come back. Please, don't leave me." Eyes closed against the pain, she experienced a surge of the power she'd only glimpsed every time she'd opened the spell books in her grandfather's library, humming through her body. Her grandmother had found the strength to return, to offer one last gift. Violet nodded her acceptance.

The energy within her spectrum buzzed just under her skin. Bubbling and exalting in the moment, every part of her released her full power. Holding nothing back, she breathed deeply and transformed. Her entire body allowed the change, and she gloried in the turning of her skin from pale white to bright purple. The tips of her hair flared in all shades of violet, releasing all connection to her human body.

Raging with vengeance, she called forth the prisoner for his final judgment.

"Locked within Sorcha's shield
Dark matter you will yield
Sorcha's spell be done today
Our combined power will not sway
From your darkness we are freed
As I will, so mote it be"

The Ukrainian appeared at her feet, a mere shadow of the human he'd once been. Black ooze poured from every orifice—ears, nose, mouth. The murky matter swirled all around him and leeched toward Violet.

A scratchy voice filled her head. *"If you destroy me, you'll destroy everyone. Each Elemental diminished under your radiant waves. Those powers you hold within are too strong. Radiation burns. Gamma-rays kill."*

Hair now fully black, Sorcha clasped her hand. "Destroy him. Avenge my mother."

"You'll kill Flint in the process. Is that what you want? With each spectrum layer tapped, you release more radiation. Magic has consequences, witch."

"Is this true?" In a panic, Violet turned to Sorcha. "Am I affecting the outside world?"

"Take him now." Sorcha's eyes flashed red, and she locked her nails into Violet's palms. For a moment, the skin on her face flashed in and out, revealing a horror-film skeleton. "Do you see the nightmare I've become in order to reach this day? I've haunted this earth waiting for you. For this moment."

Violet closed her eyes as Sorcha's dark will nudged against her soul. Revenge. Power. Destruction. Death. All crept along her senses and combined with her gift, eliciting the overwhelming desire to strike down the dark matter creature swaying on his knees before them.

"You've dug deep, but you've found her. What you really are—my liberation. My vengeance." Sorcha clasped Violet's shoulders and met her gaze. "This human shell holds the majority of Quint's dark matter. The largest portion of his foul existence. The other seeds he's planted will be easily destroyed by the Elementals. Before you is our greatest foe. Finish him."

With a roar, Violet charged the black miasma. Vision red, she stomped the black mass, each strike turning the black to gray, then to white. Again and again, she struck, out of control with the forces of nature's spectrum surging through her body. Every wave of the electromagnetic field poured from her fingers in stark white waves.

Sorcha's voice broke through her fury. "Yes, yes. Mother, your revenge is upon us. At last, we are freeeeee."

A booming laugh carried across the frequencies, searing Violet's mind, halting her with the truth.

"Yes, Violet." Quint's dark voice broke across her manic determination. *"Destroy me. Burn the world to hell."*

A flash of silver steel sliced through the white field surrounding the tableau of three. A loud snap echoed through the emptiness.

Cloaked in black, Death stood beside her ancestor, his scythe in hand.

Sorcha scurried backward and shrieked, "No, I won't go."

Death huffed out a laugh. "It's always the same, 'I won't go. It's not my time. What did I do to deserve this? Please, just one more hour.' Yet, the end is inevitable. An end *you* chose, remember, my witch?"

"Wait, what are you doing?" Violet stuttered out, heart exploding with fear over his words which could only mean she'd face Quint alone. "Her death is my own. *That* is the prophecy. You can't just change that now…you can't." Glaring, Violet locked both hands on her hips.

Death gave a small shake of his head, and kept her gaze.

Violet shivered from the aura of emptiness, of hopelessness, surrounding this gorgeous man. Still, she had a duty, a destiny. She stood tall before him. "You shall not take her. I need her power to destroy Quint."

"No." Death winked. "You don't."

CHAPTER 45

"I won't leave until Violet returns." Flint shoved away from Terran.

"Enough, you fool." Nodin stirred the air around them, creating a funnel that lifted them all toward the door. *"Violet made her choice. This was always her destiny. Two witches die, I've seen it."*

"Don't say that." Flint turned to smoke and swirled free of Nodin's airy grip.

A deep roar, like a dying saber-tooth tiger, erupted through the room.

Ripples like crashing waves ebbed through the air. A slight buzz zapped his skin and electrified all the hair on his body. A wave peaked from the warped wall, and suddenly, Violet erupted. Falling forward, her skin blue, hair purple, she landed on her knees.

A woman's hand pierced through the invisible barrier and clutched Violet's shoulder. *"Stay with me."*

An ancient scythe stabbed the woman's palm. Death's deadly baritone reverberated through Flint's mind. *"Sorcha, two is my due. On my honor, I fulfill my duty. I am unwavering, unceasing. Your time is at an end."*

An unearthly scream ripped through the room.

The ebbing waves disappeared with a pop, taking Death and Sorcha's hand with it.

Violet's body arched violently, and she released a howl of pain.

Staggering to her feet, she struggled to stand.

"Violet." Flint stepped closer, but was blocked by a wave of water. "Damn it, Maya. Stop. She needs me."

"Has she been infected by Quint?" Maya stepped behind Terran.

"Back away." Violet's voice broke across Flint's mind.

Black streaks slithered up and down her arms. Dark sludge oozed from her nose and mouth.

Gagging, she clutched her head in her hands and screamed. Her body pulsed white, and then black particles exploded from her core, spraying across the room.

Ebony shards embedded in his skin. Flint flinched from the pain, but he stepped toward Violet. "Red, get it under control."

"Flint, she's emitting radiation." Terran appeared before him, lacerations and red blisters forming on his skin and face. "We can't stay here."

The stray black bits reformed into a mannish shadow figure, floating and reaching ebony-tipped tentacles toward Violet.

She lifted a fist and released a pulse of white.

Flint shielded his eyes from the blast's glare as an almost unbearable heat, unlike any he'd ever known, seared through his body.

Eyes glowing bright white, Violet looked past him. "Terran, if you choose to stay, we must bind him, now."

Terran glanced at Maya, and then nodded.

Maya placed a hand on his arm, holding him back. "Terran, please. Her power will destroy you."

With a shake of his head, he closed his eyes and whispered, "It must be done."

Hair flowing in purple strands around her head, Violet held out her hand. "Make the choice, Terran. Quint's here now. I will not fail again."

Nodin stepped beside Flint and placed a blistered hand upon his shoulder. "She is magnificent. Be proud, but let her go."

Flint cringed at his brother's words, his heart sinking as he watched his beautiful Violet blossom with her destiny. "Take Maya and go, Nodin. I will stay with Terran. My time is at an end. I will not remain without her."

"I have loved you, my brother." Nodin wrapped Flint in his arms. "I will not leave you. If we die, we die together."

Flint returned the embrace, but allowed no sorrow to enter his heart. They had always been a team. Different. Stronger. As if brought together to face this day together. A solid shield against a dark enemy.

Violet's voice boomed across the room. Holding strong against the ebony figure circling her body, she spoke the binding spell,

"Goddess Isis, guide my hand

As I pierce through needle's eye

Flint heard Maya's gasp, and the rip in his heart flared anew at her pain.

Choice made, Terran limped across the room.

Flint hooked an arm around the Earth Elemental's shoulders, supporting him as he made his way to Violet's side.

Terran stopped and spoke to Nodin. "Take Maya away. Please."

"No, Terran." Maya misted then appeared at his side. "I will not leave you."

"Maya, return to water." Terran wrapped her in his arms. "With your healing gift, you may yet save Flint and Nodin. I must join Violet."

Ice-blue tears falling down her cheeks, Maya brushed her hand along his jaw. "Wait for me on the other side. I will follow soon."

Terran brushed her hair away from her face and kissed her. "I love you, Shoeless Girl." He nodded at Nodin before stalking to Violet's side.

Nodin caught Maya in his arms and whisked her toward the library's door.

Flint flicked away the tear drying on his cheek. After five-hundred years, his end had come, and he could think of no finer people to have at his side.

Terran's skin matched his own. Open wounds and burns blanketed their bodies as the continued emission of Violet's radiant rays struck against their skin.

Terran gripped Violet's purple hand, and together, they continued the spell.

"Our threads align and knot together
While we weave this binding spell
Tie the feet to hold him steady
Secure the hands against his sides
Free our minds from spider's web
Hold dark creature within our shield

Quint's sable form ceased its undulations and became static.

Steely blue bars appeared in time with their words and locked around his inky mass.

Ignoring the burns melting away his life force, Flint exalted in the power of his woman as he watched the dark matter beast disintegrate under her potent energy field.

His glorious girl lit in every shade of violet from the depths of her very soul.

Unyielding.

Vibrant.

Strong.

A human personification of Sorcha's spell.

A flame of vengeance, burning bright with her destiny.

Everything he'd ever dreamed of in a woman, lit like the brightest star.

A dull clamor reached his ears. Glass shattered. Maya screamed.

Flint watched his skin melt away as he reveled in the vision of Violet in the throes of her magic.

"May each stitch hold strong and true
Until all snares of evil yield."

Quint's inky form flashed white within his bindings.

Maya appeared once more beside Terran. On her knees,

clutching his hand, sobs pouring from her mouth. "No, it's too much. Don't go. Terran, please."

Chips, like pieces of whittled wood, splintered from Terran's damaged body.

A wall of water poured over him. "Violet, please, you're killing him."

Not responding to Maya's pleas, Terran and Violet continued their chant.

Almost completely white, Quint became a thin gray sliver within the blue bars.

"By the power within we
Led by the Earth, Fire, Air, and Sea,

Brittle, like aged wood, Terran's arm splintered. The hand holding Violet's burst into flame. He bellowed and arched in pain before collapsing to the ground.

Violet continued the spell.

"No harm—"

"No more." Nodin shook Violet's shoulders. "Stop. That's enough."

Violet's eyes rolled back in her head, and her body convulsed in a seizure.

A silver spec hovered over her form, and then shot out a broken window.

Maya lurched for Terran. Her movements crippled, her skin melted against her bones.

Hair and eyebrows bleached white, Nodin whipped beside her. After taking a deep breath, he spun and wrapped Maya and Terran into a funnel and disappeared out the open French doors.

Flint rushed to Violet and placed his ear upon her chest.

Her heartbeat weak, she heaved a deep sigh. "I failed."

"No, my love. You lived."

CHAPTER 46

Furiously throwing logs in the hearth, Violet's hands shook as she attempted to light the tinder. "Hurry, hurry."

Flint moaned. After the battle, he'd fallen and taken her down with him. She'd nudged him awake enough to lead him into the massive fireplace, then gathered all the wood and even, goddess help her, a few books.

Now, she frantically struck match after match, trying to light a fire which would rejuvenate his life force.

His skin was marred with holes and melted flesh, and nothing of her handsome fire elemental remained.

A wooden match splintered in her hand. "Enough of this! Goddess Isis, hear my cry, light this fire to the sky."

Flames erupted in the hearth, and she stepped back. "Oh, thank you. Thank you. Please, heal him. Please."

Violet dropped to her knees and breathed a sigh of relief as the red-gold flames flickered over Flint's body.

Goddess Isis had heeded her call. *Finally*

The fire crackled and popped, dancing around him. But would the rejuvenating flames be enough? Was she too late? Had she failed him, as well? And where were the Elementals?

What had she done?

Her need to destroy Quint had consumed her. Would death

come claim her now? And didn't she deserve an end?

Unanswered questions and a sense of failure had her fighting back sobs of frustration and remorse. Every fiber of her being ached with a dull, relentless pain. Her skin faded back to pink, but her hair remained violet around her shoulders. She fingered a strand, willing it to return to red.

A scream from another room pierced through her sorrow and self-pity.

Oh, dear God.

Her grandfather.

Enda.

What more could her heart take? Hadn't she battled enough? Sacrificed enough?

"Violet!"

"Enda?"

"Violet." Enda yelled from outside the library doors. "Come quickly."

After giving Flint a final glance, Violet shot to her feet and climbed over the rubble lining the library floor. Ecstatic to see her caregiver alive, she wrapped Enda in a tight hug. "What happened? How did you survive?"

"We'll talk later. Right now, your grandfather needs you." Enda wiped at the tears on her cheeks, her face filthy with soot and dust.

The words filtered through Violet's traumatized mind. Her grandfather? Wait, hadn't her grandmother...Violet gasped. "Grandmother came to me. She was with me in the field. She spoke this—"

"No, Violet." Enda shook her hand. "It's your *grandfather* who needs you." That said, she flitted down the corridor to the kitchen.

Violet glanced back at Flint still simmering in the raging fire. "I should...Flint is still...Enda, wait." Violet moved to follow her, but faltered as she took in the castle's destruction. She sank her fists into her hair. "I can't...it's too much."

"Violet, come." Enda ordered then disappeared through the

kitchen door.

Smoke and dust still clogged the air. Violet's safe haven, her home, had been touched by a dark, menacing hand, but she would mourn the loss another day. This castle could be rebuilt, could stand tall once more. Her grandfather, however…she shuddered at the thought of what awaited her in the depths of the kitchen.

Violet drew a deep breath and followed Enda's trail.

Opening the kitchen door, she bumped against Enda's back. "What is it?" She eased into the room and glanced over the woman's shoulder.

Pots and broken pottery remnants lay scattered across the kitchen floor.

Grease-stained cookbooks were burnt to ash.

Upon hearing a low, pained moan, Violet gasped.

Her grandfather lay face down on the kitchen tiles.

A woman with stringy black hair stood over him, fists clenched.

"Who?" Violet whispered.

The woman detected the sound and turned.

Her mother.

Eyes fully black, veins of ebony shooting under her pale, emaciated skin, Freesia snarled and clutched at her head. "Get it out. Out." With a mad scream, she headed for the counter and grabbed a knife. Before Freesia could plunge the blade into her heart, she wailed as her entire hand turned fiery red.

Flint stood beside her mother, knife now in his hand.

Violet huffed out a breath and shooed him away. "No, Flint. Go back to the fire. You're not fully healed. Go back." She flicked a finger toward the library.

Amber eyes met her gaze. "A certain goddess said I was needed in the kitchen. I don't think she meant to scramble eggs. Do you?"

"Flint, please be serious. Is my grandfather…?"

Freesia screamed and shoved against Flint's chest. "Get away from me."

Her grandfather still hadn't moved.

285

"What did you do to him?" Though exhausted from the earlier battle, Violet experienced a resurgence of energy. Moments earlier, she'd tamped down her gift for fear of hurting Enda, but she still trembled for full-throttle release as a current sizzled at her fingertips.

Somehow, Quint was near. Not strong. Not complete. A sliver, a tiny seed, but still close.

Freesia's head snapped up, her jaw tight, her hands squeezed into fists, her mouth mumbling incoherent words.

No, not incoherent.

A spell.

Against her.

Flint swayed at Freesia's side, his gaze locked on Violet's. *"Damn, Red, I want to strip you down and make love to you right now. That purple hair is hot."*

"Have you lost your mind?"

"Yeah, a few times actually."

She glared at the cocky bastard. He had survived. Her light. Her beacon in the darkness. Her everything.

She fought back a smile until the stupid man winked.

Winked.

What was with these men and their flirty winks in the midst of terror and destruction? Yet, that small glimpse of Flint's true nature brought forth her own.

She shoved her shirtsleeves up her arms and faced her mother. "I see you've moved on to stronger prey, Quint. What you've failed to recognize is that I keep beating you back, diminishing your existence, and I will finish you." She paced closer to her prey. "You've taken too much from this world. Too much from me. I do have Sorcha's blood in my veins, and as you very clearly just experienced, we don't appreciate when people fuck with our mothers."

"Young lady, such language. Shall I wash your mouth out with soap?" Quint's chill baritone taunted through her mind. *"I see Flint's foul tongue has tainted your innocence. Speaking of Flint, look what you've done. Do*

you think he'll forgive you for your madness? You would have destroyed him, had that Elemental air-bag not stepped in. I'm pleased to discover you and I are not so different, after all."

Her mother shrieked, her entire body quivering, and then her eyes rolled back in her head, incantations pouring from her lips.

Violet raised a brow and pursed her lips at Quint's characterization, all while batting away her mother's attempts to weave her magic around Enda, her grandfather, and Flint. "You're right, Quint. You and I do belong together. Our destinies bound. So release my mother, and we'll see where the winds take us."

"Violet," Flint growled, his displeasure evident.

"Did they ever tell you how your grandmother really died? She wasn't strong enough to defeat me, and neither are you."

Violet gasped at the implication, a silent *no* falling from her lips.

A loud snap sounded behind her, and icy chills from a different source rippled down her spine.

Pounding footsteps bore down, drawing ever closer.

With a snap of his cape, Death sauntered over to Freesia and clutched her chin in his heavy hand. "Dark man, I order your departure from this witch and this realm. I tire of your games." His black cloak rippled across the kitchen floor, cracking each tile it touched.

"The second debt is paid," Death declared, in a voice so deep the sound vibrated through Violet's body and shivered through each vein.

Violet remained stunned, locked in place by fear, by anguish, by something beyond her control. Death had chosen her mother to fulfill Sorcha's prophecy. To fulfill *her* destiny. She fought for air as the truth of the moment became crystal clear. "No, please. My mother, she…"

Death's face remained hidden inside his cloak. "Do not question my decision, young witch."

Her mother choked and gasped for air, black muck trickling over her lips. "Vi…Violet," she gurgled past the flow.

Quint's voice, though faded, as if muffled by a pillow, once more pierced her mind. *"When my seeds blossom, we shall meet again, my flower."*

Shaking off that ominous warning, Violet found the strength to stand at Death's side.

"Violet, don't touch his cloak," Flint warned.

Being careful, she steered clear of the waving black fabric, but dared to look Death in the eye. "May I say goodbye?"

From behind burgundy-colored eyes, Death paused for a moment, and then nodded. "As a reward for your bravery."

Violet caught a fleeting glimpse of sorrow, of unending sadness before he blinked and stepped back, pulling the cloak farther over his breathtakingly handsome face.

Pulling her gaze from the striking giant, Violet reached out and took her mother's hand.

Her mother blinked away the black specs in her eyes, and her irises once more turned indigo. Freesia reached up and touched Violet's face, her voice a whispered rasp, "I-I...I'm s-so sorry."

Violet bit her lip and offered the only solace she could in these final moments. "I understand and forgive you."

A weak smile touched her mother's lips. "Be...be stron...ger." A weak gasp followed the word, and then her head lolled to the side.

Violet brushed the red strands from her mother's face. "I'll try, Mother. For you." Frantic for more time with the mother she'd never had, she waved away Death. "Just one more moment, please."

Death shook his head. "The debt is paid."

"Flint, stop him. Freeze time. I need more time with her, please." Sobs racked Violet's body as the day's events overwhelmed her spirit in an unceasing flow. "I want her back."

Flint's warm arms wrapped around her from behind, and he whispered words of comfort that did nothing to appease her agony. "Though I wish it were otherwise, I cannot stop death. I'm so sorry, love."

So much death. So much waste and agony. Why?

With each tear shed, her warped world faded farther from reality, and she welcomed the emptiness. The end of misery.

This magic curse had always asked for too much and, in the end, had almost taken everything. The power still existed within her. Quint had not been defeated. She'd failed in her duty and left a trail of bodies behind. Schwarz, pyro-girl, the Ukrainian, Pillar, and now her mother.

Her mother.

And what about that stupid black dog? Who was taking care of Schwarz's beast now?

Violet laughed, barreled over at the stomach, with mad hilarity pouring from her lips. The dog. Why in the midst of all this madness was she worried about a dog?

"Violet, what's so funny?" Flint's voice held a tinge of concern.

She practically snorted with unrestrained laughter. "It's just…it's just…that dog…the black one…" She couldn't finish her thought, too lost in hysteria.

Flint pulled her to the ground and held her head in his hands. His bloodshot eyes tried to meet her gaze. "Violet, stay with me. I'm here."

Manic laughter overwhelmed all rational thought, even resisted the heat emanating from Flint's body. A flare of fire seared across her ice-cold skin, but didn't penetrate her self-imposed shield.

Lost in a haze of madness, she closed her eyes and begged the goddess for mercy, and a leash.

For the dog.

CHAPTER 47

Salt-scented breeze fluttered across Violet's skin.

Two deep male voices murmured, and then came to a sudden stop.

Footsteps creaked on what must be wooden floors then a tanned hand brushed away the sheer curtain surrounding the bed.

Flint stood beside the bed, looking hale and whole again. Hair black, skin once more a deep tan. All injuries from her death rays healed. She opened her mouth to speak, but only croaked out a gasp.

"Here, Maya left some water."

With a shaky hand, Violet took the glass, but spilled a bit on her chest.

"Here, let me." Flint steadied the cup and held it to her lips.

In a refreshing splash, Maya's healing waters flowed down her throat. Greedy for more, Violet tipped the cup and drank deep.

"Hey, it's okay. Not so fast." Flint brushed her hair away from her face.

So many questions raced through her mind. *Had her grandmother really appeared in that white haze? Were the other Elementals healed? Was her grandfather all right? Had her mother really—?*

Out of all those questions, she picked the one easiest to bear. "Is the castle completely destroyed, or can we rebuild?"

Flint sank against the headboard and pulled her into his arms.

"We can always rebuild." He kissed her temple. "However, the explosion did knock down some of the castle's inner structure."

The rumble of his voice comforted her. She pressed their hands together, aligning them before linking her fingers with his.

"How are you feeling?"

Violet took a deep breath, though she still felt weighted down. "I feel numb. Like I have endless questions and no real answers, so why bother asking?"

"Violet, don't." He squeezed her fingers then he kissed her hand woven with his.

She didn't deserve his comfort. She'd almost destroyed everything. "My grandfather...is he?

Flint ran his free hand up and down her arm. "He was knocked unconscious by the blast. His heart..."

Her own heart thundered in her chest. "Oh, please...don't tell—"

"Listen." Flint turned her in his arms and clasped her head in his warm grip. "Mother Nature will heal him. He's had quite a shock. And since they've been gone three days, I imagine he's—"

"Three days?" Violet sat upright. "I've been out three days."

"Yes." He leaned forward to kiss her.

She turned away, unable to accept his affection. How could she ever accept anything again? She'd let her mother die in her place, practically irradiated the entire Elemental crew.

Her entire being was a monster menace who should be locked in solitude.

Flint sighed and ran his fingers through his thick black hair. "I brought you here, to San Bartolo, so I could recuperate beside you. A secluded island where the volcano rumbles every day, on the edge of eruption, yet flowing still and deep with fire, with an unending flame. Like you, like me." He brushed a finger over her bottom lip. "We'll stay as long as you need. Together, we'll find peace."

Violet turned from his touch and glanced out the window at the seemingly endless ocean just steps away from the open bedroom doors. Waves whooshed against the shore, the sound meant to calm and reach into your very soul, a sacred lullaby if only you heeded its call. But she didn't deserve solace.

Refusing to accept Flint's comfort, she shifted off his lap, then cleared her throat, and plucked at the snowy down comforter. "So, my grandfather, he'll be okay?"

Flint locked his finger under her chin and used slight pressure to turn her face. "Yes, your grandfather *is* fine. Are you?"

Violet gazed into Flint's amber eyes, and saw so much, too much. Concern, worry, forgiveness, mercy, but she didn't deserve any softer emotions. She took a deep breath and pulled away. Shuffling off the bed, she moved to lean against the door frame and breathed in the tropical air. Could the crisp breeze sweep away all she had done? And all she hadn't?

"Violet." Flint came to her side and braced his hand at her waist. "You should be resting."

Mt. Stromboli's leaking lava left a faint smoke trail in the distance. The magma locked inside was the only reason Flint still existed. He was here repairing damage she had caused. She'd come too close to snuffing his flame forever. "I failed."

"No." Flint turned her into his arms. "You made the selfless choice. In the battle against the greatest adversary ever, you chose to protect the greater good. I let Nodin wrench you away. I did nothing to stop him. If anything, we are the ones who failed you."

Violet shoved Flint away. "Don't you dare say that. If I were strong, in control of my gifts, I wouldn't have needed Terran. My grandfather wouldn't need to recuperate. My home wouldn't be in shambles. If I were strong, I—"

"That's enough." Frowning, Flint gripped her upper arms.

"No, I'll never be enough. Don't you see?" Her voice faltered. "If I were strong, I could have spoken the binding spell on my own. As it was, I almost destroyed Terran. Almost destroyed you." She faltered and crumpled against the bamboo floors. "If I were strong, my mother wouldn't be...I wouldn't have ..."

"Don't do this, Violet." Flint knelt beside her, brushing a hand over her shoulder.

"Pillar, Schwarz, my mother are all dead, because of me."

"They made their choices."

"My mother. She didn't—"

"She chose a long time ago, Red."

Choice, reason, logic, none of those things had any place in her mind right now. Not when so much guilt weighed heavy on her heart. "Don't you Red me." Violet pounded a fist against Flint's chest. "I won't be your Red anymore. I won't be anyone's Red. I don't want this."

"Pain? Heartbreak? Fear? You think you get to choose? You don't want burdens? Loss? Who does, Violet?"

She tried to shove away again, but he held her close.

"Humans throughout all time have taken that pain, that sheer despair, and used it to become stronger. To rise like a phoenix from the ashes."

"Stop." Slumping against his embrace, she shook her head. "I'm not some fire Elemental."

"No. You're more." Flint kissed her cheek. "Always have been. I expect that more from you, and I will have it. No regrets, remember?" He skated his thumb over her lips, and then kissed her.

A gentle brush of warm lips against her own. She accepted the heat, pulling him closer. Frantic for escape, for passion, she drove her tongue into his mouth over and over, until he hummed out a moan.

"I'm out of control. I don't know myself anymore. I had such a structured life and now...I'm an absolute disaster."

Pulling back, Flint licked his lips then kissed the tip of her nose. "I'm liking this new you. Liking her a lot." He winked.

"Oh please, stop with the winking already."

He furrowed his brow. "Why?"

She groaned and flopped her head against his chest.

Sitting quietly for a moment, she let the sounds of the tide soothe her soul. Perhaps she could heal here, after all. Study the full power behind her spectrum, now that she understood the energy latent within. Maybe she'd discuss the science with Terran. Perhaps take up meditation.

"Meditation, babe?" Flint chuckled as he kissed her temple. "Violet, be honest with yourself. We will suffer losses, because we are at war. An ongoing war, so mourn, scream, rail against the unfairness of it all, and then be done." His amber eyes flickered with red glints. "No one expected you to be ready. No one even expected you to come as far as you have." He stood and drew her to her feet. "You've only used your gift a handful of times. Enough of this wilted flower routine, I want my vibrant violet back, and I'll remain by your side until she's ready to bloom." He hauled her over his shoulder, carried her to the bed, and dropped her with a plop. Rising above her, he locked her arms over her head.

"I hurt."

Flint bent until their foreheads met. "So do I…for you."

Violet closed her eyes and took a deep breath.

Flint shifted positions until he lay on his back and moved her so her head rested against his chest.

Silence reigned again for a moment. The ocean lapped against the shore, matching the gentle sway of Flint's hand up and down her back.

"I started this journey with you." His husky voice vibrated through his chest. "I chose to be at your side as you traveled across Europe. I chose to remain at your side as you faced death. Literally." He chuckled and mumbled, "That is a nightmare for another day."

Violet smiled and shook her head. "I know…still, he was magnificent."

"Magnificent, was he?"

"Undeniably."

"Whatever," Flint huffed out. "Maybe, if you like broody giants."

Violet snickered. "Oh my gosh, was that insane, or what?"

Flint's full laugh had her head bouncing on his chest. "Welcome to my world, Violet. Fuck me, that dude was big."

She giggled again.

"There's the girl I love." He gripped her hand, brought it to his lips, and then laughed.

"What's so funny now?"

He shrugged. "Not too long ago, a certain earth Elemental warned me you'd burn me, and you did." Flint shook his head, his thick hair swooshing across the pillow. "Burned me multiple times, in fact."

With a frown, Violet plucked at his T-shirt. "I'm sorry if I don't find that amusing."

"I was just——"

"Let me say one thing, please." Violet rested one elbow against his chest and met his gaze, worry tightening her throat. "The rest...the rest I'll deal with as you've said. I'll lock everything away in a box, and open it again during our next battle. But I need to say this...I'm so very sorry for hurting you."

"Violet——"

"No, let me finish." She placed her fingers over his lips. "I need you, Flint. I need the Elementals. I understand I can't defeat Quint on my own. The sacrifices you were willing to make, that Terran almost made...I want to fight smarter next time. I am not defined by Sorcha's spell. I'm defined by the choices I make, and I want to make them by your side."

Flint nodded. "I agree."

"That's it? I say all that, and you just say, 'I agree'?"

"Violet, I'm kind of stuck on the whole purple hair thing. Big turn on."

"Oh my gosh, is it still purple?" Violet shot up and looked around the room for a mirror.

Flint simply hummed out, "Mmm-hmm."

She whipped back around and glared. "Don't joke about this."

"I know, right?" Flint wrenched her closer and flipped her onto her back. Rising above her, he looped a strand of her hair around a finger. "I'm standing in the middle of all this destruction, my body destroyed by radiation burns, my friends all but dead, but my dick...rock solid."

Violet huffed out a laugh. "I have no difficulty believing you thought of sex the second before you died. Now get off me, I need a mirror."

"No. Stay still a moment. I have something for you. A gift."

"I've received enough gifts to last one lifetime, and if by gift, you mean that very hard situation nudging my stomach, I will smack you."

"Oh, you'll like that gift." Flint bumped her with his hips. "But, I'll give you this one first." He sat back and dangled a glass pendant hanging from a thin twine strand before her eyes.

"What's this?" She studied the red glass twinkling in the light coming from the open doors.

"The other one cracked, split in two, so I thought I'd try again." Flint dropped the piece into her hand. "Renew our vows, so to speak. This time, it won't break. I asked for your grandfather's blessing, so the glass is protected by magic. By love."

"It's beautiful." Violet clasped the sparkling glass heart in her hand.

"I flipped it."

"Flipped it?"

"Yeah, this time the violet's inside the heart." Flint cleared his throat. "I thought...I figured it was a more accurate representation."

Violet turned the red heart pendant over in her palm, traced a finger over the smooth glass, and studied the purple violet locked inside. "So...I'm inside your heart?"

"Dug in there deep, Red."

"I'm not so red, anymore." She tugged a strand of hair before her eyes. *Yep, still purple.*

"Is that so?" He leaned down to kiss her, his breath heating her lips. "Wanna bet I can make you red again?"

As his lips touched hers, she felt the burning flare pour over her skin and welcomed the heat.

Though she'd recall, and mourn, the losses from this journey for the rest of her existence, she'd found her beacon, her light in every storm.

Her hearth.

Her fire.

Her heart.

EPILOGUE

"I can't believe you talked me into this." Violet watched Terran slide down the volcano, following a trail of mist left by Maya. Along the rumbling side of Mt. Stromboli, Violet brought the safety goggles down over her eyes.

Staring down the volcano, she thought of the day, five years ago, when her grandfather had returned, his left side permanently damaged but his spirits healthy. He and Mother Nature had sat her down and explained the significance of her grandmother's spell.

Time had frozen.

She would remain twenty-five until the final battle with Quint, if there ever was one. Regardless, she cherished each moment with her ever-bright flame.

They'd fought, loved hard, and reveled in every nuance of their new life together.

Flint had just returned from a forest fire in California. He'd trudged along with the volunteers, though for some reason, had been more skilled at snuffing the flames.

The first two years following their battle with Quint, they'd hunted down what they could of his remaining seeds.

There were more, so many they couldn't see, but Nodin's duty—one he had put off for far too long—was destined to be their vision in the darkness.

Mind once more in the present, she smiled at Flint as she zipped up her protective orange jump suit.

"You look like an escaped prisoner." Flint tweaked her nose with his finger. "Prison sex has never been a fantasy of mine, but seeing you in this outfit, I might reconsider."

With him newly returned from his elemental duties, any sex sounded just fine.

Flint tilted his head, gleaning her mood. "So, prison sex? That works for you? Guess I left you alone too long."

Violet stepped close, her lips hovering just under his. "First one down gets to play the warden." She shoved away with a loud whoop, and surfed down the side of the volcano on a thin Plywood board.

Adrenaline rushed through her body, and she gloried in Flint's shout of joy behind her. Though wishing she could raise her hands in victory, she kept her arms at her sides for fear of falling and getting cut by the rough volcanic ash. Arriving at the bottom of the hill, she stood and slapped palms with Maya.

Flint slid to a stop beside her, lifted her in his arms, and kissed her. "What's next, Warden?"

As Violet stared over his shoulder at the Elemental crew, she felt her heart stretch wide, encompassing all she'd never dreamed to be, yet all she'd become. What came next no longer mattered, she had everything right here. She glanced at Flint, his eyes glinting with flecks of gold, lighting every facet of her life.

Never fading, never burning out.

"What's next?" She shot him a cheeky grin. "We go again!"

# # #

Weary, and still very unclear of why he had agreed to this mission, Nodin traveled back to his native tribe.

For years, he'd questioned his decision to stop Violet. For years, though he was air, he still couldn't catch his breath or remember his purpose.

He hadn't visited his homelands since the invasion by the

Europeans in 1645, back when his people had looked to him to stem the tide of marauding pale faces.

No. Nodin shook off those recollections. He wouldn't get lost in memories of the past. His people dying from foreign diseases, dying by gunfire…dying, just dying.

Mother Nature had directed him to this place. Five years may have passed with only whispers from Quint, but that meant nothing.

Murmurs echoed across his mind as he entered the town's diner. *"Outcast."*

An odd sensation like the touch of a winter breeze shivered down his spine. He turned and saw her with flowing ebony hair, diminutive facial features, her body buried in an oversized blue sweater.

Opaque eyes.

A small sliver of apple pie and half cup of milk sat on the table before her.

She couldn't see him, yet she was looking right at him.

Nodin gleaned into her mind and saw, *shadows and forms moving in the darkness. Swirling, spinning before her eyes.*

What did a blind girl see?

Thank you for reading *Fire's Field*. I hope you enjoyed Violet and Flint's story. If you did, please leave a review at your purchase site. Reviews are very appreciated by the author. I'm "moose"-assuredly grateful.

Visit **www.jillianjacobs.com**
for all titles available.

Please enjoy the following excerpt from *Water's Threshold,* **Book #1 in The Elementals Series.**

Since arriving in Wyoming only a few months ago, Maya had experienced a strange energy pattern that interrupted her sense of peace. A consciousness never felt before, as if something attempted to anchor her in place—a pull unlike anything she had experienced since starting this new life nearly one hundred and fifteen years ago.

This internal strife was because of him—Terran Forrester. Mother had warned this would come. He was part of her purpose in being in this place at this time. Her orders were to guide him, because their destinies were entwined. Having Mother Nature set her up on a "fate date" left her feeling like a contestant on a game show. During her human life, Maya strove to control her own destiny, never handing over power. As an Elemental, she remained determined to give her all to their cause, but it chafed when Mother asked for more—to open her heart. Why now? Why was this burden of love thrust upon her with a mate she had not chosen?

Mate. What a ridiculous word.

Maya blew out a breath, causing a bevy of bubbles to dance their way to the surface. She couldn't have children so Mother using that specific word made the whole idea more ludicrous. Yet, Mother's wishes had come to fruition and that fact rankled. When spying on Terran, Maya experienced emotions surfacing she'd thought buried in a deep well long ago.

Her duties included watching him as he went about his daily human life. She enjoyed observing his frequent visits to the banks of the Snake River where he filled little glass vials. A soft hum raced through her body each time she spied him doing ordinary things, like working up a sweat at the gym or grabbing a cup of coffee at the local café. Since her last sexual adventure occurred in the free-love laced 70's, she was more than overdue for male attention. Terran would, no doubt, approach sex with the same care he did his experiments—meticulously and thoroughly.

That trickle of lust thrummed especially strong tonight at the gas station, when he'd touched her shoulder, all concerned citizen, seeking to offer assistance to an unfamiliar woman. Her waterlogged heart had pumped like a steam engine traveling uphill.

About the Author

In the spring of 2013, Jillian Jacobs changed her career path and became a romance writer. After reading for years, she figured writing a romance would be quick and easy. Nope! With the guidance of the Indiana Romance Writers of America chapter, she's learned there are many "rules" to writing a proper romance. Being re-schooled has been an interesting journey, and she hopes the best trails are yet to be traveled.

Water's Threshold, the first in Jillian's Elementals series, was a finalist in Chicago-North's 2014 Fire and Ice contest in the Women's Fiction category.

Jillian is a: Tea Guzzler, Polish Pottery Hoarder, and lover of all things Moose.

The genres she writes under are: Paranormal and Contemporary romance with suspenseful elements.

Connect with Jillian Jacobs online

Website: www.jillianjacobs.com

www.ingramcontent.com/pod-product-compliance
Lightning Source LLC
Chambersburg PA
CBHW071445170626
46811CB00007B/2482